MY HEART TURNED COLD

Happens to be a: *4 Figure$ Production L.L.C.* Product.

Created By: Willie James Evans Junior
Illustration By: Willie James Evans Junior
Written By: Willie James Evans Junior
Edited By: Willie James Evans Junior

PRINTED IN THE UNITED STATES OF AMERICA

For information regarding special discounts for bulk purchases, please contact a *4 Figure$ Production L.L.C.* Special Sales Representative At 314-585-5733 or at *4figuresproduction@gmail.com*

4 Figure$ Production L.L.C. Can arrange for authors to appear live at your special events. For more information or to book an event, please contact a *4 Figure$ Production L.L.C.* Live Speaker Bureau Representative at 314-585-5733 or email us at *4figuresproduction@gmail.com*

ACKNOWLEDGEMENTS

*A*lthough the stories I share with you all may not be your everyday religious type of reading material, I first and foremost would like to take a moment to give all praises and thanks to the most high of the highest, creator of all creations, my GOD.

*T*hank you for blessing me with the gifts and abilities to be able to not only read and write, but also the ability to be able to entertain other people through stories that some folks are easily able to relate too and may have even experienced.

*W*hile at the same time, although the stories I tell are visible to all of those who are able to use their imaginations, some folks are still going to find it next to impossible to even begin to believe, understand, or overall just to imagine having to experience the situations through the journeys that I take each individual reader through; but I thank you all too for not only the support of my works, but any feed back I get as well.

*T*hough our journeys in life may be different or perhaps even be one of the same, it's nothing like having one motivate you because you are an inspiration to them; and although one may know not that they inspire you because of their strong belief in you and encouragement numerous of times is the only reason you are the accomplisher that they believed you could be. I personally think and feel like that it would only be fair to accommodate them with at least a line of thanks and gratitude. That being said, I personally would like to take a moment to thank 23 year old Mr. Neikos C. Walker for his every helping hand and thoughts that he gave me to use to push me forward to bring this very book into existence. Without his consistency and effective effort to help develop this project, never would have such characters personalities such as DaMesha been created. Thank you my friend for all of your help.

*L*ast but certainly not least, let me give a special acknowledgement shout out to 17 year old Cortez Tiarel James Evans for not only allowing me to use a photo of him as part of my main cover image design, but also for being the very reason this book was created in the first place.

*R*emember it's easy to blame others for that which you choose not to control; but here's the proof that anything you believe in and strive forth to achieve, with true determination you can bring whatever you vision into existence.

~Willie James Evans Junior~

<u>*Prologue*</u>

*A*pproximately six minutes had past and I was still stretched out in the middle of the streets. I was sure the shooters were long gone; but what was bothering me besides the pain that I was in, was the fact that I still didn't hear or see a police or ambulance. I knew from that moment that if I was planning on surviving, then it was going to be up to me to get to a hospital.

I struggle effortlessly to stand up, but with the burning pain in my legs and hand I just continue to fall. Having no other choice, I dragged myself out of the streets to a nearby parked car for support to lift myself up; but I still was unable to do so. All that kept replaying in my mind was how I was caught slipping and left for dead. Those thoughts quickly came to an end when a young boy appeared out of nowhere. I just knew he was about to finish me off! So I replied the only thing that came to my head. "If blood gone shed, then let it shed. Show no sympathy, because I have no pity. As for as religion, may it be with you. 'Cause place death upon me, and six times worser will be my vengeance."

The young boy just stood and looked in disbelief. Then he replied, "I didn't come to hurt you. My name is Elijah. I came to help you. I know who you are."

Even though Elijah looked as if he could have been innocent, I was still defensive; but could you blame me? I was just shot down and robbed by three youngsters. All I could manage to ask him was, "How do you know me?"

Elijah quickly responded, "Everybody knows you. You the man they call Boom with the tricked out cars. Besides, I know your son." At the mentioning of my son, my mind flashed out. All that kept replaying in my head was the promise that I made to Lil' Threat about never leaving him. Now here I was dying not too far from the crib. Elijah spoke again, "You don't look alright!"

Indeed he was right. I knew if I didn't hurry up and make it to my feet, I would surely die. I weakly asked the little youngster, "You think you could help me stand up?" He just nodded his head as he began trying with all of his strength. Once I was standing I thanked Elijah, and then told him, "Now you go ahead and get in the house, and make sure you take a bath first before you do anything else. Anyway, it's too late for you to be out here," with that being said he ran off.

I struggle to reach my car as I kept my balance on other park cars. When I reached mines, the alarm went off and Cortez came running out the house saying, "Daddy, I see you trying to creep out! Where you think you going?" but then froze in his tracks when he saw me bleeding and screamed.

"I'm okay son; just open the door for me."

Cortez replied while crying, "What happen to you?"

"I just got to make it to the hospital and everything is going to be alright." I replied as I got in the car.

"I'm coming too; but what happen?"

I didn't see any sense in being argumentative with him; besides I knew this could very much have been the very last time that I might have been able to share anything with him. Once he got inside the car, I told him, "First, put on your seat belt. You never know when it might be able to actually save your life." As he fasten his seat belt, I lower the music so he could hear every word that I was about to tell him clearly. "Now Lil' Threat, I want you to listen to me real good because what I'm about to tell you can make a difference in the rest of your life."

"I'm listening" he replied with a sincere expression on his face.

"When you get older, I don't want you to be like me. I want for you to be better than me. So learn all that you can about anything and everything that you get involved in beforehand. Knowledge is your most important tool son. Second, always remember that anything possible is always possible even when it don't seem like it. So never count anything out as impossible." I replied as I swirled across the highway causing a state trooper to turn on their bubble gum lights in pursuit of me.

"*Ooh* dad! The police got they lights on behind you!"

I continue driving ignoring the state trooper. Then said with sharpness in my voice, "I hope you paying attention to me; because it's a lot of stuff that you are going to have to watch out for, and the police are one of the main things! Never believe them a hundred percent; and never ever under no means give them information concerning anything or anybody even if they promise to help and protect you!" Feeling a little more weaker, I swirled towards the exit ramp and then continue, "Never trust anybody completely son. You never can know what's exactly on someone else's mind; but you can always be positive about what you say, and what you do. That's it. Always keep your word son! Your word should mean everything! So whenever you give your word to someone, keep it! You understand me?" Cortez just nodded his head so I continue. "Son no matter what, always finish what you start. That way you won't be caught sleep by anyone that feels like you are too much of a threat to them. The last thing I want you to know before we make it to the hospital son, is to always remember where you lay your head at."

"I know both your address and my momma's too."

"That's not what I'm talking about. What I mean is never do any dirt close to where you stay and sleep. But the most important thing I want you to always remember, is always think before you react. You got that?" but before I could hear his answer I lost control of the car and crashed into a parked car in front of the emergency room side of the hospital.

Chapter One
(A New Start)

$\mathcal{N}$ow here it was six years later, and I was still waking up in cold sweats recalling the last hours that I spent with my father. For some reason, I just couldn't seem to erase the memory of seeing my father bleeding as he sincerely gave me a lecture on the principles that he wanted me to live by. You couldn't have convinced me that that's how our relationship would've ended as I recalled the nurses and doctors scrambling trying to revive him. Blood was everywhere. At the time, I didn't quite fully understand how seriously injured my father was when I heard the nurses yelling out, "Hurry up, we're losing him!" I just knew everything was going to be alright and my father was going to pull through even though the hospital staff refused to allow me to enter into the surgery room with him. How wrong was I?

Life quickly had changed for me after my pop's funeral. Things just weren't the same. Although my mother was already married to Tony at the time of my father's death, she still took it hard. On several occasions, my momma would look at me and then just out of the blue break down crying saying, "You look just like your father."

I knew that was true. I looked like a splitting image of him; so I didn't know how to console her. She constantly would burst out in tears, and that led to Tony and her constantly getting into it. One day, my mother was going through one of her emotional break downs and Tony snapped out on her.

"Bitch, you sitting around here crying about another nigga'; when ho', you suppose to be my motherfucking wife! Keisha, if you don't stop this shit, I swear to fucking God you going to be joining that nigga' since you love him so fucking much!" At least that's how their last argument went that I witness before they physically began to fight.

They must have fought every other day; at least three times throughout a week. Their relationship became so full of domestic violence, that it led to them filing for divorce. I was glad when I found out that they were serious about getting divorce; because hearing Tony talk the way he talked to my mother and about my father, only made me want to brutally murder him. I knew if my father was still living, that he wouldn't have said a single word out of line about him; and most definitely not in front of me. He wouldn't even be putting his hands up with the intention of fighting my momma; but what could I do? I just use to think to myself, *His time coming, he just don't know it yet; but soon enough, he going to get his.*

Once the divorce was finalize Tony went his separate way, and mom and me were on our own. The first week, moms kept mentioning that it was time for a new start; but being that we where in the slums, I didn't see how much change we were going to be able to make in New Orleans. Besides, New Orleans was all we knew. I guess my mother had more faith than me, because moms kept on talking about it was time for us to meet new people; go to new places, and just do new things.

I overheard her talking on the telephone to her sister, auntie Keniesha who stayed in Saint Louis, Missouri about the divorce being finalize; but I didn't really pay it any mind until I notice how excited mom seem to have gotten. "Sis, are you for real? I don't know! It's just Cortez and me now. I was just telling him we need a new start; but I don't want us to be a burden to you! I'll think about it. If anything, it'll be temporary. Okay. I love you too sis! Talk to you later." My mother said, and then hung up the telephone.

From what I got out of their conversation, I figured auntie Keniesha must have been trying to convince my mother to bring us up there like she usually did; or at least until she knew that we were situated. Either way, I personally felt like if we were going to get a fresh start, then moving out of town would have been our best option. I didn't want my momma to know that I was somewhat ease dropping on her conversation; so I played it off once I heard her set the telephone down, I yelled out of the room that I was in, "Momma, tell aunt Keniesha I said hello!"

"Cortez, you are a second too late. I just got off the phone with her; but you can call her back if you want. Come here anyway; before you do anything eles, I need to talk to you first."

I walked into my mother's room not knowing exactly what she was about to say, and quickly replied, "Huh momma. How auntie Keniesha doing? I see you been talking to her a lot lately."

"She's doing just fine; I told you that you could call her back if you want too, but first I want to talk to you. Have a seat." Keisha said patting on the bed next to her.

Instead of sitting on her bed though, I took a seat in the blue lazy boy recliner chair that sat in the corner in her room and asked, "What's wrong? Is everything alright?"

"Ain't nothing wrong boy; just listen up! Anyway, now I know that you are probably tired of hearing me talk about we need a fresh start; but today your auntie and me were talking, and she invited us to come stay with her in Saint Louis until we get ourselves situated. I didn't want to make that big of a decision until we sat down and talked about it; because it's important to me to see how you would feel about a change like this."

"I don't know momma! I don't know nothing about Saint Louis besides my father was from there. Have you ever been there?"

"Nope; but that's the beauty of it! I've never been, and you've never been; so it will be brand new to both of us. Then from what my sister tells me, it's quite a few good job opportunities there for me and kids your age along with good schools." Keisha said as if she had pretty much had already made her mind up about the whole ordeal.

"All of that sound good to me momma; but what about all of our stuff? How are we going to get it all there?"

Keisha looked around her room slowly in disappointment; and then replied, "Things are going to be tight baby; so we can only take our clothes, and you can bring your video game system because I know how much you love that thing."

I was like, "That's it!" with what I imagine was a total look of disbelief expression written across my face.

"Yeah baby, that's it! We going to start all over and get everything brand new!"

Three days later, we were on the Greyhound Bus headed to Saint Louis, Missouri.

Chapter Two
(Da Move)

*W*hen we first enter Missouri, I saw a sign that read, "Welcome to Missouri the Show-Me-State." I don't know what it was about that sign, but it stuck out to me. I wanted to know why they called Missouri the Show-Me-State.

As we continue heading towards our destination, I just looked out of the bus windows in excitement thinking to myself, *I hope it ain't going to be country where we going,* as we passed a field full of all Black cows. It was about the thirty-six one I had seen. I was starting to lose hope, as we continually passed fields after fields for awhile. I thought to myself, *I can't believe we had came this far to be getting ready to move on a farm. Auntie Keniesha or momma ain't never mention nothing about a farm, cows, chickens, and sheeps to me.* I felt like they played me for a fool.

It seemed like it was getting worse until I saw a sign that read "St. Louis City Limits." At that moment I knew that we were in the city and shouldn't have been seeing any more farms. As the bus driver switched highways and approached his exit, I saw some tall shinny grey thing that looked like reflecting mirrors going high up into the sky and coming back down to the ground. I became full of excitement and said, *"Ooh* momma, you see that?" pointing at this new object. "You know what that is?"

She looked in the direction of this object in amazement as well; but at the same time, my mother nor me knew what it was until another passenger who overheard me asking about it informed us. "It's called The Gateway Arch. It's the third tallest monument in the world. Isn't it a beauty?" the older lady replied. I just nodded my head in agreement.

Within minutes, we had arrived at the Saint Louis Greyhound Bus Station. My auntie Keniesha was already there waiting on us sitting inside her platinum gray Chrysler 300C. After a brief exchange in greetings, hugs, kisses, and getting our luggage settle into the trunk of her car, my auntie said, "I know ya'll probably hungry as hell after that long as ride! What ya'll want to eat?"

"I could go for an ole shrimp poor-boy." Cortez answered.

"A shrimp poor-boy! Boy we don't have that up here. What else do you got in mind?"

"Ya'll don't have shrimp poor-boys up here; aw man auntie! Ya'll sell crawfish up here; don't ya'll?"

"We do; but not anywhere around here. I got a place for ya'll. Ya'll want some pizza for now?"

"Sure, I can go for some!" Keisha calmly said.

"Can we get some with hamburger on it?" Cortez questioned.

"We sure can! Bacon, extra cheese, and hamburger is my favorite kind." Keniesha replied.

Within moments, we were pulling up to a building with the letters IMOE'S on it. "I-Moes! I never heard of this. Is they food good auntie?"

"First off, it's pronounced E-Moes; and their pizza is the best! You can only get it here in St. Louis. Wait until you taste it, you'll see." We finally entered the restaurant and I saw that it was quite a few people inside of there already. My auntie looked at me and asked me, "Cortez, what do you want to drink?"

"It don't matter to me auntie; I'm not choosy."

"Okay then, well go find us a table." Auntie Keniesha instructed me to do. I chose a table that set in the corner, but near the window. After a couple of minutes, both my mother and auntie joined me. Once they got seated and comfortable, Keniesha said in a serious tone, "I think that this would be a good time to discuss the house rules with ya'll before we even much get there." She then paused until she knew for sure that she had both of our undivided attention before carrying on. "I don't really expect much. All I ask of ya'll is: Whatever ya'll mess up, clean up. We all are old enough to clean up behind ourselves, and don't neither one of us sitting here have a maid. Second, don't leave anything on in my house if you are not using it because my bills are high enough. Third, I don't mind ya'll having company from time to time, but lets keep it to a minimum. I really don't want and I don't like having a bunch of people running in and out of my house. Overall, just respect the house; that's all I ask. Ya'll don't feel that I'm asking too much of ya'll, do ya'll?"

"Not at all!" momma replied.

"What about you Cortez?"

"Nope! Momma had way more rules than you do." I truthfully answered causing all of us to burst out laughing.

After we all got a good laugh in, momma asked her sister, "How are we going to split the bills? Cause as of right now, I have eight hundred dollars."

"As far as the bills go, as long as ya'll do what I asked and keep everything off when ya'll are not using something, then everything should be just fine. I make enough money at Southwestern Bell to cover the household bills. Remember this is about me helping ya'll; not ya'll helping me." Auntie Keniesha replied.

As soon as that conversation was established, the food arrived. We had pizza and hot wings. Off the flip, I was tripping off how thin the pizza was; but at the same time, it looked good as hell! The wings didn't look bad either. They were smoother in an orange color sauce. Auntie Keniesha said, "Don't just sit there and look at it, dig in!"

We all grabbed a piece and began eating. Momma was the first one to break the silence by saying, "Damn this pizza good!" and grabbed another slice.

Aunt Keniesha smiled and then asked, "What about you Cortez? What do you think about it? Do you like it?"

"Un huh! They should sell this in New Orleans!"

"Well that's good ya'll like it because I eat this all the time. We have one right by the house, but you can't go in there and sit down and eat in that one; it's only pick-up or delivery." She then said in between bits, "I'm happy ya'll came up here; I haven't seen my lil' sister and nephew in awhile now. I thought I was going to have to come down there and kidnap ya'll!" she said jokingly. "When we get to the house, I have a surprise for you Cortez."

"Well what we waiting for, we finish eating ain't we?"

"I'm just waiting on ya'll to say ya'll ready to go."

"Well I think I speak for both of us when I say we ready to go auntie." I held the door open for both my auntie and mother and ran to the car to open up the doors for them both again so we could hurry up and leave. I was so excited and couldn't wait to find out what my surprise was going to be, but I soon learned that auntie Keniesha drove like a bat out of hell as we flew down the highway passing cars.

We were all pretty quiet as if we all where in each of our own world until my auntie Keniesha broke the silence. "Keisha, you ready for tonight?"

"What do your crazy ass got up your sleeve?"

"You'll see!" aunt Keniesha responded with a smurf clearly visible on her face.

As we got off the highway, I noticed a big white tower was built in the middle of the street as cars drove in a circle around it. "What is that place called auntie?" I questioned eager to learn more about my new surroundings.

She said, "Oh that place been closed probably more than a hundred years now; but it's called *The Water Tower*. That's one of the places they sold slaves out of back in the slavery days. You see this street right here," she said pointing to a street that sign read 20th Street "everybody here in St. Louis calls this street *The Dub!* It's very dangerous over here, so stay from over there."

"I hear you loud and clear auntie"

My momma just being herself had to say something as If I didn't understand what auntie Keniesha just explained. "Your ass better! 'Cause Keniesha he likes to roam all over the place."

I just kept my mouth shut. We went down two or three more blocks and I noticed the streets signs read Grand Blvd. and Lee Ave., as we made a right turn onto Lee. I was happy to see so many kids my age outside playing and then all of sudden, the car started to slow down as auntie Keniesha made a U-turn and pulled in front of a nice house that looked better than most of all the other ones on this part of the street. She cut the car off and said, "Well, this is it! It ain't much, but its home!"

I said, "It looks good to me." as I opened the car door.

My momma said, "Yeah girl, this is a nice ass house. It looks like it was just built."

"It was; it's only about five years old." Aunt Keniesha said. "Wait until I show ya'll the inside." she continued as she popped the trunk so I could retrieve our luggage.

In the process of doing so, an older lady in the next house over from us yelled over the fence to my auntie, "This must be your handsome nephew and his momma?"

"It sure is!" auntie Keniesha responded back to her. "Ain't he a cutie pie? "

The older lady said, "He gone have all the girls calling all times of the night!" We all laughed as she came across the yard so my auntie could properly introduce us.

"This here is my sister Keisha and my nephew Cortez." My auntie Keniesha said.

"Well how are ya'll doing? My name is Rosemary; but just call me Rose. I stay next door, and just wanted to introduce myself. By the way, welcome to St. Louis. If ya'll need anything, just knock on my door; I'm always home."

As we entered the house, Keniesha said, "Just sit ya'll bags by the couch so I can show ya'll around the house real quick. This house has: two bedrooms, one bathroom, a dinning room, and a big kitchen."

I must admit that it was a nice house. She showed us her bedroom first, and than showed us the other bedroom. Upon seeing it, I said, "Momma, I want to sleep on the side by the window! "

Auntie Keniesha intervene and said, "You ain't sleeping with her; you got your own space down in the basement! I got it set up real nice just for you; plus you got a few gifts waiting on you down there."

"The basement! What the hell is that?" my mom asked as the exact same question ran through my mind.

Sensing the concern in her sister's voice, Keniesha answered, "It's the lower part of the house that people usually use for storing things. But instead of that, how I got it set up, it's going to be like Cortez own lil' apartment." All I could do was smile because I felt super special. We walked into the kitchen, and she opened what I thought was just a closet door. Instead of it being a closet though, it was the entry way to my room. The basement. As we walked down the steps, the rest of the room came into view. I thought this hidden room was off the chain even though it wasn't much in it. Auntie Keniesha said, "Now this is your room! I know it's not much in here right now, but next week I'll take you to get a few more things to make you feel even more comfortable. But for now, you got a brand new bedroom set, and a few more gifts that I know you going to love. As a matter of fact, go ahead and open your gifts and tell me if you like them or not. They right there in the corner."

I turned around and seen a television stand with no television on it; but sitting next to the stand was two nice size boxes. One was wrapped in some Christmas paper wrapping; while the other one was wrapped in some happy birthday design wrapping paper. I asked, "Which one should I open first?"

"Which ever one you want!" auntie Keniesha replied.

Keisha then said, "You should open the smallest one first."

I grabbed the smallest box first. I noticed that it had a nice bit of weight to it, as I picked it up and set it on the bed. Once I begin opening it, I saw the words play station; and out of excitement I yanked the rest of the paper off as fast as I could. "Look momma!" I yelled "Auntie Keniesha got me the brand new PS3 that I been asking for."

Auntie Keniesha said, "Opening the next one."

The next box was two times the size of the first one and weighted more too I quickly pull the paper off and underneath was a brand new Sony 32" flat screen television. I was out done. "Thank you! Thank you so much auntie Keniesha! I love them!" I said and gave her a hug and kiss.

"Why you spoiling him like that Keniesha?" my momma asked.

"Because I missed my nephew sixteenth birthday; and Christmas. Plus, he's my only nephew. Anyway, I'm glad that you like your gifts; but now I have somewhere I want to take your momma, and I need you to stay here and hold the house down cause you the man of the house now."

"I got you!" I said.

"Okay. It's late, so stay in the house and play your game. Don't go anywhere Cortez, because we won't be gone long."

"I'm about to play my game auntie. I ain't going outside, not tonight."

"Okay. Your momma and me are about to go get dress. If you want something else to eat or drink, the refrigerator is always full and some snacks are in the closet. We'll yell down here and let you know we gone before we leave."

As soon as they began walking back up stairs, I began hooking up my new video game system and began playing Grand Theft Auto as I sat on my brand new queen size bed. I guess about thirty minutes later, momma and auntie Keniesha came back down into my room to get my opinion on how they looked. I took a quick glance at them both and said, "Ya'll look good." Which they did, but turned my focus back on my game.

"He ain't paying us no attention; he all up in that damn game!" My mother said.

"Oh well, we gone! If you need to reach us, I wrote my cellular phone number down on a piece of paper on the dinning room table."

"Okay." I replied but kept my focus on the television screen.

Chapter Three
(Ladies Night)

"Girl, where in the hell are we going anyway?" Keisha questioned Keniesha.

"We about to go to the *Royal Palace*; so we can have a few drinks, and a lil' fun sis. From our conversation we had over the phone, it sounded like you needed a change of pace. Plus with all the extra hours I've been working, I need this break too! Besides, I seen you had your hair and nails done already, so I said fuck it; we out here tonight! Anyway, when was the last time we kicked it? It's been a hell of a long time!"

Thinking about that, I knew she was right and said, "I really feel like this is a good ideal. I should've been and came up here when you first asked."

"Well you don't need to worry about it now, cause ya'll here now; and you know big sis got some shit lined up for you already as far as work goes, but we can talk about that shit tomorrow. Tonight, we are just going to have fun!"

We arrived at the Royal Palace and the parking lot was packed with all kinds of brand new cars. I was excited to go in because I could hear the music jamming. When we finally got in, I could see the place was jammed packed, considering that it was pretty small on the inside. I quickly looked passed that after I down my first drink and my song *Step in the name of love by R. Kelly* came on. "This is my shit!" I said feeling the vibe.

"Girl, you look like you ready to start stepping. You still know how to dance, don't you?"

"Hell yeah! I can still get down!" I said with confidence. That's when I noticed that this spot was full of nice looking men. I told Keniesha, "Watch my drink while I get my step on sis."

"Okay girl, don't break a leg."

"Yeah right!" I said over my shoulder as I stepped my way onto the dance floor. I couldn't help thinking it felt good to be dancing and having fun with my big sis without all of the extra drama.

I noticed this fine ass nigga' looking at me from across the room. I assumed he had to be every bit of six feet, and two hundred pounds. He had a light brown skin complexion; sporting a wavy low hair cut just like I like. His outfit looked as if it was made just for him. He was the hottest nigga' in the whole damn club from my point of view.

He started walking towards me and I could feel this shyness hit me like a ton of bricks, because I just knew that he was coming to introduce his self. I tried to play it off like I didn't notice him, but it was too late. He approach me saying, "Excuse me Ms.; how you doing tonight? I don't mean to cause you any trouble, but I've never seen you in here before. My name is Quincy, but everybody calls me Que. What's your name?"

I quickly pulled myself together and answered, "My name is Keisha."

"Damn Keisha, I love your accent. Where are you from; and are you in here by yourself? If so may I dance with you?"

"No I'm not in here by myself, I'm with my sister; but I would love for you to dance with me, and by the way I'm from New Orleans." Just as soon as we started to dance, the song went off. Thank God it did because I felt a tingle between my legs as he brushed up against me and I smelt his cologne. I said, "It was nice meeting you." and turned to walk away.

"Hold up sweetie, can I at least buy you a drink since we didn't get to finish our dance?"

"Only if you're planning on buying my sister one too!"

"I'll buy the whole motherfucking bar if I have too! Just say whatever it's going to take for me to get to know you. Ms. Keisha from New Orleans!"

She blushed as she began walking back towards the bar where her sister was watching her from the side line, with Que right on her heels. "Oh shit, I see you! You ain't been here twenty minutes and already found somebody to talk too!" Keniesha said teasingly; and then turned her attention towards Quincy who was revealing his perfect even white teeth and smile. "Now who the fuck are you, trying to talk to my lil' sister?" she said jokingly.

"Calm down big sis; they call me Que. I hope it's okay with you for me to talk to your sister."

"Girl quit bullying him; he came over here to buy us a drink!" Keisha interrupted saving Que from being interrogated on the spot.

"Us!"

"Yeah, us!"

"Bartender." Quincy shouted over the blaring music.

The bartender quickly made his way over and asked, "What can I get for you today Que?"

"You already know what I want; but I want you to give these two beautiful women whatever it is that they want."

"No problem Que! Well ladies, what can I get for you?"

Keisha responded, "I would like a Long Island Ice Tea. Keniesha, what do you want?"

"I'll take the same thing she's having." Keniesha replied to the bartender who was checking her out.

"So you must come here all the time; you got the bartender calling you Que and shit." Keisha said striking up a conversation.

"Yeah, I do actually. I love the music and the food here. Speaking of food, would ya'll like something to eat? If so, order whatever ya'll want. I got ya'll."

"We straight; we already ate before we got here."

"That's cool. How long ya'll been up here?"

"I just got here today, but my sister been living here for a few years now." As Keisha was answering Que's question, their drinks arrived.

"So you just got here today; well how long do you plan on staying up here before you leave?"

"I'm here for good. My son and me needed a change in environments."

"So you have a son; how old is he?"

"He sixteen; going on twenty-six! His name is Cortez and he's my everything."

"That's good to hear; but you know that I have to ask you, are you still with his daddy because you are too beautiful to tell me that you are single unless something is wrong with you and I just don't know it?"

"Que, ain't nothing wrong with me boy; but for real, my son father past away a few years ago."

"Oh I'm sorry. I'm sorry to hear that."

"It's okay."

"Well, I'm single; with no kids. I just help my sisters with their kids. I have three nephews and one niece. My oldest nephew is sixteen like your son. Maybe, one day they might get a chance to meet each other."

"That might be possible; but anyway Que, what do you do for a living?"

"I'm a." just as he began to answer Keisha's question, someone interrupted their conversation by calling out his name. It was an older guy who had on more gold than the law should allow.

"Que, I need to talk business with you as soon as possible." The older guy said.

"Give me a second, and I'll be right with you. Say Blue, take care of these two! Whatever they want give it to them and it's all on me. Excuse me Keisha; I'll be back in a minute."

"I got you bro." Said the bartender. "Ladies, my name is Blue. Do ya'll need anything?"

"We good right now!" Keniesha replied.

"Well, whenever ya'll change ya'll minds, let me know. Just give me a holla'!"

While Blue was talking to us, I noticed Que and the older gentleman walked into a room behind the bar; and shut the door behind them. From what I could see, Que was a pretty well known guy; which is good most of the time, I was just hoping he wouldn't be gone too long.

"So what do you think about him sis?" Keisha asked Keniesha.

"Since you asked me, I say he's worth trying to learn more about. Now you can stop smiling so hard love bird!"

"I want another drink; what about you?"

"Hell yeah!" Keniesha replied and then said, "Say Blue!"

"How can I help you sweetie?" Blue asked as he came over.

"I would like another Long Island Ice Tea please."

"And you honey?"

"Another Long Island as well."

"I get that right away ladies!"

"Anyway Keniesha, I'm really feeling Que right now; if he ask me out, do you think I should say yes or would I be moving too fast?"

"Hell nor you wouldn't be moving too fast! That is what I brought you here for; to have fun and meet new people. So far you doing good at that, but I ain't telling you to go fuck him tonight that'll be on you."

"Girl quit playing; you know he ain't ready for none of this pussy. His sexy ass wouldn't know what to do with all this." Keisha said but briefly allowed her mind to wonder on how fucking him would feel before Blue came back with their drinks. "Thank you Blue."

"Anytime ladies."

"I know one thing, you got the hottest nigga' in here." Keniesha begin before Keisha cut her off.

"Oh shit, he's on his way back over here girl."

"I hope I didn't take too long; is everything going okay? Blue been getting ya'll whatever ya'll needed?" Quincy said as he returned.

"You straight; and Blue is one of the best bartenders I've ever seen." Keisha answered trying not to reveal how much she was anticipating him coming back.

"As long as ya'll are having a good time, then I'm good. Are you ladies driving home tonight? Do ya'll stay near by?" Que asked out of concern because he notice Keniesha appeared to be a lil' tipsy.

"We stay close by, so we gone be okay." Keisha answered.

"I was just asking because I wouldn't want ya'll to get too drunk and couldn't make it home safely." He replied honestly. That scored him a couple of more like points in Keisha's book. Then he continue, "I'm really feeling you

Keisha, and really would like to see you again after tonight. I personally be all over and busy a lot, but I would love to show you around the city. I know a lot of places we could go."

"Oh yeah; like where?"

Before Que could answer, his cellular phone rang. "Oh shit!" he said out loud and then told me, "Give me one second." as he took the call walking away. It had to be something important because he came back with a whole different expression on his face. "Look Keisha, something just popped up and I have to go. I'm sorry I have to leave like this, but can I at least get your number so we can talk more?"

Keisha firmly said, "No; but I'll take yours!"

"Fair enough! Blue, I'm out; but I need you to make sure these ladies make it to their car safely for me." Then he dug into his pocket and pulled out what had to be at least ten thousand dollars in all one hundred dollar bills. He peeled off five crispy bills and then handed it to Blue saying, "Three of that put in your pocket; the other couple of hundred should cover my tab."

"Thanks Que!" Blue said then turned around and began walking off.

Que then peeled five more hundred dollar bills off his knot and tried handing it to Keisha while saying, "Take this right here, just in case ya'll end up needing to catch a cab or anything else."

Keisha quickly decline his offering saying, *"Naw*; we good!"

As soon as I said that, Keniesha elbowed the shit out of me saying, *"Naw*; we ain't good!"

That was my clue to get the money as I said, "Thank you Que."

"You welcome. Get my number from Blue and call me whenever you get ready." We hugged and then he left.

"Keniesha, he wants your sis!" I said feeling myself just a bit.

"You better make sure you get his number and call him then."

"Okay I plan too, trust me."

"And just for future reference sis, when a man offers you that kind of money with no strings attached, you don't ever turn it down!"

"Since when did you become an expert in men? Where's your man at?"

Feeling insulted and all in her feelings, Keniesha snapped, "I ain't got one, and I don't need one. I've been having fun just dating around; but tonight was all about you. Whenever you ready to go, just let me know."

"I'm ready now! Let me get this phone number from Blue and we can go."

I called Blue and asked for Que's phone number. He wrote it down for me, and asked, "Can I get anything else for either one of you?"

"Naw, we about to go; but thank you for everything."

"Well hold up one moment and let me get security to escort ya'll out to ya'll car."

"Cool!"

Security came and walked us to the car, opened the doors for us, and even watched us pull off safely. We were quiet the whole ride home which was only about six minutes if that. Infact, we actually made it home at 2:46a.m.

When we went inside the house, I said, "I'm about to check on Cortez." but Keniesha didn't say a word. She just straight into her room and closed the door. I got halfway down the stairs that led to Cortez's room, and heard a low snore coming from him. I thought to myself, *Ain't this cute; my baby sound asleep.* Then I went to my room, undressed and fell out thinking, *I'll call Que tomorrow!*

Chapter Four
(Settling In)

I don't know what time it was when I felt asleep or when I woke up; but momma and Keniesha had already made it back in without me even knowing it. I went upstairs to use the bathroom, and then brought my suitcase down stairs in my room and unpacked. Next, I hooked up my X-Box that I had brought with us and began playing it until I heard foot steps. Once I knew that they both were up, I decided to slide on some clothes and see what they were up too.

As soon as I made it up stairs, I seen auntie Keniesha was in the kitchen pouring her a cup of coffee. "Good morning auntie Keniesha." I said and caused her to jump.

"Good morning baby! How did you sleep?"

"I slept so good; that I didn't even here ya'll come in last night." I said as my stomach made a loud growling noise.

"Oh baby we got to do something about that; I can't be having my nephew stomach making them type of noises."

"What you about to cook auntie?"

"I ain't about to cook nothing! We're about to get your momma up; so we can go get something to eat at Goody Good's."

"Goody Good! What's that?"

"Only the best breakfast spot in St. Louis!"

"Well I'm about to get her up right now!" I went down the hall and burst into her room, "Momma get up!"

"Boy, what do you want?" She said aggravated as she set up.

"I want you to get up and get some clothes on so auntie can take us to get some breakfast from Goody Good."

"Goody Good! What the hell is that?"

"It's a restaurant and auntie Keniesha said they got the best breakfast in St. Louis."

"Okay Cortez, I'm up!" she said as her head started pounding from last night drinking. "I'm about to take a quick shower and brush my teeth. Hand me my Black bag please." After Cortez handed her the bag, she opened it and pulled out a matching bra and panties set and then asked Cortez as she got up to walk to the bathroom, "Can you please do me one more favor and look in my suitcase and grab my red Polo shirt and Polo blue-jean shorts, and just leave them on the bed when you find them?"

"Okay momma, but hurry up!"

I felt like shit from those damn drinks from the night before. I hadn't drunk any liquor in awhile and now I was remembering why. As I turned on the shower and waited on the water to get hot, all I could think of was Que and how much of a gentleman he was to me and Keniesha last night. I said to myself, "I'm going to call his sexy ass after breakfast."

I shower and got dressed as fast as I could, and then went into the living room where Keniesha and Cortez was joking around as they waited on me. "Girl, your sleepy ass ready; because my nephew hungry? Plus we got business to take care of. I spoke to my friend, Derrick, this morning about you a job, and he said to bring you up there today so you can fill out an application."

"What kind of job is it?" Keisha questioned.

"Girl get your shit so we can go! I can tell you about it over breakfast. All you need to know right now is you can get paid twelve dollars an hour to do shit!"

"Well that sounds good to me so far." Keisha stated. As we arrived at Goody Good, I noticed that the line was wrapped around the whole damn building. "Damn Keniesha, we got to wait in this long ass line? It's too early for all this shit!" I said bitchingly because my hangover was kicking my ass.

"Girl, stop all that crybaby shit! We gone walk straight in and order; I'm a regular here every Saturday at nine o'clock a.m.! They already have a table ready and waiting for us, lil' ugly!"

Keniesha and Cortez found that to be funny, but I sure in the hell didn't. I just got out of the car and tried my best not to slam the door. I could smell the food from outside the building as we walked up to the door; and that alone made me have a craving for some grits and eggs with a biscuit or two.

As we walked in and straight up to the counter, an older white man yelled out, "Keniesha, we've been waiting on you. You running a lil' late this morning I see."

"Yeah, I got my big headed lil' sister and my nephew with me today; and she slowed us down a bit. But you know that I wouldn't miss my Saturday breakfast for nothing in the world."

"I know; that's why I kept your favorite table open for you. You all can just go get settled in, and I'll be over shortly to take ya'll orders."

"Okay; and thank you Tom."

"Girl, this is a cool lil' spot and their food smells good as fuck. What's the best thing to order?"

"Everything is good in here; so order whatever catches your eye."

"Okay now, how are you all doing this morning? My name is Tom and I'll be taking your order this morning. Are you all ready to order, or do you all need another minute?"

"Oh we ready!" Cortez answered as if starving to death not even glancing once at the menu.

"Okay, so the regular chicken and waffles for you right?" Tom asked Keniesha.

"Yes sir!"

"Chicken and waffles!" Keisha repeated.

"Yeah girl, it's good as hell. I get it every Saturday."

"Okay! Well I'll try that."

"Me too!"

"Okay, three chicken and waffle plates. What would you all like to drink?"

Cortez and Keniesha said at the same time, "Orange juice!" then looked at each other and smile.

"I'll take a cup of coffee with lots of sugar and two creams."

"Okay, your food will be here shortly; and I'll be right back with your drinks."

"Now are you ready to hear about the job?" Keniesha asked her sister.

"Of course!"

"Well first off, the job is at Aldi's grocery store. You will be a cashier, but at least you will be able to sit down while you ring their stuff up. You will get at least forty hours a week, and they start you off at twelve dollars an hour. The bummer part is that they get paid bi-weekly, so every two weeks you would get a pay check; but my friend said that he would see to it that you make at least a thousand dollars every pay period or close to it as long as you are willing to work. I told him, I need him to come through on this one for me, and I know he's going to look out for you because he' dying to get a sniff of my dirty panties!"

Cortez just shook his head in disbelief that this was how his auntie actually talked. By then Tom returned and placed each of their drinks in front of them as he said, "Okay ladies and gentleman, here are your drinks and your food is almost ready as well" and then walked off just as quickly as he appeared.

"Okay, so how long do you think it's going to be before I'll be able to start?"

"I can't say for sure, but we going to go straight there when we leave from here so you can fill out the application and I can introduce ya'll to each other; but I'm kind of sure he'll start you the next day, well I know he will if I tell him too!"

Tom returned to their table again, this time bringing them their plates. "If you all need anything else, just let me know!" and he was gone again.

They each looked at each other's over filled plate and thought, *Wow! What a breakfast this is about to be!* As they each began digging in. After a couple of bits, Keniesha licked her fingers and said, "After we leave from here and get done taking care of business, I want to take my favorite nephew out to get the new Jordan's that came out this morning."

"Now that's what I'm talking about auntie; I love Jordan's! Can I get a hat too?"

"Yes sir; you sure can! The faster we get through eating, the faster we can get business handle."

"Oh man, we need to hurry up then!" Cortez said excited.

"Boy, you are something else! First, you rushed us to get here; and now you trying to rush us to leave." Keisha said jokingly as she realized her headache had gone away.

About fifteen minutes later, breakfast was paid for and they were on their way to Aldi's. Keisha was shocked to see how close the grocery store was to their house. She thought to herself, *I'm very happy with the fact that I'll be able to walk home from work and it'll only take me about fifteen minutes tops; until I get my own car.*

Before we got out of the car, Keniesha called Derrick and told him we were on our way in. I could hear him say, "I'm on my way up front right now."

When we walked in and I seen how easy the job looked, I was happy as hell. All of a sudden, I heard whom I assumed had to be Derrick call out, "Keniesha!" as he walked u and gave her a hug. "And how are ya'll doing today? Everything good?"

"Yeah! This is my sister Keisha and my nephew Cortez, and ya'll this is Derrick." Keniesha quickly introduced everyone.

"How are you doing today, Derrick?" Keisha asked.

"Oh, I'm blessed! I've been waiting on you to get here and you are right on time. Lets go back to my office and discuss business; shall we?"

"Sure; lead the way!" Keisha said with confidence.

"Okay Cortez, if you see anything you want, you better get it while we are in here." Keniesha said as they began walking off.

Derrick showed me to his office and said, "Shut the door behind you please. Okay Keisha, I brought you back here so you can get the special treatment."

"Special treatment!" Keisha repeated with a look of confusion on her face.

Derrick noticed her face expression and quickly replied, "The special treatment is, I'm not going to run a background check on you and have you take a million and one unnecessary tests. You know how to add and subtract don't you?"

"With no problem!"

"Well see, you just passed all of them unnecessary tests." He smiled and then continue, "Are you comfortable with counting money?"

"I can count money with no problem."

"Great! So if I hire you as a cashier, when will you be ready to start?"

"I can start as soon as tomorrow morning, if you would let me."

"That'll be good. I'll give you a t-shirt now." He said as he pulled a shirt out of his draw. "I hope a small fits."

"A small is perfect." Keisha said ready to start.

"Now all I need you to do is get a pair of Black slacks and show up here at seven o'clock tomorrow morning. Your hours will be seven a.m. to three p.m. if that's okay with you."

"That's perfect for me."

"Well, you got the job Keisha. Just take this application home with you and bring it back filled out tomorrow so I'll be able to put you in our system."

"Thank you Derrick!"

"It's no need to thank me; anything I can do to help, consider it done. Now I know your sister probably in a rush and I got quite a bit of paperwork to do, so ya'll go ahead and get out of here. Tell Keniesha I said I'll call her when I get off."

"Okay, and thanks again Derrick." On my way back up front, I had the biggest smile on my face thinking about how I haven't even been up here a full two days and already got a job. That's when I spotted Cortez eating some candy.

"Well what did he say?" Keniesha asked as I approached.

"He said I got the job and I start tomorrow morning. He seems hella' cool too! Why you ain't made him your man yet?"

"Because he ain't ready for me yet; but I been thinking about giving him a chance. Anyway, congrats on your new job."

"Yeah momma, congratulation! Now can we go please?" Cortez asked.

"Yeah bad ass lil' boy; come on!" Keisha said.

"Auntie Keniesha, can we go get my Jordan's now?"

"Yes sir; we sure can!" Keniesha said as she started up the car. "We got to hurry up, because everybody and they momma want these Jordan's. Marty's here we come." Keniesha said as she turned up the radio and sped off the parking lot. Bobbing their heads to Lil' Wayne's "Go DJ", they pulled up to Marty's. Keniesha said, "Ya'll go ahead and go in and order the shoes, while I find a parking spot." Surprisingly, Marty's wasn't packed; so it didn't take long before Cortez had his box of Black and red Jordan's number twelve's.

As Keniesha walked into the store, Cortez was trying his new shoes on. "Damn those fire! Can I get a size seven in women's please sir?"

"Yes ma'am; you sure can!"

"You might as well grab me a size six in women too while you at it." Keisha added on.

"Yes ma'am, I'll be right back with them." The clerk said.

"We gone be fresh as hell. Cortez go and pick you a few Jordan shirts out to go with your shoes." Keniesha said as the clerk brought back their shoes to them. They tried them on and both pair fitted perfectly. "Okay Cortez, are you ready?"

"Yeah auntie; I got three shirts, but they ain't got no hats in here."

"I know." Keniesha said, "We gone go down the street to Gus for that." as they began to check out.

"Your total is $507.87." the clerk said after ringing up everything. "Will you be paying with cash or credit?"

"Cash!" Keniesha replied.

"Un-un, I got this!" Keisha interrupted.

"*Naw*, I'll pay for everything this time." Keniesha insisted.

"No you ain't!" Keisha carried on the brief argument while the cashier just looked at them both in total disbelief.

After a couple of minutes of discussing who would pay for what, they finally came to an agreement. Keniesha would pay for her and Cortez's shoes since she originally planned on getting them; and Keisha would pay for her own shoes and Cortez's three shirts. They separated the stuff, and then paid separately. The sales clerk simply said, "Ya'll must be sisters!" as we grabbed the bags and left out the store.

"We gone walk to Gus, because it's right on the corner." Keniesha said once we all were outside.

"Well lead the way." Keisha said looking around.

When they walked into Gus, the first thing Cortez saw was hats. As he picked through them, Keniesha went and picked out a pair of black Levi jean-shorts to go with his shoes. After that, she made her way back up to the counter to pay when she seen Cortez only had one hat in his hand and Gus was trying to cut him deal if he would choose to get another one. "Go ahead!" Keniesha shouted out "Pick out another one." Once Cortez picked out another hat, Keniesha asked Gus, "How much is my total?"

"Well I told him that I'll give him the hats for two for forty; and you got these shorts. The shorts normally go for forty as well, but I'm going to give them to you for thirty five. So your total is seventy five even and I'm not going to charge you any tax. Next time if you buy your shoes and everything else from me, I'll give you an even better deal."

"Well I'll keep that in mind Gus, and thanks for the deal." Keniesha said as we walked out the door and back to the car. As we pulled off down Washington and made a right turn onto Tucker Street, auntie Keniesha said, "Now it's time for your surprise Cortez."

"Dang auntie, you got something else for me?"

"*Naw*, I don't have anything else for you, but I want to take you somewhere." She said as she continue driving.

When they hit Market Street, Cortez said, "Look momma, you can see that big silver mirror thing from here."

"You sure can." Keisha replied.

They parked downtown on the landing along the Mississippi River, and then they walked up the steps that led to the Gateway Arch. "Wow momma, look at how tall it is!"

When Keniesha seen how fascinated her sister and nephew was she asked, "Do ya'll want to go inside there and go to the top?"

"You can go to the top of this thing?" Keisha and Cortez asked at the same time.

"*Yep* and it's pretty cool too. So ya'll want to go in it?"

"Yeah!" Cortez quickly responded.

"What about you sis?"

Keisha was still staring up in the sky looking at the arch when she lowly replied, "I guess so."

"Well let's do this then!" Keniesha said cheering them on but on the inside was really afraid of heights herself.

Cortez was amped to get to the top, but Keisha was a lil' nervous about it. As they got on the elevator and it started going up, Cortez asked, "Auntie, how many times have you been up here?"

"None!" Keniesha honestly confessed.

Keisha snapped, "None! What the hell you mean none? You were just saying outside, that it looked cool from here."

"Girl I know what the hell I said and why I said it!"

"So why in the hell did you say it then?" Keisha continue snapping.

"Because I knew if I didn't, your scary ass wasn't going to come up here."

"Well, I think we at the top now!" Cortez said as the elevator doors opened. They stepped out of the elevator and seen other people were looking out of the windows and joined in. "Dang auntie, you can see all of Saint Louis from inside here!"

"Almost." Keniesha responded.

"I think this is the most coolest place I've ever been." Keisha said.

"Well I'm happy ya'll like it; but now let's get out of here before it breaks." Keniesha replied as the wind slightly shook the arch. Once they made it out of the arch, Keniesha noticed it was almost 6:30 p.m. "Let's get out of here so we can get your momma some work pants; and then we can get some Chinamen."

"Okay."

As they was pulling off, Keisha said, "You know I don't really care for Chinese food girl; they be having too many vegetables in their rice."

"I don't like the rice down in New Orleans either; but these Chinamen places up here ain't nothing like down there. The rice come way different and I promise you gone love it. If not we'll get you something else."

Pulling up to the St. Louis Center Mall, Keniesha said, "We got to hurry up and get in here before Dots closes."

"What's Dots?" Keisha questioned.

"It's a female clothing store that's pretty reasonable for what you need."

They went in the mall and went straight to Dots to get Keisha pants for work. On the way out, Keniesha spotted a booth in the middle of the mall that made copies of keys and had copies made for each Keisha and Cortez. After giving them their own copies Keniesha said, "Please, whatever ya'll do try ya'll best not to lose them."

After they got back in the car and began driving, Keniesha asked, "What kind of meat would you like in your rice Cortez?"

"I don't know; what kind can I get?"

"You can get: beef, chicken, ham, duck, pork, shrimp, or you can just get some special fried rice which has some of all the meats in it."

"I'm feeling special, so I'm going to say special."

"Okay, what about you sis? What kind do you want?"

"I'll take the shrimp."

"Okay, let me call our order in so it will be ready by the time that we get there."

Keniesha called a Chinese restaurant and order: a half of an order of shrimp, beef, and special fried rice; two orders of cheese fries; and a shrimp St. Paul sandwich. When she got off of the phone I asked her, "Auntie, what is a St. Paul?" she explained to me that it was some type of sandwich that they sold only at Chinamen in St. Louis. When they pulled up to the Chinese restaurant, Cortez said, "Dang auntie, you got everything by your house!"

"I know, that's one of the reasons I like it over here. I just don't like this park on Sundays. Anyway, I'll be right back because I'm sure our food is ready."

Right across the street from the Chinese restaurant was the park, but it looked harmless to me. Auntie Keniesha came right back out the restaurant carrying three bags that looked like they were full of stuff so I opened the door for her. Once she got in the car, she pulled off cutting across the park heading straight home.

Once we reached the house, Keniesha said, "Home sweet home!"

"I'll do the honors and open the door so I can try my keys." Keisha said. "And Cortez you need to try yours too!"

"Okay momma, I'll try them as soon as I sit these bags down in the house."

After I freed my hands, I tried my set of keys. Once I seen that they worked, I went straight into the dinner room to eat. "Damn, this shit fire!"

Keisha said with a mouth full of food.

"Yeah, I'm loving these St. Louis food." Cortez said.

"I told ya'll it was going to be good and it wasn't nothing like New Orleans rice. I'm glad ya'll like it though. Oh yeah nephew, cut this sandwich in half so you and your momma can see what a St. Paul sandwich taste like. Pour a pack of sweet and sour sauce on it first before you cut it, that'll bring the taste out."

After I did everything auntie Keniesha said and tasted the sandwich, I was hooked without a doubt. Then I knew where to get it from, I knew they were going to be seeing more of me. I said, "Auntie I don't know who turned you on to all of this good food you keep coming up with, but I'm glad they did because so far everything been good."

"You know I got to make sure my family gets the best of anything I'm going to give them. Anyway, eat all ya'll want, I had enough! Plus I got to get ready to go to sleep because I got to get up at five o'clock in the morning to get ready for work."

"I guess I'm going to call it a night because I got to get up early too." Keisha said out loud.

"Cortez, I don't want you around there at that park tomorrow, because it's dangerous over there. You can go outside, but stay on Lee please."

"Okay auntie!" I replied; but auntie Keniesha just didn't know that I had already made up in my mind that I wanted to see what the park was like and why she thought it was so dangerous.

Chapter Five
(Exploring Da Hood)

The next morning when I woke up, I noticed that I was the only person in the house when I went up stairs and yelled out, "Momma. Auntie Keniesha." and got no response from neither one of them. That's when I remembered that they both had to go to work this morning. I said to myself, "Oh what the hell" as I walked to the refrigerator to grab something to eat.

Stuck to the refrigerator freezer door was a not that read, "Cortez" in really big bold red ink. "I left $50.00 on your television stand for you; and remember I said stay away from that park. Love you."

I was happy as hell about the money. I proceeded to go through the refrigerator, and eventually decided to make me a quick ham and cheese sandwich; with a cup of Sunny Delight. As I was eating, I thought not only am I going to the park, but I'm going to look fresh as fuck when I do get there; plus have a pocket full of money. "I can't wait to see what these St. Louis girls like up here." I said out loud but to myself walking back down to my room eating my sandwich.

I got downstairs and went straight to my T.V. stand to see the fifty dollars my auntie left me. I picked it up and went to a pair of all white Air-force 1's where I kept my money that I had been saving up for a PS3, which my auntie ended up buying me, and removed the money from inside them. I counted out three hundred and sixty dollars as I thought to myself, *Yeah, let me hurry up and get dress so I can get the hell out of here.*

After taking a shower and brushing my teeth, I got dressed. I felt fresh as fuck with my new Jay's and outfit on. The president himself couldn't have told me that I wasn't the shit. I looked at my clock and seen that it was 10:08 a.m. and was like, "Yeah, I got plenty of time to do whatever I want too." as I put my three hundred and sixty dollars in my pocket and walked out the front door.

Outside, it was about eighty-five degrees and everybody was out. I heard Ms. Rose yell out, "Hey Cortez; how are you doing this morning?"

"I'm a lil' bored; but I'm fine other than that. What about you; is everything okay?"

"Yeah everything okay; I'm just waiting on my bad ass grandkids to get here. When they get here, I'll introduce ya'll. I promise you, you won't be bored when my two grandsons Ej and Corey get here."

"How old are they?"

"They about your age; they're sixteen and seventeen. How old are you?"

"I'm sixteen."

"Oh yeah, ya'll should get along just fine. They know everybody around here too."

I got happy when she said that; because I was dying to meet some new people in the neighborhood. As I sat on the front porch thinking to myself, I saw a black Dodge Magnum pull in Ms. Rose driveway. Two girls and two boys jumped out saying, "What's up grandma?"

"Nothing much" Ms. Rose replied, "but I have somebody I want to introduce ya'll to. Cortez, come over here and meet my grandkids. Corey, Ej, DaMesha, and Raykel, meet Cortez. This is Keniesha's nephew from out of town; and he's looking for somebody to show him around. Can ya'll show him around the neighborhood?"

"Yeah." Ej said as he went on to say, "Those Jay's super hard. Where you get those at?"

"I got them yesterday from some store ya'll got up here." I responded.

"Well, I'm going to let ya'll do whatever teenagers ya'll age do; I guess." Ms, Rose said as she turned to go in the house.

As soon as she shut the door behind her, Corey looked at Ej and said, "You got the money right?"

"Yeah nigga'!" Ej replied. "Let's go get the shit, so we can hit the park. DaMesha and Raykel, we'll be right back. Are you gone come with us Cortez?"

"Yeah; just let me lock up the house first." I ran back across the lawn and locked up the house. As I walked back down the steps where they were waiting on me, I asked, "Where we about to go anyway?" as I noticed DaMesha looking at me as if she wanted to just run up and rape me.

"We're going to go get some weed." Ej said as we hit the corner.

"Do you smoke?" Corey asked.

"Hell yeah I smoke! I ain't had no weed since I been up here though."

"Do you got some money to put in on some?" Corey questioned.

"Yeah; how much you need?"

"We got ten dollars a piece." Ej cut in.

"Since ya'll got twenty dollars, I'll match ya'll twenty. Is that cool?"

"Damn right! That way we can get a quarter ounce, blunts, and a pack of Newport's." Ej said.

"Where is all of that music coming from?" Cortez asked.

"Oh that's coming from the park around the corner; and we definitely gone go there. But first, we gone go get some weed; then go to the store. Once we leave there we gone go back to my granny's house and roll up and get the girls; and from there we going straight to the park." Ej answered as if he already had this planned out in advance.

When we got to the weed man's crib, Ej asked, "Where your twenty dollars at Cortez?"

As I went into my pocket I said, "Are ya'll sure twenty dollars gone be enough, because I'm trying to get high?"

"Yeah." Ej said as I pulled twenty dollars out of my knot.

"Damn nigga', you balling!" Corey said staring at my money as I put it back in my pocket.

"*Naw*, I wouldn't say that." I responded as Ej went up a set of steps and inside the weed man's house. While waiting on Ej to come back, I asked Corey, "So do you and your brother come over to your granny's house all the time?"

Corey corrected me, "He's my cousin; not my brother. DaMesha is my sister; and Raykel is Ej's sister. But yeah, we come over every weekend just about. We love going to the park on Sundays."

Before I could ask anything else, Ej came out and said, "Alright lets go; he plugged us!"

"Plugged us! What does that mean?" I asked dumb founded as they laughed at me.

"That means we got more than what we paid for." Corey explained.

"Where you from?" Ej asked.

"I'm from New Orleans!"

"What part of New Orleans?"

"I stayed in the third ward."

"For real? We heard about the third ward before." Corey joined in.

As we walked up to the corner store, Ej said, "Yeah, there go that bitch ass nigga', Lil' T, right there; I'm about to whoop his ass!"

"Man chill out." Corey said "We ain't on that shit today Ej; we got Cortez with us. Plus I ain't trying to get dirty before we hit the park. Let's just get our shit, get high, go to the park, and pull some hoes. Ain't that right Cortez?"

"Yeah, but I'm down with whatever!" I said.

"Alright, but next time he getting his ass whoop!" Ej said as we walked in the store.

When we got in the store, the man behind the counter said, "What's up Ej? You ain't starting no shit in front of my store today, are you?"

"*Naw* Ali, not today; but you need to keep those chump-ass niggas' from in front of your store."

"I'm trying." The clerk said. "What can I get for you today?"

"Let me get a pack of Newport's long, a box of Swishers Sweets, plus two single Swishers, and that's it."

"Okay, your total is ten dollars and fifty cents."

"Okay, cool Ali. Just keep the change." Ej said. "Remember I owe you from last week."

"Oh yeah, we even now." The clerk said.

As we were walking out of the store, four guys were coming in. one of them was the boy Ej wanted to fight. That dude looked at Ej and said, "Yeah nigga' you don't wan'na see me!"

Ej stood his ground and replied back, "*Naw*, you don't wan'na see me! You only talking shit 'cause ya'll deeper than us; but you gone see me soon enough. Today just ain't the day." Then continue walking out. As soon as we got outside Ej continue, "Lets hurry up and get back to granny's house so I can roll up; Lil' T got me pissed the fuck off."

Before you knew it, we were back at Ms. Rose's house where Raykel and DaMesha was on the porch waiting. "Damn," DaMesha said, "it took ya'll ass thirty minutes to go get that shit and come back. Ya'll hella' slow; or did ya'll get into some more bull shit?"

"Almost! I wanted to whoop that nigga' Lil' T ass, but Corey oh good Samaritan ass stopped me. Lil' T tried to stunt on us 'cause they were deeper than us, but fuck them. Let's go in the back so I can roll up and we can smoke." Ej replied, but clearly was still upset.

"Why don't we just go in my auntie's house and roll up; that way won't nobody see us." Cortez suggested.

"That's cool because it's hot as hell out here." DaMesha said. When we walked in, we went straight to the dinning room and sat while Ej and Corey rolled up. "So Cortez, how long are you going to be up here?" DaMesha asked.

"Me and my momma up here for good."

"Are you coming to the park with us?" Raykel asked.

"Hell yeah, I been waiting to hit the park up!"

"We done rolling up;" Corey said, "Can we smoke in here?"

"Fuck *Naw*; but we can go on my back though!"

"That's cool." Ej said.

As we all made our way to the backdoor, I offered everybody a cold soda in which everybody accepted; and then we went outside to smoke. "We got seven fat ass blunts;" Corey said, "so me and Ej gone keep one for the road. Cortez, we gone give you one to keep; and the other five we gone smoke."

"That's cool," I said, "but before we even start smoking give me my blunt so I can go put it in my room."

"Here, pick one." Ej said. They all looked fat as hell; so I just grabbed one and took it to my room.

When I came back, we began smoking. We smoked two blunts back to back; everybody except Raykel. "It's eleven twelve ya'll." Raykel said. "Let's go; ya'll can smoke at the park."

"Yeah!" DaMesha agreed.

We all got up and walked to the park. The park was packed. I know it had to be at least a thousand people out here. I was hella' amped to finally be here, and to see what goes on in this park that made my auntie feel that it was so dangerous. Ej said, "Corey, there go Kayla and Re-Re. Lets go get them *cuzz!*"

"We'll be right back." Corey said. "Don't go nowhere ya'll."

"We ain't." Raykel replied.

"Cortez, can I just call you Tez?" DaMesha asked.

"Yeah, I don't have no problem with that. Back home, my friends use to call me that or Lil' Threat."

"So Tez, did you have a girl friend back home?"

"*Naw*, I wouldn't say that; but I had my fair share of female friends."

"Boy, how old are you?"

"I ain't nothing but sixteen."

"Well sixteen or not, I'm only seventeen and I think you are sexy as fuck! I love your accent!" DaMesha said as they both smiled.

"Girl, don't nobody want you!" Raykel said with a jealous expression glued to her face.

"Shut up lil' girl! Don't be mad because I look better than you." DaMesha replied.

Raykel was at a lost for words because she knew hands down that DaMesha looked better than her body wise and face wise. DaMesha stood about five feet five, with a smooth dark milk chocolate skin complexion, with the body of a young goddess. On top of that, she had sexy hazel brown eyes, with dreads that were just starting to touch her shoulders.

"Whatever!" Raykel said, "Its cool!"

"I know it can't be nothing but cool, lil' girl." DaMesha continue their small argument.

"Chill out DaMesha!" Cortez interrupted trying to squash their argument.

"Okay, I'm done. Anyway, just call me Mesha 'cause that's what everybody else calls me."

As we were talking, we heard an out burst of commotion. We turned around and seen that it was a group of females beginning to fight. It had to be at least eight of them fighting from what I could see as the crowd gather around. All of a sudden in the mist of the fight, three of the girls that were fighting, just broke out running and jumped into a car. I just knew that they had to be getting ready to grab something to use, until I heard the car starting up; but the other five girls wasn't finished yet. One of the five girls grabbed the driver hair through the window and proceeded punching her in the face. As the driver tried to back out of the parking spot, she hit the car that was parked behind her. *Boom!* The girl on the outside, still had her hair in her hand; punching her as she put the car in drive and smashed into the car that was parked in front of her. *Boom!* I couldn't believe what I was witnessing; but in the process of her doing so, the girl on the outside let her go. That's when I noticed the owner of the first car, running to his car as the girl who hit his car finally got control of her car and began pulling off.

We could hear the owner of the car that got hit yell out, "Oh fuck *Naw*; I'm gone kill that bitch!" as he jumped into his car and chased her down shooting at her car.

I couldn't believe how live shit was. We could see everything. All the way up to the point the girl crashed into the light pole at the end of the park, and the guy in the other car kept going. Everyone else in the park remained calm, as if this type of stuff happened all of the time. The police and the ambulance arrived on the scene, but they didn't stop anything.

"Tez, it get crazy out here sometimes." Mesha said.

"I can see, but it's cool. I'm from the third ward, so I'm use to seeing crazy shit."

"The third ward, where is that?"

"It's in New Orleans! So where ya'll from?"

"I'm from the projects." Raykel said proudly.

"Yeah, Raykel and Ej are from the projects downtown; and me and Corey are from Penrose which is the next street over from Lee." DaMesha said.

"What school do ya'll go to?"

"Corey and me go to The Mount which is right there across the." DaMesha pointed out.

Raykel added, "And me and Ej go to Vashon; its downtown by our house."

Just when I started thinking, this park ain't as dangerous as my auntie made it seem like it could be, Raykel said, "Oh fuck *Naw*" running pass DaMesha and me.

As DaMesha and me turned around, we seen Ej and Corey fighting against three other guys and began running towards them. Ej was fighting the same dude we saw at the store earlier that he had exchange words with; and Corey was fighting two people at the same time. To my surprise, Ej and Corey appeared to be winning the fight. Just as we got a few feet away from them, one of the guys fighting Corey pulled out a small Black gun and shot Ej twice; and then broke out running with his friends following behind him as we all froze in shock in our tracks.

Everybody came back to reality when Mesha and Raykel burst out screaming for help. My high was instantly blown from everything that was going on. Corey ran over to Ej side and prompted him up asking, "Are you okay? Can you move? Talk to me Ej!"

Raykel just kept screaming, "Oh my God! Oh my God! Please help us!"

Mesha started screaming out of anger, "Them niggas' dead! Fuck that, they gone get theirs; on my momma!" as everybody crowed around us.

It was so many people around us that we couldn't even see the street any more; but we could hear the sirens from the ambulance and the police cars approaching the scene. All I could think was, *Damn, my auntie told me not to come to this damn park. Now how in the hell am I going to get myself out of this mess?*

As the crowd opened up and the paramedics came to Ej's aid, I started having flashbacks of seeing my father in the same bloody position, but only he didn't make it. That's when I really started to worry about Ej and if he was going to live.

The police kept asking random questions to the crowd. "Do any of ya'll know who did this? Do we have any witnesses on the scene? Come on folks, we know somebody had to have seen something. Give us a name." but nobody had even much attempted to sneeze a word.

Seeing how everyone that was present remained silent, made me recall part of my father's last lecture very clearly. "Never ever under no means give them information concerning anything or anybody; even if they promise to help and protect you!" Even though that was Ej and I witness what had happen to him, I remained silent when the police questioned me.

After awhile, they let us go, and we began running home. Right before we got there, I told DaMesha, Raykel, and Corey, "Listen up ya'll, I need ya'll to cover for me. Whatever ya'll do, don't tell anybody that I was with ya'll because mw auntie specifically told me not to go to that park and I don't want to hear her mouth. Ya'll got me?"

"We got you." Everybody agree at the same time.

Before I went in the house through the backdoor, DaMesha said, "Tez, give me your number so I can call you and let you know what's going on and if my cousin is going to be alright."

I quickly gave her my auntie's house phone number and said, "Make sure you call me."

Once I got inside of the house, I saw that it was 3:14p.m. and I had made it home before my momma and auntie Keniesha did. Just as soon as I started going down the steps that led to my room, I heard my mother and auntie coming through the front door. My auntie was saying loudly, "Now see, that's why I told Cortez to stay away from that damn park. Somebody had done shot Ms. Rose's grandson, Ej, up there today."

"Cortez, come here." Keisha yelled.

I came up stairs and said, "Hi momma; hello auntie Keniesha."

"I was just checking on you." Keisha said.

"You know somebody done shot up Ms. Rose's grandson today?" Keniesha said staring at me.

"For real?" I said trying to play like I had the slightest ideal of anything had happen to him. "I just met them earlier today, and they seemed pretty cool. What did he get shot for?" I asked.

"I don't know." Auntie Keniesha responded.

"Ain't you glad you listened?" my momma said, "If you would have been with him at the park, they probably would have shot you too."

"Yeah momma, you right! Thanks auntie for giving me the heads up."

"You welcome baby."

Then I asked, "Is everybody else okay auntie?"

"Yeah I guess." Keniesha said. "I seen Corey and DaMesha on the front, but I didn't see Raykel out there. But I'm sure she's okay because Rose would have told me if something would've happened to her."

To quickly change the subject I asked, "So how was your first day at work momma?"

"It was good. Infact, it's the easiest job I ever had in my life. I can get use to it!"

"That's good to hear. I had a cool lil' day myself. I met Ms. Rose's grandkids and hung with them a few hours. We went down to the store and hung out on the front. Speaking of the store, thanks for the money you gave me auntie."

"You don't have to thank me Cortez. As long as you listen to what I tell you, I'll give you anything you ask for."

I then said to myself, "I can't wait for Mesha to call me." I wanted to find out if Ej was okay; but I really wanted to get to know Mesha better because I liked the fact that she stayed close by. After about thirty minutes had passed, I went down in my room to clear my head.

As soon as I got down there, I went to turn on my television and seen the blunt from earlier that I had hid on the side of it, and said to myself, "Damn right, I'm about to smoke this motherfucker right now." But then I thought, *Damn, how in the hell am I'm going to light it?* I thought about it for a quick second and then thought, *My auntie smoke cigarettes, so I know she has to have a spare lighter somewhere in this house.* I went up stairs and began searching the house like a burglary trying to find a lighter, but I didn't have to look to hard though before I found a pack of matches in the kitchen cabinet.

"Yes!" I said t myself; and then I yelled out loud, "I'm going outside on the front ya'll"

"Okay, but don't go too far." Auntie Keniesha responded.

"Yeah, don't go nowhere Cortez." My momma said as I shut the front door behind me.

I walked outside and saw that the front was nearly empty. A few folks were down the street, but not that many. I wonder if DaMesha and them had gone home already, but I wasn't about to knock on Ms. Rose's door to find out. Instead, I eased around to the side of the house, and fired up the blunt.

Spooked that Ms. Rose nosey ass might be lurking in a window and come out and bust me; I smoked a lil' more than half of the blunt, and then put it out. Unlike earlier, I was high as hell. I made my way back to the front of the house and just sat on the porch thinking to myself and watching cars go by.

After about an hour had passed, my auntie came to the door with the cordless phone in her hand and said, "The phone is for you; it's DaMesha." as she handed it to me and then walked back inside the house.

"Hello, is everything alright?" I asked as I anxiously spoke into the receiver.

"Yeah, everything okay; and my cousin is going to be alright. The doctor said that he'll be able to come home in a few days."

"That's good." I said feeling slightly relief.

"Just so you know, I made sure didn't anybody say shit about you being at the park with us."

"Thanks Mesha; because my auntie would've been disappointed and upset with me."

"I got your back! Tez, I know we just met today and all, and you probably gone think that I'm tripping; but I'm gone go ahead and put it out there. I really like you, for real. You don't have to say anything; I just wanted you to know it. I also wanted to know, if we could hang out tomorrow after my momma and me get done at the mall?"

"Sure; I'll like to hang out with you." I said with a big ass smile on my face. Who was I kidding; I was excited about seeing her tomorrow?

"Well, I'm about to go do these damn dishes real quick so I can have my way at the mall tomorrow. I'll see you tomorrow; and Tez!" she quickly yelled catching me before I hung up the telephone.

"Yeah." I answered.

"Feel free to call me whenever you feel like it. This is my own private line. Do you have caller ID?"

"Yeah."

"Well you can get the number from there; and I'll see you tomorrow." She said and we both hung up.

After the phone conversation with Mesha, I went inside. I went down to my room to pick out a pair of jeans to wear with one of the other Jordan t-shirts my momma had brought me. When I found my Black True Religions, I ironed them and sat my outfit to the side. After that, I started playing *Midnight Club Dub Edition*.

As I was playing, all I could think of was all the tight ass cars I seen at the park today. It seemed like every car out there had rims, beats, and candy paint on them. After all the crazy shit that happened today, I still wanted to go back to the park. Hell, I knew I was going back.

Chapter Six
(A Long Time Cumming)

I had just jumped out of the shower and freshen up, as I finally started to relax. I thought to myself, *Damn, I never called Que.* I quickly picked up my phone and called him. As the phone rang, I felt nervous as hell. After the forth ring, a man finally picked up.

"Hello; who is this?" the man that answered the phone asked.

"This Keisha; may I speak to Que?"

"Awe shit, what's up Ms. New Orleans? I thought you wasn't gone ever call!"

"*Naw*, it ain't like that! I just have been busy as hell, trying to get settled in. Plus, I started my new job this morning."

"So you already are working now? That's what's up! Where are you working at?"

"At some store called Aldi's!"

"Do you like it?"

"It's cool; plus, it's as easy as it can get."

"Well, that cause for a celebration. Would you like to go out with me tonight, Ms. Keisha from New Orleans?"

"Where would we go on a Sunday night?"

"Now that's a surprise you will have to wait and find out; but I promise you will enjoy yourself. Have you ate dinner yet?"

"No, I actually haven't ate anything yet; Mr. Que from St. Louis!"

"So is it a date?"

"Yeah, it's a date."

"Well, when can I come pick you up?"

"I can be ready in about thirty minutes; so any time after that is fine with me."

"Okay, it's 6:15 p.m. right now; so is seven o'clock cool?"

"Seven o'clock is perfect." Keisha said anxious to see Que.

"Where am I picking you up at?"

"5039 Lee."

"Okay, you right in the hood. Well you go ahead and get ready, and I'll call you when I'm outside."

"Alright." Keisha said and they both hung up.

Soon as Keisha put the telephone down, she ran to her closet to find her something to wear. She quickly chose a sexy red floor length dress that had Black and gold beads around the neck, with the back cut out. She then pulled out her Black and gold beaded sandals to match the dress. After getting dress, she looked in the mirror and knew Que wouldn't be able to take his eyes off of her.

Keisha was five feet eight. She weighted about a hundred and thirty seven pounds; but had the body of a Victoria's Secret model, with the exception that she had a lil' bit more ass on her. The dress she chose, hug every curve in her body perfectly. Keisha was flawless and she knew it.

"Keniesha." Keisha called out.

"What?"

"I need you to come do me a favor real quick; please!"

Keniesha entered the room and said, "Now what do you need with me; and where you going all dressed up like that?"

"I'

M going out with Que, thank you; but I need you to style my braids for me."

"I got you." Keniesha said. "Turn around; I'll braid them into two pigtails."

"That's cool!"

"Where are ya'll going anyway?"

"I don't know, he said it's a surprise; but he promised that I would enjoy myself though."

"You better not forget you got to go to work in the morning and come in with a hangover. And you bet not give him no pussy either!"

"Yes ma'am! Anything else mother?" Keisha said sarcastically joking. "Girl, you know it ain't nothing like that. We just are celebrating me finding a job already."

"Okay sis, you just" Keniesha started, but before she could finish her sentence Keisha's phone started ringing interrupting her.

"Hand me my phone sis."

"Here you go."

"Oh shit girl, it's Que. Hello!"

"You said your address is 5039 Lee; didn't you?'

"Un-huh!"

"Well, I'm outside."

"Okay, give me one moment and I'll be right out." Keisha said and then hung up. "He outside already; so hurry up and finish Keniesha!"

"I'm just about done now." As soon as she finished the braid, she looked at her younger sister and smiled. She then said, "Now all you need to do is go in my room and look on my vanity table, and spray on some of my Juicy Couture perfume and you gone kill him dead."

They both laughed as Keisha ran into her sister's room and found the perfume; sprayed some on, and then ran towards the door saying, "Thank you sis; and keep an eye on Cortez for me."

"It's a lil' too late to be asking that; but I'll do it anyway. Enjoy yourself!" Keniesha said and locked the door behind her sister.

As soon as Keisha stepped out the door, Que got out of the car. "God damn!" Que exclaim. "I knew you looked good, but you killing the game tonight! You got me wishing you were mines and shit!" Que said as he opened the door for Keisha.

Before Keisha got in the car, she looked Que in the eyes and said, "I just might be, if you play your cards right!" and then she got in the car and sat back as Que shut her door for her. When Que got in the car and pulled off, Keisha said, "This is a nice car. What kind is it?"

"It's a BMW 750LXI. It's the biggest BMW they make. I'm glad you like it."

"This car look like it cost a hundred thousand dollars."

"You can say that." Que responded. "Do you like steak?" he asked.

"I love steak! Steak and potatoes; steak and eggs. Hell, I like steak like I like chicken; and you know Black people love them some chicken." She said causing them both to laugh.

Que jumped on Interstate 70 and did a 100mph all the way downtown. When they got off of the highway, they pulled up to the Lumiere Casino front doors where a valet attendant opened their doors for them to get out. "How are you doing today, Mr. Quincy?" the attendant asked.

"I'm doing just fine." Que answered as he went in his pocket and handed the attendant a hundred dollar bill. Then Keisha and him proceeded into the casino.

"Why are we at the casino?" Keisha asked.

"Because they have a good ass restaurant inside; and with you on my side, I feel lucky! Do you like to gamble?"

"No, well I never tried. I don't be having money just to blow or give away. I told you I have a sixteen year old son; and he costs me more than I can afford."

"Well not tonight! Tonight I want you to play as if you don't have a worry in the world. I'm going to show you how to play poker."

"Poker! I guess it's never too late to learn something new!" Keisha said. "Well, count me in; I'd love to learn."

They walked into the restaurant and was taken to a table immediately as if they were awaiting for there arrival. They both quickly order their food so they could get back to their privacy. As they waited on their food, Que asked, "So Keisha, what is it going to take for me to make you all mines?"

"Well for starters, I want to get to know more about you before I even much consider that ideal. Second, I need to know whoever I choose to be with, loves me and my son three hundred and sixty five days a year. Holidays included!"

"Well that's fair, and I understand that you and your son come as a package. Any real man should." Que began "But, I know there has to be more."

"Oh believe me, there is!" Keisha said as if she been asked this question plenty of times.

"Like what?" Que asked really curious of what else she would come up with.

"I need a man who can help me out from time to time when I'm in need without all the extra shit; or who gone throw it back in my face that he helped me."

"That's reasonable and understandable; carry on."

"Oh, I need good sex too! That's important!" she said and they both laughed in an unnecessary to be explained agreement.

"Diner is served." The waitress said placing their plates in front of them.

"Thank you." They both said and the waitress turned to walk away.

"This steak looks good and juicy." Keisha said.

"Yeah, but not as good as you." Que replied.

"But I ain't on the menu though, so you can't eat me; at least not yet." Keisha said with a very seductive smirk on her face.

The look on her face really turned Que on as he said, "On the menu or not, don't look like that cause it makes me feel some type of way."

"Oh yeah, so tell me how it make you feel."

"Lets just say it makes me feel a lil' razzed dazzle if you catch my drift." Que replied as his dick started to rise instantly.

"I know you ain't getting hard over there!" she jokingly teased.

"Actually, I am. You just don't know it!"
Que said so seriously.

"If we weren't in here, I'd tell you to show it to me." Keisha teased as they continue to make sexually and casually conversation until they finished their meal and left to try their luck on the poker table.

On the way to the poker table, Que couldn't help replaying the conversation they just had over diner in his head and said, "You know, as far as helping you goes, I'll help you do whatever you need help with as long as I see you trying to help yourself first. And sex, oh my God; I promise you great sex and head!" Que said licking his lips and then continue, "I also would love to meet your son. I told you my sister have a son his age. Anyway, just think about it. If you need anything that I can help you with, please feel free to let me know. If I can help you, I got you. If not, I ain't gone lead you on. I'm might can't perform miracles or do magic tricks, but I'm straight when it comes to something money can fix."

"You talk a good game, but I can't wait to see how everything works out. You know they say Jesus puts people in your life for a reason, so I'm dying to know why he allowed me to meet you." Keisha said as they reached the poker table.

"Okay this is poker." Que said going into his pocket and removing a knot of money. He counted out two thousand dollars and said, "Here, this your cut. Watch and learn!"

"You want me to gamble all of this money?"

"Yeah! Win or lose, I don't care; just as long as you have fun."

"What if I lose it all, then what?"

"Don't worry about it! It's plenty of more where that came from."

Que tried to explain to Keisha the rules of the game as he placed bet after bet. After Keisha felt as if she was catching on, she placed a few bets herself until she got frustrated with trying to keep up with the rules and losing. She quickly convinced Que into trying their luck on another game.

As they made their way through the casino, they ended up stopping at a Blackjack table. A waitress walked up and asked, "Can I get a drink for you all?"

"Sure, I'll take a eighteen hundred on the rocks." Que replied.

"Okay, and you ma'am?" she asked Keisha.

"What do you have that's not too strong, but I can still get a buzz?"

"Do you like Hypnotic?"

"I don't know, but I'll try it as long as it's not too strong."

"No ma'am, it's not strong at all." The waitress ensured her and then said, "I'll be right back with your drinks."

They got their drinks and hit the Blackjack table only to lose even more money. Keisha ran out of money first, but didn't notice it from the drinks the waitress kept bringing them. Before Keisha even realized it, she was drunk; and they had lost more than seven thousand dollars.

A guy in an all Black suit with some type of ear piece on, walked up and asked, "How are you doing Mr. Quincy? Is everything going alright for you tonight sir?"

Que quickly turned around only to recognize that it was a casino employee. He then answered, "*Naw*, I've seen better days! I'm down almost ten thousand dollars."

"Whoa! That's a lot of money to lose in one night. Can we at least accommodate you with a presidential suite for the night? It'll be totally on the house sir."

"Sure." Que said. "I need somewhere quiet to sit back and relax as I collect my thoughts."

"Well sir, I'll get everything set up and have a staff member bring you your key and escort you to your suite shortly."

"Okay, I'll be in the bar area."

Keisha didn't really catch the conversation between the casino host and Que because she was too busy watching an older woman on a slot machine who was winning big, wishing it was her. About twenty minutes later, a different casino host walked up behind Que and said, "Mr. Quincy." causing Que to turn around instantly.

"That will be me."

"I'm here to show you to your room sir."

"Okay, just give me a second to grab my company and I'll be ready." Que said. "Keisha come on, were going to the 4 Season."

Once Keisha grabbed his hand, the host asked, "Are you ready now?"

"Yeah, lead the way."

"Okay, right this way." The host said as he led them to their room. As he opened the door to the suite and handed Que the key he asked, "Is there anything else I can help you with sir?"

"No;" Que said "but if you make sure that you are the only person to come to this room Mr."

"Oh, Jones; I'm Mr. Jones!"

"Yeah, only you Mr. Jones; I promise to take real good care of you before I check out."

"That will be no problem sir!" Mr. Jones said excusing his self.

When Keisha stepped into the room, she was very shocked to see how spacious and plush the room was. The suite itself was the size of a three bedroom house with an upstairs and downstairs. She hadn't ever been in a hotel room the size of this one. "Why did you get this big ass room?" Keisha asked "I know it cost a fortune."

"Actually, it's free to me;" Que said "so make yourself at home. I'm about to run down stairs to the ATM right quick, I won't be long. Do you want anything while I'm down there?"

"No." Keisha replied.

"Okay; well, I'll be right back then."

When Que walked out the door, Keisha went for a tour around the penthouse suite. After finding the master bedroom, she jumped in the extra luxury California king size bed like a grown ass kid. *Oh my God, this bed is so comfortable.* She thought to herself. As she laid there enjoying the softness for a moment, she started thinking about Que and what she was about to do to him when he came back in the room.

Unaware that fifteen minutes had passed since she started fantasizing about what she wanted to do with Que, Que came back into the room to find Keisha naked as the day she was born sitting on the diner room table with her legs spread wide open and feet relaxing in two different chairs.

"What are you doing?" Que asked as his dick got rock hard in a matter of seconds from looking at the perfectly evenly shaved phat pussy in between Keisha's legs.

"Well you treated us to dinner already, so I figured that I'd give you desert on me." Keisha replied with that seductive face that she knew Que liked. "You do like sweets, don't you?"

"Hell yeah! Who don't like a good sweet desert specially made for one?" Que quickly answered while walking towards the table.

Keisha slowly rubbed her fingers in a circular motion around her click until juices flowed freely from her pussy; and the she put the same fingers she was using in her mouth and said, "Yeah, it's good and sweet for you! Come and get you some of this pussy, since you promise me good sex and head! On the way up here from New Orleans, I saw a sign that said *The Show-Me-State,* so I need for you to show me why it's called that, Mr. Saint Louis!"

Que walked up to Keisha and laid her back as he began to kiss her from her first set of lips, to her second private set of lips. Yeah her pussy lips that is. "Yeah, this pussy taste good and sweet." Que said as he continued to suck on the pearl of her pussy and finger her with two of his fingers at the same time.

Keisha couldn't believe how good his head game was, she thought as she enjoyed rubbing the deep waves in his head. After a few minutes, Que sat down in one of the chairs in front of her and said, "I've been a bad boy. I forgot to say grace." as he placed her legs on his shoulders. "God is good! God is great! Let me thank you for this pussy, I'm about to eat!"

"Amen!" they both said at the same time.

After saying his version of grace, he went back to eating her pussy from the end of the table like Jesus in the last supper. Fifteen to twenty minutes into it, Keisha couldn't keep quiet, so Que reached up and put two of his fingers in her mouth. She sucked his fingers warming her jaws up for the dick she was about to suck; but from the head he was giving her, to the sight of seeing him do it, gave her a rush as she screamed out loud, "I'm about to cum!"

"Good, cum on!" Que said, "cause I wan'na taste it" a few licks later, Keisha squirted all in his mouth like a squeeze juice.

"Oh my God!" Keisha kept saying as she kept cumming. When she sat up to see Que, she saw he was swallowing every drop of her cum turning her on even more.

"Stand up!" Keisha order Que.

"Yes ma'am! Whatever you want."

Keisha unbuttoned his pants and pulled his dick out in disbelief of how big it was, but there was no time to ask how long it was. She knew it had to be nine inches or longer. She just got down on her knees and started licking and sucking. As she sucked his dick, she took her pigtails down with her left hand letting her sandy brown micros hang loose before placing Que's hand in it.

Que grabbed a handful of her hair and pushed her head down on his dick until he seen her eyes water up. He repeated this process three or four times before saying, "Damn, you got some fire ass head."

"This the way you like it?" Keisha asked with a mouth full of dick already, but yet was forcing Que's dick head down her throat while using her muscles in her throat to massage the rest of his dick.

Que couldn't say anything at first; he just curled his toes up tight. After a few seconds he said, "Fuck yeah, you got that fire!"

Keisha was ready to feel his dick inside of her; so she let it be known. "Que, I can't take it any more. Please fuck me; I need it now!"

Que stood her up and looked her in her eyes as he slid into her warm wet pussy. After a few long deep strokes, he asked, "Are you ready to go airborne?"

"Yes!" she said, "I'm ready for whatever you do to me."

That's when Que picked Keisha up with her legs in his arms and began to pound in and out of her pussy. She couldn't control herself at all. She tried to keep quiet but Que said, "All *Naw*, let it out. Talk to me; tell me how this dick feel." but Keisha was at a lost for words. The only sounds she could make were moans of pleasure that she been holding in and waiting to release. Que kept fucking her as he carried her over to the couch and sat her on top of it. He then told her to bend over so he could see his self go in and out of her. That's when he really started fucking her hard as he pulled on her micros. She kept screaming how much she loved his dick, not knowing that it was only turning him on more. He was drilling her like this could be his last nut; and then just roughly flipped her onto her back and said, "Now just lay there as I fuck you, so I can read your face." After penetrating her and playing with the pearl of her pussy while talking dirty, Keisha went into an orgasm. She started shaking like a fish out of water, screaming as if he was killing her.

"Keisha; Keisha." Que repeated as he tapped her on the shoulder "Wake up!" As Keisha eyes blinked open and close Que said, "Wake up, it's almost two in the morning and I got to get you home."

Keisha was lost for a moment; she didn't remember going to sleep. She looked around confused as if looking for something, and then asked, "What time is it?" as she pulled herself together and realized she'd been dreaming a dream that she didn't want to wake up from.

"It's almost two in the morning." Que repeated. "Come on so I can get you home; I wouldn't want your sister to think that I kidnapped you." He said causing them both to laugh. "You ready?"

"Yeah, I'm ready." Keisha said as she thought to herself, *Damn, a dream or not, I'm wetter than a motherfucker; and he ain't even bust a nut!*

As they got in the car and begin pulling off, Que turned on the radio as *Sam Cooke "It's been a long time coming"* started to play in the background.

Keisha asked, "How long was I sleep; and why didn't you wake me up?"

"You were sleep for almost three hours." Que answered. "I was only gone for about fifteen minutes, but when I came back in the room you was knock out. I was gone wake you up, but it looked like you was sleeping so peacefully that I just let you sleep for awhile."

"I'm so sorry; I hope you ain't mad! I don't even remember falling asleep; but that bed was just so soft I couldn't resist it I guess."

"Well let me know when you are off and I'll take you to get the exact same kind of bed, so you can have your own soft plush ass bed." He said as they both smiled.

"You don't need to do that." Keisha replied.

"Yes I do!" Que said. "A beautiful hard working such as yourself has to get her beauty sleep." Keisha didn't have a come back line for him after he said that.

They pulled up to Keniesha's house and Que got out an opened up the door for Keisha as he asked, "Can I walk you to the door?"

"Of course you can!"

As they walked to the porch Que asked, "Well did you have a good time night?"

"No!" Keisha said flatly. "I had a great time! It's been a long time coming since I had a date with a real gentleman like you; I'm really hoping to see more of you."

"You can bet you will. What are you doing this weekend?"

"I don't have any plans as of now, but I don't know what my work schedule is going to be like yet." Keisha true fully answered.

"Well, if it's okay with you and you happen to be off, I would love to take you out again."

"That will be cool. Infact, I'm all for it."

"Okay, just let me know when you got time."

"Que, for you I'll make time." Keisha said with a warm smile.

"Well I don't want you to be sleepy at work tomorrow, so I'm going to let you go ahead and get in. I'll be waiting on you to call me when you can."

"Okay, I'm going to get in here and lay my ass down; but I'll be sure to call you tomorrow." She replied as she opened the door. "Oh Que!" she said before he could walk off the porch.

"Yeah." He answered as he turned around to see she was walking up to him.

"Your kiss!" she said as she stood on her tippy toes and planted a kiss on the right side of his cheek. "Thank you for tonight."

"It was all my pleasure! We'll always have fun as long as you allow me to hang with you. Now get you some sleep."

"Okay; drive home safe." She said as she went inside and closed the door behind her.

Oh my God, I had a good ass night, Keisha thought to herself as she pulled her uniform out for work in the morning. "I think I just might have found me someone special." Keisha said to herself as she smiled.

As she laid awake in the bed trying to go to sleep, she just kept thinking of the dream she had at the casino. Replaying image after image in her mind, she thought, *Damn, I can't believe how he made me cum!* Then she felt asleep.

Chapter Seven
(Hidden Secrets)

*A*fter going to sleep so early the night before, Cortez woke up to an empty house. He didn't know anything about his momma going out on a date with Quincy. He woke up at nine eleven and went up stairs to grab a quick bit to eat. When he made it to the kitchen and realized how peaceful it was, he thought to his self, *I can get use to this.*

After Cortez finished eating a ham, egg, and cheese hot pocket, he ran and grabbed the cordless phone out of the living room to take back down stairs with him. Out of boredom, he went through the caller ID to get DaMesha's telephone number so he could call her. For a second, he thought that it had gotten erase because he hadn't came across it after the first ten numbers he stroll through; but there it was, the very next number. He quickly dialed the phone number, but the phone just rung until the answering machine came on. As bad as he wanted to speak to DaMesha, he didn't leave a message.

Maybe she's at the mall, he thought as he noticed a door in the middle of the back wall of the basement. "Now I wonder what's in there." Cortez said to his self out loud. When he opened it, he was shocked to see that it led straight outside to the middle of the back yard once he walked up a few steps.

Damn right, I can smoke out here without them even knowing I went out, Cortez thought. Before closing the door he quickly thought, *Fuck it, I'm fin'na smoke the rest of my blunt right now.* He went and got the piece of blunt that he had saved, along with the pack of matches that he had found the day before in the kitchen. As Cortez was smoking, all he could think of was DaMesha; and what they were going to do when she got there. That's when he thought to find a movie for them to watch, but quickly dismissed that ideal and said, "Fuck it; we'll just go with the flow."

He went back in the house and ran up stairs to take a shower. He carried the telephone with him everywhere he went. Cortez jumped in the water and allowed the warmness of it to mellow him out. As soon as he started to get out, the phone rang. Once he seen DaMesha name show up on the caller ID, he quickly answered it. "Hello; what's up Mesha?"

"Nothing! I just walked in the house and seen you called."

"Yeah, I was just calling to tell you good morning."

"All that's so sweet!" DaMesha said while blushing. "What are you doing?"

"I'm drying off and about to put my clothes on. Did ya'll go to the mall yet?"

"Yeah, we just got back."

"So what did you get?"

"You'll see when I come over. Speaking of that, I'm about to come over my granny's house as soon as my momma get done putting her stuff up."

"Good, cause I'm bored as hell!" Cortez said. "I'm fin'na put my clothes on and wait on you. Hopefully, ya'll won't be too long."

"We're not!"

Cortez hung up the telephone and put his clothes on as fast as he could. He grabbed his Jay's and ran out the front door. He was in so much of a rush that he put his shoes on, on the porch. About five minutes later, the Black Dodge Magnum pulled up in front of Ms. Rose's driveway.

DaMesha jumped out the vehicle, and as soon as she shut the door the Magnum pulled off. Cortez's eyes were stuck on DaMesha. She was dressed in her a pair of Black 501 skinny legs jeans; an all red and Black Polo shirt; and to top it off, she had on the same red and Black Jordan's number twelve's that Cortez was rocking with her dreads hanging.

She walked straight up to the porch where Cortez was as he said, "So you trying to be like me I see!"

"If that's how you want to look at it!"

"It's cool! You're looking good as fuck trying to follow my lead!" Cortez jokingly teased.

"Boy, whatever! Thank you anyway; I was hoping you would like it." DaMesha said with a big smile on her face. "Your eyes are red as the fuck! Are you high?"

"Yeah; I got a lil' buzz going on."

"Well share that shit! Where it's at?" DaMesha asked wanting to be on the same level that he appeared to be on.

"That shit gone! That was just a piece of blunt I had; it wasn't even a half."

"Well, I got half on a sack."

"You don't have to spend your money; if you know where to get it from, I'll buy it."

"I know where to get some from."

"Well soon as you ready, I'm ready."

"Okay, let me let my granny know I'm here and see if she needs something from the store. I'll be right back."

As DaMesha went inside of her granny's house, Cortez ran inside of his house to get his money and keys. When he came back outside, DaMesha was already waiting on him as he locked the door. On the way to the weed man's house, Cortez noticed that they were going the same way him, Ej, and Corey took the day Ej got shot.

They were talking for a second when Cortez asked, "Where Corey at?"

"He's at boxing training." DaMesha answered. When she said that, Cortez thought, *so that's why he was beating those two niggas' asses like that.* "Okay, we're here." DaMesha said as they walked up to the same building that Ej went too. "What you want to get?"

Cortez handed her a fifty dollar bill and said, "Get whatever you can with that."

"Are you sure?"

"Yeah; spend it all if you want too."

"Okay." DaMesha said as she walked up the steps and knocked on the door.

"Who is it?" a male voice came from the other side of the door.

"It's Mesha."

Cortez could hear everything that was said clearly as it sounded like somebody was running down some stairs behind the close door. When the door opened a dude around their age if not a couple of years older appeared saying, "Well, well, well; if it ain't Mesha. Long time no see!"

"Yeah, yeah; let me get seven grams!" she said and handed him the fifty dollar bill.

"Come in."

"*Naw*, I'm good! I'm gone stand right here."

"Okay, I'll be right back with your shit in a second." He said then vanished behind the door as he closed it. When he came back, he handed her twenty five dollars and what had to be damn near a half of ounce if not more; and then said, "When you gone give me a chance, Mesha?"

"Never!" DaMesha flatly said and added, "Add you already know this!"

The dude just shook his head and looked at me as he replied, "So who is he; your lil' boyfriend?"

"Yeah he is." DaMesha answered as she turned to walk away. I just stared at him then lifted my shoulders as if saying I don't know what to tell you bro.

That's when he replied, "Well, you know where I'm at."

DaMesha never responded. Instead she said, "Come on Tez, we got what we need from him." When they turned the corner DaMesha said, "Here

Tez." and handed him his change and the weed.

"Damn, this ain't the same shit from the other day! This shit smells good as a motherfucker."

"Don't it? I can't wait to see what it smokes like. Anyway, when we get to the store, I'm going to get the blunts because Ali ain't gone card me."

"That's cool!"

The store front was full of a bunch of motherfuckers. It had to be eight or nine motherfuckers just posted up. One of the lil' cats out there said, "What's up Mesha?" as we approached.

"Not shit!" she replied and kept walking.

Once we got in the store, DaMesha walked to the freezer and got her a huge freeze pop and then went straight to the counter. "How are you doing today, Mesha?" Ali asked.

"I'm okay."

"I heard your brother beat some ass at the park yesterday. Is it true Ej got shot?"

"Everything you heard is true. Can I get two boxes of Swishers Sweets, and this freeze pop?"

"Yeah, it's on the house today." Ali said as he handed her the Swishers.

"Thank you Ali." DaMesha said. "How you know what happened at the park anyway?"

"You know I know everything; I keep my ears in the streets! Tell Ej, I said keep his head up."

"Will do." DaMesha responded as they walked out of the store.

When we walked outside, everybody was silent and just staring at us as we walked off. For a second I felt awkward, but I guess that was because I didn't know any of them. To break the silence that had formed between us I said, "So I take it everybody around here likes you."

"Yeah, you can say that; but ain't none of them got a chance. It's only one person out here that I'm feeling right now; and you know who he is." DaMesha said looking Cortez in the eyes.

"Oh really?"

"For real!"

Walking back up to the porch, Cortez said, "We can go in and roll up instead of trying to sneak and do it out here."

"You right on point. I damn sure don't need my granny catching us in the act."

"I'm pretty sure I wouldn't hear the end of it either." Cortez replied as he opened the door for them to go inside.

They went straight down stairs to Cortez's room. When DaMesha seen the bed she said, "So this must be your room."

"Yeah, this my lil' honeycomb hideout. It ain't much, but I can do just about whatever I want to down here."

"You gone have to sneak me in some times." DaMesha joked.

"Whenever you ready." Cortez seriously replied. "You can even spend a night if it was up to me as long as you not gone get in trouble."

"We'll see because I'm gone hold you to that."

"You do that!"

After they rolled a box of the Swisher Sweets up, they went out of the basement back door and sat on the steps and smoked. "So have you spoken to Ej yet?" Cortez asked.

"*Naw*, but my momma said he was coming home today. He might be home now, come to think of it. He told Corey, him and a few of his homeboys gone shoot Lil' T's house up Sunday when his momma and brothers coming out for church; so he can get rid of the whole damn family at once to get it over with."

"Damn, he gets down like that? Tell him I'm down if he need some more help!"

"You can tell him yourself if you want too. I'm going to his house to see him when I leave from over here, but you can come too if you want."

"How we going to get there?"

"We can catch the bus! The Lee bus will drop us off right down the street from their house."

"Well, let's roll the other box of Swisher up for the road; and we can split whatever that's left. Matter of fact, I'm going to put these four blunts up, so whenever we come back we will have something ready for us to smoke."

"Okay." DaMesha said.

"I'll be right back. I'ma run up stairs and grab a sandwich bag right quick." Cortez said. When he came back with a sandwich bag, he took some weed out of the other bag and said, "Just take this weed and start rolling up while I split the rest." He looked at how much weed he had placed on the T.V. stand and asked, "You think you can roll a whole box out of that?"

"Hell yeah; and might have a little left."

"We'll see." He said and began helping her roll up.

Once they were finished rolling, Cortez split what was left as evenly as he could and then said, "Here Mesha, go hide this in your granny's house. I'm gone put mines up too, so we won't have so much on us."

"Okay, I'll be right back." She said.

As DaMesha went to do what Cortez said, he ran and looked at the clock. It was two twenty three. He quickly called his momma on the job and told her that he was going to the mall with Corey, DaMesha, and Raykel. "How are ya'll going to get there?" Keisha asked.

"We going to catch the bus that rides pass the house. They say it'll drop us off right in front of the mall."

"Okay Cortez. Just don't be gone all night; and don't get in no trouble."

"I ain't." He said and then hung up.

Once he put his stash of weed under his mattress, he went back outside. DaMesha was standing in her granny's doorway yelling, "I'll be back in a few hours granny." and shut the door. She then asked, "Are you ready?"

"Yeah."

"Okay. The bus stop on the corner, and one should be on the way because they run every thirty minutes." Once we made it to the bus stop DaMesha asked, "Do you want to stop and get something to eat before we make it to my auntie's house?"

"Yeah, we can do that."

"Okay, cause we can get off at Union Station and eat; and when we done we'll just have to walk right across the bridge."

"We can do whatever you want, Mesha."

"I like that!" she said with a smile on her face as the bus pulled up and they got on.

The bus ride was fast. They were at Union Station within fifteen minutes. "What's the Hard Rock Café?" Cortez questioned reading the sign.

"It's one of the restaurants they have inside of here. They got McDonalds; Hooters, and a few more other food spots in here."

"I want to check this place out; it looks nice. Plus we don't have one back home, and so far all the places that we don't have back home got some good ass food."

"It's cool you chose this café because to tell you the truth, it will be both of our first time eating here."

"The Hard Rock Café it is then!"

It took about twenty minutes for them to get a table. They placed their orders and as they waited DaMesha sparked up a conversation. "So this our first date!"

"So you really serious about us dating huh?" Cortez replied.

"Yeah; I really want you!" DaMesha came back. "To be honest, I ain't gone stop trying until I get you."

"Well, if you wan'na give it a try, let's do it."

"So you telling me, you my man?"

"Yeah!"

"Tez I promise you, you gone be happy you gave in." she said with a sexy smirk on her face. "Is there anything you wan'na know about me?" she asked as the waiter brought them their food and drinks.

"Yeah, actually it is. Out of all the niggas' that want you, why you choose me? What makes me so special?"

"I like the vibe I get from you; and your accent. You just different; and I like different."

"Are you a virgin?"

"No! I have had sex twice; but I ain't never sucked nobody's dick before, before you even much ask me! I ain't saying that I wouldn't ever try it with you; I just didn't like the person I was with enough to suck his dick. Can I ask you a few things?"

"Sure, go right ahead."

"I very seriously doubt you are a virgin; but it's killing me to know if you know how to eat pussy, because I love it and your lips just do something to me."

"*Naw*, but I'm sure it can't be too hard."

"Is your momma cool like your auntie; because I wan'na have a good relationship with my future mother-in-law?"

"Yeah she cool. She probably cooler; but every now and then she have her moments."

"Good, I guess I can work with her."

"What about your brother?"

"You don't have to worry about him. If I like it, he loves it!"

"Alright; is your daddy around?"

"*Naw*, but my momma got a man though. He's good to all of us; so yeah, I know how to treat a man if that's what you're wondering. I can cook! I'll clean and do anything else that'll make you happy. Just don't play me Tez!"

"I'll never do that Mesha! I like you too much."

"Well, we can finish this conversation later tonight on the phone. Let's get out of here."

"Well I'll pay for our first date, since it wasn't too bad." Cortez said jokingly.

"Tez, come on; we pay on the way out." She said. When they got to the front of the restaurant, DaMesha grabbed Cortez hand and yelled, "Run!" as she pulled him and they burst out the door as if they just had robbed the place.

They ran out and halfway across the bridge. When they stopped to catch their breath, Cortez said, "Mesha, you crazy as hell; but it was fun though."

"I know; that's why I did it." DaMesha replied. "Tez, I got something that's bothering me that I got to tell you before we make it to my auntie's house."

"What is it? What's wrong? What's going on?" Cortez asked in concern.

"I know you just met us and really don't know that much about us; but you don't owe me, Ej, or none of my family nothing. I like you because you seem different from the rest of these niggas' up here. Don't place yourself in a situation you can avoid just to try to prove yourself to any of these niggas'. My cousin and Lil' T been beefing for years. They use to be best friends back in the day. So if you tell Ej and his boys you gone ride with them, they gone hold you to it because your word means everything up here."

He thought about what she said, and knew she was right. Was I really trying to prove myself to a few niggas' that I barely even knew? Would they do the same for me if the shoes were on the other feet? Questions quickly flooded

Cortez mind as he was facing reality from a different point of view. DaMesha was the only other person other than his father who gave him the advice to think things through before just acting upon instinct; and right now was the time to decide. "That nigga' could've shot all of us; but you know what, you right. That ain't even my beef!"

DaMesha looked up at Cortez and smiled. "I'm happy you thought about it because I don't think Ej know his friends like he think he do. Niggas' ain't loyal as they claim to be; and a lot of niggas' our age just be doing a lot of talking these days." She said as they approached the end of the bridge and Cortez seen what appeared to be two different apartment complexes.

"This where they stay; this the projects. It's crazy down here; these niggas' all claim gangs. Most of them are bloods or either deuces." She said.

Cortez had a lost and curious face expression when he asked, "What's the differences?"

"The deuces wear blue and orange, and the bloods wear red; but they both get along." DaMesha explained. Cortez looked down to see actually what he had on and then at what DaMesha was wearing again. DaMesha noticed what Cortez just done and said, "With all this red we got on, we gone fit right on in; so you don't have to worry about nothing."

Cortez noticed that it was a lot of people outside dressed in red as they walked up a street name Hickory in the middle of the complex. Tiny little kids were running around cussing and playing in the street as if they didn't have a care in the world.

They walked up to an apartment that door was wide open and DaMesha walked right on in calling out Ej; but he didn't respond. Raykel came out a room and said, "What's up Mesha?" and then spotted me and said, "What's up Tez? What you doing over here?"

I didn't even get a chance to reply back before DaMesha said, "Damn, you nosey! He didn't come to see you; he came to see Ej! So where is he at now?"

"Juan and him just went to go get some weed. They'll be right back."

"Where auntie at?"

"She over her friend house, so ain't no telling when she coming back. You know how she is."

"Well we fin'na chill in Ej's room until he come back."

After a few minutes Ej walked in surprised to see Mesha, but even more surprised to see Cortez. "What's good Tez? Mesha got you hanging in the projects already?"

"I don't know about that. We just came to check on you and blow a few blunts with you."

"That's what I'm talking about. We just got some weed too, so we'll match ya'll. My bad, let me introduce ya'll. Tez this is Juan; and Juan this Tez. He just moved out here."

They nodded heads at each other and then Cortez told DaMesha,

"Here" as he passed her a blunt "Fire up!"

After smoking eight blunts and playing a few games of NBA2K, DaMesha noticed it was almost eight o'clock. "Shit Ej, it's getting late and I told granny I'd only be gone a few hours so we about to go in a minute. I don't want her getting all worried because you know how she gets."

"Yeah you right." Ej said. "As a matter of fact, why don't you meet us in the living room; while I holla' at Tez real quick." Ej said dismissing his cousin out of his room.

"Okay, but don't take too long cause I don't want to miss the next bus that should be about to come." DaMesha said as she walked out the room.

"Juan, shut the door and lock it." Ej order as he stood up to lift up his mattress. "It's like that for that nigga' Lil' T." Ej said as he picked up an all Black Ar15 and a blue steel 357 magnum. "We sliding on him, his momma, and his brothers. I want them all dead! We gone do it next Sunday. I'ma let my arm heal another week like the doctor said, but know that nigga' dead blood."

Juan cosign with Ej saying, "Yeah we on 'em. They ain't gone even see this coming."

Ej continue, "We gone wait on everybody to get ready to leave for church and smoke 'em all. I know Lil' T gone be home too cause he always drop them off."

"You better keep your head up and be fast about it." Cortez said. "If you need anything though, give me a call. Where something to write on so I can give you my number and you can give me yours?"

After exchanging numbers Ej said, "Alright Tez, ya'll go ahead and get out of here before ya'll miss ya'll bus. Also, don't tell Mesha what I told you."

Cortez replied, "My lips are zipped." As he walked out the room thinking to his self, *Mesha already knows.*

"You ready to go?" DaMesha asked.

"Yeah!"

"Okay, let's hurry up because the bus will be here in about fifteen minutes."

After leaving out of the projects, they ran across the bridge and caught their bus just in time before it pulled off. "Whoa! That was close." DaMesha said while catching her breath. "If we would've missed this bus, the next one wouldn't have came for another hour; and by then my granny would have started worrying to death."

"I know my mom and auntie Keniesha probably wondering where I am too. My momma told me not to stay out all night."

"When am I going to get a chance to meet my mother-in-law and see what she is like for myself?"

"I don't know, but you can whenever you want too. Are you spending the night over your granny's house; or, are you going home tonight?"

"Most likely I'm gone end up going home because I didn't bring no other clothes to change into. Why; you were going to sneak me in your room tonight?"

"I told you, I don't have a problem with sneaking you in. I just don't want you getting in trouble. But if you just so happen to sneak over, it ain't like I'm gone tell on you. I'm just curious as to what you going to do when morning comes?"

"Leave that up to me; I'll figure something out. Anyway, what Ej tell you when he put me out of his room? Did he tell you about what he got plan?"

"*Naw*, actually he didn't. Now that you mention it, he didn't even much bring up the whole situation." Cortez lied while trying to figure out what else he was going to tell her. Just his luck, he recognized their house was coming up ahead and quickly changed the subject by saying, "Ain't we suppose to get off somewhere down here?"

"*Naw*, the bus stop we get off on is right after we pass your house. You gone see it; it's close to the corner."

As the bus road passed our house, I saw my mother was sitting on the porch it looked like talking on her cellular phone; while my auntie Keniesha was plucking away a cigarette. I didn't know what to think. I was just hoping they weren't about to embarrass me in front of DaMesha. As we got off of the bus and begin walking towards the house, my auntie Keniesha went inside. I suddenly thought, *Maybe they're not waiting on me after all.*

Feeling a lil' more comfortable, I looked at DaMesha and said, "Besides your eyes being red and low, if you were serious about meeting my mother, I mean your future mother-in-law, here's a chance because she's sitting right on the porch."

"You for real; my eyes red and low?"

"Yeah! Even though it's getting dark out here, you ain't gone be able to hide it. You look blowed clear as day! Are my eyes red and low too?"

"They are a little low, but not as red." DaMesha said. "I think I'll wait until another time to meet her; I don't want her to see me like this!"

"Whatever suits you!" Cortez said as they got closer to their front yard. "I guess I'll talk and see you later Mesha. Have a good night."

"You too!" DaMesha replied back as she walked into her granny's yard and waved to Keisha acknowledging her.

Cortez watched DaMesha go inside before he began walking up to his own porch. Whoever his momma was talking to on the phone, had her blushing and smiling ear to ear before she quickly ended their conversation. "Hi baby." Keisha said "I see you and that girl kind of dress a like. What, she your new girl friend or something?"

Not wanting to have to answer a million and one questions about her, Cortez replied, "We cool; but I guess you can call her that if you want. She wants to be your daughter-in-law anyway. Look at me!" Cortez said as he dust imaginary dust off of his shoulders and popped his collar causing his mother to laugh.

"Boy, you're something else! Where are the rest of the kids at that you went to the mall with?"

Keisha caught Cortez off guard with her question, but he quickly responded, "They stay closer to mall, so they caught the bus going the other way."

"Okay. Well it's some Popeye's in there if you hungry. Keniesha and me already ate, so you can eat whatever you want. I'm going to sit out here a lil' longer before I call it a night."

Chapter Eight
(Da Conflict)

*A*lmost a week had past since we moved from the south, and I was just really starting to get use to things. Almost everyday I would wake up to find my momma and auntie already gone to work leaving me with nothing to do but look forward to seeing DaMesha. The only problem that I started to notice that I had was every time I wanted to get high, I had to wait on DaMesha to come around to go to the weed man's house; and that shit was starting to strike a nerve.

I didn't mind smoking it with her, nor kicking it with her. What the hell she was my girlfriend! It was just some days were I just woke up wanting to do my own thang. For example, here it was Friday morning, and I woke up fully energize. The house was empty; I had money in my pocket, and I had a single Swisher Sweet but not a crumb of weed. I didn't even have any weed roaches saved up for hard times like these. I must have called DaMesha every bit of ten times, but her telephone kept going straight to the voice mail before the phone would even ring once. I was straight pass being drove, and tempted as hell to go knock on the weed man's door myself. What the hell was he gone tell me, "Nor, I don't want your money" after seeing me damn near a week straight. I had to figure something out and fast.

Fed up, I finally figured fuck it. I'll go to the store and see if any of the niggas' that be posted out there have any weed; that way I could kill two birds with one stone if I need to get some more Swishers. I locked the house up and made my way to the store. As soon as I got there, I saw a crew of young thundercats hanging out like always. I didn't notice any of them in particular, so I asked them all at the same time, "One of ya'll got some weed for sale?"

"I got you; what you trying to do?" one of them responded.

"I'll spend twenty dollars with you."

"I'll give you five bags for your twenty dollars."

"Okay, cool. Let me get that." I said exchanging the money for the weed and then went inside of the store.

I grabbed a bag of hot Lay's potato chips and went straight to the counter. "What's up my man? I see you ain't got your friend with you today." Ali said.

"*Naw*, not today."

"So what can I do for you?" he asked.

"I want these chips, a box of Swisher Sweets, and a Bic lighter."

"I normally wouldn't sell people your age any kind of smoking products; but since you know Mesha and Corey, I'll sell it to you."

"Thanks Ali." I replied.

"Your total is seven dollars and seventy-seven cents."

I handed him a ten dollar bill and told him, "Keep the change." as I walked out.

When I stepped out of the door, I noticed there were more people posted on the store front then when I came in. I said, "Right on bruh, I'll fuck with you again if I see you out here." to the guy who sold me the weed and started to walk off.

Out of nowhere, I heard a voice say, "Tank, don't fuck with that bitch ass nigga'! He hang with Ej and Corey bitch asses!"

When I turned to see who it was, I seen it was Lil' T. "You got me fucked up!" I said "I ain't no nobody bitch, nigga'!"

"You a bitch if I say you is!" Lil' T said as he lifted up his shirt and flashed a gun.

Even though I knew Lil' T was strapped now, the way he flashed it on me, only made me pissed. I couldn't control myself as I said, "Cause you got a gun, I suppose to be scared of you now nigga'! What you gone do; shoot me?"

"Yeah, I'm gone pop your ass; if you don't stay your ass from down here. You and that bitch DaMesha!"

Now I was already mad, but he straight struck a nerve when he included DaMesha name in this too. As bad as I wanted to show him I had some hands and could fight good, I knew I was out numbered as I peeped niggas' starting to huddle up. "You know what, you got this; it's all good!" I said as I walked off.

When I got home, I could hear the telephone ringing from outside. As soon as I got inside, I looked at the caller ID and seen it was DaMesha; but I was so mad that I didn't even answer it. Instead, I rolled up a blunt and went out on the back to smoke.

I tried to let the confrontation with Lil' T go; but I couldn't. All I could think about was revenge. It kept running through my head how he tried to play me like a straight bitch ass nigga' in front of his boys. I knew him and his boys weren't scared to shoot anybody. Shit, I seen them shoot Ej in a park full of people in broad day light. That's when I made up my mind and said, "Fuck it! I'ma get him before he gets me."

I ran inside right quick to get Ej's number off my television stand, and then hit him up. *Ring! Ring!* "Hello." answered a female.

"May I please speak to Ej?" I politely asked not sure if I was speaking to his mother or not.

"Who is this?" the female voice questioned.

"My name Cortez. Is Ej home?"

"What's up Tez? This Raykel; you sound so proper on the phone. How you doing?"

"I'm straight; but I really need to talk to your brother. Is he around?"

"Yeah, I'm fin'na give him the phone. Hold on!" Raykel replied.

I could hear Raykel in the background calling out Ej's name and telling him that I was on the phone before he picked it up. "What's up Tez? What's good my dude?"

I didn't waste any time telling him, "Ain't shit good! This bitch ass nigga' Lil' T had the damn nerves to flash his burner on me today. Talking about me and Mesha better stay away from the store are he gone shoot us. He got me fucked up!"

"You for real?" Ej said in disbelief. Then he replied, "I'm on my way over there."

"*Naw*, you stay at home and let your arm heal. I'm going to handle this. I just called you because I need a favor."

"What's up? Talk to me!"

"I need you to sell me one of your guns."

"I don't sell guns Tez; but I'll let you use one until Sunday."

"I-ight! Is it cool if I come get one now?"

"Yeah! I'ma be waiting on you."

"Okay, I'm leaving out now."

When I hung up the phone from talking to Ej, I quickly called DaMesha back. Her phone didn't ring twice before she picked up. "What's up boo? I saw you called me, but my momma and me was gone grocery shopping this morning. What you got going on?"

"Check this out Mesha, I need you to listen to me and do what I tell you."

"Okay; what's going on?" DaMesha replied with concern in her voice.

"I want you to stay in the house today; and whatever you do, stay away from Ali's store. You hear me?"

From the tone in his voice, DaMesha could tell something was definitely wrong and replied, "Yeah, I hear you; but what's wrong?" she questioned.

Ignoring her question, Cortez replied, "Look, I have to make a run right quick; but I'll explain everything to you when I get back. Infact, I'll come over to your house so we can smoke and I'll fill you in on everything."

"Okay Tez; I ain't going anywhere. I'ma be sitting at home waiting on you to get here."

"Oh yeah, tell Corey to stay in too!"

"Okay, I'll tell him; but Corey gone to boxing practice already." DaMesha said not knowing that Cortez had already hung up the phone not hearing what all she said.

Once I hung up the telephone, I ran to the corner to catch the bus. I wasn't at the bus stop a good four minutes before the bus pulled up. I briefly thought to myself, *this motherfucker right on time.* In a matter of minutes I was pulling the chord to get off the bus; and running across the bridge that led to the projects.

As I was approaching Ej's apartment, I seen he was sitting on the porch waiting on me with Juan. "Damn Tez, you got here faster than a motherfucker! What you get a ride?" Ej asked.

"*Naw,* I told you I was leaving out as soon as we hung up. It just so happen, I didn't have to wait long on the bus to come." Cortez replied and then continue, "What's up Juan?" acknowledging him.

"I'm cooling." Juan replied giving Cortez some dap.

"Now tell me what all happen again." Ej said still not believing what Cortez already told him.

Cortez started telling both of them the story again from the top. "I woke up this morning in need of some weed, so I went to Ali's store trying to find some. It just so happen to be a lil' dude out there with some, so I spent dub with him. He gave me five bags for the twenty dollars and I went in the store."

"What this nigga' look like?" Ej interrupted.

"He was dark skinned with dreads in his head, but Lil' T called him Tank or something like that."

"Okay, go ahead; I know who you talking about. His name Tank." Ej said.

"Anyway, as I was leaving out of the store" Cortez continue "I told the dude I got the weed from, good looking out and I was gone fuck with him again if I seen him out there. That's when I heard somebody say don't fuck with that bitch ass nigga'; he be with Ej and Corey. When I turned around I seen it was Lil' T and said some shit back to the nigga'. That's when his bitch ass flashed his strap on me, talking about me and Mesha better stay away from down by the store or he gone pop us."

"What?" Juan replied after hearing the story.

"What he put Mesha name in it for? What you and her been walking around together or something?" Ej questioned.

"Yeah, we been chilling together almost everyday since I met ya'll.

Plus without her, I haven't been able to get no weed so she been taking me over to that one house you and Corey took me to the day you got shot to get the weed. From there we hit up Ali's."

"Man, what you think Juan? You want to ride down on this nigga' this Sunday instead of next weekend?" Ej asked.

"You know I don't give a fuck about peeling this nigga's cap back. It's whatever!" replied Juan.

Cortez spoke up, "Look, I ain't asking ya'll to ride down on this nigga' for me. I don't even rock like that! I just came down here to get a strap from you. I told you I'll buy one from you if I have too."

"You talking like you gone ride down on him yourself or something Tez." Juan replied staring at Cortez.

"I am!" Cortez said heated. "What you think I'm trying to get a gun for? I don't ask nobody else to handle my problems; especially when it comes to a motherfucker beefing with me. Shit, ya'll wouldn't know nothing about this if I already had a strap or knew where to get one from."

"I feel you!" Juan replied. "Go ahead and let the lil' nigga' hold down a strap for a few days until we run across somebody selling one."

"Usually I wouldn't even do this or even much consider doing this by you not being from the hood; but I like you and actually feel like it's kind of my fault that you even in this mess to begin with. So I'ma let you hold down one of the hood's guns."

"A hood's gun! What's that?" Cortez asked lost and confused.

"A hood's gun is a gun we keep in the hood, meant to be used by those in the hood or from the hood. It probably been around longer than God knows his self; and most likely has more bodies on it than can be counted. If you get caught with it, then whatever crimes they link up to it and charge you with, are on you. But the number one rule that comes along with this gun is, if you don't die using this gun, then don't lose it. Make sure it makes it back to the hood."

"I ain't gone lose it! Hopefully I'll run across another one real soon so I won't need it no more." Cortez replied.

"Don't be bullshitting Tez! Don't have me go get this burner and you really ain't ready to use it." Ej said really debating on breaking the hood rules about the hood's guns.

"Ej, look me in my eyes." Cortez said with a serious face. "Nigga', I ain't playing! I'm serious as a motherfucker; I want this nigga' dead! I can't let this nigga' threaten me and think he gone walk around here like it's all good. Fuck that! My father died telling me to finish whatever I start, and I might didn't start this shit, but I be damn if a motherfucker gone initiate some beef with me and I ain't gone finish it. I'm standing on that!"

"Juan, go get that nine!" Ej said with no hesitation.

When Juan left to go get the gun, I said, "Ej, I need another favor too."

"Yeah, what's up?"

"Can you get me a half ounce of weed from over here? I got fifty. Plus I can get some Swisher from the gas station right across the street before I leave from over here; that way Mesha and Corey won't have to go to Ali's until this shit gets all cleared up."

"Oh, that ain't shit! I thought you really was about to ask for something. As soon as Juan comes back, we can go snatch that; but let me ask you something. Are you talking to my cousin, and don't lie?"

"We talk and see each other just about everyday. We real cool."

"If you dating her, that's cool because I know she's a good girl. Just don't hurt her or let nothing happen to her."

"I got you." Cortez said as Juan walked back up.

"Here, hurry up and tuck it." Juan said as he handed Cortez a fully loaded all chrome nine millimeter.

As Cortez tucked the nine, Ej said, "Be careful because it's loaded and dirty."

"I-ight. Now let's get the weed so I can hurry up and get up out of here and make it back home to make sure Mesha and Corey good."

"Alright, let's go get it. It's right across the street from the gas station anyway so it's right in route." Ej said. "Once you get what you need from the gas station, we gone walk you to the bus stop and chill with you until it comes."

Once Cortez got everything that he needed they walked him to the bus stop but didn't have to wait long before the bus came. As soon as he made it home: he went straight in the living room and grabbed the cordless phone, stopped in the kitchen and grabbed a sandwich bag, and then headed straight down stairs to his room. He put everything down on his bed, including the four sacks from earlier. Wanting to get a feel of the nine millimeter, Cortez thought, *I guess I'll just give Mesha half of the half ounce that I just got from the projects. Then we can just smoke these other four sacks.*

He noticed the clock on the telephone read 1:36 p.m., so he hurried up and bagged up DaMesha's share of the weed. As soon as he was finish doing that, he quickly checked out the nine millimeter and all of its features. Once he was satisfied in feeling comfortable with being able to properly operate it, he called DaMesha to let her know that he made it back.

The phone rung about four or five times before DaMesha picked it up. "Hello, what's up baby? Is everything alright?"

"Everything is everything! Anyway, I just got back and was about to come your way if it's okay."

"Yeah silly! I been waiting on you since earlier. You remember what house it is; right?"

"*Naw!*" Cortez said jokingly. "Of coarse I do. How am I gone forget where you stay and I was just over there two days ago. I'm on my way."

"Okay, but hurry up. I'll be on the front waiting on you." DaMesha said and then hung up.

On the way to DaMesha's house, Cortez felt real confident now that he had a pistol. He just kept thinking to his self, *I wish this bitch ass nigga', Lil' T, try me now. I'll kill him and every motherfucker that's with him. I'll teach him about flashing a pistol and not using it; on my momma!* as he continue walking. Once he saw DaMesha big ole smile, it helped him lose a lil' anger; but not enough to let it go completely.

DaMesha ran up to Cortez as he approach, and gave him a big hug.

"You had me so worry!" DaMesha said and then asked, "What's going on?"

"Before we get into that, where is Corey? I came to smoke and talk to both of ya'll."

"I thought I told you he gone to boxing practices. He goes five days a week."

"Okay, that's what's up. Let's go on your back then."

"That's cool, but we got to go through the house to get back there."

As they walked inside, Cortez handed DaMesha her half of the weed that he had gotten for her and seven Swishers, and then told her, "Go put that up; we got something else to smoke."

"Thank you baby!" DaMesha said and did just as Cortez told her too. When she came back in the kitchen where Cortez was waiting, she seen he was standing at the back door with a blunt in his hand already beginning to roll it up.

They walked outside and Cortez lit up the blunt; and from there, he began choking and coughing. Once he caught his breath, he said, "Damn, that's that fire!"

"I hope so if it got you doing all of that; but are you gone tell me what happen?" DaMesha questioned.

Cortez told her most of the story, but he fell to mention the fact of Lil' T flashing a gun on him. He didn't want DaMesha to get any more worried. Just as he was looking at DaMesha while they were getting high, he came up with a plan. "Mesha, I need you to show me where Lil' T stay, so I can catch him by his self and whoop his ass."

"Are you serious?"

"Damn right I'm serious!"

At first DaMesha was against it; but after smoking another blunt and Cortez insisting she show him, she said okay. Little did DaMesha know what Cortez had in store for Lil' T with the burner he just had gotten from Ej.

Chapter Nine
(Truth Be Told)

Saturday had creep around before Keisha even realized it with her working so much. She couldn't wait to hook up with Que so they could have a lil' fun. Looking at her watch, she seen she only had thirty more minutes left before she got off. All she kept thinking is I'm off tomorrow so I don't have to rush home this time. Even though, last time she was out until about three o'clock in the morning.

The last ten minutes seen to drag on forever Keisha thought. She was so much in a hurry for her sift to be over with, that she almost told her last customer to just take the food and go without her even ringing him up. "Calm down!" she had to say to herself "This shit about to be over." She finished ringing up her customer items, threw her closed sign up, and quickly began counting down her draw. As soon as she was finished, she clocked out not saying bye to anyone and called her sister. "Keniesha, where you at?" Keisha asked but not waiting on her to give an answer before continuing "Can you swing by the job and pick me up?"

"I can, but it's gone be about fifteen minutes though; because I just got on the highway. I would've been home, but I had to stop and get some gas. It's your call though. Are you gone wait on me or not?"

As bad as Keisha wanted to get as far away from her job before anybody could ask her anything else, she didn't feel like hiking across the park; so grudgingly she replied, "Yeah, I'll wait! I'll be sitting right ion front of the doors so you will see me as soon as you pull up."

"Okay, I'll be there in a few minutes." Keniesha said and then she hung up.

About ten minutes had past when Keniesha turned onto the parking lot and picked up her sister. As soon as they got home, the first thing they both noticed was Cortez wasn't there. Without saying a single word between them, they both thought and knew that he was somewhere close by with that damn girl DaMesha.

"Well big sis, what you have planned for the day?" Keisha asked Keniesha.

"I was planning on going out with Derrick today, but right now I don't know. I need to clear my mind for a minute."

"What's wrong?"

"I've been pissed off all day because I haven't heard from my friend Trina, and this bitch owes me three hundred dollars! I've been ripping and running all damn day trying to catch up with her, and I still haven't. But I'm not gone take it out on Derrick; I'ma lay down until he calls me. What about you? Was there something you wanted to do?" Keniesha asked while rubbing her feet.

"Yeah, and I'm gone do it; it just doesn't involve you." Keisha said sassy but joking. "*Naw*, but for real, I'm planning on spending some time with Que again tonight. Then tomorrow, I want me, you, and Cortez to catch a movie and go out to dinner. My treat this time though."

"Okay that sounds good to me, and I know the perfect place for us to eat were ya'll gone love it." Keniesha said.

"Okay, it sounds like a plan."

"But speaking of this Mr. Que," Keniesha said dragging out his name "You gave him some pussy yet? Cause you stay trying to spend a lil' time with him like he got you sprung or something. What, he got a big dick?"

"Girl, I don't know!" Keisha said as she walked in her room thinking, *but I'm thinking about fucking him.*

Keisha changed into a pair of shorts and a T-shirt, and then she plopped down on her bed and called Que. The phone rang a couple of times before he answered the phone saying, "I've been waiting on your call."

"Boy stop it; I just got in from work! What are you doing?"

"I'm just riding around seeing what I can see; but you know I'll rather be seeing you."

"And you can, whenever you get ready!" Keisha said with a big ass smile on her face.

"Oh, so you don't have any plans?"

"Nope; I plan on chilling with you!"

"Okay, that sounds like a good plan to me. I have a few things to do over around your way, so I'll be close by in an hour or two. Can you be dressed and ready by then, or is that too early for you?"

"*Naw* it won't be too early; I can be ready whenever you need me too be."

"Okay, so five o'clock I'll be there; and be dressed for fun. Meaning no dresses or hills, cause we are going to be doing some walking around."

"Alright, if you say so." She said but had no ideal what he had in storage for them to do. "Well, I'ma let you go handle your business. Just call me when you on your way."

"I will do." Que said "I'll see you soon." and they both hung up.

Keisha already knew what she was going to wear. She pulled out her new Jordan's number twelve's, with her red and Black Polo T-shirt that that had the Black horseman on it, and a pair of Black Polo skinny legs. Keisha was the queen of Polo she thought.

About forty-five minutes after finding her outfit, Cortez walked in her room. "Boy, where you been?" Keisha asked.

"I been over Corey and DaMesha's house chilling. I just came home real quick to check in and to see what you and auntie were doing; that's all."

"Well your auntie is in her room resting. We're both going out later." She said as if they both were going out together.

"Where to?" Cortez asked being nosey.

"I don't know; but I do know all three of us are going out tomorrow for dinner and a movie."

"That sounds good to me momma. Well, I'm about to fix me some pizza rolls and go back around the corner. Do you need anything?"

"No, but you might come home to an empty house because we gone be leaving out in a few hours."

"I-ight, that's cool! I'm big enough to watch the house by myself anyway. I got this!" Cortez thought out loud with the nine millimeter still tucked in the back of his pants.

Keisha thought to herself, *Yeah, my baby growing up; looking more and more like his daddy too.* Keisha knew sooner than later, she was going to have to tell Cortez that she was dating again because she liked Que. She just didn't know how her son was going to react to her dating already; especially after the divorce she just went through. No matter how he would react though, she knew she needed to be the one to tell him.

After warming up some pizza rolls, Cortez left the house heading back to DaMesha's crib. Keisha quickly jumped in the shower, but had to cut it short because Que was calling back already. She jumped out of the shower and got ready. Once she got dressed, she went outside and sat on the porch looking for the navy blue 750LXI Que drove.

Keisha was shocked to see Que pull up in a Range Rover Super Sport, which just so happened to be her favorite truck. She knew what it was, and how much they sold for. Que jumped out and greeted her at the passenger door. They hugged and then he opened the door for her as she said, "I love this truck!" in an excitingly girly voice.

That's when Que asked, "Do you know how to drive?"

"Yeah, I can drive!" Keisha answered feeling a tab bit insulted.

"Well, you wan'na drive it?"

"Hell yeah I'll drive it; but I don't know where we going."

"Good, cause I been driving all day. I'll direct you where to go."

Hitting corners felt good to Keisha because she haven't drove in a few weeks, and then she was driving her favorite hundred and twenty-five thousand dollars Range Rover. She just knew that she looked good behind the wheel.

Que directed her to the City Museum downtown. Inside Keisha was fascinated. She felt like a big kid again, running all over the damn museum. They kicked it there for awhile before Que asked, "Are you ready to eat?"

"Hell yeah; I than worked up an appetite!"

"Okay, let's go then. What kind of food do you have a taste for?" Quincy asked.

"I don't know why, but I got a craving for some shrimps right now."

"Okay, Red Lobster it is."

"Oh I love Red Lobster. I didn't know ya'll had that up here. Do ya'll have a Joe's Crab Shack as well?"

"I know where one is. Since I see you like seafood, I guess we can go there on our next date." Que hinted that he wanted to go out with her again.

After dinner, Keisha thanked Que and then told him that she really just wanted to go somewhere quiet and chill out with him. "I really want to spend the rest of the day getting to know you more." Keisha said.

"That's fine! I had just got a penthouse suite at the Hilton Hotel earlier. I was tired and said fuck it. I rode past the museum and figured we could go there today, so if you want to we can go to the room or we can go post up at a park and find a quiet spot. But it's all on you. What you want to do?"

"*Naw*, I don't want to go hit up no park. I'll rather go to the room so we can chill in some A/C and kick back and conversant."

"That's what's up; but the Hilton is back downtown." Que said as he guided her.

When they reached the Hilton's penthouse suite, Keisha quickly took noticed of all the luxuries it came with. As she made her way through the suite, she noticed that one of the beds was partially messed up and playfully asked Que, "So who you slept with in here?" pointing to the bed.

"Oh, I forgot her name. Is she still in there?" Que joked back.

"Don't play!"

"I'm just saying, if I slept with somebody in there, the bed most definitely wouldn't look like that afterwards. I would be lucky if I wouldn't have to replace the whole bed once the people who work here come in and find that I rearrange the whole frame. I can see them now, charging my credit card." Que laughed as he joked with her.

They continue to make small talk and jokes back and forth while getting comfortable. After they had a few drinks, Keisha finally exploded with all the real questions that she had been letting build up. "So Que, let me ask you a few things that been slightly bothering me; and be real with me. I don't want you to sugar coat nothing or blow me off if you feel I'm getting to personal."

"What's up boo; what's bothering you?" Que said sitting his drink down.

"When are you going to bring me into your world? Your real world! I ain't blind and far from a fool; but it's something, well a few things about yourself that I know you ain't telling me. Since I met you, you have been nothing more to me but a gentleman. So why is it you don't have a woman? Are do you really have one, and just playing me stupid?" Keisha said while rolling her head and focusing on Que. Que was about to say something when Keisha cut him off. "Hold up one minute and let me finish." Keisha continued "Am I your mistress; or do you just spoil and treat every woman you meet extremely good. Look at you; as sexy as you are, you just throw money around without a care. I know you have all kinds of women throwing their self at you!" *Damn, I'm tempted to throw myself all over you and just fuck you until your dick can't get back hard.* Keisha thought as she seen Que flex his chest muscle through his shirt. "You drive top notch fancy whips and hundred thousand dollar trucks that most motherfuckers can only dream to have. Plus you stay getting these expensive as suites like they nothing. What, you don't have your own place? What the hell do you do for a living?"

Que slightly laugh and then took a long drink. As soon as he opened his mouth to begin to say something, his cellular phone began ringing. Que looked at the phone number and debated on answering it; but instead he pressed ignore. The caller didn't let thirty seconds pass by before calling back again; and again Que pressed ignore.

Keisha was sitting next to Que, so she saw him press the ignore button repeatedly and snapped the third time the same caller called back. "You ain't got to keep ignoring them because I'm with you! What that's your wife or something? What you need me to be quiet so you can answer her call? Just take me home; or do I need to find my own way home?" Keisha said as she jumped up and began gathering her things.

For a second Que was lost. He was trying to figure out how things went from them having a good time and conversation, to seeing Keisha grabbing her things talking about finding her own ride home. He knew if he wanted to have a chance with Keisha, then he was about to have to expose his hands to her and right now. "Hold on Keisha!" Que said as he stood up and grabbed her arm gently. "If you want the real, I'll give you the real; just sit down." When Keisha sat down, Que began telling her almost everything as if he'd known her all of his life. "Okay Keisha, I'ma keep it gutter with you. I'm a drug dealer! I'm one of the biggest dealers in St. Louis."

"So now you a big time drug dealer!" Keisha said as if she had heard enough bullshit for one night.

"Yeah; I sell dope! My phone keeps ringing because a motherfucker been trying to get some dope from me all day and I keep lying to him saying I'll send it to him."

"So if you are so much of a big time drug dealer, then why you don't go and get that money?" Keisha asked waiting to hear his next excuse.

"Because he's in the county and where he's at, it's hotter than fish grease out there. I ain't about to go out there, nor am I about to send any of my workers either. That's ten thousand dollars I just won't get."

"Ten thousand dollars! Que are you crazy? So you just going to miss out on that kind of money like it ain't nothing?" Keisha questioned in disbelief of what she was hearing.

"*Yop!*" Que calmly replied. "All money ain't good money! If one of my workers or me get caught up out there, between bond money and lawyer fees I'll be out of way more money than ten thousand dollars."

"Okay, that makes sense. So why are we at this hotel; you ain't got a trap house?"

As Que laughed he said, "Yeah, I got quite a few; but you'll never catch me in *'em*. I get these rooms because it's more convenient for me to rent a room and make money, than to drive home and miss out on money."

"So you do have a house!"

"Yeah; I own quite a few pieces of properties. I'm into real-estate too!"

"What, you like some kind of Scar Face or something?"

"You can say that! But, I like to think that I'm better then Face."

"Now I see why you got that fancy car and expensive truck."

"Keisha, I got seven whips! I got three cars; two trucks, and two SUVs'. All of them sitting high and paid for. I drive a different vehicular everyday; and every few months I swap them out for something newer."

"So I know a nigga' like you got to have a woman if not a few of them Mr. Smooth Talker! You ain't got to lie to me since you coming clean."

"I have a few females I fuck around with from time to time; but nobody can say I'm their man. Every one of them knows what it is. I ain't had a girlfriend or been in a relationship since I was in the seventh grade. By eight grade, you can say that I was marry to the game. I was out in the streets getting it and haven't looked back since. I got a model I live by."

"And what's that?"

"If you can't keep it real with a motherfucker, then don't deal with the motherfucker!"

"So where do you find the time to hang out with me and why?"

"I make time for what and who I want too. I like you because you seem different from all these females up here. Most of the females up here are moochers! They always got their hands out looking for a motherfucker like me to take care of them. But you on the other hand, I can't say that about. I guess you just seem different to me because you came up here with a plan and you trying to make it happen. You a beautiful hard working single mother, and I wan'na help you get to where you are trying to get in life; because I feel like you deserve it."

"Help me how?"

"Well, I know you just got you a job; but I want you to work for me! I know you can't be making any more than seventeen or eighteen thousand a year, if that. If you work for me, you could make that every month and you wouldn't be doing too much of shit!"

"Oh yeah; what exactly would I be doing to make that kind of money a month?"

"Give me one second, and I'll show you exactly what you would be doing." Que said as he went into another room and came back carrying a Black and white Nike duffel bag.

Que sat next to Keisha and opened the duffel bag. He pulled out what looked like four white powder bricks wrapped in plastic. "What the hell is this; because it looks like flour wrapped up?" Keisha questioned.

"It's dope! Well its heroin. Each one of these, are whole kilos. One of these go for thirty thousand dollars. I might sell a few for twenty-five grand depending on how I'm feeling. I want you to break each one of these down to thirty-six ounces; which means by the time you finish these four kilos, you should have a hundred and forty-four ounces exactly."

"Okay, well I'm a fast learning; so when are you going to show me how to break '*em* down?"

"Right now!" Que said as he removed a fish scale from the duffel bag and begin showing her what everything should weight from start to finish.

As Que showed her the process, it turned Keisha on seeing how focus he was as if he was a scientist and making cuts like a chef. After carefully and closely watching Que break down and bag up a few zips, she showed him she could do it too. Keisha was damn good at it; she seemed like a nature or have at least done this plenty of times before and was just playing Que stupid now.

After she quickly broke down the second kilo by herself, Que said, "Okay, I see you got it down pat; so I'ma pay you for these two now. I'ma set up a spot for you to work out of so you can get to making some real money." Que stood up and walked back into the room he got the duffel bag from and came back with eight thousand dollars cash. "Here Keisha; this is your days pay, eight thousand dollars. You get four thousand dollars for each kilo you break down every time."

"Oh my God, this all mines! Are you for real?"

"*Yop*! So are you my new employee or what?"

"Hell yeah; especially if you paying like this!"

"Okay then. In two days you start. I'ma change your life Keisha, just stick with me."

Between the money and Que, Keisha was so turned on that her pussy was soaking wet. She couldn't decipher whether the drinks was keeping her juices flowing, or the fact that she was long over due for having her pussy explored was the cause. Either way, she couldn't control the throbbing in her pussy as she felt herself reach another orgasm. The only thing Keisha could say was, "I wan'na lay down for awhile and let this liquor wear off some; is that okay Que?"

"Sure, come on. I'll show you to the master bedroom." When they got to the room Que said, "Make yourself at home. I'ma be finishing up things up front if you need me." About thirty minutes later, Que came back in the room to check on Keisha. "Are you okay? Are you feeling better now?"

"Yeah! Come lay down with me; I want your company!" Keisha said patting the bed.

"Alright now, no foolish stuff." Que said as he jumped in the bed and began playing with her which really turned her on because she loved to play around.

"Que, now I'ma be real with you." Keisha said causing Que to instantly stop playing and become so serious by his body language.

"What's up Keisha; what you got to tell me?" Que asked as he rolled onto his side facing Keisha and his chest muscular jump as they tighten.

Keisha for a moment was stuck staring at his chest before she finally spoke. "I know we've only known each other a week or so, but I really like you."

"I really like you too." Que replied.

"No, I don't think you really understand. I really like you! I'm not asking you to be my man or nothing to that degree; but I want you right now!"

"What exactly do you want from me?" Que asked making sure she was on the same page as to what he was thinking.

With a mischievous look in her eyes as she slightly bit down on her bottom lip, she said, "I want to see if we can rearrange this bed frame. The truth be told, I want you to fuck the shit out of me!" Keisha said as she stood up and pulled her shirt off. "Can you help me pull my pants off?" she asked seductively.

"Yeah, I got you. Just lay down."

Que slowly begin pulling her pants off, while letting his eyes roam over her body. He was fascinated with Keisha's six pack, as he noticed that he couldn't find not one single flaw about her body. Once Que got Keisha's pants completely off, his lil' soldier stood at attention as he took in the sight of her beautiful caramel butterscotch complexion skin body.

Ready to be the judge of Que's sexual experience and the moment to reveal Que's actually dick size, Keisha stood up and quickly undressed Que. She was happy as hell to see his dick was as big as she thought it would be. *I can't wait to feel this dick inside of me.* Keisha thought.

Keisha looked so good to Que in her sexy see through matching Black and red thong and bra set, that he didn't waste any time asking her, "How you want it?" as he thought to his self, *I'm about to fuck the shit out of her.*

"I want it from the back! I want you to start off slow, and then speed it up."

Que was so amped; he didn't even pull her thong off. Instead, he just slid them to the side and proceeded to rub his dick up and down the juices that flowed freely from her pussy before entering her. Upon entering her pussy, it felt so good to Keisha that she creamed instantly. That was unusual for her, but Que was so big and it had been a few months since Keisha last had sex. Once she got use to the feeling, she started throwing her ass back saying, "Okay, speed it up."

Enjoying the grip feeling her pussy had, Que sped up his stokes. They both tried their best to hold in their moans, but Keisha couldn't hold hers in any longer. She let out a high pitch scream of pleasure as she spasm into an orgasm. From the way she started shaking, Que knew he did his job thoroughly which caused him to nut all inside of Keisha.

After sex, they laid next to each other with both of their minds in two different directions as they made small talk. Keisha was thinking: *I can't believe I gave this sneaky ass, smooth talking ass nigga' some pussy already; but damn, his dick was good. And ooh we, the way he made me cum, I didn't know it was gone be that damn good. Fuck, we should've used some protection though. I don't know how many bitches he out here fucking. And shit, this nigga' came in me! I hope I ain't pregnant.*

Now at the same time Que was thinking: *Yeah, I just fucked the dog shit out of her. It's about time she quit playing around with me and gave me that pussy. I just hope it wasn't because I just gave her all of that money. Speaking of money, I need to get my ass up and make a couple of moves, and collect my shit from these niggas'.*

Just as soon as silence fell amongst them, Que's phone began ringing. He got out of the bed and retrieved his cellular phone. As soon as he saw the telephone number, he did a double take and said, "We need to go!"

"Is everything alright?" Keisha asked.

"Somewhat, I just need to make a couple of moves right quick."

They quickly got dressed and left the room. When they reached the Rover, Keisha walked over to the passenger side and was waiting on Que to open the door for her when he said, "What you think you doing?"

"What you mean, what I think I'm doing?"

"Didn't you say you like this motherfucker?"

"Yeah!"

"Well act like it and drive it! You know you look good behind the wheel anyway."

"You keep saying stuff like that and you gone have a hard time getting your keys back." Keisha said ready to drive her favorite vehicular anyway.

"You know what; since you like this ride so much, you can have it. Consider it a sign on bonus for you coming to work for me."

"Nigga' quit playing! I'll believe that when I see a title with my name on it!"

"We can make that happen first thing Monday morning."

"Whatever!" Keisha said.

"For real; I'm dead serious! Infact, you can just drop me off at the Royal Palace where we met since that's closer to your house; and I can go from there." Que said as he gave her directions.

Chapter Ten
(Sunday Massacre)

*S*unday morning, I woke up feeling possessed by an evil dark spirit named Doom. I climbed out of the bed right at six o'clock on the dot, so I knew that I had plenty of time on my side to make my move. I had a problem and this morning was the day I was going to handle it no matter what.

I couldn't keep it out of my mind how Lil' T called his self threaten me in front of his crew. I made up my mind, just like my daddy told me to think before I reacted and to finish whatever I started, I was about to do everybody a favor and get rid of Lil' T and whoever else with him. I didn't give a fuck.

I noticed everybody in my house was still asleep on at least still in bed by me not hearing any footsteps, so I quietly got dressed. I put on a pair of my all Black blue jeans, a Black hoodie, with a Black T shirt under it, and my all Black Air Force Ones. I then tucked the nine millimeter in the front of my pants and creep out the backdoor in my room and head straight towards Lil' T's house.

As soon as I stepped out the house, I noticed that it was still dark outside which made it pretty easy for me to make it to his house without being seen. It was like a ghost town outside. Not a soul was out on at least insight. It was like the word had been passed along to the streetwalkers not to be roaming the streets because death was lurking and I was the enforcer.

When I made it to his block, it looked just as dead as the previous one that I came off of. As I made it half way down his street, I spotted someone come out a house and jumped into a can headed in my direction. As they got closer, I ducked down and hide behind a park car, until they where out of sight. Once the coast was clear, I quickly jogged the rest of the way down the street. When I made it to the third house before I would house reached Lil' T's house, I spotted a boarded up building directly across the street from his house and decided that ill hide in the gangway there and wait.

While waiting in the gangway, I came up with a quick plan. I figured if I walked up on him while his momma was looking, then most likely he wouldn't pull his gun on me. I knew that he knew or at least assumed that I didn't have a gun how things played out Ali's stone and I didn't do nothing; but this time things was going to be different I was going to have the advantage. Once I got up on him, I figured I'll just up and shoot him; and then his brother along with his momma too.

For a second I consider spearing his mother because I knew she would be hurt enough witnessing the murder of her two halves; plus she really didn't have anything to with what was going on. For some reason, this evil spirit that seemed to be possessing me and controlling my actions, kept telling me "Fuck spearing her, the old bitch wouldn't save you! So kill her too!"

Before I realized it, the voice in my head had convinced me to say, "Fuck it! I didn't have shit to do with Lil' T and Ej beef, yet Lil' T threw me in it. So fuck his momma! The bitch shouldn't had his ass!" I rationalize.

I definitely couldn't let his brother slide. I refuse to have to constantly watch over my shoulders anticipating the moment he would try to seek retaliation, knowing that sooner or later he would try to retaliate. On that note, I knew I couldn't be nice to anybody. I was so deep into my thoughts that I wasn't even tripping off the fact that the sun had came out.

I glanced at my watch to see it was seven eighteen. I had been out here for over an hour. After about another twenty or thirty minutes past, I saw Lil' T's front door open. My adrenaline started pumping as his momma came out the house saying, "Come on T! You know I have to teach Sunday school this morning."

I pulled my hoodie over my head and placed the gun inside my hoodie pocket so that it was already in my hand after I made sure the safety was off and walked across the street. While I was crossing the street, Lil' T brother had came out the house and walked to the car. Him and his mother stood next to Lil' T's car doors while they waited on him to come on and unlock the doors. That's when I decided I had to change my approach to make sure shit went smoothly.

As I was walking towards them Lil' T brother turned and face me; so I nodded my head at him in a friendly speaking gesture. Once I took about three steps pass them, I turned around and walked back upon them saying, "Excuse me ma'am, can you tell me what time it is?" since I spotted she had a watch on.

"Sure baby, it's a quarter to eight!"

"Thank you." I replied and then said, "I like your dress; it looks good on you. Are ya'll about to go to church?"

"Yes indeed we about to go give God his praise." Lil' T mother said as he finally came out of the house and locked the door, heading our way.

"Well ya'll enjoy ya'll self and get ya'll praise on." I replied as Lil' T and me locked eyes.

I didn't break my stare as he unlocked his car doors with a remote for his mother and brother could get in. As soon as his mother took a seat in the car, Lil' T said, "Nigga', what you doing on my block?" as he continued to walk towards me.

"Nigga', I didn't know this was your block, but why you keep fucking with me; I ain't never did shit to you."

"Cause you hang with the enemies!" and then he leaned close to me and whisper, " I'm at you today, if it's the last."

Before he could finish making his threat, I swiftly pulled the nine out of my hoodie pocket and let him have it. *Boom! Boom! Boom! Boom! Boom! Boom!* Was the only sounds heard as I shot him from the chest up. His mother let out a scream as his brother opened up the back door. I quickly aimed the gun at him releasing two shots which both struck him killing him instantly. Their momma was now screaming historically trying to draw attention. That's when I fully snapped, "Shut up bitch and say a prayer!" as I released a few rounds in her until she was completely silent and motionless. For a split second I thought I seen Lil' T brother move, so to make sure he was dead, I shot him two more times. I ran over to Lil' T and kicked him over then empty the remaining shells into him before I quickly search him.

Just my luck, he had four hundred and ten dollars on him and an all Black Glock forty. "Jackpot!" I said as I quickly stuff everything in my pockets and broke out running.

I was nervous as hell. I didn't have a sense in what directions I was headed, I was just running trying to get as far as possible from the crime scene as I could. I cut across a few yards and jumped a couple of fences, just to ensure myself that I had a nice distant between me and Lil' T's house. As I made my way back towards Lee, I spotted the bus coming down the street and quickly ran to the nearest bus stop.

I hopped on the bus damn near out of breath and thought that I was about to have a panic attack as I heard sirens coming into the neighborhood. I took a seat all the way in the rear of the bus, looking out of the windows as I regain my composure. Within fifteen minutes, I was getting off of the bus and walking across the bridge heading to the projects.

Folks where already out in about in the projects young and old. Even little kids were running around playing and cursing. I made my way to Ej's apartment and knocked on the door a few times before he came and answered. "Who the fuck is it?" he said as if he was mad at the world.

"It's Tez!" I replied while looking around.

"Tez!" He repeated and then opened the door. "What the fuck you doing over here so early?" he asked while rolling his eyes.

"I just came to bring you that burner back." tapping on it, but he didn't pay the sign any attention still halfway asleep.

"This early! I thought I told you, you can hold it down for a few days; just don't lose it!"

"You did, and it has been a few days. I know I ain't from ya'll hood, so I'm just making sure that it makes it back just in case somebody else needs it. I honor the hood's rule about it. Besides, I don't need it no more."

"Awe nigga' you don't need it no more! What you than got scared?" Ej said, but was clueless of what Cortez just done. "Don't worry about nothing; we still gone handle Lil' T next week."

Cortez wanted to tell Ej bad as hell that next week would be a week too late. Instead he replied, "Whatever you say. Just get this gun so I can catch the next bus back home." After he gave him the gun, he shook and headed back home a little relieved that he no longer had the murder weapon on him.

Chapter Eleven
(Ultimate Hustler)

*E*arly Monday morning, Keisha woke up excited and full of energy. She was ready for work; and not at Aldi's either. She was ready for her new job with Que. Keniesha knocked on Keisha's bedroom door and asked, "Keisha, am I dropping you off at work this morning? Cause if so, we got to leave early; because I'm going to Trina's house to get my damn money!"

"*Naw* sis, I'll walk." Keisha replied as she opened her door. "I need the exercise anyway. It'll only take me ten or fifteen minutes anyway. Damn, you dressed already? You ain't playing about that money huh?"

"Hell naw! I need all of mines and she can't borrow shit else from me since the bitch wants to play games! Call me if you need a ride home, and be safe."

"Okay, I will; and the same to you." Keisha said as Keniesha ran out the door.

With only her up and Cortez sleep, she hurried and got dressed herself. Once she got ready, she counted out a thousand dollars; and hid the rest of her money in her Prada high heel box. She put eight hundred dollars in her bra, and then snuck downstairs in Cortez's room and placed the other two hundred dollars on his T.V. stand.

When Keisha walked outside and saw her new all Black Range Rover Super Charge, with the Black twenty-two's and one hundred percent tint, she smiled from ear to ear. *I can't believe this; this my shit!* She thought opening the door to get in. As soon as she got in and situated, she called Que.

Ring! Ring! "Hello, what's good ma? Where is your sexy ass at this morning?" Que asked.

"I'm about to pull off and go to my job so I can let Derrick know I quit; and not to tell my sister because they talk. I know if I don't say shit, he'll most definitely tell her about it, and I don't want to hear all of that extra shit right now. After that, since I know how to get to Goody Good, I was going to get us something to eat. Have you eaten anything yet?" Keisha asked.

"Nope!"

"Okay, well as soon as I get to Goody Good I'll call you back to see what you want to eat."

"Okay, don't be long because I'm hungry."

"I won't be." Keisha said and they both hung up.

Keisha pulled off feeling like a million bucks. When she pulled up to her job, she quickly thought, *I can't let Derrick see me driving this,* so she pulled off of the parking lot and parked on the gas station lot right across the street from Aldi's. She quickly ran across Grand while no traffic was coming and walked into the store looking for Derrick. "Derrick!" she called out once she spotted him.

"What's up Keisha? Why don't you have on your uniform; is everything alright?"

"Yeah everything is okay. I actually came in to let you know today is my last day, and to personally thank you for the opportunity."

"What happen; was it the hours because if so I can change them?"

"No, it's just me! I found a better job that pays more, but I do appreciate everything you've done." Keisha said as she pulled out the money from her bra and counted out five hundred dollars. "Here Derrick, take this for your troubles; and please don't tell Keniesha because I want to surprise her when the time is right."

"Okay Keisha, I won't. If you ever need me or want to come back, I'm here; and congratulations on your new job."

"Thanks for understanding Derrick. Now I got to get out of here so I won't be late. I'll see you around." She said as she walked out the door. *Whoa, well that went smooth,* Keisha thought as she climbed in her truck. "Now Goody Good, here I come."

Pulling up to Goody Good, she noticed that the line wasn't that long. She got out and walked to the front of the line and asked the young couple that was next to order if she could jump them if she'd paid for their meal. "Hell yeah!" the young man said excited that he didn't have to pay for their on meal.

"Thank you!" Keisha said and gave him forty dollars as she started to call Que.

Que didn't even let the phone ring twice before he answered. "Hello, tell me something good! Did you handle the lil' job situation?"

"Yeah, and I'm at Goody Good now. I order next, so what do you want?"

"Just get a table; I'm about ten minutes away. We can just eat there. This way once we are finish I won't have to direct you, you can just trail me."

"Okay, sounds good to me. I'll see you when you get here."

The waiter took Keisha to a table by a window, which allowed her to see Que pull onto the lot in a brand new Porsche Cayenne truck. It had all Black everything, just like the Range Rover he just gave Keisha. "Damn, this nigga' balling for real!" Keisha thought out loud.

Que walked in and glanced around to see Keisha standing up waving her hand to get his attention. As Que walked up, he hugged her super tight as if he hadn't seen her in years. "How your lil' sexy ass doing this morning?"

"I'm feeling better than ever riding around in my new truck." Keisha said with a huge smile on her face.

"Well it's good to see you smile; I plan to always keep a smile on your face." Que said before the waiter approach.

"Nice to see you again, Mr. Quincy. How are you guys and gal doing today?" the waiter smile while asking.

"Just fine!" Que replied.

"Are ya'll ready to order, or do ya'll need another minute?"

Keisha quickly spoke up saying, *"Naw,* we ready now."

"Okay ma'am, what can I get for you this morning?"

"I'll have the chicken and waffles platter with an orange juice please."

"Okay, and will you be having the Quincy special this morning sir?"

"Yeah buddy, with a pink lemonade."

"Okay, I'll be right back with your drinks in a second."

"The Quincy special! What the hell is that?" Keisha questioned Que.

"It's eggs, grits, waffles. Shit, it's a lil' bit of everything."

"So you think you are a super star having food named after you?" Keisha asked jokingly.

"By no means at all! The last thing I need is fame; too many people know me already."

"I think it's cool how everywhere we go people already know who you are." Keisha said as the waiter returned placing their drinks in front of them on a napkin.

"Sometimes I think its cool; but not always. I make a lot of investments around here; that's how a lot of these people around here know me. If I like a place or business, I try to invest in whatever they may need. Sometimes I lose; but most of the time I win."

"So do you call yourself investing in me?"

"You can say that if you want; but I wouldn't."

"Why not?"

"Because when I invest in something, I'm looking to make a profit. With you, it's not about making money." Que explained.

"What's it about then?"

"It's about building a friendship for starters; and seeing where things could possible go from there. I'ma be real with you. I want you to be my woman; and if you ain't noticed yet, I'm working hard on making that a reality."

Shit you already got me, Keisha thought to herself. "Um huh, we'll see!" she said as their food came.

"Yeah, we will." Que said as he began eating.

After breakfast, they left with Keisha following close behind Que to the spot where she would be breaking down the dope. They pulled up to a shotgun house that looked vacant; but once Que took Keisha inside, she couldn't believe her eyes. This place was decked out from front to back, top to bottom.

"I thought this was suppose to be some kind of trap house or something. Why does the inside look so good, but the outside look like shit?"

"I did the inside like this so you would be comfortable while you work. The outside looks fucked up because I don't want any attention on us. So with that being said, look around and tell me what you think."

After a tour around the whole house, Keisha confirmed that she loved it. "Shit, I could live in here." She said.

"No indeed; I have something way better than this for you, just give me a few weeks! I got a four bedroom house in the Central West End. It's super nice and I know you'll love it. I need two more weeks before I can do what I have in mind to do with it. My current tenants there lease is up next week and they get on my nerves, so I'm not going to renew their lease. Once they move out, I'm going to rehab the whole place, and get brand new everything for you and your lil' one." Que said. *I can't believe this,* Keisha thought with tears in her eyes. "What's wrong; why you crying?"

"Cause it's like you my angle! Every since I met you, you have been nothing but good to me; and nobody has ever been so nice to me in my life. I'm just happy, that's all."

"It's cool, you just been dealing with the wrong ones; but don't worry about nothing. Just wipe those tears off your face because I don't want to see you crying. Besides, we got work to do. Okay."

"Okay." Keisha said drying her eyes.

Que went in the bedroom and removed a picture from the wall. Keisha was surprised to see a safe was behind it built into the wall. Que opened it and pulled out three kilos and asked, "Do you think you can break these down before three o'clock?"

"Yeah, I should be able too."

"Okay, well do what you do. I'm about to make a few moves. I'll be back soon with some food. Have you ever ate White Castles?"

"No, what's that?"

"Don't worry about it; I'll just bring you some of everything they sell when I come back. Oh yeah, nobody knows about this house but you and me, so nobody should knock on the door or disturb you. Whatever you do though, don't bring anybody in here or to this place."

"I won't, I got this! Just go handle your business and hurry back."

"Will do." Que said as he walked out the door.

Keisha locked up the house and went straight to work. She felt like a pro already. Once she got her rhythm together, you couldn't tell her that she wasn't on top of her shit.

About three and a half hours went by before Que came back to the house with a few bags of food and a Louis Vuitton book bag. "Have you been working hard?" Que asked striking a conversation.

"I guess you can say that, because I'm almost done. I got two of them out the way."

"Damn, you're working way faster than I thought. I know you got to be ready to grub. Come sit down and eat right quick while the food still hot."

When Keisha saw the little square burgers and fish sandwiches she asked, "Why in the hell all these sandwiches so damn small and squared?"

"I don't know, that's just the way they make them. They actually are very popular and good; just try them."

After eating a couple of them, Keisha said, "They're actually not bad!" while grabbing another one. While eating Keisha asked, "So, when did you come up with the ideal of me moving into one of your houses and why?"

"I came up with that thought the other day when we were at the Hilton. Plus I peeped the way you sneaking around your sister, and I can't have you sneaking around working for me. Besides, I know ya'll need ya'll own space, and I won't charge you much. Anyway with all the money you making now, you might as well live good!"

"Yeah, you right about that shit! I want that book bag too." Keisha said admiring the Louis Vuitton bag.

"And you can have it after I empty it out."

"What's in it anyway?" she asked Que as he began dropping ounces on the scale to make sure they all were on point.

"Oh I see you got this and gone with it. You sure you ain't never did this before you came here?"

"I told you I learn real quick. Now what's in the bag, a million dollars?"

"Not quite." Que said as he opened the bag and dumped its contents onto the floor.

"Damn, how much money is that?" Keisha asked while her face let it be known that she never been around so much money in her life.

"It's a hundred thousand right here, and twelve thousand of this is yours when you get finish with that last kilo."

"Say no more; I'm about to knock that out now." Keisha said as she hurried to get back to work. Que started helping with the last kilo when Keisha said, "I got this! You just sit down and watch me do my thang!"

Que laughed and said, "We on a schedule ma, and I'm a man of my word, so I'm just trying to help speed things up so we can go get all the paper work done on that truck so you can legally own it."

"Boy that can wait; we got money to make." Keisha said with a smile on her face.

"I'm happy you feel that way. If you keep that kind of attitude, you'll be a millionaire like me in no time. Speaking of money, do you want your twelve thousand today, or do you wan'na wait until you got a nice lump sum? It's your call."

"I'll take it today."

"Cool. Oh yeah, you moving pretty fast, but I'ma need you to break down twice as much over the next week because it's gone be the first; and in between the first and the fifth, I make most of my money so we need to come up with a plan."

"Well, I can come back later on and meet you here after my son makes it home."

"That's cool, but check this out. I got a spare key for you, so you can come and go as you please."

"Okay, that will work too. Just tell me what to do and I'll get it done."

"I-ight, well check this out. I'ma give you the safe combination and by tomorrow morning it will be fill with thirty kilos. If you can have all thirty of them ready for me by the first, not only will I pay you for them; but I'll give you a bonus as well. Does that sound like a plan?" Que asked as he put twelve thousand dollars in Keisha now Louis Vuitton book bag.

"Sounds like a plan to me."

"Well let's hurry up and knock this out for we can be done for the day. We still got a few hours before it'll be three o'clock, so we'll have plenty of time to bend a few corners and see what we see."

It didn't take them long to finish after all. Before you knew it, Keisha was grabbing her new Louis Vuitton book bag following Que out of the door while thinking to herself, *I don't know if this nigga' really a millionaire; but shit, so far he is the ultimate hustler!*

Chapter Twelve
(Word on Da Streets)

*L*ying awake in my bed staring at the ceiling, I kept replaying the scene of the murders over and over. *I bet Lil' T bitch ass wish he wouldn't have fucked with me now;* I thought as I just laid there. His face expression was priceless when he realized I had than up a strap on him, and the tables had turned; but this time I was determined to use mines, and it wasn't shit he could do about it.

I can't lie, I was nervous as hell at first. As the day began, I was hoping nobody seen me. I just planned on staying in the house for a few weeks until shit blew over. That way if anybody did see me, they would have forgotten what I looked like if they ever saw me again.

When twelve o'clock hit, my phone started ringing. When I looked at the caller ID, I saw that it was DaMesha and quickly answered. "Hello."

"Tez, did you hear about Lil' T and his momma and brother?" DaMesha asked before allowing Cortez to greet her properly.

"Well first of all, how are you doing this morning?"

"Oh, I'm sorry. I'm fine!"

"Okay, now that I know my future wife is feeling good, I can answer your questions. No, I haven't heard shit about Lil' T. Fuck that nigga'!"

"Well somebody killed him yesterday; him, his brother, and his momma in broad daylight!"

"Are you for real? You bullshitting! When did this happen; and who told you?" Cortez questioned acting as if he knew nothing about it.

"It happened yesterday. It's been all over the news; and on every channel! It's crazy how they did them. Straight executed them in-." DaMesha was saying before Cortez interrupted her.

"Fuck them! I don't want to hear about what happened to them! Who did it?" Cortez snapped.

"They don't know. The news said the police are still looking for a suspect."

"Well all I can say is, he had it coming."

"True; but fuck that! Can you come see me? I just got some fire ass weed from my momma's boyfriend, Chicago, and I wan'na smoke it with you."

Scared to leave the house still, Cortez made up a quick lie and said, "I can't, I lost my key yesterday and don't wan'na leave the door open; but you can come over. I'm bored as hell! Plus my auntie and momma at work."

"Okay, just give me about thirty minutes and I'll be over. I'm fixing to straighten up my room and get dressed because I still got my pajamas on."

"Okay, well I'm here. I ain't going anywhere!" Cortez said and then hung up.

As Cortez started to fix his bed he thought, *Just because the police don't know who murder Lil' T and his family, didn't mean the streets didn't. Shit, the police didn't know who shot Ej, but the streets do.* Just as he was having that thought, his phone rung and to his surprise it was Ej.

Cortez hesitated, but then answered anyway. "What's up Ej, my dude?"

"Man, I know you heard about Lil' T and his family!"

"Yeah, I just found out about ten minutes ago. That shit all over the news."

"Yeah, well it's all over the internet too. Then I've been getting calls all last night and this morning from a few of my folks from over there."

"Okay, well what they all talking about?"

"They all pretty much saying that the word on the streets is everybody thinks that I did it because Lil' T shot me last week."

So what; fuck what they think! They don't know shit; and if they do, fuck *'em.* Let *'em* think what they want."

"Tez bruh, they said they got shot with a nine seventeen times Sunday morning. Did you-." Click, before Ej could finish asking Cortez hung up on him.

What in the hell is wrong with this nigga'? I know he knows better to be talking all reckless on the phone like that. Cortez thought and snapped out loud. The phone begin ringing again and it was Ej calling right back. "Hello."

"Damn, what happened to you phone?"

"Check this out Ej; don't talk to me over this phone about shit that supposed to have happened. When my momma gets here, I'ma just come holla' at you in person. She should be here at around four o'clock, so I'll be your way by five o'clock. Is that cool?"

"Yeah."

"I-ight; I'll call you when I'm on my way."

Cortez sat around feeling relieved that nobody knew that it was him. Just knowing that made him happy enough to go outside and sit on the porch while he waited for DaMesha to show up. When DaMesha finally did walk up, she was looking good as always, Cortez thought.

"Look at you; you look happier than hell!" DaMesha said walking up.

"I Do?"

"Yeah; you do. What got you so happy?"

"You! Plus I got a pocket full of money and read to have some fun." Cortez said, but really hid the fact of why he really was so happy.

"Well, what you going to do?"

Naw; you mean, what we going to do?"

"Whatever; you knew what I meant."

"I need to go holla' at Ej; and then we can do whatever you wan'na do."

"Okay, well smell this first." DaMesha said as she handed him the sack of weed she brought over to smoke with him.

"Damn, this shit smells good as fuck! Is Chicago selling this?"

"No, he sells dope. He just smokes weed. He buys it by the ounces, and gives us sacks every now and then; but he knows where it's at though, and he'll get it for you."

"Okay, we gone have to holla' at him later. Let's go inside."

"Good; because I don't need to get any darker than what I already am." DaMesha said causing Cortez to giggle. Once they made it to Cortez's room, DaMesha sat on his bed while he rolled up. She spotted the money his momma had left him and said, "Dang, you just got money laying around and shit."

"*Naw*, I don't do that, I keep my money in my pocket." Cortez replied but didn't know that his momma had left him two hundred dollars that morning.

"So who do this belongs too?" DaMesha asked while picking it up and showing it to him.

"I guess its mines. How much is it?"

After she quickly counted it she answered, "It's two hundred."

"Do you have any money?"

"Yeah, I got about seventy dollars. Why, what's up?"

"I was just making sure you had something in your pockets. I tell you what though. Give me a hundred out of that, and you take the other hundred."

"*Naw*, I don't need your money!" DaMesha protested.

"I didn't ask you that; just put it in your pocket!"

"Thank you baby!"

"That ain't shit; let's step out and smoke this blunt."

"Oh yeah, I got something for you too."

"What it is?"

"I'll show you when we get done smoking, so let's hurry up because I know you gone like it." DaMesha said convincingly. As they stood outside smoking, DaMesha asked, "So, why you got to go over to my cousins' house?"

"I'm going to loan him a few dollars, that's all. It won't take long at all." Cortez smoothly lied. "So what you wan'na show me?"

"You're going to see soon enough."

Cortez phone begin ringing, so he handed DaMesha the blunt and ran in the house to grab it. Once he saw that it was his momma calling he quickly answered it. "What's up momma?"

"Nothing much; I was just calling to check up on you. Did you get the money I left for you this morning on your T.V. stand?"

"Oh yeah; thanks momma! I was just talking to Mesha and Corey about going to Union Station; but I was going to wait to ask you when got home."

"What's Union Station?"

"They say it's another mall downtown and the Lee bus goes right by it."

"Okay; well I don't care, just have fun and be safe. Call me if you need anything."

"Okay, thanks momma. I love you."

As soon as he hung up the phone with is momma, he came up with the ideal to put his keys on the floor on the side of his bed and play like he just found them. When he went back outside where DaMesha was waiting, DaMesha said, "Here, fire it back up. I put it out for you. I didn't want to smoke it all from you."

They finished smoking the blunt and then went back inside of Cortez's room. Cortez went straight to the side of his bed where he just placed his house keys and acted like he all of a sudden just found them. "Here go my damn keys right here!" he said bending over to pick them up off the floor so DaMesha could see him picking them up. "I be tripping, or either I just be too high sometimes; because I swear I been looking for these damn keys high and low and they been right here all of this damn time." Cortez said as DaMesha now giggled as if she have had her fair share of doing stupid shit why being high. "Anyway, I got some more of that weed from the other day; so I'm ready to go whenever you are now that I can lock the door."

"Alright."

"Oh yeah, what did you want to show me?"

Nervous about showing him what she wanted to surprise him with, DaMesha said, "We can go now, and I'll show you when we get back."

"I-ight, I'm about to call Ej and let him know we on our way."

Upon reaching Ej's apartment, everything almost seemed as normal as the first time Cortez ever came over. The only exception this time was their mother was home. "Damn Mesha, I ain't seen you in a few weeks! You been staying out of trouble; and who in the hell is your cute ass boyfriend?"

"Auntie, this Tez. Tez this is my auntie Carla."

"How are you doing Ms. Carla?" Cortez asked.

"I'm fine and you?" Carla asked.

"I'm good and can't complain." Cortez answered.

"Well Mesha, I see you got you a sexy one; where you meet him at?" Carla questioned.

"Dang auntie you nosey!" DaMesha said with a grin on her face. "But for real, he stays next door to granny. This is Ms. Keniesha's nephew."

"Oh, so ya'll ain't fucking or are ya'll?" Carla asked not sugar coating what she wanted to know.

"Auntie stop it!" DaMesha said feeling a lil' embarrassed about her auntie's interrogation.

"Okay, don't get all in your lil' feelings now. I'ma stop and mind my own business. Anyway, what ya'll doing over here? You came to show off your new boyfriend?"

"No- I brought him to see Ej."

Speaking of Ej, he had just walked in the room. "Damn Tez, when you get here?" Ej asked while spotting DaMesha and his momma. "Is my momma bothering ya'll?"

"*Naw!*" Cortez answered.

"Yes she is! You know how she be." DaMesha spoke up laughing.

"Momma leave him alone. Say Tez, come holla' at me; and Mesha, you keep her in here."

"Okay." DaMesha replied thinking Ej just didn't want his momma seeing him getting some money so she wouldn't be asking him for any.

When they got in Ej's room, Ej shut the door and began saying, "Man, do you know exactly what happen to Lil' T and '*em*?"

"I heard bits and pieces." Cortez calmly said.

"Look man, they got shot with a nine, seventeen times, on Sunday morning. A few hours after the news said it happen, you come bringing our seventeen shot nine back empty. On some real shit, Tez did you do it?" Cortez started laughing at how Ej looked so nervous as Ej said, "Tez, this shit ain't funny!"

"Why you acting so nervous nigga'? You ain't got shit to worry about!"

"I do got something to worry about nigga'; everybody blaming me!"

"Fuck what everybody think! I thought this was what you wanted; ain't it?"

"I'm just saying!"

"You just saying what? Look at it like a motherfucker just did you a favor; now you ain't got to get your hands dirty!"

After Cortez said that, Ej didn't have much to say. All he could mumble was, "I was just trying to figure out if you did it or not because you brought back our gun empty."

Cortez snapped, "Nigga' what's done is done! It ain't got to be explained or figured out! You said you was gone pop that nigga' anyway; so just look at it like a motherfucker beat you to it. As a matter of fact, we ain't even fin'na keep discussion this shit no more. Here go fifty dollars for them shells." Cortez said as he dug in his pocket and counted out fifty dollars and handed it to Ej. "Are you good now; cause me and Mesha about to slide out?"

"Yeah, I'm good."

"Alright then, hit my line later."

Soon as we left out of their apartment and made it halfway across their yard, cops came running from everywhere surrounding Ej's apartment before kicking the door off the hinges. DaMesha and me was in total disbelief as we witness what was going on and heard the police shouting different orders. "Everybody get back!" one officer yelled as it seem like all the people in the projects started coming out of nowhere.

"Oh hell naw!" DaMesha said as she began to run back towards Ej's apartment before Cortez grabbed her by the hand just in the nick of time. "Let me go; I gotta' help them!" she yelled.

"Mesha, you can't help them; you gone only make shit worse! We need to get out of here! The best thing we can do is you go to your granny's house and let her know what's going on, so she can get them some real help."

DaMesha was just standing there listening, but watching as more and more police continue pouring in before she responded back saying, "Okay." sadly as she started to follow Cortez back towards the bus stop.

"Baby, they're going to be alright! Your granny most likely is going to get them a lawyer, and make sure they're okay." Cortez said trying his best to cheer her up, but just that soon everything got worse as they heard multiple gun shots followed by a loud scream.

"Oh my God, that's my auntie!" DaMesha screamed. "Fuck that; I gotta' help her!" she said as she broke free and ran back to the apartment wit Cortez chasing behind her.

When they got close to the door, they could hear Carla screaming, "Ya'll motherfuckers didn't have to kill my baby! Ya'll didn't have to kill my baby!"

DaMesha ran to the door, only to be stopped by a few cops telling her to get back. I noticed Raykel running towards the apartment yelling, "What's going on?" as she made her way through the crowd to the front.

DaMesha answered her saying, "They killed Ej!"

Raykel went into shock as DaMesha's words soaked in; and then she fainted when her momma, Carla, came walking out of her apartment with tears flowing like the Mississippi River and blood all over her. Carla just kept repeating, "They killed my baby! They killed my baby!" as she hugged DaMesha tightly.

It seemed as if the whole complex was outside watching in shock. I didn't know what to do as I tried to revive Raykel. Right as Raykel woke up,

Juan walked up and helped me get Raykel to her feet and begin trying to comfort her. That's when I asked Juan, did he have a phone I could use so I could call for some help. He walked me four apartments down from Ej's apartment and went inside. He quickly came back out with a phone.

I called my momma, but she didn't have a clue as to who I was as she said, "Hello, who's speaking?"

"Momma, it's me. I need you and auntie to come downtown to the Peabody's to get me and Mesha. The police just killed her cousin Ej."

"What? I'm not with Keniesha, but I can come get you. I just need to know where you at."

"We right across the bridge from where the Grey Hound bus dropped us off at. As soon as you cross the bridge, you are going to see a complex with a sign in front of it that says Peabody's. As soon as you turn in the complex, you are going to see a crowd of people and cop cars; that's where we are."

"Okay, I'm in a Black SUV. I'ma be blowing the horn, so be looking for me. I'm on my way." Keisha said and hung up.

It was like everybody was just stuck for awhile. After about twenty minutes, I saw a Black on Black Range Rover coming down the lane blowing the horn. I was shocked to see my momma get out the driver seat as she started screaming out my name. "Here I am." I yelled out so she would stop drawing attention to herself.

When they caught up to each other, Keisha hugged Cortez tightly for a moment before asking, "Are you okay; because you had me worry to death?"

"I'm sorry to have worried you; but I didn't know what else to do. I'm alright, but Mesha and them ain't. We got to get her home. They just killed her cousin."

"Oh my God; go get her baby! I'll take her anywhere she needs to go."

"Okay, I'll be right back." Cortez said then darted back amongst the crowd. "Mesha, come on; we got to go. My momma gone take you home so you can tell your momma and granny what's going on." DaMesha was so shocked and out done that she didn't even argue at all. She just got up and waited for Cortez to lead her home. "I'm so sorry Ms. Carla; I'm about to get Mesha home and tell your sister and momma what's going on so you can have some support."

Carla couldn't even hold her head up as hard as she was crying. At a sound just above a whisper and between shedding tears she said, "Thank you baby!"

Cortez couldn't imagined the hurting pain Carla was going through; but as sad as she looked, he wish he could've taken the pain away that she was feeling as he wrapped his arm around DaMesha and led her to the Black Range Rover his momma was driving.

The whole ride to Ms. Rose's house was silent until Cortez got his momma's cellular phone to call Barber, DaMesha's mother. "Mesha, what's your momma's number?" Cortez asked.

"383-3297." She replied as Cortez quickly dialed it.

A male answered, "Hello." but Cortez knew that it wasn't Corey and figured it had to be Ms. Barber's boyfriend.

"How you doing; is this Chicago?"

"Yeah, who is this?"

"My name Cortez. I'm calling to see if you and Ms. Barber can meet me and DaMesha over Ms. Rose's house to help break the news?"

"Break what news?"

"Ej just got killed!" Cortez said as Keisha was pulling up to the house.

"We're on our way right now." Chicago said hanging up.

Cortez helped DaMesha out the truck and walked her to her granny's door before ringing the doorbell. When Rose came to the door and saw DaMesha's face she asked, "What's wrong baby?"

"They killed him granny!"

"Killed who? Who got killed, baby? What's going on?" Rosemary asked confused looking at DaMesha, Keisha, and Cortez.

Cortez had to tell her, "Ma'am, the police shot and killed Ej."

"Oh my God!" Rose screamed as she fell to the floor in the door way.

"What happened baby? Tell me what happened." I heard coming from a woman voice behind me. I turned around to see Corey, Chicago, and Ms. Barber running towards us.

"Tez, what happened?" Corey asked this time. As I told them everything that we knew, all Corey could do was shake his head with tears in his eyes repeating, "The police! The police kill my damn cousin!"

DaMesha said, "I need to lay down." as she walked in her granny's house with her head hanging down.

"Ms. Barber, I don't know how close you and your sister are," Cortez began, "but your sister, Carla, really need ya'll right now. My momma and me will keep an eye on Ms. Rose and Mesha so ya'll can at least go check on her."

Keisha nodded her head in agreement with her son before Barber replied, "Yeah baby, you right! Thank ya'll. Chi, we need to go; and momma we'll be back."

"Oh hell naw, ya'll ain't leaving me! I'm going too! I need to see my baby." Rose snapped.

"Okay momma, come on." Barber said as they all begin to walk towards their car.

Keisha said, "Ya'll just lock the door and I'll keep DaMesha over here with us until ya'll get back. She really don't need to go back over there; and she don't need to be by herself either."

"Yeah you right." Barber agreed as she went to go get DaMesha. When they came out, DaMesha went right to Cortez and laid her head on his shoulder.

After locking the door and thanking us Keisha gave Barber her cellular phone number and told her, "We got DaMesha for you. She's in good hands; so don't worry about her, and just go handle your business. Take as much time as you need; it's no need to rush back."

"Thanks again." Barber said and then they pulled off.

Walking into our house, my auntie was in her room asleep. After hearing us making noise, she woke up and came into the living room where we were. Upon seeing the blood on DaMesha's shirt Keniesha said, "Oh my God, DaMesha what happened?"

Cortez spoke up saying, "Not now auntie; she okay. I'll explain to you later what's going on."

"Come with me DaMesha." Keisha said as she took DaMesha in her room and gave her a different shirt to put on.

While they where in my mother's room, I filled auntie Keniesha in on what happened. She didn't say anything back; she just looked and listened in disbelief. After DaMesha and my momma came out of her room, I walked DaMesha down to my room so she could lay down and free her mind.

Before I knew it, it was almost one o'clock in the morning. I went upstairs to see if Ms. Barber or Chicago had called my momma, but everybody in the house was sound asleep. I eased into my mother's room trying my best not to wake her, and grabbed her cellular phone off of her nightstand and creep back out of her room. Once I got in the hallway, I looked through her phone to see if they had called; but there were no missed calls listed so I took the phone with me back to my room.

When I got back inside of my room, DaMesha was up. "Baby, why you leave me?" she asked.

"I just went upstairs for a second. I'm not going anywhere." I said as I placed the phone on my television stand and turned on the T.V.

DaMesha sat up and said, "Come hold me baby."

Feeling obligated to provide her comfort; Cortez climbed in the bed behind DaMesha and held her tightly while telling her, "Everything is going to be alright, baby." While holding her between his legs, Cortez gently placed a kiss on her neck before whispering in DaMesha's ear, "I still got some weed. Do you want to smoke?"

"Yeah, that just might be what I need to do." DaMesha replied, while Cortez got up and rolled them a blunt. As soon he finished rolling up, they creep out the basement door to smoke. That's when DaMesha said, "I just can't believe the police killed my cousin! We were just joking around with him."

Before even realizing it, it was going on three o'clock. At exactly three thirty, Barber called and said, "I'm sorry to be calling this late; but you can tell Mesha to come on, we outside. And thank you for everything."

"It's no need to thank us; but I'll tell Mesha that ya'll are waiting on her." Cortez replied.

As DaMesha got up and made her way to the front door she said, "Tez baby, please call me when you wake up."

"*Naw*, just call me when you get up; that way I won't be disturbing you, if you are still resting."

"Okay, I'll talk to you later."

"I'll be waiting on your call."

Before walking out of the door, DaMesha hugged Cortez and said, "I love you Tez!"

"I love you too!"

"Don't say it unless you mean it."

"I do."

DaMesha kissed Cortez and walked out the door and climbed into her momma's car as Cortez watched until they pulled off. After they where out of sight, Cortez returned his momma's phone; and then went back to his room thinking to his self, *this been one crazy ass day; I wonder what the word on the streets gone be tomorrow.*

Chapter Thirteen
(Da Reason)

*W*hile eating breakfast and watching the Fox 2 News, Cortez caught a recap of the breaking developing story involving Earl Johnson, which was Ej, as they flashed his picture across the screen. The reporter was interviewing Chief Deputy Lieutenant Shaw who was explaining why homicide detectives shot and killed Ej which caused Cortez to tune in and closely listen.

Chief Deputy Lieutenant Shaw said, "While our Homicide department was investigating a triple homicide that occurred early last week, involving a mother and her two sons being executed in front of their home," Fox 2 News flashed a picture of Lil' T, his mother, and younger brother posed together "our investigation team received a good tip from an anonymous reliable source saying that Earl Johnson was previously shot a week earlier by our deceased victim, Terrance Walker, which led to Earl Johnson retaliating. While our investigators team continued to look deeper into this matter, we were able to locate our suspect of interest inside his resident in the Clinton Peabody's Housing Development. Upon entering the resident with a search warrant to apprehend our suspect for questioning, Earl Johnson armed with at this time appears to be the murder weapon used in the Walker's case aimed at officers which caused them to open fire killing our suspect. At this time no charges will be brought against any officers involved in this matter as we continue to do a full investigation."

After listening to the lieutenant explanation of justifying the killing of Ej, Cortez thought, *that's some bullshit; I know Ej ain't aim no empty gun at them.* At the same time though, Cortez felt guilty as hell. *I should've; I mean; what If;*

he could've; Cortez was thinking trying to come up with a way the situation could have been played out differently; but the facts remained that he couldn't turn back the hands of time. A big part of Cortez felt like what he did had to be done for his and DaMesha safety; and no matter who got the job done, Ej was going to be the one everybody blame whether he did it or not. That's just how words traveled in the streets he rationalized; but no matter what, Cortez thought, *Mesha could never find out the facts of what really happened that Sunday morning.*

All of a sudden, Keisha came out of her room and walked in the living room where Cortez was at eating some cereal. She scared the shit out of him, causing him to spill some milk on his lap. "Dang momma, I didn't know you was still here! I thought you was at work. What happened; you got the day off?" Cortez asked while cleaning up the milk.

"*Naw,* I still got to go to work; but I wanted to talk to you though."

"About what?" Cortez asked thinking she was about to say something about him hanging out with DaMesha and her family.

"About us!"

"What about us, momma?"

"I know since we moved up here, I been doing a lot of ripping and running and sometimes it seems like I barely have time to spend with you; but I don't want that to effect our relationship."

"Ain't nothing going to come between us. I know you just be taking care of business."

"Most of the time. I was just thinking about what happened to your friend, and God knows I pray that I don't ever have to experience nothing like that because I would lose my mind."

"I hope don't nothing like that ever happen either."

"Anyway, what I wanted to tell you is, I'm going to try to start spending a little more time with you even if we have to include your girlfriend DaMesha. My bad, Mesha as you call her." She teased.

"That's cool; plus I think you would like her too."

"We'll see; but that's not all I wanted to tell you."

"I'm listening."

"I got a new friend too! His name is Quincy, but everybody calls him Que." She paused so she could see how her son was taking her news.

"For real; that's who truck you was in?"

"Kind of. Well it's Que's truck until the paperwork comes back. He owns his own shipping and manufactory company and offer me a job paying way much more than Aldi's could pay me; and when I told him that I would love to take the opportunity but didn't have transportation to get back and forth, he pretty much gave me the truck as a sign on bonus since I was willing to start immediately."

"Oh that's cool, and that truck tight too. We gone be styling!"

"That's not all." Keisha continue. "He owns a few pieces of properties too, and said he'll rent a house out to me for the low if I like it after he finish remodeling it. So most likely we won't be living here with my sister much more longer if everything goes as plan."

Although Cortez was happy to see his momma excited, he didn't really want to move out his auntie's house. Not trying to kill her vibe, Cortez said, "That's great momma. You tell auntie Keniesha yet? She's going to be happy to see everything falling into place for us."

"*Naw*, that's another thing; I don't want you to tell Keniesha shit about what we talking about as far as my new job, that truck, or even us moving. Do I make myself clear? I want to be the one who tells her!"

"Yes ma'am; I won't say nothing!"

Shortly afterwards Keisha left; and Cortez went outside on the back to smoke. While sitting on the steps smoking and listening to cars blasting music as they passed by, Cortez thought, *I can't wait to get me a ride so I can blast my music and go where I please. Then next month, I'm going to be seventeen; ain't nobody going to be able to tell me shit;* but his thoughts were cut short by the ringing of the phone.

It was DaMesha. As soon as Cortez answered the phone he could tell something was wrong from the tone of DaMesha's voice as she begin venting. "Baby, I can't believe my got damn auntie Carla!"

"Baby, what's going on now?" Cortez asked clueless.

"Baby you ain't going to believe this shit! Why the fuck my auntie Carla trying to say you part of the reason why they killed Ej?"

"Huh, what the fuck would make her think some shit like that? I just met her!"

"We all know this; but she trying to say Ej ain't never had no gun. All of a sudden, you came over and gave him one. Ain't that some shit? But on top of that, she's trying to say you the one who had the police run up in their house."

"Mesha, I didn't have shit to do with that."

"I know because he told Corey exactly what he was going to do. We just didn't think that he was serious, and that's what Corey and me tried to explain to her, but she ain't trying to hear us. She trying to say Ej was at home Sunday; but like Corey and me said, she don't know where Ej was because she ain't never there. My momma even told her you only been here a few weeks. You ain't got him into shit! He got his self into that mess and almost got Corey in it too."

"I would have never called the police and told them shit about a motherfucking thing! Fuck that; I don't rock like that at all! That's on my dead pops!"

"Don't trip, she just in her feelings right now; she'll get over it. You know they say the truth hurts. Anyway, I'm sorry I didn't call you earlier, but my auntie called here with that bullshit and fucked up my morning for a second, But, I'm good now that I'm talking to you. I'm going over my granny's house in a few hours, are you going to be at home?"

"Yeah, I'm gone be here all day unless something pops off; and I'm out of weed. Do you think Chicago can get us some of that weed we smoked yesterday? I got a hundred to spend on some!"

"I'll ask him. I know he'll go and get it, if he ain't already got it. Either way, he bringing me over there later; so I'll make sure we get something before I come that way and just pay for it with the hundred dollars you gave me."

"Cool and I'll give you the money back as soon as you get here."

"Okay, then let me get dressed so I can hurry up and get over there. I'll see you soon."

"Alright. I'm here just knock on the door."

DaMesha said, "Okay." and they hung up.

Chapter Fourteen
(Shocking News)

Que did just like he said he would do. When Keisha arrived at the trap house, everything was already in the safe for her to get started. As it got closer to the first of the month, she was getting closer to reaching her goal. Everyday Keisha been putting in work six to eight hours straight before leaving only to return shortly and put in another four hours just to make sure that they would reach their goal on time.

Que been running in and out of town over the last few days, trying to spread his empire as he calls it; so we been speaking on the phone in brief periods. At first I didn't see anything wrong with what he was doing, but that was before I started to miss him. I wanted him to be happy when he finally would return and see that I been on my grind for him. Besides, I was looking forward to getting a hundred and twenty thousand dollars cash, plus a bonus. Shit'd, I ain't never had that kind of money; so I was hustling hard!

"What's up sweetie; how are things going?" Que called me out of the blue and asked me putting a smile on my face.

"Oh nothing much; I'm just trying to knock out the last of this stuff before I call it quits. Why; what's up? When are you gone make it back because you know tomorrow is the first?"

"I can't say 4-sho what time it's going to be when you'll see me; but I'll be there by tomorrow night. I just got a few more things to wrap up, up here before I'll be headed back that way."

"Okay, well be careful and I'll see you when you get here. I'm about to finish up." Keisha said before hanging up in slight disappointment.

It took Keisha damn near the whole day to finish the remaining kilos of heroin. By the time she finish and got everything cleaned back up, it had already got dark and she was hungry as hell besides sleepy and feeling like she had caught a contact. She neatly stacked all one hundred and forty four ounces in the safe as she counted and reweighed each one to make sure she was all the way on point before leaving.

Once inside her ride, Keisha couldn't make up her mind on what she wanted to eat, so she decided to call home. Cortez answered the phone on the second ring. "My fault, Mesha. Hello."

"My fault Mesha." Keisha repeated before saying, "Boy this is not no damn Mesha; and that's not how you answer a phone!"

"Oh I'm sorry momma. My bad. How you doing?"

"Boy, you're something else. You almost made me forget what I called for. Oh yeah, have you and your auntie ate anything?"

"I haven't ate anything. I don't know about auntie Keniesha."

"Well ask her is she hungry; and what do you have a taste for?"

"It don't matter to me, I can go for anything; but hold on and let me go ask auntie Keniesha." After a couple of minutes went by, Cortez came back to the phone and said, "Auntie Keniesha said, just come home because she's about to order some Imoe's because she wants to use some coupons she have before they expire unless you want something different."

"Well that will work for me; I'm on my way home then." Keisha pulled up at the house at the same time as the Imoe's delivery man did. When she got out of the Rover and the delivery man got out of his vehicular, Keisha told him, "You right on time! How much is everything?" before the driver could check the price on the ticket, Keisha said, "Oh don't worry about it; forty dollars should be enough and just keep the change." The driver didn't argue at all as he handed her the two boxes of pizza and a bag of hot wings. As Keisha walked through the front door she yelled out, "Special delivery!" causing Keniesha and Cortez to come in the living room immediately after they heard her voice.

"How much was it again?" Keniesha asked.

"Don't worry about it; let's just eat." Keisha replied as her stomach growled.

While eating Keniesha asked Keisha, "Where you been these last few days? I noticed you ain't been asking me for a ride to work or to come get you. What's going on with you; talk to me?"

"I been working doing my thing; plus I got a lil' side job cleaning. I was going to surprise you, but since you asked, I'll tell you now. If this girl quit this week, then I'll be working there full time. They pay more than Aldi's; so I'ma quit working there."

Cortez just stared at his momma while thinking to his self, *A cleaning job! That ain't what she told me;* but he didn't say anything as he continue to stuff his mouth with pizza. As the conversation came to a halt, Keniesha said, "Somebody's birthday is coming up soon if I ain't mistaken."

Cortez quickly responded, "Sure is; so ya'll need to be getting ya'll money right before it gets here!"

"Oh yeah; is that right? So what is it do you want this year; some more money?" Keisha asked.

"Nope! I want a car with some rims on it. I seen one around the corner, and they only want twenty-five hundred. I got'ta have it!"

"Son, I don't know about that one. We need to get a place first, don't you think?" Keisha said.

Cortez just didn't know, but in Keisha's mind she told herself, "If it's a car my baby wants, then it's a car my baby gone get. A nice one too!" Cortez took his momma's answer as a no; so he started making plans of his own. He thought to his self, *I'm getting a car this year. I ain't fin'na keep riding the bus. Then once I get it, I'm going to shit on everybody at the park;* but only if he knew what Keisha was planning for him.

The next day began, which was the first of the month and Keisha woke up patiently waiting on Que to call her. She couldn't get her mind off of him, but didn't want to seem like a bug of boo and call him first. As the day went on, she started getting impatient; but maintained her control and didn't dial his number. By the time it got dark and she still haven't heard from Que, she thought, *Fuck that;* and started calling him; but every time she called, she got his voicemail on the first ring. "Yeah, you reached Que; you know what to do" followed by, "We're sorry, but the mailbox you're trying to reach is full. Please try your call again later. Good Bye." and then it just disconnected their call.

After trying several more times and getting the same results each time, Keisha began to worry. "I hope everything alright with him." She said out loud to herself. When night fall hit and she still hadn't gotten a phone call from Que, she really began to worry as she thought of all negative types of things that could've happened.

Six o'clock the next morning Que finally called Keisha's phone. "Hello." Keisha answered halfway asleep.

"Wake up sleepy head! I see you did your thang and got the job done; but get up, we got work to do." Que said.

Keisha was so upset and frustrated but happy at the same time, that she didn't know what to say as she took a moment to get her thoughts in order. "I'll be ready shortly. Where do you need me to be?"

"I want you to meet me at the trap house a soon as you can, and be looking sexy for me!"

"Whatever, I'll be there in about thirty minutes." Keisha said and then she hung up.

Keisha jumped up and got dressed super fast. After getting dressed, she threw on her Louis Vuitton book bag and darted out the door. She flew to the trap house like she knew St. Louis streets like they were the back of her hands. Upon pulling in the driveway, she saw a navy blue Audi A8 with twenty-two inch chrome rims already parked in the driveway and smiled because she knew who it belong too. Just the thought of being about to see Que, made Keisha happy enough to say forget about yesterday.

As she walked in the house Que said, "Come sit down" as he pulled out a chair for her at the dinner table which had pancakes and fresh fruits sitting on it. Keisha was lost for words once again. "I need you to eat up because we gone be doing a lot of running around today and I want you to drive me around. I already got your money ready for you in the safe, so you can get that whenever you ready for it."

Keisha completely blew off what Que said, and replied, "I was trying to call you all day yesterday, but your phone kept going straight to voicemail. For a second, you had me getting worried about you."

"Oh shit, so you care?"

"Yeah I care! You the sweetest man I ever met. Plus I wanted you to see that I was able to take care of business before we reached the dead line."

"It's good to know we feel the same. Shit'd, if you wanted too, you could have easily taken everything out the safe; and got your sister and son together and went back to New Orleans with over a half a million dollars worth of shit." Que said jokingly.

"I wouldn't ever do no shit like that! I make more money and have more fun working with you; so you don't have to worry about me going against the grain. Now you can fuck around and play with my hard earned money and feelings and that'll be another story!" Keisha said jokingly but serious at the same time.

"I'm not. Anyway, let's get out of here because we got a big day ahead of us, and then your surprise is almost ready so I'ma give you a sneak peak of it and get your input."

"I'm ready." Keisha said as she stood up and went to put the leftover fruits in the refrigerator and made her way to the door where Que was waiting with two Prada duffel bags.

Today going to be a good day; Que thought as he watched Keisha walk to the car in her skin tight True Religion jeans. After locking the door to the trap house, Que hit the automatic start button and unlocked the car doors; and then he handed Keisha the keys as he opened her door for her, while watching her sit on the soft all peanut butter leather seat. With Que giving directions, Keisha was whipping everywhere as they picked up cash and made drops. Everything was going smooth as butter until we pulled up on his main man, Antwon, to make a drop and collect all the money from Antwon's side of town.

"What it do my nigga' Tweezy; you got everything under control?" Que shouted out the window follow by exchanging hand shakes of some type of code with him.

"You already know I do. I got everybody on point especially after what

happen." Antwon a.k.a. Tweezy said. "If its anything I can do for you, just let
me know and I got you."

"What the hell done got into you; what happened that I missed?" Que
replied.

"What? You ain't heard about Carissa and the kids?" Antwon asked
removing his shades.

"*Naw*, what my sister and her kids done now? Don't tell me Lil' T done
did something stupid and had them laws run into my sister's house."

"*Naw* fam; I wish it was that simple. I hat to be the one who has to tell
you this, but a nigga' shot and killed all of them last Sunday coming out the
house."

"What the fuck did you just say to me? Nigga', I'll smoke you out here
if you ever play with me like that again!" Que snapped.

"Calm down fam; you know I wouldn't joke around like that. We don't
get down like that! I'm serious!"

"Who the hell did it and why in the fuck ain't nobody told me shit?"
Que said pulling out his phone to dial his sister up.

"As soon as I seen that shit on the news, I tried getting in touch with
you, but your phone being going straight to the voice mail. Hell, I thought
Joseline would've most definitely got in touch with you. You ain't seen or talk
to her yet?" Tweezy asked but Que didn't respond. Antwon knew Que was
hurting and most likely was thinking of murder, so he said, "Shit'd every since
this shit happen, we been trying to find out who did it. By the time word got
around on who Lil' T had beef with, the police beat us to him."

"I don't give a fuck if Jesus got him; I want him dead! I don't care how
much his bond is, I'll pay to get him out just so I can touch him!"

"Fam, I don't know where you been; but you need to slow down for a
minute and check to see what's going on. It's obvious you haven't been
watching the news, but it's been on every news channel how the police already
have killed this motherfucker. Remember that white boy cop lieutenant Shaw?"

"Yeah, the one we got into it with a few years ago. What about him?"

"He got on the news and said they got an anonymous tip on who it was
and kicked the lil' nigga' momma crib in. When they went in this lil'
motherfucker room, he up the banger on them; so they didn't have a choice but
to shot and kill the nigga'. Come to find out the gun he suppose to had, was the
same gun he used to kill Carissa and them. So they got the right nigga'"

Keisha was shock to find out that the family that got murder was Que's
family. She just kept quiet as Que went on, "Where was the nigga' from?"

"He was from the Peabodies."

"Okay, well whoever stayed with him, I want '*em* dead. I got ten grand
on his momma's head."

"He got a sister too."

"Fuck her; I got ten grand on her head too; and I want it done A.S.A.P..

If anybody try to get in the way kill '*em* too! Can you do that for me?"

"Say no more; I'm on it. You know how we do; you just go try to clear your head and get in touch with Joseline so you can find out what's going on as far as the funeral arrangements. Let me worry about all this shit out here."

"Alright bro; I got to go. I need you to go collect from all the niggas' on the south and drop this shit off. I got a list I been checking off of who get what. When you done, call me and I'll send for it."

"I got you." Tweezy said as Que rolled up his window and told Keisha to pull off.

Que had a look on his face like he wanted to kill everybody. For a moment Keisha was somewhat scared to talk; so she surely wasn't about to tell him what all she knew. Instead, she said, "I'm so sorry to hear what happen baby; I wish I could do something."

"It's nothing you can do; I don't even know what to do."

"Where do you want to go now?"

"To my sister's house. I'm about to go hard on her!"

"Baby, please don't do anything crazy cause your sister wouldn't want you to do that. Ya'll need to pull together on this."

"Yeah you right; I won't clown, but it's no reason in the world why she ain't got in touch with me." Que said as he had Keisha bus a u-turn and directed her to Joseline's house.

Joseline and Que didn't really get along at all; and it had been almost two and a half years since they last spoke. Once they made it onto Joseline's street, Que spotted her getting into her car and directed Keisha to pull right up on the side of her as he let the window down and called her name, "Joseline."

Que startled the shit out of Joseline; but once she recognized that it was her older brother, she snapped on him, "Nigga' don't be having nobody pulling up on the side of me and I don't know who the fuck you are sitting behind this tint! What the fuck wrong with you?"

"Fuck that! What in the hell going on; and why didn't you fucking call me as soon as you found out about Carissa and them?"

"Call you! Quincy, I ain't had a number on you in over two years; so don't get to acting like we buddy buddy or best friends. I'm your own motherfucking sister and you don't fuck with me! By the time I did get your number out of Carissa's phone," Joseline said as she begin to cry "I did call you, but you wouldn't answer. Where you been? I been trying to do everything!"

Que got out of the car and hugged his younger sister. Even though they had their differences, he couldn't stand to see his baby sister cry. As his sister tears begin to subside, Que said, "I been out of town for a few days; I just got back this morning. I just ran into Tweezy, and he just told me what happened; so I came straight over here. I didn't have the slightest ideal that none of this even took place; but I'm here now so don't worry. I'ma handle everything."

"Quincy, he shot them all in the head! Carissa didn't deserve that at all. All she did was go to church. Then the way he shot Lil' T all in the face, he's going to have to be in a close casket because can't nobody reconstruct his face as bad as it was rearrange. It don't make no sense! I told you to talk to Terrance cause he just felt like he could do anything he wanted to because you his uncle. That's why I kept Sam from hanging over there."

"Where were you about to just go?"

"To talk to Mr. Jones to get prices on everything."

"I'll call him and let him know I'm paying for everything. We want the horses and carriage; the Phantom, everything! You know Carissa's favorite color was red; so if they got a red casket, get it. What do you need?"

"I don't need anything, but my big brother back! You and the kids are all I got now. It's just us now!"

"I know, I'm here now; and I promise to be around more for you and the kids." Que leaned in the car and pulled twenty thousand dollars out of his Prada bag and handed it to Joseline. "Here take this! That's for you and the kids. Where are they anyway?" Que asked not knowing that they were seated behind the tinted windows of her Chevy Impala SS.

"They're both in the car."

Que poked his head through the driver side door to see Sam and Tiffany. "What's up ya'll? Ya'll alright?"

"Yeah!" They both said at the same time.

Sam then said, "We ain't seen you in awhile. Where you been uncle Que?"

"I been a lil' bit of everywhere; but I'm here now, and ya'll going to be seeing more of me from here on out. I got to go now; but we gone all meet up tonight for dinner if it's cool with ya'll momma."

"Yeah, I'd love that!" Joseline replied before Sam and Tiffany could even ask her.

"Good, dinner it is! Just call me at six o'clock and we can meet wherever ya'll want to go."

"I-ight; just make sure you answer your phone."

As Que got back in the Audi he said, "I will, I promise." and shut the door.

"Thanks for not clowning Que. Where are we going from here because you need to chill and collect your thoughts? My surprise and money can wait!" Keisha said as she began pulling off.

"Okay, well let's go to the 4 Seasons. I need to have a few drinks anyway and lay down till about five o'clock. I ain't slept in two days. Is that cool with you?"

"I'm cool with that."

"Shit'd, while I'm asking, will you go out to dinner with us too?"

"I ain't got nothing planned anyway; and with all the shocking news you received today, I 'm down to do whatever you need me to do."

Chapter Fifteen
(Stick 'em Up)

*A*ll Cortez could think of was his momma saying she didn't know about buying him a car, and how he could come up with the money his self. He sat around and thought for hours, before he came up with the thought, *Fuck it, I got a gun now; so I'll just rob a motherfucker and take their shit. I'll rob the motherfuckers that be posted in front of Ali's store.*

After awhile he realized that was a dumb plan, and thought of another scheme. Fuck it, I can rob the store. I know Ali and them got at least ten thousand dollars in there; and then I can get a car, rims, beats, and probably still have a lil' money left over to play with.

Cortez grabbed his Glock forty and left heading to the store to scope shit out because he never actually went all the way through it; or never noticed how many people actually worked there. Ali and another guy were the only two people he'd ever seen working there. When he got to the store, he noticed that there was only one lil' cat hanging out front when he went in.

Upon entering the store, he went straight to the back where they cut up and made cooked pizzas to go. Seeing Ali and the other guy up front ringing up the people in line, Cortez rung the bell on the meat counter for service. Bing, was the sound that came from the bell. A few seconds later, a Black man came from out of a room behind the counter talking to somebody that Cortez couldn't see; so he knew it was somebody else back there. He was just clueless as to how many more people or what was actually back there.

"What's up young brother; what can I get you?" the Black man asked.

"I'm trying to get a pizza. How long will it take to be ready?"

"It takes up to twenty minutes to cook depending on how many you order."

"Alright, that's cool. Let me get a small meat lovers pizza then."

"Is that it?"

"Yeah; that's all I need."

The cook then wrote small meat lovers pizza $6.99 on a piece of paper and said, "Here, take this up front and pay for it; then bring me the receipt back so I can start cooking it."

"I-ight." Cortez said grabbing his ticket.

As Cortez walked back up front to pay for the pizza, he noticed Doe, the weed man Ej and Corey first took him too, standing in line as he got right behind him. Standing next to each other in line, Doe bust out and said, "Ain't you the lil' nigga' who came to my house with Mesha and got that half?"

"Yeah; what's up?" Cortez replied.

"How is she doing?" Doe asked with a smirk on his face trying to piss Cortez off. "Tell her Doe said he got that Kush on deck so holla' at me!"

The first thing Cortez thought was, *I should fuck this nigga' up!* and then he quickly changed his mind and thought to his self, *Let me test this motherfucker.* "Alright, I'll tell her when I see her. What's the prices on it?"

"I got ounces for three fifty, halves for a dollar seventy-five, and quarters going for a hundred even. I don't sell nothing less!"

"I-ight, I got a hot hundred I can spend with you."

Doe moved up to the register and said, "What it do Ali? Let me get a pack of Newport shorts and a box of White Owls" and then he went in his pocket and pulled out a fat ass knot of money and handed Ali a fifty dollar bill. "Yeah lil' nigga', I'll sell you a quarter real quick. Just come around to my crib whenever you ready; and know I ain't taking no shorts!" he said as he walked out the store.

Mad that Doe was asking him about DaMesha and addressing him as a lil' nigga', Cortez kept his composer as he stepped up to the counter and paid for the pizza, and then he took the receipt to the cook. "Okay, give me about twenty minutes." The cook said.

Cortez went outside on the front and tried to come up with a plan on how to rob the store, but every plan that he came up with wasn't good enough. He knew it could be done, but he just had to figure out how. He went back into the store about fifteen minutes later and got a box of Swisher Sweets and a soda. When he went to check on his order, it was ready to go.

As the man handed him his food he said, "Come next week, we going to start selling hot plates."

"That's what's up! I'll have to come check ya'll out." Cortez said as he turned to leave.

After leaving out the store, Cortez made his way around to Doe's house for the Kush. When he got there and rang the door bell, Doe opened the door super fast like he was standing right behind the door waiting on his arrival.

"Step in." Doe said. "You got the whole one hundred right?"

"Yeah." Cortez said as he counted it out.

"Okay, stand here. I'll be right back." Doe replied. Cortez watched him go down the hall and into the second room on the right. He then started to notice that it looked as if no one else lived here besides Doe. Just as he started to noticed the lack of evidence that anybody else may have also lived here, Doe came out the room. "Alright, which kind do you want? This here is OG; and this one is called Blue Dream." He said handing Cortez two quarter bags.

"They both smell and look good; so I'll roll with which ever one you think is the best."

"Well, I'll say get the OG; it's super fire! Well they both fire; OG just tastes better."

"I-ight here." Cortez said handing him the hundred dollars and the bag of Blue Dream. As he turned to leave he said, "Right on; I'll be back to fuck with you."

"You better hurry back and get what all you want because I only got like five pounds of this shit left and it's gone go fast."

Cortez said, "Alright." and left out the house. before he could make it to his house he thought to his self with a smile on his face, *I know what I'm going to do now. I'ma rob that nigga' since he figure I'm such a lil' nigga.* Walking up to the house, he saw DaMesha and Corey sitting on Ms. Rose porch. "What's up ya'll?" Cortez yelled out.

"Nothing." DaMesha responded "We about to walk to the store for my granny. What you on?"

"I ain't on shit! I just came from the store. When ya'll make it back, knock on my door. I got a Kush blunt I'll smoke with ya'll."

"I can't smoke right now." Corey said. "My coach should be here in about thirty minutes. I got a big fight coming up next week at 12th and Park. You should come!"

"I'll be there; just let me know what time."

"I will; also I'm going to call you when I get back home. I wan'na holla' at you."

"I'm gone knock on your door when we get back from the store." DaMesha said.

"I-ight; I'm here!"

Cortez went in the house and went straight to his room to roll up a blunt and put his gun back under the mattress. Once he was done rolling the blunt, he put it behind his ear; and then ran back upstairs to eat his pizza while he waited on DaMesha to come back. He kept thinking about if Doe was going to be an easy lick or not because he wasn't trying to have anybody trying to retaliate on him. That's when he said to his self out loud, "I just got away with killing three people; putting another motherfucker under my belt ain't going to hurt nothing!"

After eating two slices of pizza DaMesha knocked on the door, bringing a smile upon Cortez's face as he quickly opened the door for her. "What's up baby?" DaMesha said as she gave him a hug.

"Shit; I was just thinking about getting a car for my birthday."

"Oh yeah; when is your birthday?"

"August the sixth. I only got twenty eight days until then."

"Well, I can't get you a car, but I can get you something else. What you want me to get you?"

"Nothing!"

"For real Tez! Tell me now so I can have it by your birthday."

"I got everything I want except a car. What I want from you, is for you to spend my birthday with me."

"I wouldn't miss it for the world; I'm looking forward to it!"

"Let's smoke real quick so we can eat."

"I already ate." DaMesha said as they went out the back door to smoke.

"Here, light it up." Cortez said. After hitting the blunt twice, DaMesha damn near coughed up a lung. "You alright?" Cortez asked patting her on the back.

"Yeah; I'm good. Where you get this from?"

Cortez didn't want to tell DaMesha where he got it from because of what he was about to do; so he lied and said, "I got this from some dude at the store. I got a few more sacks of this shit, so I'll give you one to go home with."

"That's what's up. You know Ej's funeral this Friday; can you come with me?"

"Yeah, I'll go. You sure his momma ain't gone trip out? I don't want to go and fuck his funeral up being that his momma is already blaming me for his death."

"I'm sure. You gone be right next to me and my momma, so my auntie Carla ain't gone say shit!" DaMesha said as if she knew for curtain. "Oh yeah, my momma know we go together too! We talked about it last night; and she told me to tell you, that you are welcome over to our house any time. So I'm expecting to see more of you!"

"Oh that's cool. My momma knows we talk too. We haven't talked about it, but she knows." Cortez said with a smile on his face.

After spending all day with DaMesha, Cortez started putting his plan together for the mission he was going on the next morning. He wasn't going to waste any time putting it off; he knew he wanted and had the tools to get the job done. Cortez laid back thinking, *I'll go over Doe's house early in the morning and catch him off guard. Once I get him to let me in, I'll make him show me where everything is at; and once he does that and I get what I want, I'm going to knock him off. Fuck that, I'ma show him how this lil' nigga' gets down!*

Cortez called and spoke to DaMesha once more before laying down and going to sleep. When he woke up, it was six o'clock in the morning and he was ready to put in work. He felt like the money was already his; he just had to claim it. He got dressed in all Black once again, grabbed his Glock forty, and left out the basement door.

It didn't take Cortez seven minutes to make it to Doe's crib. Cortez stepped to the door and rang the door bell twice; after standing there for a minute, he rung it two more times. The forth time got Doe's attention, as you could hear him storming to the door. Unlocking the door with an attitude Doe asked, "Who in the fuck is it?"

"It's Tez!" I replied as he opened the door.

"What the fuck you doing over here so got damn early for; ringing my motherfucking door bell, like you done lost your rabbit ass mind lil' nigga'?"

"I came because I got a hundred and seventy-five dollars to spend this early."

"I'll serve you this time lil' nigga'; but next time you ain't getting shit! Step in."

"I-ight, it won't be a next time." Cortez replied as he thought, *You ain't gone see a next time nigga'*.

"What you want anyway? Some more of that OG, or do you want to try that Blue Dream?"

"I want the OG; that shit was on point. I had to come get some more!"

"Next time, don't come so damn early! I don't get up till around twelve." Doe said as he was walking down the hall and went in the same room on the right as he did yesterday.

Once he went in the room, Cortez pulled out his gun and quickly made his way down the hall. When Doe came out of the room it was too late for him to try to run. Cortez was right in front of him with his gun damn near touching Doe's nose. "Don't make this turn into a murder; you know what I came for. So give it up!" Cortez said boldly but direct. "Now you can play games if you wan'na, and I'ma pop the shit out of you; and still gone get everything, so just give it to me and you won't get hurt!"

"Alright man, you can have it. I thought we were cool bruh."

"Oh, I was just a lil' nigga' a minute ago; now we cool! Stop talking nigga' and get the shit!" Cortez said as he grabbed Doe by the shirt so he can lead him to it.

"Okay, it's right in my safe; and my safe is right behind my T. V. stand."

Once Cortez got Doe to the safe, he told him, "If you try anything stupid, I'ma put one in the back of your head; and that's on my dead daddy!" From the look on Cortez's face and the tone of his voice, Doe knew he was dead serious and meant business; so he did exactly what he was told, while thinking to his self, *Please don't let this lil' nigga' see that gun*. Doe had a blue steel .38 special sitting on the nightstand next to his lamp on the other side of the bed. "What you want me to put it in?" Doe asked as he opened the safe.

Cortez immediately saw that it was way much more than what he thought he was going to come up on; so he quickly grabbed a pillow off the bed and dumped the pillow out. He then threw Doe the empty pillowcase and told him, "Fill it up and don't leave shit out or it's your ass."

Looking around the room, Cortez spotted the .38 special on the nightstand. When Doe handed him the pillowcase back, he said, "Here, you got it all. The money and everything."

"Bullshit, this ain't every motherfucking thing! Where the fuck are them pants you had on yesterday?"

"They're on the floor, on the other side of the bed. I got like fifteen hundred in those, but you can take it too."

"Motherfucker, I don't need your permission on what I can take! Keep playing me fucking stupid and its gone be the last motherfucking game you play! You understand me?"

"Yeah."

"Now I'm gone ask you one last got damn time, is this every motherfucking thing?"

"Yeah, that's it."

Cortez smacked the shit out of Doe and then replied, "So what about that motherfucking gun over there; what you forgot about that?"

"I thought you seen it already. Take it; it's your. Just please don't shoot me!" Doe begged.

"Alright, lay down and don't move." Cortez ordered. Doe laid on his back nervous as hell, then Cortez snapped, "Nigga' you steady playing me fucking stupid! You must want me to pop your ass. Turn your monkey ass over face down. Matter of fact, kiss the fucking floor!"

"Come on bruh don't" Doe started saying before Cortez cut him off.

"Come on bruh my ass! Act like the floor Mesha nigga' and kiss it!" Cortez ordered. Doe kissed the floor once causing Cortez to spasm out, "Oh fat ass motherfucker, I don't recall telling you to fucking stop. Keep kissing that bitch! You thought I was just a lil' nigga' huh? I bet you wish you never met this lil' nigga' now."

Cortez slid the .38 special into the pillowcase and picked up the pants Doe wore yesterday to get the fifteen hundred. After he got the money he stepped over Doe and bent down resting the barrow of his gun on the back of his head as he asked, "Okay, now where is the rest of the shit?"

Cortez knew from the fear he had installed in Doe that if it was something else he'd for sure tell it. "I swear I ain't got shit else bruh. If you want, take the flat screens; they worth some money."

"Punk ass motherfucker, I don't want no got damn televisions. I already got flat screens. Where the rest of the shit at?" Cortez asked with the barrow of his gun still resting on the back of Doe's head.

"Bruh, I promise you; you got it all!"

"Now I do." Cortez said shooting him dead smack in the back of the head.

Blood scattered everywhere, even getting on Cortez's pants and shoes. Luckily they were Black so you couldn't see it as clear as if it would have shown up on a bright color. Wasting no time to flew from the scene, Cortez ran out of the back door straight down the alley.

He wasn't in Doe's house not even five minutes, so it was still kind of dark outside as he ran threw the alleys all the way to the crib. Once he made it back inside of the house and locked the doors, he felt super good. He knew that he got away with it. He took off his shoes and pants and put them in a garbage bag, while quickly changing into another outfit. Cortez then quietly left back out of the house with the bag to throw away, but only he threw it away in a dumpster that was three blocks over.

On the way back home, Cortez felt no remorse. Instead, he was amped to see how much money he came up on all together. When he got back inside, he couldn't wait on his momma and auntie Keniesha to wake up and leave so he could go through the pillowcase. The moment he knew they both were gone, he grabbed the pillowcase dumping out its contents on his bed and began counting.

When he was finished counting, he had a grand total of $17,974.00. That's when he started to go through the rest of the stuff that he had gotten. He had: a zip-lock freezer bag filled with thirteen individual sandwich bags containing a hundred X-pills a piece all different kinds; two ounces of crack cocaine, two and a half pounds of OG and Blue Dream Kush, four pounds of regular weed, and a new blue steel .38 special to add to his collection.

Cortez didn't know what to do with half of the shit that he got; but he didn't care too much at this point. All he wanted was a car. Cortez quickly thought, *I need to find a stash spot.* He looked around the basement, but there wasn't anywhere to stash all the shit he had; so he went up stairs in hope of finding a nice spot, but came up short.

Feeling like fuck it, cause he was running out of ideals, he decided to stash everything under his bed mattress. When he saw that the bed still looked normal with all the shit stash under the mattress, he thought, *All I need now is some incenses to keep the smell down, and I'll be good.*

After coming to his conclusion, he ran up to Ali's store to get some smell goods. Once he got some and made it back, he lit up an incense and then called DaMesha. "Hello; what's up boo?" DaMesha said answering the phone.

"Shit; I'm bored to death and trying to see if I can come over."

"You don't have to ask; just come over."

"Okay; I'm on my way." Cortez said and then hung up and made a fat ass sack of OG to smoke out of. He put two hundred dollars in his pocket, and left headed straight for DaMesha's house.

Once he got there, they had a normal day. Cortez acted as if he hadn't done anything out of the normal, but all the rest of the day he frequently thought to his self, *From here on out if I catch a motherfucker stunting too hard, I'ma stick 'em up!*

Chapter Sixteen
(Back 2 Business)

*T*he day after Que's family funeral, it was back to business as usual.

Que was still upset, but he knew he had to let it go; because by Ej being dead, it wasn't much he could do. Keisha gift was also ready; so Que stopped by to make sure everything was perfect, before he brought Keisha over to see what would be her new house, if she liked it herself. Plus since Keisha had been so patient about getting her money and surprise, Que went to Frontenac Plaza to pick her up a fourteen karat gold women's Rolex for all the support and time she had been giving him.

It was time to make his rounds, but Que refused to make Keisha wait another day for what she earned and deserved. Since Tweezy had handled everything smoothly, Que called him and told him he needed him to pick up everything south and west for him again. Que then picked up everything north his self. Once he was finish, he called Keisha.

"What's up boo; what you doing?" Keisha answered the phone and asked.

"I'm around your way, and want to know if I could slide on you so I can take you to see your surprise?"

"Yeah, you can come get me!" Keisha said full of excitement.

"I'm coming down Grand now, so I'll be there in a few minutes. I'm in a red G-wagon with Black rims on it."

"A red G-wagon! What the hell is that?"

"It's a Mercedes G-class truck. Just be outside, and you'll see me." Que replied. Four minutes later Que was out front and Keisha jumped in giving him a big hug and kiss. "You sure all cheesy. You smiling harder than a kid in a toy store. You happy?"

"Damn right; I love surprises!" Keisha replied wiggling like she had ants in her pants. "I can't wait to see what it is. I just hope you didn't go to far out of your way for whatever it is."

"I didn't, I got it from the gas station. Infact, you can share it with me. Look in the glove department and give me a piece of your gum." Que said jokingly.

"Don't play! You want some gum for real?"

"*Naw*, I was just teasing; but maybe I did or didn't go out of my way, but I'll rather you be the judge of that." After about a fifteen minute ride, Que pulled up to a big three story brick house that looked like it was out of the future and said, "Lets run in here real quick."

"Is this your house; because it's beautiful if so?" Keisha asked as walking up to the house admiring its unique structure.

"Yeah, this one of mines; but come on we won't be long." Que answered as he opened the stain glass front door.

Upon entering the house, Keisha's mind was blown away. The house whole first floor was marble including the base of the windows seals. Even the ceilings were custom made out of oak wood built in multiple different levels leading to two different sets of spiral steps. It was hands down the best house Keisha ever seen in person or been in with one exception as she addressed it. "Que, where in the hell is your furniture at?" she asked in disbelief that the house was empty.

"Well I figured since it's your place now, you could furnish it any kind of way you wanted."

"Are you serious?" Keisha asked with a facial expression that was priceless and should have been recorded.

"*Yep*, it's all yours if you want it."

"For real Que, don't play with me like this." Keisha said not believing him for one moment.

"I'm serious! It's yours if you want it."

"Hell yeah I want it!" Keisha burst out, but then after a quick thought replied, "*Naw*, before I even jump the gun; how much is the rent gone be?"

"How much is the rent gone be?" Que repeated as if feeling insulted and then replied, "Shit! I'm giving you this! This your surprise!"

"Oh my God; thank you Que. I don't even know what to say."

"You ain't got to say anything, but when you are ready to move in. Go check out the rest of the house."

Walking through the house, Keisha thought to herself, *Cortez is going to love this place; it's so spacious.* After looking all through the three story house, Keisha claimed the master bedroom out of the other three bedrooms. Then she bluntly said, "I'm ready to move in as soon as possible. Is tomorrow too soon?"

"Not if that's what you want to do; but if you want to move in tomorrow, I think we need to be going shopping for some furniture now. What you think?"

"I would love to go shopping, but I know it's work that needs to be done. I don't want to hold you up."

"You ain't holding me up! Today is all about you. So whatever you want to do, then that's what we doing."

Keisha said, "Okay. Well if that's the case, let's hurry up and furnish my new crib so I can fuck you in it."

"In that case, I'll race you to the truck." Que replied as they both laughed and then took off running like some track stars. Pulling up to the House of Denmark Que told Keisha, "Don't hold back when we get in here. Get whatever you want; I got you cover."

Keisha fell in love with a brown and cream sectional coach with the matching center and two end tables. She pictured that it would look perfect sitting on her marble floor and even compliment her oak wood ceilings. She also picked out a very exclusive bedroom set that had columns that looked as if they would touch the ceiling in her bedroom. The next item Keisha chose was a dinner room table, which looked like the table Jesus ate the last supper on. It seated twelve people. Keisha next picked out a king size bed that had a Black leather pillow top head board and foot board for Cortez. She figured that's all she would get for him so he could pick out his own stuff and add his own style to his room.

"Okay, that's all I want." Keisha said to Que.

"What about the other two rooms; they need beds and shit too; don't they?"

"You gone furnish the whole house?"

"Yeah; if you see something you like, get it."

"Well I'm going to turn one of the rooms into my own office."

"If that's what you want to do, then do it. I told you it's your place now; so I don't have any objections to whatever you decide to do with the place."

After Keisha picked out all of the stuff she wanted, the grand total for everything after taxes was $22,704.16. Que pulled out a credit card and paid for everything like it was just twenty-two dollars and seventy cents. Once they left there, Keisha just knew they were done shopping; until Que pulled up to HH Greg's for flat screen televisions and stands.

Keisha look at Que as if she wanted to say something, but before she could even get a word out Que said, "You got to at least have a T.V. in the house; I know you and your son don't want to just stare at walls!" Keisha didn't have a come back; she just proceeded to follow Que into the store. Once inside, the first television she picked out was a ninety inch flat screen for her living room. She then chose three Sony fifty-five inch smart televisions for Cortez, her, and the additional room. In the process Que suggested that she got one for the bathrooms and the room she planned on making into her office; so she got two twenty-two inches and a thirty-two inch television to complete the house as for as televisions were needed. The only thing she figured she was missing now was a television stand for the ninety inch flat screen she picked out since she planned on having the rest of the televisions mounted on the walls; and some surround sounds as well as a few Blu-ray systems. They did a lil' more shopping for that, and by time night fall

begin to hit Que took her to Joe's Crab Shack for dinner since he remember that she mentioned it before.

As they waited on their food, Que began to thank Keisha for all of her support. "Keisha, I really want to thank you for being here for me. You've worked hard and been patient with me; so I got you another gift." Que said as he pulled out the Rolex box and opened it.

"Is that a-." Keisha said as her voice faded out.

"*Yep*; and I hope you like it." Que said before she could finish getting her words together.

"I always wanted a Rolex, but I never figured I would actually get one. I love it!" Keisha said putting it on. "Why are you doing all of this for me?"

"Because you mean a lot to me. Besides, you gave me the best gift anybody could ever give me; and I want to show you that I'm grateful."

"What have I gave you to deserve everything that you have blessed me with?"

"Your time and loyalty was the greatest gift I could ever had gotten. You can give me cars, clothes, money, and everything else that man can make, but you can take all of that back. You on the other hand gave me not only your time, but loyalty as well; and that's something you can't just take back, and I'm loving every second of it."

As the night ended, Keisha was very much satisfied with how her day had played out. She couldn't find a single thing to complain about. When Que pulled back up to Keniesha's house to drop her off, he told Keisha, "Remember you need these." and handed her two sets of keys to her new house. He then said, "Also remember you need to be at the house by twelve o'clock so you can let the delivery people in so they can set up everything."

"Again, thank you for everything Que!"

"Stop that; don't thank me! Tomorrow if ya'll feeling up to it, I would like to take you and Cortez out so I can finally get a chance to meet him."

"We'll be waiting on you." Keisha said as Que got out of the car to open her door for her, and then walked her to the porch and waited on her to open it; Keisha gave him a kiss and said, "Call me when you get where you going."

"I will." Said Que as he walked back to his Benz climbed in and pulled off.

The next day, Keisha woke up early and went down stairs to Cortez's room to find him still asleep; so she woke him up. "Cortez!" she called out but he didn't respond. "Cortez, wake up!"

Blinking his eyes trying to gain focus, Cortez finally answered, "What's up momma? What's wrong?"

"Boy, ain't nothing wrong! I just need you to get up, and get ready to go; because I have a surprise for you and we have a lot of stuff to do. It's ten o'clock now, and we need to be where we are going before twelve o'clock; so get up and get ready!"

"Okay, I'm up!" Cortez said grudgingly. "I'll be ready in a minute, but can we at least get something to eat on the way to wherever we going?"

"Yeah, if you hurry up!" Keisha answered as she returned back up stairs.

Cortez quickly got dressed not caring if he was matching or not, as he made his way up stairs to let his momma know that he was ready. Upon seeing her child, Keisha shook her head at how he was dressed; but didn't say anything about it because she had other things on her mind. About twenty minutes later, they were out the door.

Keisha went the same way she remembered Que going yesterday. When she made it to Kingshighway, she stopped at White Castle's. She was going to go through the drive through, but figured since they still had a little over an hour they could dine in. While eating, Cortez asked a million questions. Keisha thought to herself, *I wish this boy tongue hurry up and get tired, so he'll stop asking me all these damn questions and just eat!* as she answered another question.

When they left White Castle's she told Cortez, "Now listen, you need to pay close attention to where we are going now; so you'll know your way back."

Cortez didn't ask any more questions; he instead tried to remember every corner and street name they drove passed. As they turned down a couple of streets, Cortez realized that he wouldn't be able to remember every street they passed; and then decided to just remember the main ones. As Keisha made a left onto a street named McPherson, Cortez easy remembered the name because he had a friend with the same last name back in New Orleans, and then he noticed that the houses on this street were different than any other street he had been on in St. Louis.

"Dang, these some big cribs over here! Momma, one day I'ma buy you a house that big." Cortez said as he pointed to the first house he seen.

Halfway down the block, Keisha pulled over and parked. It was eleven forty-two on the dot, and so far she had beat the delivery trucks. "Come on baby, let's get out."

"Who house is this? "It's hella' big!" Cortez asked as he viewed the house in amazement while following his mother.

Keisha got up to the door and pulled out both sets of keys Que gave her, and then handed Cortez a set and said, "Surprise! Open the door to our new house!"

"Are you for real?"

"Yes sir; and I need you to hurry up and pick out a room on the third floor. That's your floor!"

Cortez was totally amazed with the inside of the house. he quickly chose the room with the wall size windows and sliding door. As they were talking about the new house, one of the delivery companies arrived right on schedule. Just as they begin to unload, the second delivery company truck pulled up and was ready to set up too. Cortez just stood back and watched in disbelief until both companies were finish unloading everything and had set up their stuff. That's when he said, "All we need now are some televisions."

"Oh don't worry! We got some coming; they just haven't made it here yet. I picked you out a fifty-five inch Sony smart T.V. for your rooms and one for mines too; but wait until you see our living room T.V., you gone love it!" Keisha said excitedly. "After they get here and set up the televisions, we gone go get us some covers sets from Macy's in the mall. Do you know what color you want your room to be?"

"*Yop!*" I want them to be red and Black."

Once the television where delivered and mounted where they wanted them, the house was almost complete so they shot out to the mall. When they got to Macy's, Cortez chose two different design king size red and Black Ralph Lauren cover sets. Keisha chose a green and purple king size bed cover set along with other knick knacks for the house before heading home.

On the way there Keisha called Que, who was waiting for his car to get finished washed and waxed. "Hey Keisha; how is everything going?"

"Good! We got just about everything we need for the house. Infact, we on our way back home now. Where you at?"

"I'm at the car wash right now; but as soon as they get done here, I'll be headed your way."

"Okay, we're waiting." Keisha said and then hung up.

"Who was that?" Cortez questioned.

Your future father-in-law. Keisha thought before she caught herself from actually saying it out loud. "Oh, that was my friend Que; I want ya'll to meet each other. I know you are going to like him, because he can be just as silly as you can be."

"I hope he ain't no lame wan'na be!"

After laughing Keisha said, "*Naw*, actually he's far from a lame! I just want you to give him a fair chance before you pass judgment on him."

"Don't worry, I will; but if he a lame, I'm going to talk about him something bad!" Cortez said so serious. Keisha just laughed because she knew her son was for real; but at the same time he was in for a surprise.

Once they made it home, Cortez ran straight to his room and put his new sheets and covers on his beds. He was loving his new room, even though he was farther away from DaMesha now. All he could think was, *She'll get her chance to see it in due time.*

When Que arrived, he rung the door bell and waited on someone to answer. Keisha opened the door and gave Que a hug and a kiss before he stepped in and congratulated her on decorating the house. Wasting no time to introduce Que to her son, Keisha yelled up the stairs, "Cortez, come down here."

As Cortez was coming down the steps, he spotted Que's Arctica watch flooded in ice and thought to his self, *Damn, that motherfucker tight!* "Yes ma'am." Cortez said reaching the last step.

"Cortez, meet my friend Que. Que, this is my son Cortez."

Extending his hand out to shake Cortez's hand, Que said, "What's good Tez? It's nice to meet you."

Following his watch with his eyes, Cortez replied, "It's nice to meet you too; but it would be even better if I had one of those watches!"

They all laughed as Que said, "I paid a pretty penny for this one."

"I bet you did; it looks like it costs a million dollars!" Cortez blurted out.

"Not quite a million; I ain't got it like that." Que responded with a smirk. "Are ya'll ready?"

"Yeah I am." Keisha said, and then asked Cortez, "Are you ready?"

"Yeah, you know I was born ready!"

"Okay then; let's do this." Que said as he opened the door and hit his unlock doors button to his Mercedes CLS55AMG.

This car was red and Black like his G-class. "Dang Que, that mug hard; and I'm loving the color! Momma, I want one of those for my birthday!"

"Boy dream on! It ain't no telling how much that kind of car costs; you better be happy if you even get a car."

Oh I'm getting a car; you just ain't gone know. Cortez thought. "I'll get one someday." Cortez said.

"When is your birthday?" Que asked.

"I'ma be seventeen August 6th!"

"Can you drive yet?"

"Yeah I can whip; I love driving!"

"Well I'll tell you like this, I'll let you drive it for your birthday; but you can't have it. I actually got a few whips. I'll show you all of them, and then you can choose which one you wan'na drive for your birthday. What you think about that?"

"Do they get better than this?"

"Yes sir! I got a few foreign whips that I consider nice." Que said as they pulled off. "We about to go eat and have fun; you are hungry, ain't you Tez?"

"He always hungry; he'll eat anything you give him." Keisha said with a smile on her face.

"Well that's cool with me. Tez eat the whole damn place if you can; I'll pay for it."

Keisha phone rang; and to her surprise it was Keniesha, so she answered it. "Hello, where ya'll at?" Keniesha questioned.

"We out chilling with Que; why, what's up?"

"Shit, I was just being nosey. I ain't want nothing; ya'll have fun." Keniesha said and then hung up.

"We will." Keisha replied before just saying out loud, "That was sister with her nosey ass!"

Pulling up to Dave & Buster's, Que said, "Tez, I got five hundred dollars say I out shoot you in basket ball."

"Put your money where your mouth is, and you gone loss it; cause ain't no way in the world I'm going to let you beat me. But if you feel like you got it to lose, then it's a bet!"

"I see I'm going to have to show you some sports; lets go have some fun."

Rushing into the place, they ended up having a great time. Que surprise Cortez with his basketball skills; and when it was all over with, Que beat Cortez in the basketball contest but still gave him the five hundred dollars as he told him, "You might want to put this towards you a car, because you ain't got nothing on me when it comes to basketball! You got to get your game up!"

Cortez couldn't say anything back because Que straight out shot him hands down; but he was more surprise when Que actually gave him the five hundred dollars anyway. That won him over and Keisha was very much pleased that they were getting along. She thought to herself, *If shit keep going like this, I'ma have to make it official.* As she whisper to Cortez, "You still think he's a lame?" smiling.

When they left Dave & Buster's the night was still young, and Keisha was ready to make her move with Que. She wanted to get rid of Cortez for the night, and she just how to get him to go along with her plans without him even knowing so. Keisha just came out and said, "Cortez, when are you going to tell DaMesha that we move?"

"I don't know; but I'ma do it soon though."

"Well me and Que going out tonight; so if you wan'na go over to Keniesha's house you better speak up now, or forever hold your peace!" Keisha said while making eye contact with Que.

"Yeah I wan'na go over auntie's house tonight. I'll tell Mesha we moved tomorrow; and you ain't even got to come pick me up until I call you."

Que interrupted their conversation by saying, "Now that I'm thinking about it, I'ma be around that way tomorrow; so if you want me to, I'll pick you up. Just put my number in you phone and call when you ready to make a move."

"I don't have a phone yet; but I got to get me one a.s.a.p. though."

"*Okay*, well I tell you what then. I'll pick you up tomorrow at six o'clock and we gone go to the mall and get you one; and if you want you can bring your girlfriend too."

"Now I'm down for that! I want an I-phone."

"So we're gone get you an I-phone then. You see I got one. All players got'ta have one." Que said jokingly.

As they pulled up to Keniesha's house, Keisha said, "Don't tell your auntie about the house yet. We going to show her tomorrow; and tell Mesha I said she welcome over any time she wants to come over."

"My lips are zipped. I'll leave that all to you. Anyway Que take care of my momma; and it was nice to meet you. Next time though, I'ma have to show you some real skills with that basketball and not take it so easy on you and let you win! I'm out."

Cortez jumped out the car and went in Keniesha's house. As soon as Que pulled off he asked Keisha, "So where are we going out too?"

"To my new house; I got a surprise for you, so I hope you are ready." Keisha said with a seductive look on her face.

Que flew to Keisha's house. When he pulled up he let her out and followed her to the door. Once inside, Keisha wasted no time. She pushed him on the couch and said, "Don't move; I'll be right back."

Keisha ran up to her room and took a quick shower. She then put on a see through American Apparel bra and panties set. She looked fierce and she knew Que wouldn't be able to resist her. Next she made her way back down stairs to see Que was watching the nine o'clock news so he wasn't paying attention to her until she walked up to him and sat on his lap. "Damn, you're looking so fucking sexy!" Que said as he rubbed his hands through her micros.

"I'm happy you like it because I got this just for you. I want us to Christian every room in here except for Cortez's room." Keisha said smiling.

Que said, "Well I'm ready and willing; just say when."

Keisha could feel Que's nature rising as she moved her ass side to side on his lap. That's when she turned around on his lap to where they were face to face and started to kiss him. She then began sucking on his neck and unbuttoning the three buttons on his Polo collar shirt at the same time. From the look on his face, she knew she had him right where she wanted him. She then told him to put his hands up so she could take his shirt off. As she did so, she told Que what she wanted. "Que, I already had you for a snack; but now I want the whole five course meal. I want you to go hard on me until you can't go any more." As Que began to talk, Keisha put her finger on his lips shushing him as she said, "Just enjoy this!" as she slid to her knees and undid his pants and pulled his dick out.

Keisha began sucking Que's dick as if her life depended on pleasing him. She was taking in as much of his thick manhood as she possibly could until her eyes began to water up. She didn't know it, but she had Que's toes curling up in his low top Air-Forces. Just before he was about to bust, he grabbed her by the hair and said, "Now it's your turn."

Que quickly stood up with the thought in his mind, *Yeah, we gone Christian every room alright.* That's when he picked Keisha up and carried her to the kitchen and placed her on the marble island. He was so excited to be getting ready to put his tongue game on her as he played his part in helping blessing her house as she wanted. Que gently slid Keisha's panties off and then just through them as he began eating her pussy.

After only a few moments, Que had Keisha started feeling better than any man had ever made her feel in her life. It was almost as if Que was trying to eat the DNA out of her the way he was going in on her. Keisha just kept rubbing the deep waves he had in his head as she began to cry out how good it felt. It felt so good to her, that tears even begin to run from her eyes as Que continue serving her. When Que saw the tears of joy running down Keisha's face, he knew that he kept part of his promise but it wasn't over with. That's when he told Keisha, "Now take me up to your room so we can continue there."

Keisha grabbed his hand and did just as she was told with cum running down her legs. When Que got her in the bedroom, he picked her up with ease and laid her in the bed before removing his pants and boxers. Que commitment in pleasing Keisha really turned her; and once she got a glance at Que's dick standing damn near as tall as he was, Keisha proceeded to suck it once more leaving it wet and throbbing.

Que started fucking Keisha real slow to keep his self from cumming too soon as he watched her flex up and her six pack form to its best. Keisha couldn't even keep her eyes open, nor did she try to keep quiet as she enjoy

the feeling of Que inside of her. "Fuck me faster and pull my hair!" Keisha shouted out.

Que roughly turned her around in a doggy style position, and did just that. He had fist full of micro braids in one hand, and with the other hand he put it on the top of her back to keep her face down right where he wanted her as he drilled in and out of her. Que was becoming rougher with each stoke; but Keisha was loving every bit of it.

Keisha started to use her hands to push Que back, so he let her up and turned her back around before picking her up off her feet and re-entering her wet warm pussy. Keisha felt like she was falling into a trance the more Que bounced her up and down on his dick without breaking his rhythm. "Oh shit, I'm about to cum!" Keisha screamed repeatedly.

After bouncing her up and down a few more times, Que felt her reach another orgasm before he let her down and laid back his self so she could ride him. Feeling the urge to quickly get him back inside of her, she quickly jumped on his lap with both of her feet flat on the bed and her hands on his chest as she begin riding him. She rode him until she couldn't hold back reaching another orgasm. Upon reaching it, she fell over shaking and squirting like a super-soaker-water-gun.

When she stopped shaking, Que said, "You ain't done yet; I ain't got mines off yet!"

Keisha mind was blown away. As much throbbing and swollen as her pussy felt, she quickly decided to give him some more head. As she begin, she said, "I want you to nut on my chest so I can see it and feel how warm it is." When Que did bust, he released what had to be a set of twins all over her chest; he then rubbed it around her breast with the head of his dick.

After they freshen up, they laid in the bed and talked until Keisha dozed off. Once Que knew for sure that Keisha was out, he started to get up and leave but Keisha woke up in the nick of time and said, "Where you going? You staying the night with me ain't you?"

"Yeah!" Que said, "If you want me too."

"Well I want you too; so lay back down."

Que laid back down, and shortly afterwards they both fell to sleep; and they both slept better than they either had in a while, especially Que.

Chapter Seventeen
(Da Come up)

Once I woke up the following morning, I kept thinking of how cool my momma's friend Que was. I also wanted to know exactly what the hell he did to make his money. That's when I thought to call DaMesha so I could break the news to her that I had to move, but I figured I'll do it face to face; so I got dressed, bag up a nice sack of Blue Dream, and then called and told her to meet me on her porch. I rolled up on the way to her house so that would be one less thing I had to do when I got there.

When I hit her block DaMesha said, "What's up baby? I was looking for you yesterday; why you didn't call me?"

"My momma woke me up early and had me ripping and running all day. I'm sorry I didn't call you. What you do yesterday?"

"I didn't do nothing for real. I went to check on my granny, and then I went to the nail shop with my momma and got my nails painted and my feet done. Do you like them? I was gone get your name on one of them, but I didn't know how you would feel about that."

"I like the way they done, and it would have been cool to see my name on your nails. Next time you should do it; just let me know when you going again and I'll pay for it."

"Okay I will. Oh yeah, did you hear somebody killed Doe fat ass the other day? They found him face down on his bedroom floor, dead with a hole in his head!"

"*Naw* I didn't hear about nothing like that. Who is Doe anyway? I don't even know who you're talking about." Cortez replied playing dumb.

"Doe is the nigga who house we went over to get the weed that day. Somebody ran in his shit and robbed and killed his nasty ass. He was always trying to pay me to eat my pussy with his trifling ass!"

Cortez quickly thought, *Huh is that so; that's why I made that fat ass motherfucker kiss the floor.* "Well that's all on that motherfucker; fuck him. Here fire this up so I can tell you what I really came to tell you."

"I hope it ain't nothing bad." DaMesha said as she fired up.

"Okay, yesterday me and my momma moved into our own house; she surprised me with my own key."

"So now I ain't gone never get to see you." DaMesha replied with a sad look on her face.

"No, you still gone see me all the time. It's not far at all; and my momma told me to tell you, you welcome over anytime. Plus you know I'm fin'na get a car for my birthday, so I'll pick you up everyday if you want me too. Don't look so sad! As a matter of fact, if you want to, you can go to the mall with me and my momma friend. That way we can stop by my house so you can see it. It's hella' big!"

"*Okay*, you just better make sure you call me everyday; or I'ma be mad at you."

"Don't worry, that's why we going to the mall so I can get an I-phone. What the hell, I'll buy you one too so you can call me from anywhere."

That's when Chicago came out the house and seen them smoking. "What's up Tez? Damn, so y'all out here holding out on the good shit huh?"

"*Naw* it ain't like that." Cortez said as he handed Chicago the blunt.

After hitting the blunt twice Chicago asked, "Where the hell you get this shit from? I need some of this like right now! What is this shit called?"

"That's that Blue Dream shit. My folks got it on deck for three hundred and fifty dollars an ounce."

"So your folks got ounces of this shit right here?"

"Yeah, they got that and some OG. The OG is better then this, but they been charging three hundred and seventy-five dollars an ounce for the OG."

"So I can buy an ounce from your folks right now, or is you faking?"

"I ain't gone even fake it with you. If I said it, that's what it is! We can go right now if you ready."

"Yeah, I'm ready right now; come on. Mesha, we'll be right back; tell your momma I'm making a run real quick." Once in the car, Chicago asked, "So where we going?"

"We going to my auntie's house. I didn't wan'na do to much talking in front of Mesha, but I got this shit! I got some fire ass Reggie too."

"Be real with me Tez; because if this is your shit, I'll help you move it. But I ain't trying to help no nigga I don't know move shit!"

"On my daddy this all me! And if you help me get it off, I'll look out for you."

"I don't need nothing from you; I get money out here! So I'll pay for everything I get from you. If you wan'na help me out, take care of Mesha and keep her out of my pockets and I'll help you do whatever you trying to do."

Pulling up to Keniesha's house Cortez said, "Wait right here; I'll be right back." Cortez ran in the house and grabbed a sack full of each kind of weed for Chicago to smell. Once he got back to the car he handed Chicago three different bags and told him to smell them, as he told him which one was which.

"They all smell good; but what's up with the ounce?"

"I broke my scale, so I need you to take me to the store so I can get another one right quick. While we are up there, I'ma get some more blunts so you can taste the OG and the Reggie as well; that way you can see it's all good, and then we can get down to business."

"Sounds like a good idea to me." Chicago said as he pulled off headed to Ali's store. After getting the scale and Chicago smoking a blunt of the Reggie and the OG he was sold. He quickly counted out seven hundred and twenty-five dollars and said, "I want an ounce of the OG, and an ounce of the Blue Dream. Hold up, while you in the house I'ma make some calls to a few of my associates who I know gone spend; that's if you wan'na bust a few moves today."

"Yeah that's all good; just know I'm trying to get all this Reggie off as fast as possible, and they can buy whole pounds of that shit."

"I-ight, so what's the price on the Reggie?"

"I want a hundred dollars an ounce, or a thousand dollars a pound. I'll be right back." Cortez said before taking off.

He ran inside and quickly bagged up each ounce weighting them on twenty-eight grams a piece; and then he put everything else back where it was, and came back out to the car as if he never did anything.

"Check this out, I got a partner who wants an ounce of that OG and a pound of Reggie. Then I got this other lil' nigga' that I fuck with who gone call me back in about thirty minutes for a pound of Reggie as well. So you need to go get two pounds of that Reggie, and another ounce of that OG; because by the time we make the first drop, my lil' nigga' should be calling for his order." As Cortez was about to get out the car Chicago's phone rang. "Hold on Tez, this might be another order. Hello; what's good nigga'? I got a partner with them Christmas trees on deck."

"What he working with?" The caller on the phone asked.

"He got onions of the loud for three hundred and fifty, and three hundred and seventy-five depending on what flavor you choose. Then he got whole things of Reggie for a thousand, or onions for a buck; and it's all A1." Chicago replied.

"Well bring me an onion of the loud; and I want the best shit he got! Meet me at the Citgo on Goodfellow; and just call me when you on your way." The caller said.

"I got you, give me about forty minutes." Chicago said then hung up the phone. He looked at Cortez and said, "Grab two ounces of the OG."

Cortez went and got everything Chicago told him to get and put it in a Nike bag he had. Then he thought to his self, *Let me grab one of these guns, because I'll be damned if a nigga' try to take my shit!* He chose the .38 special to roll with because he hadn't used it yet; and then he made his way back to Chicago's car. About two hours later they pulled back up to DaMesha's house, and Cortez was three thousand four hundred and seventy-five dollars richer than when he left.

Once they walked in the house, the first person they seen was DaMesha sitting on the couch. "Dang, I thought ya'll were coming right back! I was just about to call ya'll." DaMesha snapped while rolling her eyes.

"Everything is all good; we just made a few runs, that's all. Anyway, are you going to the mall with me; because if so, we need to go around to my auntie's house so we'll be there when Que pulls up." Cortez replied.

"Yeah I'm going; just let me tell my momma and put my shoes on. I'll be right back." After putting on her shoes, DaMesha went to her mother's room and said, "Momma, I'll be back. I'm going to the mall with Tez."

Barber said, "Are you asking me, or are you telling me?"

"Come on momma; you know I'm asking."

Chicago butted in and said, "Barber, quit playing and let her go to the mall." because he knew Cortez was going to get DaMesha something that he wouldn't have to buy her his self.

Listening to Chicago as always Barber said, "Okay, just don't come home at no one in the morning like your brother."

"Come on momma, you know I ain't fin'na be gone until no one o'clock in the morning. I ain't no fool! I'll be back way before that." DaMesha said before thanking her momma for allowing her to go. She then ran back downstairs and told Cortez, "Okay, I'm ready now; let's go."

It was only 5:20p.m. when they made it around to Keniesha's house; which she wasn't there, because she was with Keisha checking out the new house. They rolled up another blunt and sat on the porch smoking while waiting for Que to pull up. As six o'clock hit, Que came rolling down the street in a Black on Black four-door Porsche Panamera. DaMesha seen the Porsche first and said, "That motherfucker hard! I wonder who in the hell is in that, to be cruising down the street like that."

"I don't know, but that motherfucker is hard though." Cortez said as the car passed the house and bust a U-turn before it pulled right in front of Keniesha's house.

The window began coming down slowly before Que became visible and said, "What's up; ya'll ready to go?"

Shocked to see that it was Que inside the Black on Black Porsche Panamera, Cortez tried to hide the blunt and put it out; but Que had already spotted them smoking it. "Yeah we ready." Cortez said as him and DaMesha made their way to the car.

Once they got in, Cortez introduced DaMesha to Que. Que said, "How you doing Ms. Mesha?"

"I'm good; I really like your car."

"We both do." Cortez said.

"Thanks; but why ya'll put ya'll blunt out? I don't care if ya'll smoke. I use to smoke when I was ya'll age! I ain't gone tell if ya'll don't." Que said with a smile on his face.

Pulling off Cortez said, "So we can smoke in here?"

"Yeah, just don't burn nothing. That iPod got all the new shit on it; so find something we can bump!" Cortez grab the iPod and found *Lil' Boosie, Better Believe It*. Que turned it all the way up and jumped on the highway. He flew all the way to the exit nearest to the Galleria Mall before saying, "When we go in here, ya'll can get whatever ya'll want. So if you want it, you better get it!"

"Hold up Que, did you just say ya'll?" DaMesha asked.

"Yeah, you too! You good with Tez; so then you good with me."

After finding a parking spot and entering the mall, Cortez and DaMesha had Que all over the mall. He got them both iPhones, glasses, and clothes. They got everything they wanted. Then as they were in Champs getting the new Air Forces DaMesha said, "If Ej was still alive, he'd be on his head to get these."

When she said that, it really got Que's attention. "I know it's only been a week or so, but you gotta let it go. He's in a better place now. Shit, he's probably watching over us right now; okay." Cortez said.

"Yeah you right; I just miss his crazy ass, that's all."

Que played it off like he didn't even hear them, but in the inside he couldn't wait to drop DaMesha off so he could get as much information on Ej as possible from Cortez. Once he paid for their stuff he said, "Ya'll think ya'll got everything that ya'll want?"

"Yeah!" they both said at the same time.

"Okay then, let's get out of here. I know ya'll ready to sit down after all this walking."

Once they were leaving the mall Cortez asked Que, "Can we swing by the house so Mesha can see it?"

"Yeah we can do that; I need to holla' at your momma anyway."

DaMesha was shocked when they pulled up and she seen how big Cortez's new crib was. She was really surprised with the inside. When she saw Cortez's bedroom she thought, *Damn I can't wait to sleep in here.* "So when can I spend the night over here with you in this big ass bed?" DaMesha asked as she sat on the edge of his bed.

Cortez pushed her back on the bed, then stood in between her legs and lean over in her face and said, "Whenever you want too." as he kissed her on her lips. Then he pointed to the top left side of the bed and said, "That's your spot right there. I'm saving it just for you."

DaMesha could feel how hard Cortez was as he was leaned up against her; and she wanted him so bad, but she was afraid to let it be known. "Tez, I'ma see if my mama will let me spend a night with you. She be letting Corey spend the night over his girlfriend's house and shit. Then I'm sure if Chicago tell her to let me, she gone say yes."

"Well you let me work on Chicago." Cortez said as he began kissing her again.

DaMesha was so turned on that her pussy became instantly soaking wet. When she notice how horny she was she said, "What if your momma or Que come up here?"

"This is my floor; they ain't coming up here. You don't have to worry about them."

"Do you have any condoms?" DaMesha asked.

"*Naw*." Cortez said as he thought, *Damn, why I ain't got no damn condoms?*

"If we gone do it, we gone need a condom. I ain't trying to get pregnant; not yet at least. I don't wan'na be like the rest of these girls running around here with babies they can't even take care of. I do wan'na have a baby though; just not now."

Cortez totally understood where she was coming from and said, "Same here. We don't have to do it today; I can wait. I wan'na do it with you whenever you feel like you ready. I want you to be comfortable when we do it." DaMesha thought to herself, *I want it now. I just don't wan'na get pregnant.* Tez stood up and asked, "Are you hungry?"

"Yeah I can go for something to eat." DaMesha said as she looked at the time on the G-shock watch that she stole from Corey. "Oh it's ten o'clock, and I need to be home by eleven because I want my momma to always be cool with me coming over to see you."

"I-ight, I'll have my momma take you to get something to eat and then we'll drop you off. Is that cool with you?"

"Yeah that's cool. I got a taste for some McDonald's."

"Well McDonald's it is." Cortez said as they walked back downstairs to see Que had brought all of their bags in the house and left.

Keisha was sitting in the living room watching *How High*; so when they came down stairs she said, "I see ya'll love birds creeping down here; so what ya'll up too? Have ya'll ate anything?"

"That's what I was about to ask you. Can you take us to McDonald's? Then we need to get Mesha home by eleven o'clock too."

Looking at her new Rolex, Keisha saw that it was five after ten and said, "Well we better get going now, because it's getting close to that time; and by the way, Que told me to tell ya'll that he had fun with ya'll. He also said for you to call him Cortez when you charge your new phone up."

By the time that they got to DaMesha's house, it was ten minutes before eleven. Cortez helped DaMesha take her bags in the house; while

MY HEART TURNED COLD

Chicago sat back and peeped out all of the stuff that she brought in. "Well I'm fin'na get out of here, I don't wan'na have my momma out there waiting to long. Go let your phone charge up, and I'll call you when I get home to let you know we made it."

"Okay Tez." DaMesha said as she gave him a hug and said, "I'ma be waiting on your call." and turned toward her room and walked off.

"Alright; Chicago come lock the door."

"I'm about too; plus I wan'na holla' at you on the porch." As they walked outside Chicago said, "What are you doing tomorrow; cause everybody calling my phone trying to get some of that loud and the Reggie?"

"Shit!" Cortez said.

"Well can you come over tomorrow?"

"Yeah."

"Well try to come as early as you can, so we can get out here before everybody else do."

"I-ight; I'll be here by nine o'clock." Cortez said walking down the steps and jumping in the Rover.

Once Cortez made it home, he called DaMesha who was already sleepy. "Hello." she said with the sleepiest voice Cortez have ever heard.

"Were you sleep already?"

"Yeah I dozed off, but I'm up now."

"I was just calling to let you know we made it home; but I'm about to lay down too, so I can get up early in the morning because I have something to do with Chicago. So I'll be over there in the morning to smoke to with you."

"Okay baby, I'ma be waiting on you." she said.

Right after they hung up, Cortez ran down stairs to ask Keisha if she could take him over to Keniesha's house in the morning. "Yeah; but you gone have to get up at about seven a.m. because I got'ta go to work."

"That's cool because I wan'na be there by nine o'clock any way." he said as he turned to go back up stairs. On the way to his room he thought, *Fuck waiting, I'ma buy me a damn car A.S.A.P.*. The next day Cortez was at Keniesha's house by seven thirty, and Keisha went to the trap house to get to work. Cortez went to his old room and sacked up sack of OG, and then called DaMesha. "Hello; who is this?" she asked not noticing Cortez's new cellular phone number.

"It's Tez sleepy head! This my new number; anyway wake up cause I'm on my way around there. And save this number in your phone, and call me so I can program yours in mines."

"*Okay*, I'm up and I'm fin'na call you right now so hang up." DaMesha said and called right back from her new phone for Cortez to program her number in his phone.

"Is Chicago up?"

"Yeah; he always up by 6:00am. You wan'na speak to him?"

"Yeah let me holla' at him real quick."

Mesha made her way to the kitchen and handled Chicago the phone, "Here; it's Tez."

"What it do my nigga? I see you up early this morning; which is good. You ready to go to work or what?"

"Yeah I'm ready; what I need to bring with me?"

"I got four different orders; well five, if you got it."

"Well run it by me."

"You need six ounces of OG; eight ounces of the Blue Dream, and another whole thang of Reggie. If you got it, get it ready because I'm on my way."

"Alright, I'll be ready when you get here. Are we going straight to work, or are we going back to your crib for a minute?"

"*Naw*, we going to go ahead and get this out the way so we can chill; and then I have a business proposition for you too, but we'll talk about that later."

"Well do me a favor and give Mesha a sack and a blunt so she can have something to smoke on."

"I got you. Infact, I'm fin'na do it now; and then I'm out the door. So hold on, I'm fin'na give Mesha back the phone."

"Hello." DaMesha said grabbing the phone back.

"Yeah I'm here; but Mesha baby check this out. I ain't about to come right now because me and Chicago got a lil' work we about to do right quick. But he fin'na give you something to smoke on until we get done; and then I'll be over there to kick it with you."

"Okay baby. You know I'ma be waiting on you." she said, "I'll see you when you get here." then they hung up.

Chicago pulled up to Cortez sitting on the porch waiting with everything he told him to bring, plus his Glock-forty on him. Everything went smooth as it did the day before, and they sold all of Cortez's weed. Chicago was even selling his own shit too. As they were on their way back to the crib, Cortez said, "Say Chicago, I need you to help me find a car."

"What kind of car you trying to get? Are better yet, what you trying to spend on one?"

"I don't care what one going to cost me; I just want something real nice."

"Of coarse I know you want something nice; you to use to riding around in Rovers and shit big baller! I'll take you to my partner Sam when you ready; he got some nice shit!"

"I'm ready today! I just need to stop by the crib real quick."

"Alright." Chicago said headed straight for Keniesha's house.

When they got there, Cortez ran in the house to count up everything he had, so he could decide exactly what he was going to spend. He counted out

MY HEART TURNED COLD

$28,940; so he decided to bring ten thousand with him to spend on a nice whip.

"Alright, I'm ready." Cortez said to Chicago as he made it back to his car.

"You sure; because I just spoke to Sam and he's waiting on us."

"I'm good to go." Cortez said a lil' cocky feeling his self.

Pulling up to Sam's garage, Sam was sitting inside an all Black 1996 Chevy Impala with 24" rims on it. It was super clean. As they all got out of their vehicles, Chicago introduced Cortez to Sam; and then they got straight down to business. Sam showed Cortez four different cars, in which one was a newer model Lexus. Cortez didn't like any of them. He wanted the Chevy Impala Sam was sitting in. "Do you see something you like?" Sam asked.

"Yeah; I want that Impala you were sitting in. I don't want anything else."

"That's my baby! If I sell that, I'd have to get at least eight grand for it. It only has sixty thousand miles on it; plus I got it sitting on rims. The blue book value for its type of condition is ten thousand dollars."

"I'll gladly give you eight thousand for it." Cortez said rubbing his hands with a smile on his face.

"I hear you talking; but when are you going to be ready?" Sam asked not really believing Cortez was capable of producing that kind of money.

"I'm ready now!" Cortez said as he pulled out the ten thousand dollar knot he had and counted out eight thousand dollars. "Go get the title."

Sam looked at Chicago and said, "This nigga' about his business huh?"

"Yeah, lil' bro doing the damn thing! He papered up!" Chicago vouched for Cortez.

"Alright, I'll be right back with the title." Sam said surprised that he was selling his most pride and joy vehicular.

As Sam went to get the paper work that he needed to sell the car, Chicago told Cortez, "That's a nice choice you made. That's a classic car; and it got a LT1 Corvette motor under the hood."

Cortez was speechless. When Sam came back they signed all the paper work that was needed, and then Sam gave Cortez the keys and title as Cortez handed him the money. "It was nice doing business with you, Sam." Cortez replied.

"*Naw*, it was nice doing business with you. Come back anytime you want to do business again. I stay getting dependable cars."

"Alright Sam, we about to slide out." Chicago said.

"Good looking out my nigga'! Be safe here." Sam said as Chicago and Cortez started their cars up.

When Cortez started up his new car, he could feel the power coming from the Corvette engine he had under the hood. Chicago said, "Follow me to the highway; we gone run them so you can see what you are working with."

"I-ight!" Cortez said feeling excited.

Cortez followed Chicago to the highway; but once they got on it, he knew his way back to DaMesha's house so he smoked the Dodge Magnum R/T Chicago was driving. When Chicago made it to the house, Cortez was already parked calling DaMesha telling her to come outside as he leaned up against his new pride and joy. Chicago pulled up and said, "Damn, you ain't have to leave me like that." as he parked in front of him. Before he went in the house he said, "Don't forget I need to holla' at you about my business proportion before you leave."

"I ain't fin'na go no where yet." Cortez said as DaMesha came walking out the house.

"Boy, you don't know who car that is and you all on they shit! You better get off of it before somebody come out tripping!"

"What you talking about?"

"Do you know who car you leaning all up against?" DaMesha asked.

"Of coarse I do!"

"Well who's is it?"

"It's mines." Cortez said as he flashed her the keys.

"When in the hell did you get that? That motherfucker fire!"

"I just got it today. I hope you can drive, because we about to go for a ride in a minute and I want you to drive."

"Yeah I can drive; but let me go get fresh real quick before we do anything." DaMesha said as she ran up the steps and back in the house.

Remembering that he was supposed to call Que, Cortez called Keisha. "Hello." He said as she answered the phone.

"Who is this?"

"It's you son! Who else is it going to be calling you, that sound like me? Anyway, this my new number so program it in your phone so next time you will know it's me. How is work going?"

"Boy, you almost made me tell you something! But anyway, it's going good. What are you up too besides calling and bugging me?"

"Nothing! I'm just over here chilling with Mesha; but I was calling to get Que's number so I can give him my number, and thank him for getting me the phone."

"Oh okay. His number is 632-0122. Tell my daughter-in-law I said hi; and I'm looking forward to her coming over again soon."

"I will; but she upstairs right now."

"Alright; well let me get back to work. I love you."

"I love you too!" Cortez said as they hung up. He then called up Que.

"Hello; who am I speaking too?" Que asked upon answering the phone.

"What's up Que; it's Tez. I'm calling to give you my new number and thank you for the phone."

"Don't thank me; like I said, every player needs an I-Phone." Que said

MY HEART TURNED COLD

as the both laughed. "*Naw* for real though, where you at?"

"I'm over Mesha's house chilling with her."

"Well what you think about me picking you up in a few hours, and you help me pick out me a new whip?"

"Dang, you fin'na get another car?"

"*Yep*; and I want you to help me pick it out. Plus I wan'na holla' at you about some shit too!"

"Okay, I'm down!"

"That's what I'm talking about. I'ma call you at five o'clock; you think you can be ready then?"

"Yeah, I'll be ready. Just call me."

"Okay, five o'clock it is. I'll talk to you then." Que said and then hung up. One minute later he sent a text message to Cortez saying, "Be alone."

Chicago came back out and said, "Are you ready to hear me out yet?"

"Yeah shoot; I'm listening."

"Well I'm trying to see what you think about going in on a package with me?"

"A package like what?"

"Crack! I sell girl and I'm buying like three and four zips at a time, but I need more! I was thinking me and you can go half on a pack, and I'll sell it. You won't have to do shit, but sit back and collect your money. You'll get paid at least twice a week. So what you think?" Chicago said as if he had already mapped out all of the ins and outs.

"So you telling me I ain't gone have to do shit, but collect huh?"

"*Yep.*"

"And what do you need me to give you to make this happen?"

"I'll need three thousand dollars from you."

"What you gone do with three grand?"

"It's gone get me the three extra ounces I need to keep up with the clientele I got."

"What would you say if I tell you I already got two ounces? Would you believe me?"

"Yeah; you got everything else you said you had. So do you have it?"

"Yeah I got it."

"So can I have one of my customers test it out to make sure it's A1?"

"Sure, but this gone have to wait until tomorrow because Mesha and me about to slide out. Then when we get back, I got'ta meet up with my momma's friend."

"That's cool; can you come early like you did today?"

"Yeah; that won't be a problem." Cortez replied.

Right as they were finishing up their conversation, DaMesha was walking out the house with one of her new outfits on. She was wearing her Couch shoes and had her sun-glasses on. "Damn Mesha!" Chicago began

BY BOOM

before DaMesha cut him off.

"I know, you ain't got'ta tell me!" she said knowing what he was about to say.

"We'll be back in a hour or two." Cortez said to Chicago while handing DaMesha the keys.

They pulled off and DaMesha asked, "Where we going?"

"I don't know; just take me for a ride and show me around." A hour and a half later Cortez said, "This was cool, but I got'ta meet up with Que. I'ma let you drop me off, and pick me up later. I shouldn't be gone that long."

"You gone let me keep your car for real?"

"Yeah; you can drive damn near as good as me. Just try not to mess it up." he said.

"I ain't; I'm just gone go home and wait on you to call me. I ain't got shit to do."

"Okay, well take me to my auntie house so I can be there when Que pull up. I don't want to have him waiting on me."

When they pulled up to the Keniesha's house and Cortez was about to jump out, DaMesha said, "Damn, I don't get a kiss or nothing?"

"Yeah, get out of the car so I can give it to you right." Cortez said. "You should know I ain't gone forgot to give you a kiss by now. You my baby!" As DaMesha made her way around the car Cortez said, "Now you know I had you get out of the car just so I can see that sexy ass body of yours; come here." he said as he reached out to hug and kiss her. "Oh yeah, I know what you can do while I'm gone."

"What's that?"

"Go back to the nail shop and get my name on your nail; here." Cortez said handing her an one hundred dollar bill."

"Thanks baby."

As they stood there talking Que pulled up in his white on white BMW 750 LXI and blew the horn. He then let the window down and asked, "Are you ready?"

Cortez and DaMesha were impressed with his BMW. "Damn baby, how many cars does he have?" DaMesha asked.

"I don't know, but I'ma be back soon so be looking for my call." Cortez replied. Getting in Que's car Cortez said, "Now this sweet right here. This the 3rd car I done seen you in."

"You only saw half of my shit! We fin'na go to the car lot right now and I want you to help me find something new." Que said.

Pulling up to the car lot, Cortez felt like he had died and went to heaven. Once Que parked and got out of his car, a salesman greeted him and Cortez. "How's everything going Mr. Quincy? It's nice to see you again; and you to sir." he said addressing Cortez.

"Nice to see you again too." Que said. "This here is my good friend

MY HEART TURNED COLD

Tez; and we come to see what you got new. I want something I ain't seen on the streets yet."

"Okay, I've got four new cars that are pretty rare. Follow me." The salesman replied.

He took them to the back of the lot where he had: an Audi R8; a Dodge Challenger R/T; a Lexus GS 450; and a Jaguar XF. All of them were brand spanking new; fresh off the line with no miles on them. "Okay Tez, which one you think I should get and why?"

"Well I love the Dodge Challenger because it's pure American muscle; and it come with 22" on it already."

"I think that's cool, but I like foreign shit! What you think about the other three?"

"I normally don't even like Jags, but I like this one. It kind of reminds me of an Austin Marten. It's the sportiest Jaguar I've ever seen. Then on top of that, I ain't never seen it in a book or nothing. Plus it's white like the 750LXI."

"I-ight, you ain't got to say no more; we getting it! How much is it gone cost me?"

"Well they start at a hundred and thirty thousand dollars, but we can make a nice cash only price of a hundred and twenty thousand dollars; and that's fully loaded everything."

"We'll take it; get the paper work ready." As the salesmen went to get the paper work ready Que said, "Okay Tez, I hope you can drive for real because I need you to follow me to your momma's house and I'ma park that one there for a few days."

"That ain't no problem; I can drive for real!" Quickly grabbing Que's car keys.

Once they took off and made it to parked both cars in front of the

house, Que said to Cortez, "Come get in this car, I need to holla' at you."

"What's up?" Cortez asked as he kept looking at the Arctica watch Que was sporting.

"Check this out, when we were at the mall yesterday I over-heard you and Mesha talking about an Ej; and I just so happen to be looking for a nigga' named Ej. Tell me what you know about him that ya'll were talking about."

"The Ej Mesha and me were talking about is Mesha's cousin, but he's dead! The police killed him a few weeks ago; so you can't be looking for this Ej."

"Okay, so we are talking about the same nigga'. He killed my two nephews and my sister; so I wan'na know everything you know about him. If you give me some good info on him I'll look out for you."

"What kind of information you talking about; and what you mean you will look out for me?"

BY BOOM

"I wan'na know everything about him, and his family. I also wan'na know why he did it. If you tell me what I wan'na know I'll give you five grand; and since I see you keep looking at my watch, I'll get you one of these too. It ain't gone be the same as this one, but I promise you'll love it though."

Being that Ej was dead, Cortez decided to blame everything on him. He knew he could never let Que find out that he was the one who really murder his sister and nephews no matter what. So he replied, "I know where you going with this, and that's cool with me. As long as you leave Mesha's household out of it."

"I promise you nothing will happen to them! Do we got a deal?"

After a quick thought, Cortez replied "Yeah; as long as you keep your word." he said staring Que in the eyes. "The day I met Mesha and Ej we went to Fairground Park. When we was all chilling Ej and Corey, which Corey is Mesha's brother, walked off and started talking to these girls that they knew; when your nephew and a couple of his friends came walking up on them. Before you knew it, Raykel starts screaming; and as me and Mesha turned around to see what was going on, we seen Ej was fighting Lil' T, and Corey was fighting the other two dudes that was with him. By time reality set in and we really grasp what was going on, Ej got shot."

"Who shot him?"

"I'm not sure because it was so many people crowded around them when they broke out fighting; but word was Lil' T did it. Then Ej told me his self that he was gone kill them; but I thought he was talking about the dudes that they were fighting at first, not your sister and other nephew."

"What you mean by at first?"

"At first I thought he was just referring to the ones that was involved in the fight from jump, but he was on some other shit! Talking about taking out Lil' T and his whole family."

"So his original plan was for him to kill all three of them?"

"Yeah, I guess. I told him that ain't nobody have nothing to do with him and Lil' T's beef, but he wouldn't listen. He said point blank, fuck his momma; she's dead! She shouldn't have never made him; and fuck whoever else riding with him! I didn't know how serious he was. I personally thought he was just letting off some steam until the day I went to his house to get some weed and when I was leaving out the police kicked his door in. About three minutes later, all shots were fired; and his momma came outside screaming they killed him."

"Okay, you said enough. Now all I need to know is was anybody with him when he killed my people; and where does his momma stay?"

"To my knowledge, he did it on his own; and his momma lives in the Peabody's."

"I know that much, but can you show me their apartment?"

"Yeah, when you want me to show you?"

"Right now." Que said starting his car and heading straight for the Peabody's. Once they got there and Cortez pointed the apartment out, Que pulled his phone out and called in a hit. After leaving Que told Cortez, "I fuck with you hard for this; and I'm gone meet up with you tomorrow with your money and shit. Where am I taking you to?"

"Just take me back to my auntie's house." Cortez said.

On the way there he called DaMesha and told her to meet him at her granny's house. When Que dropped him off, DaMesha was parked in front of her granny's house sitting on the porch already. Cortez got out and he went straight in the house and bagged up the rest of his money and drugs. When he came back out he told DaMesha to pop the trunk, and placed his bags inside.

Once in the car, DaMesha showed Cortez her nails. Cortez was happy so he said, "Let's go somewhere and kick it. I wan'na talk to you about some shit when we get there!"

"Where you want me to take you?"

"I don't know; I ain't from here! We can go anywhere. Out to eat, to a park, anywhere. You the driver."

"Okay then, I know where we going." DaMesha said. DaMesha drove to Tower Grove Park and parked near a pond so they could see the ducks. "Before you say anything, this the good park. They don't do no shooting over here." DaMesha said jokingly. "But for real, what is it that you want to talk to me about?"

"You know I just got this whip; but now my momma and auntie don't quite know I got it yet, so I want you to keep it for me. Chicago already knows it's mines; but if your momma ask you about it, just tell her it's mines. This way you can come see me everyday; and if you need to go anywhere you can just go."

"Okay I'll do whatever you say; but just know, I'm coming to see you everyday."

"That's cool, you would have me wondering if you didn't."

"I hope you don't mind me asking; but since your momma and auntie don't know anything about this car, how did you get it? I know you ain't steal it!"

"I prefer not to discuss that. Just know I got it, and hell naw it ain't stolen! It's all good!" Cortez said as he quickly hugged her and changed the subject. They kicked it at the park and went to Cortez's house afterwards for him to drop off the bags he put in the trunk.

Chapter Eighteen
(A New Age)

$\mathcal{A}$ugust the 6th had finally arrived and I was ready to celebrate my seventeen birthday; but I was clueless as to what I was going to do. The only thing I was looking forward to besides spending the day with DaMesha was seeing what my momma was going to surprise me with for my seventeen birthday. Every year she made it her business to try to get me something special, if not exactly what I asked her for; but this year was different because I already had everything I wanted.

I got dressed in my fresh all white Air-Forces; with my camouflage Polo cargo's, and then slid on my white Polo shirt. Plus I put on my Arctica watch with the diamonds in the face that Que gave me, and I had a pocket full of money. The only thing I really cared to do today was cheer DaMesha up as best as I could for the simple fact, she had just lost two more family members and I was the main reason why.

A part of me felt like shit! I had already let DaMesha know that I wanted to spend the day with her; but earlier she told me she wasn't feeling to good and she didn't really wan'na do anything. I tried my best to understand how she felt and said, "Okay; I'll just come see you after my momma does whatever she has planned for me."
At around noon, Que pulled up in the 750 that I wanted to drive. Him and my momma asked upon seeing me was I ready to go. When I said yeah, Que gave me the keys to the 750 and then he jumped in his truck with my momma. I was hella' happy. I was just wishing DaMesha was here with me.

They pulled on the side of me and told me to follow them closely. I followed them to a place called Six Flags. It kind of reminded me of Jazz Land back home; only Six Flags was much bigger. When we walked in the theme park, I was super surprised to see DaMesha, Corey, and my auntie Keniesha was already there. I was really ready to kick it and have fun.

"Happy birthday nephew! How does it feel to be seventeen?" Keniesha asked.

"It feels good! I'm excited about it."

"Yeah baby, happy birthday! You thought I wasn't coming huh?" DaMesha joined in.

"Yeah; ya'll got me good!"

"I told you I wouldn't miss it for the world; me and Corey had to be here!"

Corey joined in and replied, "You know I had to come. I was like it's Tez's birthday and we going to Six Flags; I had to be here. I needed a day to chill any way after all the fighting I been doing."

Que said, "Okay then; let's get started." and then handed Cortez a map and asked, "Which ride do you want to get on first? They all are on the map."

"I don't know; which one do you think we should ride first?" Cortez asked Que.

"Let's just ride them all." DaMesha suggested. "Everything we walk pass, we get on; that way we end up riding everything until we get tried of walking."

"That sounds good to me." Cortez replied.

After a few hours of enjoying our selves on a few rides my momma asked was everybody ready to eat; which on the low, made me happy because I had already had enough of the roller coasters and the long ass lines we had to wait in to get on them. Before anybody could state their personal opinion I quickly spoke up saying, "Yeah momma; my stomach straight turning! What we going to eat?"

She didn't say anything; instead we end up going to Hurricane Harbor which is a water park inside of Six Flags. They had a special spot by the pool for me on the sand already reserved. My table had gifts all over it, and the waiters brought us out food and everything as we arrived. When they brought my birthday cake out and started singing happy birthday to me, it seemed like everybody in the whole park was singing it to me. I was out done, but couldn't wait to start opening my gifts.

I end up getting all kinds of gifts. Clothes, shoes, money, I even got a brand new laptop computer. Que watched me open up everything, and then he dipped off only to return a few minutes later looking like he had something up his sleeve. For a second I tried to read his face expression, but then I blew it off as I continue to enjoy the rest of the day.

We stayed at the park until it turned six o'clock. That's when my momma asked me was I ready to go in which I was. I had done everything I wanted to do at the park; and now I just wanted to spend the rest of my day with DaMesha, so we begin to leave. Walking back to the car Que told DaMesha and my auntie Keniesha to just follow us since we was parked so close to the door, and he would drive them to their parking spot.

When we got to the car, next to my momma's truck was a brand new Dodge Challenger R/T like the one I saw at the car lot when we got Que's Jaguar only this one was all Black with red stripes and a special front and back bumper kit on it. "Dang Que! You see that Challenger? It's harder than that one we saw when you got the Jag."

"Yeah, I see. You like that one huh?" Que asked.

"Yeah; you should get one of them. You would have all types of lil' dudes hating hard on you though!"

Que pulled out a set of keys from his pockets and threw them to Cortez saying, "Well get ready for them to hate on you because that's yours! Happy birthday from your momma and me."

I was so shocked I couldn't speak. You could've sold me for a penny and I wouldn't have been able to protest against it. I finally muster out the words thank you as I asked them both, "What made ya'll get this for me?"

"You did ask for a car right?" Keisha said.

"Yeah; but-." Cortez began before Keisha cut him off.

"But what? Que told me how much you liked it when you seen it; so we went and got you one. I know that you love Black and red, so we got it in Black and red. Then Que had them put those bumper kits on it; and it's got navigation so you won't get lost. We hope you like it!"

"I love it! Here Que, you got to drive your own car home!" Cortex exclaimed.

Que laughed and said, "I figured that was coming next!"

"Okay Mesha, you ride with me; and Corey, you drive the Impala." Cortez ordered.

"We rode here with your auntie; I didn't drive." DaMesha quickly spoke up and informed Cortez.

"Well jump in; what ya'll waiting for?" Cortez replied ready to pull off and see what his new car drove like.

Keisha must have caught a motherly vibe of what her child wanted to do and said, "Before you pull off, be safe and don't be speeding and driving like you than lost your mind!"

"I won't!" Cortez replied and then pulled off. He had DaMesha put his address in the navigation system and they went to his house for a while. After ten o'clock came, Cortez said, "I guess I'll take ya'll home before it get too late."

But on the way out the door, DaMesha said, "Corey ain't going home; he going over his girlfriend's house to spend the night."

"I guess that's cool; but where do she stay at? Do you know how to get to her house from here?"

"Yeah; of coarse I do." Corey replied. "It's not far from here; it's right off South Kingshighway. I'll guide you."

On the way there Cortez kept thinking, *why couldn't DaMesha send the night with him; and how he should've talked to Chicago about it.* After they dropped Corey off DaMesha asked Cortez, "Do you think your momma will let you spend the night with me?"

"Yeah; I know she will, as long as she knows where I'm at."

"Well call her and make sure it's okay." DaMesha said. Without hesitation Cortez called Keisha and got her approval; that's when DaMesha told him, "Let's go downtown for a minute." as she begin giving him directions.

DaMesha guided Cortez straight to the Hyatt Hotel. As soon as it registered to Cortez what this building was that they had pulled up to, he ask DaMesha with a strange look on his face, "What are we about to do here?"

"Don't ask any questions; just come on and follow me." DaMesha said getting out of the car. Cortez jumped out of the car and began following right behind her as she enter the hotel. Inside the hallway, DaMesha handed Cortez a room key as she continue leading the way to the room. Once they reached the room DaMesha said, "Go ahead and open it."

Before Cortez could figured out that the card that DaMesha just gave him a few minutes ago was actually the key to the room, he just tried to open the door and said, "It's locked."

DaMesha burst out laughing before she said, "Silly, use the card I just gave you. That's what you need to unlock the doors in here"

"Oh okay; tell me something because I didn't have a clue on how we were going to get inside." Cortez replied while quickly reading over the words written on the card on how to use it. After he finished reading the directions, he did just like it had instructed for him to do and heard the door unlock. Once he opened the door and stepped into the room, he was out done. The room wasn't anything like he expected it to be like; and when Cortez finally saw the chocolate covered strawberries and a bottle Red Berry Ciroc waiting for him, he again was out done. All he could say was, "Damn Mesha! You did all of this for me? How in the hell did you manage to pull this off?"

"Well I saved the money for the room myself; and then I talked Chicago into renting it for me. He was cool with it; and then him and me came up with a story for my momma to go along with it. She thinks you are having a hotel party, which you are. It's just a private party." DaMesha said with an I'm slick too smirk on her face. "I had to get you alone for your birthday; I've been planning this for a while now."

"Well you did a damn good job at surprising me all day today. Thanks for making time for me after everything that's been going on."

"Tez, you been with me through it all; and you've been trying your best to keep me happy, which you have so it's my turn. As a matter of fact, wait right here." DaMesha said as she ran to the back and grabbed the box of Kush blunts she had.

They begin to smoke, drink, and eat on the chocolate covered strawberries before DaMesha jumped up again and went in the bathroom. Cortez didn't pay her any mind as he continue to smoke; but he just didn't know that DaMesha had her own plans for them. Inside the bathroom, DaMesha changed into her sexy pink and cream bra and panties set that she had just gotten from Victory's Secret just for Cortez and this occasion. She then sprayed on her some Armani perfume and looked at herself in the mirror. She knew she looked damn good, but she was super nervous. She wanted Cortez so bad that she felt butterflies in her stomach, but she quickly pulled herself together because she convinced herself that this is what she wanted.

When DaMesha walked out of the bathroom, she went straight in the bedroom and laid across the bed before calling Cortez to come into the room. Upon entering the bedroom, Cortez saw DaMesha and said, "Damn! You look sexy as fuck right now!"

"I know right!" DaMesha said as she stood up and continue, "And I'm all yours tonight. You can have me any way you desire."

From the looks of DaMesha's dark chocolate skin which didn't have a blemish in sight and her perfectly built body, Cortez couldn't control his self. He was ready to explore her body. "Damn, let me run down stairs and get some condoms." Cortez replied.

"It's no need for you to run anywhere; I came fully prepared." DaMesha said as she pulled out a box of magnums. "All I need for you to do is just come here."

As Cortez eased closer to DaMesha, she gently pushed him back onto the bed and began slowly undressing him. At this point she thought to herself that Cortez could have been a sponsor for Chevy because his seven and a half inch dick was like a rock. She was very much pleased with his size as she began to stroke it with her hand. "What do you want me to do first baby? I'll do anything you say!" DaMesha said seductively.

"I want you to do everything!"

"Remember you said you want everything!" DaMesha said while steady stroking his dick up and down before licking around it and then placing it in her mouth and start sucking it as best as she could.

Cortez mind was blown. He wasn't expecting DaMesha to go this far, so he just laid back and enjoyed the feeling for a moment; before sitting up to watch her as her head went up and down and in circular motions. While DaMesha was bent over, Cortez caught a glimpser of her perfectly heart shape ass with her panties that looked like they were painted on her body in the mirror. He was too turned on. Without wasting any time or breaking DaMesha rhythm, Cortez leaned to the side and began playing with DaMesha pussy.

DaMesha let out a sighs of pleasure repeatedly from the way Cortez's finger game felt to her. Before now, DaMesha's pussy had barely been tamper with, so just the mildest touch felt super good to her. After awhile of doing her thang to Cortez and Cortez doing his to her, DaMesha stood up to find her pussy juices flowing like the Nile River down her legs. That's when Cortez attempted to go down on her, but she stopped him before he could get a taste of her wet pussy and said while pulling him up by his arms, "No; not tonight. Tonight is all about you. Now get up here and fuck me good!"

"Trust me, I'ma fuck you good alright!" Cortez said a lil' anxious. "Especially after how good you been to me today, you got that coming!"

"I here you talking; but I'm not a pro, so you are going to have to take it easy on me baby. Let me get use to you inside of me before you start dicking me down hard as a motherfucker!"

"I-ight!" Cortez replied.

Cortez enter into DaMesha's warm pussy and did just as she asked. He started off fucking her nice and slow with each stroke barely applying pressure. He had her laying on her back with her feet barely touching the floor on the corner of the bed as he stood up in her. Cortez was turned on even more from the facial expressions DaMesha was making and the way she kept trying to stop herself from screaming.

DaMesha kept saying, "Oh shit baby! Keep fucking me like this."

As Cortez started to speed the pace up, DaMesha let out her screams and started trying to get away. That's when Cortez slid her up to the center of the bed and lifted both of her legs in the air. DaMesha didn't know what to do because she hadn't ever been fucked like this before. With Cortez holding her legs in the air and going easy but deep as he could inside of her, it felt to DaMesha like he was in her stomach. DaMesha tried her very best to take everything Cortez was giving her; and so far she was doing good, but she didn't know how long she was going to be able to keep up.

DaMesha's pussy was so warm and wet it almost felt like Cortez didn't have on a condom to either one of them; but neither one of them dared to stop or broke their rhythm to make sure that they were still protected. Instead, Cortez bent DaMesha over in a doggie style position, gripped her pretty ass checks, and commenced to pounded her pussy even more. That's when DaMesha lost control of herself. To keep from screaming so loud, she just put her hands up and buried her face in the bed.

It had to be the Ciroc controlling Cortez's hormones, because Cortez was going harder than he ever had as sweat ran down his body and dripped onto her. He was turned on by DaMesha in everyway possible as he continue to have sex with her. Out of nowhere, Cortez grabbed a hand full of DaMesha's dreads, pulling her head up forcing her to get on her knees and hands as she took his dick from the back.

DaMesha had no ideal of what part of sex was this suppose to be, or what level that they had reached; but she began to feel a feeling she would come to love. She was having her first organism. It was the best sexual feeling DaMesha ever had experienced. She shook, shivered, and screamed, but

Cortez never stopped stroking or changed his pace. He proceeded to dick DaMesha down from the back as he smacked her on the ass and told her, "Damn your pussy fire! Throw that ass back Mesha baby; and keep throwing it!" DaMesha tried but began to brake down. Cortez said, "Un-un, don't quit on me now! You got yours off; so now let me get mines!"

"Okay; but let me turn around or ride you!" DaMesha begged.

Cortez quickly turned her around trying not to lose the feeling or ruin the moment between them as he allow her to climb on top of him. After about five minutes had past, with DaMesha riding him, and giving him looks of pure satisfaction, and with her pussy being so good, Cortez bust all in her.

After Cortez reached his big relief and dick stop throbbing, he pulled it out of her and took the condom off. DaMesha just laid there in silence as if she was a mute with her eyes wide open. She couldn't move. Her pussy was well pleased, swollen and sore at the same time. Cortez began to kiss her all over before he climbed out the bed and made his way to the bathroom.

When he went inside of the bathroom and saw a Ja*cuzz*i tub, he instantly began running some bath water and put some bubbles in it. After the Ja*cuzz*i filled up halfway, Cortez went and got DaMesha to get inside it with him. They freshen up and played in it for a moment before making their way back to the room. Once back in the room, Cortez turned the television on and flipped through the channels until he saw Eddie Murphy.

"*Ooh*, this my favorite movie. I love *Life*; it's hella' funny!" DaMesha said.

Without an argument or debate Cortez left the television on *Life* and set the remote controller down. He then said, "Thank you baby for tonight. This was the best birthday I've ever had!"

"I'm happy that you enjoyed yourself today because I sure did. I can't even lie to you; you fucked the shit out of me too!"

Cortez smiled and then said, "I'm happy you liked it! I get it from my daddy! Rest in peace!"

"You a fool!" DaMesha replied as she laid her head on Cortez's chest and watched *Life* until she fell asleep followed by Cortez shortly afterwards.

Chapter Nineteen
(1 Wrong Turn)

*A*s time passed by, things were going smoothly. Autumn had come and gone, and winter was now taking its place. Que and Keisha were not only coworkers in an illegal business as they first started off to be; but now their relationship had grown more into a couple type of connection. The only time you could find them separated other than when Keisha was working in the trap house, was if Que was out of town meeting up with his connection making business arrangements.

Things had also changed big time for Keisha and Cortez, as they had to adjust to the arctic temperatures that winter had brought along. Not only was it their first time experiencing temperatures as cold, but also having to dress in layers to keep warm as the first snow storm had arrived early in the winter season. It was Keisha and Cortez first time seeing snow fall, so they were quite fascinated watching as the fluffy white snow continue to come down heavy and steady for the next eight hours.

Business arrangements had also changed up for Cortez and Chicago. Cortez and Chicago were both upset about the lack of money they were making due to Chicago's connect changing up on them and now taxing them with an additional interest for the crumbs he was dishing out, but shit was about to get real.

"*M*an, I'm about to hit a lick on this motherfucker if he don't quit trying to bird feed me. We've been spending too much money with him, for him to be playing games and shit!" Chicago snapped.

"Fuck it, let's hit him. I'm all for it whenever you decide that you are ready to make a move." Cortez responded.

"You ain't ready for that type of shit! We'll have to kill that nigga'. If not, we'll have all kinds of people looking for us."

"Chicago, look me in my eyes; I'm ready! I'll kill the nigga' myself if need be." Cortez said as he pulled his .38 off his hip.

"Okay, since you say you ready; we gone see. I'ma set it up. I know just how we can get up on him; and get him by his self."

"And how are we going to do that?"

"The motherfucker is a real Trick-Tracy type of motherfucker! I know just the right bitch to get though, to get him alone. We gone have to pay her five grand up front, and tell her we gone give her another five grand after the job complete; but we gone smoke her ass too! We just need for her, when they get to where they going, to let us in."

"So I got'ta smoke two people?" Cortez replied.

"*Naw*; I want some of the action too nigga'. I feel like he been playing me the most."

"So when can you have this set up?"

"I can have everything put together by next week. Is that cool with you?"

"That's cool!" Cortez said with a smile on his face from the thought of how much money they could squeeze out of Chicago's connect.

*M*eanwhile, Que had just gotten a call from Tweezy. He answered it, "What's up bruh?"

"Shit. I'm calling you to let you know your partner Pee Wee keep coming up short. This the second time; and I ain't fin'na keep playing with that nigga' *cuzz*! He's your friend, not mines!"

"Chill out Tweezy baby! I'ma go holla' at him before I leave today. You know I'm going on one of those trips were I can't have you fucking shit up while I'm gone. Just fall back on this one! Pee Wee a good nigga'. He don't want any smoke; trust me!"

"Alright, it's your call. If you need me, call me; and be safe on your trip."

"Will do; I'ma hit your line, as soon as I get back." Que said and then they both hung up.

Que attempted to call Pee Wee, but then thought, *Fuck it; I'ma just slide on him since he right there by the highway*, as he continued to pack his luggage. After Que finished packing his stuff, he jumped in his new Jaguar and called Keisha to let her know what was going on. "Hello sweetie!"

"What's going on? Are you coming to see me before you leave out?"

"*Naw*; I wish. I got to go holla' at this fool Pee Wee about coming short. Tweezy called me ready to kill him; so I'm about to see what's going on with that. But I'll call you when I'm done with him. Also, you know I left eighteen kilos and my trap phone at the spot."

"Yeah, I'm actually working on that now. What you going to do about the people who wan'na re-up?"

"I'm pulling up on Pee Wee right now; so I'ma have to call you back. But when I call you back, I'll tell you what I want you to do. I also wan'na talk to you about us living together; and what you think Tez going to think about it."

Excited about what she just heard, Keisha said, "Okay baby, handle your business and call me as soon as you get done." and then hung up the phone and let her mind wonder.

When Que knocked on Pee Wee's door, Pee Wee answered, "Que, what's good my nigga'? I got something for you."

"That's good; but I came to holla' at you about you coming short. What's up with that?"

"That's what I got for you now. The seven grand I owe you. It's been slow down here, and I told Tweezy that shit! He act like he running shit now! It's hard for me to do business with him bruh; before it's all said and done I'm smoke his ass."

"Look, calm down! Ain't nobody fin'na shoot nobody. Give me a few days and when I get back, we all gone sit down and nip this shit in the bud."

"Yeah bruh; cause ya'll got'ta remember these broke motherfuckers I'm down here dealing with. I ain't dealing with people that own their own homes and shit! Ninety percent of these motherfucker, if not all of these motherfuckers, are on Section 8. Then half of them don't even got a job."

"Say no more; I understand where you coming from. How is Alicia and the kids doing?"

"They good. Alicia at work; and the kids somewhere around the complex."

"That's what's up. But check this out, I'ma send Keisha over here to pick up that money later on today; I got to get out of here so I can stay on schedule. Tell everybody I said what's up."

"Alright bruh. Be safe out there because it's kind of nasty in certain areas I heard."

"I will; much love nigga'!"

*L*eaving the Cochrans, Que jumped in his car and was on his way to the highway. Que made the wrong turn when he pulled on Interstate 55 South though. It would be a turn that would change his life. Upon getting on the highway, Que called Keisha back just as he promised he would." Hello."

"How did ya'll meeting go?"

"It went pretty smooth. We got an understanding, so we good. Anyway, I'ma need you to go pick up that seven grand Pee Wee owes me and put it up. As far as the other shit goes, I need you to hold it down. Nobody gets nothing, unless I say so."

"I know better baby, I ain't fucking with nobody unless you tell me too. If I get a order I'll run it by you first; and I already know how to talk to you on the telephone about it. I'ma big girl; and I got your back."

"Okay. Anyway, I've been putting a lot of thought into my living situation and I wanted to know how you felt about us finding a house together?"

"I would love to wake up to you every morning. I'm so ready for that. I been thinking about it too, but I just don't know when it would be a good time to bring it up; and what's wrong with this house?"

"Nothing; I just thought you would want something bigger that's all."

"Well no; I don't need a bigger place. Shit, you just gave me this one; and it's more than enough room here. Plus you already got all of your cars over here."

"So how do you think Cortez gone-" Que was saying before all Keisha heard on the other end was a loud boom!

Just as they conversation was getting good, Que hit a patch of Black ice which caused him to spin out of control. He dropped his cellular phone as he tried to gain control of the car, but it was too late. "Hello. Que, what's going on? Hello. Hello." Keisha screamed repeatedly into the receiver, but got no response.

All Keisha could hear was, *"Boom! Boom!* Boom; and glass breaking!" as other cars crashed into Que's Jaguar and caused a huge pile up on the interstate.

Que hit the wall in the center of the highway, and the car behind him hit him on the driver side door causing Que to Black out. Another car hit him from the back; and that's when cars just started piling up. Que's car got a taste of the impact from every last one of the cars involved in the crash.

One of the cars started to leak gas, and shortly afterwards caught fire. Before you know it, it blew up sending flames in all directions. Que was about four cars away from where the fire stopped at; but it was still spreading his way and he was unconscious, so he didn't know what was going on. By the grace of God, an older guy from the other side of the highway stopped and pulled Que out of his car before the fire reached him. He also saw Que's phone ringing, so he grabbed it as well. He pulled Que to a safe spot and put Que's phone in his pocket, and then he ran off to help other people in need of help. About five minutes later, Que's car blew up too. The Fox 2 News helicopter was catching everything as it was happening. Keisha continued to call Que's phone back to back, only to get no answer so she began to worry.

$\mathcal{M}$eanwhile, Cortez was at DaMesha's house watching scenes of the accident with Chicago. Cortez seen the Jag burning, but never in a million years would he have thought it was Que's car. The paramedics arrived on the scene from the other side of the highway, which allowed Que to be the first person that they gave aid too. As they was lifting him into the ambulance, Que phone continued to ring. That's when one of the paramedics decided to answer it. "Hello; what in the hell is going on?" Keisha franticly blurted. "Is everything alright?"

The paramedic then began to give Keisha the worst news she'd gotten since she gotten the call saying Cortez father was dead. That's when he hit her with the news. "No ma'am, everything isn't alright. The person, who we found this cellular phone on, is on the way to Saint Louis University Hospital!"

"Quit playing with me." Keisha said. "Who the hell is this; and where is Que?"

"Ma'am, this is not a game. I'm assuming the person you are referring to as Que, is the person we found here unconscious right now as we speak. Is it possible for you to meet us up at the hospital because we need a few pieces of information on him; and he's going to need all of the support he can get?"

"Yeah, I can meet up with ya'll at the hospital." Keisha said as she was locking the door to the trap house. "Just please say it's not that bad?"

"Ma'am, I'll rather not say over the phone what's wrong; but it's pretty bad."

"Where is this hospital at that ya'll taking him too?" Keisha asked as she started her truck.

"It's on South Grand; where are you coming from?"

"I'm a few blocks from North Grand right now."

"Okay. When you get to Grand, turn south and keep coming down until you see the hospital. It's going to be on your right hand side of the street. You'll see a sign that says emergency room; and when you see that sign, make a right and find you a parking spot."

"Okay; and thank you sir. I'm on my way right now." Keisha said.

Keisha was flying down Grand until she saw the hospital on the right hand side of the street like the paramedic told her she would. Once she got inside and found where they had Que at, she knew what she hope was a sick joke was very much real. Keisha saw how they had Que hooked up to all kinds of machines and she bust out crying. She was crying so hard, that her whole face turned red.

As soon as the doctor walked into the room Keisha asked, "What's wrong with him; is he going to make it?"

"Well ma'am, his left hand arm, and both femurs are broken. He also has head trauma; and quite a few scares in his face and neck from the glass. He's pretty beat up; but from the looks of things he's going to live. We just don't know if he'll ever walk again; and if so he'll probably never walk as good as he use too."

Keisha then began to explain to the doctor who she was to Que, and that she needed to get a hold of his cellular phone so she could get his sister contact number so she could inform her of what was going on with her brother. The doctor understood; and allow her to retrieve his phone. Once Joseline got word of what took place, she took off of work and came straight to the hospital to support her brother. She was there in no time.

Joseline got there and answered all the questions Keisha couldn't. She then began to comfort Keisha telling her, "Calm down sis; God got his back. He's gone be alright because he's a soldier."

About two weeks past by and Que was still in a comma. Keisha stayed with him everyday. She would only go home to shower, and then come right back. Joseline came to see him everyday after she left work as well; and Cortez came everyday after school. He would even bring DaMesha some times.

After three and a half weeks, Que woke up out of his comma. The first person he saw was Keisha looking out his hospital room window. "Keisha what in the hell is going on? Why am I in a damn gown?" Que asked not noticing where he was at."

When Keisha turned to see Que was awoke and talking, tears began to run down her face. She was so happy she couldn't control crying. She tried to pull herself together, and then started filling him in on what all happened and how blessed he was. "Baby just lay back, you can't walk."

"What you mean I can't walk?" Que asked as he looked down to see the scars on his legs.

"You were in an accident. Your left hand arm and both of your legs are broken. You were on the highway, on your way to re-up; and had a real bad accident. It was a car pile up. About nine cars hit you. Baby you are so blessed, because a man pulled you out of your car; and after he pulled you out the car, your car blew up. It was crazy; like six people died."

"How long have I been here?"

"You've been in a comma almost four weeks now."

"What was I driving? Please don't tell me it was the Panamera."

"*Naw*, you were in the jaguar you just got. Baby, eight hundred and fifty thousand dollars got burnt up in the trunk of the car." Keisha informed Que.

Que couldn't remember anything about having an accident. Quite frankly, he didn't care about the car or the money, he just kept pounding on the fact that he couldn't walk. "Don't worry about the money though; I still have all the money you gave me and I'ma give it all back so you'll be straight." Keisha replied.

"I don't care about the money, that's yours. Who all know I'm here?"

"Well Joseline and Cortez come to see you everyday. They'll be here in a few hours give or take. As for as the people that work for you, I didn't tell any of them because I didn't know if you would want me too or if you wanted them to know."

"Okay, that's what's up." Que replied.

A few hours later Joseline came in and saw Que up and talking. Her face lit up like a Christmas tree. She silently thank God for her brother recovery, and then she went in her brother room to greet him. "Boy, you know you are one bless motherfucker! You should be thanking God every time you think about doing anything! You need to be thanking Keisha too; you know she been up here everyday damn near twenty four hours a day waiting on you to recover? She really loves your crazy ass if you don't know it!"

Que didn't know how to respond, so he didn't say anything. After a while Cortez popped up too, and saw Que had awaken. "Now that's what I'm talking about! Welcome back stranger! You had everybody on the edge on their seats praying for you. It's good to see you woke; how you feeling?"

"I'm good; I don't feel any pain at all. I guess it's the drugs they giving me." Que replied halfway nodding off. While everybody stood around talking Que looked down at his injuries and thought to his self, *I never thought one wrong turn could've cause all of this; but thank you God cause I'm still alive!*

Chapter Twenty
(Da Heist)

*E*verything was in order as far as robbing Chicago's connection, Hector, went. All they had to do was make sure Shayna was still down to set Hector up. Chicago called Shayna but didn't get an answer; two minutes later his phone rang, and to his surprise it was Shayna. "Shayna what's up? I thought you was about to back out on me at the last minute." Chicago said.

"*Naw*, I'm still in. I need that money hella' bad! Now just so we clear on everything, what all you want me to do?"

"Look, I'ma give you five grand up front. All we need you to do is dance for Hector like you normally do all the time. Only this time, I need you to convince him to go to your house. Once you confirm he's coming, let him know his bodyguards can't come in your house."

"What am I'm suppose to say when he ask why?"

"Tell the Chicano motherfucker, because you don't want no random motherfuckers in your house while you fucking! Tell him to make them stay in the car and watch the house while you give him some pussy! Now I ain't saying you got to fuck him, but I do want you to leave a window open for us to come through. Do you have a basement window or something we can get in without drawing any attention?"

"Yeah, it's a window on the side of the house. I can unlock it, and ya'll can just come right in without anyone knowing."

"That's cool, but first we gone get rid of his two bodyguards that he keep with him. We then gone come in and get him; tie him up, and bring him straight outside and throw him in the car. This way we won't have to kill him in your house and have blood everywhere. After we get him in the car, we've gone need you to ride out to his house with us so it will look normal. Once we leave out the house you going to get your other five grand. Deal?"

"Hell yeah, I'm down! What time are ya'll gone get here because its nine o'clock now and I'm usually at the club by ten o'clock? I'm just asking so I can get ready."

"We on our way now; so we will be there in like twenty minutes."

"Well okay; I'm here." Shayna replied.

Chicago hung up the phone and looked at Cortez and said, "It's done; let's go." Once in Chicago's car he reached under his seat and pulled out two semi-automatic chrome and Black 380's with silencers on them. "Look at what I picked up yesterday. Ain't nobody gone hear shit! This shit gone be easy as fuck! Taking candy from a baby would be harder than this."

"I can see the money now." Cortez said. "I'm too ready to get this shit over with. Let's hurry up and get to Shayna's house."

Once they pulled up to Shayna's house, Chicago called her to let her know that they were outside. When she came outside, she showed them where the window was that they could use to climb in before they left heading to the club.

By the time they made it to the Pink Slip, any doubt Shayna had about the whole situation was out the window. She was ready to play the game to win. She went in the club's dressing room and got dress for the show she was going to put on for Hector. Shayna was hands down the stripper that all the other strippers wanted to be in the Pink Slip. Shayna was half Black and half Hispanic, with a light-browned skinned complexion. She stood five feet and ten inches; with long beautiful legs. Her ass was shaped like a perfect puffed out heart with a butterfly tattooed on it. When she shook her ass, you'd swear the butterfly was really moving.

Twelve o'clock hit, and Shayna was on the floor giving a lap dance when Hector and his two workers came in. When Hector saw Shayna, he just stood still and watched her until the song that was playing was over. "Come here!" Hector ordered in a raspy voice. "What are you doing over there dancing for that broke ass motherfucker? You know tonight is my night!"

"I know; I been waiting on you to get here. Are we going to the V.I.P. section, or are we gone stay down here?"

"Come on Shayna; don't play me like that! You know we're V.I.P-ing it up. I need my privacy!"

"Come on." Shayna said as she grabbed his hand and led him up to the V.I.P. section.

The bouncer at the V.I.P. door entrance stopped Hector and Shayna and asked, "How many dances?"

Hector handed the bouncer a thousand dollars and replied, "All night homie! You act like I don't do this same shit every week; and I already know hands off."

Hector's two workers found a spot nearby the V.I.P. section, and watched the door their boss went in like some trained defense combat specialists. They were on point as they closely observed everybody whom entered the V.I.P. section; while waiting on anything to jump off.

Shayna took Hector in the back reserved section in the V.I.P. room; and began dancing and doing her thang on Hector better than she ever have before. About eight songs past and Shayna still had Hector's full attention. Right when the eighth song finish playing, Hector asked Shayna, "What's with you tonight? I loving this new you! You're so electrifying! Where have you been hiding this side of you at?" with a fist full of twenty dollar bills. Shayna didn't say anything back; instead she turned around so he could see her ass. She then put her hands on the floor, and put her legs on his so he had a perfect private view of her fat ass as she shook it the beat of the song that was playing. "Damn Shayna; your ass so fat! When you gone quit playing games with me, and let me hit something?"

"Tonight, if your money right." Shayna replied as she stood up, turned around, and sat on his lap facing him, not missing a beat.

"You be playing too much! You know my money long; and I been trying to get this pussy from you!"

"I ain't playing tonight! Tonight, I'm for real! I need to make some extra money because I got some shit to handle; and it's going to cost me two grand."

"Oh, That's it? That ain't shit; I'll double that! Infact, I got that right now; so what's up?" Hector arrogantly replied.

Playing Hector right into her trap, Shayna said, "Well show me the money and we can go. We can get up out of here right now and go to my house; no faking or fronting! You just better know that I'm going to fuck the shit out of you though, if you can handle it."

"If I can handle it!" Hector repeated Shayna's words before saying, "So what all do I get for four grand?"

"You get the whole nine yards; head and all if you can handle it. When I'm done with you, you are going to want to marry me and never lay another eye on another woman! I promise you that it will be the best four grand you will say you every spent!"

"What the hell, let's get out of here then. I don't wan'na waste any more time. I've been trying to get inside of you long enough!"

"Just let me run in the back and grab my shit real quick. Ya'll can meet me at the front door." Shayna said and then went in the back and grabbed her bag and call Chicago to let him know she got the job done and that they were on their way to her house. After the phone call, Shayna paid her nightly dues to club owner and met Hector at the front door.

"Are you riding with us?" Hector asked as one of his workers ran to get the Black and chrome Cadillac Escalade EXT they came in.

"*Naw*; I got my own car!" Shayna said. "But, you should ride with me."

"Okay." Hector replied and then said to his workers, "Ya'll just follow us." before turning his attention back to Shayna and asking her, "So where is your car at?"

"Right there!" Shayna replied as she pointed to her hunters green Grand Prix. "It ain't a Benz, but its mines."

"It's all good love. If that pussy as good as I think it is, I'ma change all of that. You do live by yourself, don't you?"

"Hell yeah! I might not drive a Benz; but I don't stay with my momma! I got a lil' something." She said as they both laughed.

Hector worker followed Shayna to her crib, which her street was a one way, so they didn't see Chicago and Cortez because they were parked at the top of her block. From the spot that they were sitting in, they could see everything. "Okay, now we talking; they here!" Chicago said. "That's them in that Escalade. Are you ready?"

"Yeah I'm ready! I wouldn't be here if I wasn't. Just peep me out; you about to see how I get down!" Cortez replied.

As Shayna and Hector were getting out of the car, Hector's workers were getting out as well. That's when Shayna snapped, "Where they think they're going? They ain't coming in my house!"

"Why not? They good; they my bodyguards."

"Hector, they not coming in my house! I don't want no random motherfuckers in my house while I'm fucking. Ya'll not about to run a train on me anyway! You're their boss right?"

"Hell yeah!" Hector said with cockiness. "They do what I tell them too do!"

"Okay then. Make them sit out here and watch the house or something; but they not about to be posted up in my house while we do our thang!"

"Now you know they come with me everywhere I go."

"That might be the case; but they're not about to come and sit up in here, if you want some pussy from me!"

"How do I know you ain't got somebody in there trying to set me up?" Hector asked a lil' worry about leaving his bodyguards outside.

Shayna quickly responded back saying, "I would never play any games like that! I don't get down like that at all. If you want too though, you can have them come in and check around to make sure everything is cool; but afterwards you got to make they ass get out my house and wait on you in the truck or something."

"Deal!" Hector said. Shayna was on point. She was acting like she did this before because everything was working in her favor. "Okay, ya'll go in and search around." Hector order his guards "We gone be right here; so when ya'll done come back out. If everything is cool, then I want ya'll to sit in the truck and wait on me to come out."

The workers didn't say anything. They just did what they were told to do and searched the house room by room. They even went in the basement and searched around. "The coast is clear. You good to go boss." One of the workers said to Hector when they returned; and then they made their way down the steps and back into the truck.

While the workers was searching the house, Chicago had pulled off and had came up with a plan for Cortez to be able to walk up on the truck without alerting the bodyguards of what was about to go down. Once going around the corner Chicago said, "Look, this is what I want you to do Tez. I want you to cut through that yard and go through the gangway. When you come out the gangway walk towards the truck, but just walk pass it. Go to the gas station and by something big like a gallon of juice, and come back; but this time when you get up on the truck, air that motherfucker out! Don't stop shooting until you empty the clip. I'm about to drive around to the back of her house and park so I can be on the side of her house already in place. I'll be able to see everything just incase if anything goes wrong and I have to come save your lil' ass."

"Alright;" Cortez said "I'm on it."

Cortez came through the gangway like Chicago said. As soon as Hector's workers saw him, they were on him. As Cortez got closer to the truck, the guard sitting on the passenger side said to the driver, "Homes, that's just a lil' youngster. His lil' ass needs to be in the fucking house somewhere instead of out here this time of night."

When Cortez came from the gas station he was ready. Walking towards the truck with one hand holding the bag he got from the gas station and his other hand clutching the 380 in his hoodie pocket, he was ready to let them have it and they didn't even see it coming. Once the driver spotted Cortez coming back down the street through the rearview mirror he said, "I told you that lil' youngster wasn't on shit! He just went to the store." And they both took their attention off Cortez and continue watching the television in the truck.

As soon as Cortez got close to the side of the truck he slid the gun out of his pocket and ran up to the passenger door; aimed in the truck and started firing. *Boom! Boom! Boom!* Glass shattered everywhere giving Cortez a clear view of both workers as he continued shooting. *Boom! Boom! Boom!* When Cortez clip was empty, both workers were slumped over dead as a door knob.

Chicago was in the gangway of Shayna's house watching everything. He was very much impressed at how Cortez got the job done and moved smoothly. Cortez spotted Chicago in the gangway and ran across the street by him and said, "Two down, and two to go! Come on, let's hurry up and get this motherfucker so we can get paid."

Chicago didn't say anything; he just pushed the basement window open for Cortez to jump in. Once Chicago got in, they both crept upstairs. They didn't have to creep as much because Shayna had her radio on blast; as *R. Kelly's Feeling on your booty* roared throughout her whole house. When they

MY HEART TURNED COLD

got to the hallway, they saw that Shayna had her bedroom light on with her door open, which let them know what room they were in.

They got to the doorway with guns pointed, only to see Shayna butt naked grinding the shit out of Hector while his back was facing the door. Shayna just kept dancing like she didn't see anybody; allowing Chicago to walk right up on them and place his gun up to Hector's head. "Are you enjoying yourself motherfucker?" Chicago whispered into Hector's ear as he tapped him with the gun.

"What the fuck is this?" Hector asked as he realized what was going on. "Bitch, you set me up? You're dead! Wait until I get my hands on you! You're fucking dead!" Shayna didn't respond back at all; instead, she quickly put her clothes back on as Cortez and Chicago roughed Hector up a little. "Damn Chicago, I been good to you! Where the fuck is this shit coming from?"

"It's coming from the motherfucker you been playing games with. Now get the fuck up!" Chicago said pulling him to his feet.

"Chicago, look man; we can work this out! You don't have to do this shit! Somebody can get killed like this." Hector pleaded to Chicago in desperation.

That's when Cortez butted in and said, "People already been killed; and if you don't shut the fuck up, you gone be next! So don't say shit else!"

With seeing the silencer on the gun and the way Chicago was pressing it into his tempo, Hector knew not to say shit. He just start thinking to his self, *It's all good because my workers are going to kill ya'll asses!* But he just didn't know that they were already dead and couldn't help him at this point. Sensing what Hector was thinking, Chicago walked Hector over to the living room window and pulled the curtains back for him to see his workers slumped over lifeless. "Look motherfucker; are you trying to end up like your buddies? If not, you better do exactly what we say. Do I make myself clear?"

"Yeah, we're clear!" Hector quickly responded back.

"Good! Cause if not, I'll fill your taco eating ass full of holes! Now let's go for a lil' ride." Cortez said.

Not wanting to risk Hector making any kind of moves that would put their plans to get rich at jeopardy, Chicago told Cortez, "Snatch me Shayna's phone cord so we can tie him up before we leave."
Wasting no time, Cortez yanked the phone cord clean out the wall and handed it to Chicago. After Chicago tied Hector up by his hands and feet, him and Cortez then took him outside and threw him in the back of Chicago's Dodge Magnum. "Okay now," Chicago said to Hector in a serious tone "we on our way to your house to get everything you got! This is how things going to go. When we get there, Shorty is gone open the door; and you going to take us straight to your stash. If you try to play any kind of games, you ain't going to live to see tomorrow and we still going to get what the fuck we came for! So think about your life; you got about twenty minutes." Chicago said and then turned his radio up as *T.I.'s U Don't Know Me* began to play. Pulling up to

Hector's house, something seemed wrong. Every light was on, and his dogs were out in the yard roaming freely. "Who the fuck else is in your house; and you better tell me now motherfucker?" Chicago questioned Hector.

"Nobody; I always leave the lights on!" Hector nervously answered.

"Okay Tez, change of plans. I'ma open the door so I can put the dogs up. You keep him in the car. Shayna, you come with me. Tez if his bitch ass breathes on you hard, then kill him! Don't play no games with the son-of-a-bitch!"

"You ain't got to tell me twice; I got him covered! Just do what you have to do."

Chicago and Shayna got out and walked towards the gate until Shayna just stopped and replied, "I don't fuck with dogs; and look at them, they big as fuck! You didn't say anything about any dogs being involved!"

"Don't worry about the dogs; you just about to open the door for my dude. I'm about to get the dogs because they somewhat know me."

"Okay, but you bet not let them motherfuckers get loose! I ain't playing!"

Chicago went in the yard first and gather the dogs together. He then told Shayna to open the door. Once she opened it, he told her to go in and sit down and don't move so he could walk the dogs pass her without them being on high alert and go into attack mode. Scared the shit out of dogs, Shayna did just what she was told as she silently prayed that Chicago could control the dogs. Chicago contained the four dogs' full attention as he walked them into the bathroom, and then shut the door behind them trapping them locked inside. Once he made sure the door was secure, he told Shayna to tell Cortez to bring Hector in.

When Hector and Cortez made it inside, Chicago and Cortez went straight to work. Chicago said clearly to Hector, "I'm only going to ask you this one time, and one time only! Where is it; and I mean everything? I know you have dope and cash in here!"

Hector not wanting to chance his possibilities in surviving quickly replied, "It's in the floor safe that's built in my bedroom. I'll take you to it; just be cool!"

Cortez said, "Well get to moving; we ain't got all night!" Hector took them straight to the safe and told Cortez the code. Cortez then opened the safe faster than you could blink your eyes. "Jackpot!" He yelled out "This motherfucker loaded with shit! Hand me something to put all this shit in!"

"Hector, where in the fuck are all them damn bags you be having?" Chicago asked.

Hector replied, "They're in the closet."

"Shayna, get a couple of those bags for him."

Shayna opened the walk-in closet and went in and grabbed two Gucci book bags. When she came out she said, "He got guns in there."

"Oh, for real Shayna? So you holding out you slick motherfucker?"

Chicago snapped as he began pistol whipping Hector busting his head. "I said everything nigga'! Are do you wan'na fucking die?"

"No!" Hector screamed out with blood running down his forehead going into his left eye. "It's guns in the closet; and it's jewelry in my jewelry box on top of the nightstand over there. Please take everything you want; just don't kill me! I promise I won't retaliate after this is all over with; and will get lost out of town. Just don't kill me, Chicago!"

"I bet you will! You would want to get as far away from here as you possible could." Chicago sarcastically said already knowing Hector would never get that chance. When Cortez and Shayna confirmed that they had everything, Chicago asked Hector, "So where are you going to go motherfucker?"

"I'll go anywhere. I'll go to Cali with my people! I got kids out there."

Chicago stood back and said, "That ain't far enough! I think you should go to hell!" and then he shot Hector in the head twice. "Now on to you." Chicago said looking at Shayna.

"What you mean by on to me?" Shayna asked with the fear of God in her voice.

"Just what I said; now on to you." Chicago said as he shot her in the face.

"Come on Chi; let's get the fuck up out of here!" Cortez said.

They left and went straight to Cortez's house since Keisha was at the hospital with Que. They had an open house with all the privacy that they needed to count up what they just hit Hector for. Once they got inside of Cortez's room, they began counting everything that they had gotten away with. They came up on thirteen kilos of cocaine; two hundred and sixty thousand dollars in cash; plus nine new guns, and some jewelry. *This was a good lick*, they both thought to their selves.

"Tez, I'm proud of you nigga'!" Chicago said. "You played your part to the tee; so we're splitting everything!"

"I told you I go hard for my paper!" Cortez said as he smiled from ear to ear. "What are we going to do with this jewelry because I don't want none of this shit" Cortez asked.

"This is what I'm going to do. I'ma take my one hundred and thirty thousand dollars and seven kilos with me; the rest we going to leave here. Is that cool with you?" Chicago replied.

"Yeah; but what about the guns?"

"Just keep them. If I need one, I'll come and get one from you. For now though, let's drop this shit off at my house; and then we can go to the strip club and celebrate. Plus we need to come up with a plan on what we are going to do next."

"Now you know I ain't old enough to get in the strip clubs yet!" Cortez replied.

"Are you crazy? With these you are!" Chicago said holding up a fist full of one hundred dollar bills. "Come on."

They dropped Chicago's share of the packages off at his house, and the went straight across the Martin Luther King bridge headed straight to Bottoms Up next door to the Pink Slip where Shayna worked.

Chapter Twenty-One
(Da Tables Done Turned)

*T*hree months had past since the car accident, and Que was just now being released from Saint Louis University Hospital. Still unable to walk on his own, Que felt cursed being confined in a wheelchair; but at the same time he counted his blessings that not only was he living, but Keisha was still by his side.

As Keisha pushed Que to the customized van she had purchase so she wouldn't have the trouble of trying to lift him out of the wheelchair and place him in a seat, Que reality flashed before him; causing him to want to break down and cry, but his pride wouldn't allow him too. Que hated the thought of having to depend on others, but the tables had turned on him; and now he was faced with his new reality, he knew he had to depend on someone else witch he despised.

"Do you have anywhere you want to stop at or something in particular you might have a taste for while we are out?" Keisha asked Que trying to break the awkward silence that had fell between them since they gotten in the van.

"*Naw*; I just want to get as far as I can out of this city!" Que lowly mumble.

Catching the depressingly tone in Que's voice, Keisha tried to change his mood by saying, "Look, don't be sounding like you're all by yourself. We gone pull through this together! Everything is going to be back to normal in due time; but for now, can I have my good friend that joke around with me back, and you can just get rid of this snob that's sitting here."

Even though Keisha meant well, she just didn't quite understand how

Que was feeling mentally. Que had been a codependent person since he was in middle school; so for him having to depend on anybody for the slightest thing was a major mental problem for him. Que tried to play off how he was really feeling, but his acting skills could use a lot of practice as he said, "I just want you to drive me to my house, and we can go from there."

"So you ain't planning on coming home with me?" Keisha snapped.

Not wanting to tell Keisha a flat out no, Que said, "I haven't been home in awhile, and I need to check on a few things." hoping she would let it go as he gave her directions to get on the inner state headed to Lake Saint Louis.

Keisha was frustrated for a moment; and then her whole attitude quickly change at the thought of finally getting the chance to see where Que really considered his home. Finally reaching the subdivision where Que lived, Keisha thought to herself, *Damn, these some huge ass homes. I thought my house was nice, but these houses got to be some million dollar homes.*

Once pulling up to Que's house, Keisha became speechless with the size of his home. He had a big water fall in the middle of his front yard that sat in the middle of his horseshoe shape drive way. Keisha asked, "Damn baby, how in the hell did you find this house?"

"This ain't a house I found; this a house I had built from the ground up a few years ago."

"How many rooms do you got in there ten?"

"There's seven bedrooms and five bathrooms, and it's a pool in the back too!"

Keisha pulled up in front of the twelve feet double glass doors and got out. Once she got Que out, he pulled out his phone and unlocked the door. "How in the hell did you just do that?" Keisha asked because it was the first time she ever seen anything like that.

"It's apart of my alarm system. I can control the locks, lights, blinds, and all kinds of shit in my house. I can even flush the toilet from my phone if I wanted too."

"Who in the hell do you think you are Bruce Wayne or somebody?"

"*Naw*, it ain't like that. I just believe in living good and comfortable as one can get. I hustle hard, so I live good; and living good mean I got to be able to play even harder, at least that's my motto!"

"I hear you!" Keisha replied as they began to enter the house.

When Keisha got Que in the house, she couldn't believe her eyes. Now she really understood why Que didn't want to go to her house. Que was living like a king. Keisha's house looked more like an apartment when comparing it to Que's home. Que's house was more like a palace. He had marble everywhere as if his house was a marble factory itself. He actually had fish tanks built in the walls with baby sharks in them and the whole under water works. The chandelier he had hanging from his ceiling looked as if it cost at least a hundred thousand dollars; but that wasn't all his house features. When Keisha looked up to see the actual design of the chandelier, she was out done. Que's ceiling was painted like a sky with angels in it. As they made their way to the living room, Keisha saw a fire place that was shape like a lion with its mouth open. It was so big that she could sit in it.

"Oh my God; she looks just like you!" Keisha said looking at the life size picture over the fire place.

"You mean I look like her. That's my mother. She past about ten years ago. I wish she could be here to see how successful I am today. I miss her."

"I'm sorry to hear that."

"Don't be; she's in a better place now. Anyway, let's go to the kitchen. Can you hook something up for me to eat real quick?"

"Yeah baby; I'll cook you whatever you want." Keisha replied. As Keisha wheeled him down the hall she saw beautiful statues of two naked ladies. Everything was nice but what she saw next really impressed her. "I know damn well that ain't an elevator! Who in the hell has an elevator in their house?"

"That is an elevator; but I've only used it like three or four times. I'm happy I got it now! Keisha this is my palace and I'm willing to share it with you. I think we should stay here for awhile. What do you think?"

Not wasting a breath Keisha quickly replied, "I'm fine with that; I just got to run it by my son first. I'm sure he would love it!"

"And if he don't, we can just let him stay at the house in the city. I'm sure he'll take good care of it."

"Okay Que, I'll talk to him about it and see what he wants to do."

"*Naw*, let me talk to him man to man. I got some stuff I wan'na holla at him about anyway."

"Okay, I'll get him out here later. Now what do you want to eat?" Keisha asked as she spotted the pool. "Damn, now that's a pool! I'ma be in it all the time in the summer!" Que had a big ass pool with a stone wall next to it. The stone wall had a sliding board built on it that circle around before it ended in the pool. In the far corner he had living area with a bar and grill and two flat screen televisions. "Yeah baby, I wan'na stay here with you. You just got to make sure you come home to me every night."

"I will, I promise; but I ain't planning on going anywhere for a minute." Que said conscience about his current state. Keisha whipped up some bacon and eggs with cheese just like Que liked. After eating Que said, "Okay, lets jump on the elevator and go up to the room; I got a few things I wan'na talk to you about. Plus I got something I wan'na show you too."

"Okay; but give me a second so I can wash these dishes up right quick."

"Don't worry about those dishes; I'll have my servant come handle all of that!"

"So, you got a damn maid too?"

"Yeah; I got two of them. You will meet them later on."

"That's cool, but we don't need no maids! I'll take care of you and the house!"

Que didn't respond back to what Keisha said; instead, once they were on the elevator Que said, "We going to the third floor." As soon as the elevator doors opened, they were in his bedroom. It was the size of the whole floor. "This is where the magic happens!" Que said with a smile on his face.

"So you wan'na play with magic huh?" Keisha teased.

"When I'm finish telling you what I need too and you see what I wan'na show you, damn right! You ain't going to know if I'm the Black *Chris Angel!*" he said as they both laughed.

Approaching the huge cherry oak wood bedroom set that looked like *King Tut* once owned, Keisha and Que climbed in the bed and Que began speaking his mind. "I see you as loyal as it gets. You been holding me down like I need you too; and I'm thankful. It really fucked me up when you offered me your money to make sure I would be straight! You just don't know how happy I am to see money isn't everything to you; but I don't need your money. That's yours, you earned it! If I ain't got shit, I got money; that's one thing I shouldn't ever have to worry about again! I own everything you see me with. This house; those cars and trucks, everything! For real though, I feel like I can trust you with my life so I'm ready to invite you into my world full time and share everything with you. And I know Cortez means everything to you. I really like him! I think he's a good kid. I know his daddy can never be replaced; but I'm ready to take him up under my wing and treat him just like he's mine. As a matter of fact, call him and give him the address so he can come see the house; and then I can talk to him face to face." Keisha dialed up Cortez and gave him the address so he could come and meet them. Once she got off the phone with him Que asked, "So are you ready for what I wan'na show you?"

"Yeah I'm ready; where is it at back down stairs?"

"Nope, it's up here. Help me get back in the wheelchair please. I bet you this is one of the coolest things you've ever seen in anybodies house." Que wheel his self to a light switch that had a picture of a Black African woman with beautiful eyes. Que pushed her eyes in and half the wall opened up. You would have never known that the wall moved just by looking at it. "Welcome to the panic room; step on in."

As Keisha stepped into the room she asked, "What is a panic room?"

"This is where you come if the house is being robbed or something majorly wrong is going on and you need to be out of sight!" Que replied. He then pushed a button on the inside of the panic room and the wall closed up. "Now nothing or nobody can get in here; not even if they pressed the eyes on the picture out there."

Que had a ten feet safe in the panic room that he went too. Once he opened it, Keisha didn't know what to think. It was filled up with nothing but guns, ammunition, and two million dollar in cash in the floor of the safe. "See here is two million and it's plenty more where that came from; so don't worry about money, we got that. Do you know how to use a gun?"

"No, I've never shot a gun in my life!" Keisha answered in shock of what Que just exposed her too.

"Well not today, but I'ma have to take you to the gun range so you can learn because it's important that you know how to shoot!" Que said before closing the safe back and opening the wall back up for they could exit. They went back into his bedroom and talked a little more; after hearing each other out Que said, "Oh yeah, I got one more thing to show you and I know you are going to like it! Come on, it's in the basement."

They got back on the elevator and road it to another floor. When the doors opened up, Keisha saw a lounge like set up with: a bar, tables, a stripper's pole, and six flat screen televisions spread all around. She then spotted a popcorn maker next to a set of double doors that had a lit up picture of the movie *Scarface* on one side, and *Belly* on the other. "I know that ain't what I think that is!" Keisha replied.

"If you thinking a movie theater, then you right. I seen it on cribs and had to have one."

"Now this is flat out doing it big! I can get use to this!"

"Good, because that's what I'm pushing for!"

Shortly after showing Keisha the theater, the doorbell rung. It was Cortez waiting at the door. "Hey baby!" Keisha said with pure excitement in her voice waiting to tell Cortez her good news. "I see you got here pretty fast; I hope you wasn't speeding!" Keisha said already knowing that he was as she let him in the house.

Keisha wasn't paying any attention and step on a nice size pile of junk mail, so she bent over and picked it up. Cortez still tripping off the actual size of the house asked, "Momma, what in the world are you doing out here? Who's house is this?"

"Just follow me to the living room so you can sit down." Keisha replied ignoring Cortez questions.

Que was sitting in the living room as Keisha and Cortez walked in. He hadn't seen Cortez in two days so he was happy to see him. "What's up Tez? Good to see you made it here. The ride wasn't too long was it?"

"*Naw*, not at all! Who's house is this?" Cortez asked for the second time awaiting an answer.

"Keisha, can you give us a minute to talk?" Que replied, but didn't answer Cortez's question.

"Sure; if ya'll need me, just call me." Keisha replied departing the room.

With Keisha out of the room, Que got straight to the point. "Well Tez, this my house." Que began by answering Cortez's question that he left hanging. "I got to be here for a minute; at least until my legs get better!"

"This ain't a bad place to be! This place is dope! How much it cost; a million dollars?"

"Something like that; but I wan'na talk to you about something"

"Like what? I'm listening!"

"For starters, what do you think about me dating your mother? Is that alright with you? Do I have your blessings?"

"To be real with you, I thought ya'll were already dating. Yeah, you have my blessings because I see how my momma seems to be really happy around you. Plus it's been awhile since I seen her so happy."

"Okay; so what about living here? I need her here with me to help me out; and I want to know if I got the okay from you to move ya'll out here?"

"All I can say on that is if she likes it, then I love it. I wouldn't mind staying in this here; but what about my school?"

"Well we got two ways we can do this. One, you move out here and we put you in a school out here; or two, you can keep the house in the city and continue to go to school from there. What do you wan'na do?"

Cortez's face lit up as he said, "So ya'll gone just let me keep the whole house to myself?"

"*Yep*, if that's what you wan'na do. All I ask is for you not to mess it up. Look at it as if it's yours; and Mesha and you worked hard for it. I only said Mesha and you because I know you are going to wan'na have company and that's cool; but I'ma need you to keep it at a minimum because those white people ain't gone be fond of too many young niggas' all over the place around there. So this means no parties what's so ever! You and Mesha will have to stay low key. If you wan'na throw a party and shit, just let me know and I'll rent out a club or something whenever you get ready. So what you wan'na do?"

"I'ma stay in the city; and you got my word that I'll stay low key! I'll even come out here on the weekends and stuff!"

"Okay then; say no more and we are going to give it a try! You running that house now; and that's a good thing because you about to be a boss so you need to get use to having and doing boss things! Speaking of that, the 750 is down there and you can drive it whenever you want too. Just don't stunt too hard on niggas and get yourself in trouble! Tez I look at you like my son-in-law now, and I want you to know there's nothing I won't do for you. Your mother and me are going to set up an account for you were you can spend a thousand dollars a month on whatever you want; bills not included. Me and your mother gone take care of all of that! Does this sound like a good plan to you?"

"Yes sir; without a doubt! It sounds like the best plan I've heard in a while!"

They joked around for a minute until Keisha walked back in asking, "Is it okay if I come in here with my two favorite men in the world yet?"

"Yeah come on in; we were just wrapping it up. We got an understanding, and he wants to stay at the house in the city. I gave him the okay; plus access to the 750 whenever he wants to use it.

"Okay, I figured he was going to want to stay down there anyway; but Cortez, you bet not mess up my damn house! You understand me?"

"He ain't Keisha! We already went over everything, and we got a good understanding. He gave me his word, and I gave him mines."

"Yeah momma, I got this on lock; don't worry about nothing!" Cortez said as he thought to his self, *Yeah, this was just what I needed; my own crib!*

"Okay now that we all got an understanding, Cortez follow your momma so she can show you around the house; and you can pick out a room for yourself when you come out here. Also I need you to remember that nobody comes to this house with you unless it's Mesha; other than her, nobody!"

"I got you!" Cortez replied.

"Oh yeah baby, you got all kinds of junk mail; I'll bring it too you in a second. And why don't you read your mail silly; it look like you ain't been here in years."

"Shit, now that I'm thinking about it, I ain't been here since I met you; but anyway, go ahead and show Tez the house. I'm about to order us some food. I'm in the mood for some steak and shrimps. Is that cool with ya'll?"

"Yeah!" they both said as they walked off.

Shortly later, they all ate together and kicked it for awhile in the theater. Once the movie was over, Cortez said, "Alright ya'll, I'm fin'na get out of here so I can go pass by Mesha's before I go get ready for school tomorrow."

After Cortez left, Keisha and Que called it a night early and went back to their room where they discuss business. "Baby, so what's next?" Keisha asked.

"What's next as far as what?" Que questioned as he laid in the bed flipping through the channels on his sixty inch flat screen television on the wall.

"As far as selling dope goes, you done right?"

"No, there's so much more stuff that need to be done."

"But baby, you got everything people dream of having: cars, homes, and millions of dollars! Why keep going?"

"Look Keisha, this shit bigger than just me! I got about twenty niggas' and their families depending on me to keep this business running! This is how they pay their bills, and take care of their families. We don't just do this for cars and clothes; we put kids through school paying for their educations and college tuitions. We also always help the elderly with whatever they need help with too. So you see, this ain't just about me. As a matter of fact, I might need you to step up to the plate and run shit for me until my legs get better!"

"So now you want me to take over your business?"

"Not now because shit cool for now. I just wan'na take about a month or so to just try to get my legs right; and spend as much time with you as possible. But keep in mind that if I still can't walk around in a month or so, I'ma need you to step up to the plate and hold it down!"

"I-ight baby, I'll do anything you say!" Keisha said as she curled up under Que and laid around until they both felt asleep.

Chapter Twenty-Two
(Karma)

A few weeks had passed since Cortez and Chicago had knocked Hector out the picture. They didn't want to draw any extra attention to their selves, so they didn't jump right out selling weight to anybody. They kept everything as normal as they possibly could. Every now and then they might plug a motherfucker with an ounce or so; but over all they were breaking everything down.

After a couple of weeks went by, Cortez questioned Chicago as to why it was taking so long to get rid of all the dope; and that's when Chicago educated Cortez on the rules of the game and what he was doing. "Damn lil' bro, you rushing me now?"

"*Naw* it ain't like that! I'm just trying to figure out what's taking so long; and why I ain't got paid yet! That's all!"

"Well it's taking so long because I'm breaking everything down; we ain't selling no weight! Then you ain't got paid yet because I figured we'll just wait until everything was at least halfway gone before we touched any money; that way I'll be giving you a large amount instead of lil' pieces at a time."

"Shit, that sound good! You just had me used to getting paid twice a week. I just wanted an understanding on what's going on with the money, and when I was going to get paid."

"It's cool you asked; but let me put you on top of actually what I'm doing. I'm breaking every kilo down and making $72,000 off of each one. I sold three of them already. Now nigga' you do the math; I got $216,000 for us to split right now if you want too, but that's on you! I'm breaking each kilo down to make sure we can get the most we can get; but let me remind you that shit takes some time! Now six and a half of these motherfucking kilos are yours! A whole kilo goes for twenty-five to thirty thousand dollars around here. If you in such a rush, I can sell your half at twenty-five a piece and have you squared away by the end of the week! Matter of fact, I got something even better for you. I'll personally give you twenty-seven a piece for your half right now if you just don't want anything else to do with it. What do you want to do?"

Cortez thought things through for a quick second before he replied, "*Naw*, I'll wait and let you do your thang! We ain't got to rush anything; I'll just feel better if I was getting paid something every week!"

"Oh, I'm cool with that; but I got a request for you as well!"

"What's up; run it by me?"

"I need you to help me shelter, breakdown, and deliver the dope."

"I don't have a problem with still holding the dope nor bringing it to you as you need it; but I don't know anything about breaking down no dope!"

"Don't worry too much about that; I'll show you exactly what I need for you to do, and it ain't hard at all! I'ma need for you to skip school tomorrow so I can come over to your crib and we can get down to business. Speaking of cribs, Mesha asked her momma if she could come live with you. What's that about? Are do you even know anything about that?"

"*Naw*, I didn't know about her asking; but we did talk about that the other day."

"What you think your momma is going to say about her moving in?"

"My momma loves her some Mesha; but my momma don't stay there any more! My momma and her boyfriend just got them a bigger house."

"So you telling me that you got that big ass crib all to yourself?"

"*Yep*! That's how me and Mesha ended up talking about her living with me. I thought that it would be nice to have Mesha there with me on the daily!"

"I'll see what I can do for you. Shit, the girl will be eighteen on the thirty first of March. All I ask is that you make sure she stays in school. Her momma big on that."

"I will. Besides, Mesha love going to school anyway. But if you can make that happen for me, I'll owe you big time!"

"Okay, I'ma get it done so you can start paying me by taking me to get some White Owls in that new Challenger you got!"

"I'll take you, but I ain't driving the Challenger!"

"What you driven then?"

"You'll see. Come on because I'm ready to smoke too."

Once they walked out the house, Cortez unlocked the 750 with the car remote. Chicago eyes lit up for two reasons. One, because it was a 750 Cortez was driving; and two, he knew he seen it somewhere before but couldn't place it just yet. "Damn! So your ass done went out here and got a 750 already? You just got a brand new car! What in the hell made you do this? How much you pay for it?"

"Calm down Chicago; I ain't pay nothing for it because it ain't mines!"

"Stop lying nigga'; you got that money and brought it! Didn't you?"

"*Naw*! Real shit, it's my momma's boyfriend, Que, shit. He's just letting me drive it."

That's when Chicago thought to his self, *That's shole the fuck is Que's shit! I knew I seen that motherfucker before! This lil' nigga tied in with the man and probably don't even know it; but I ain't gone say shit though.* "You one lucky motherfucker! I was getting money at seventeen, but not like you. You on a whole another level!" After leaving the store Chicago said, "Fuck it, we got some free time on our hands. Barber and Mesha out chilling; so we should just go to your spot so I can show you how to break the dope down today instead of waiting on tomorrow."

"That sounds good to me; plus this way I won't have to skip school tomorrow!"

They got to Cortez's house and Chicago was ready to teach him how to break down the dope so he wouldn't have too. He just knew with Cortez breaking down the dope it would save him a lot of time, so he would be able to maneuver they way that he needed too in order to make them both more money. Cortez watched Chicago like a hawk, and in no time he had the game and gone with it. Cortez thought to his self, *I can't believe I'm doing this shit!* after he realized how time consuming it was.

"Well I see my work here is done." Chicago said once he saw Cortez break down an ounce and a half, which was enough to ensure him that Cortez now knew what he was doing.

Cortez feeling a lil' big headed about learning something new arrogantly replied, "Yeah I guess your work here is done, because breaking this shit down ain't shit! I got this!"

"I-ight then! Now that you know what you doing, you can take me back to the crib so I can give you your money and get back to work. Oh yeah, I holla' at a good friend of mines who want to check that jewelry out. He owns a pawn shop and willing to melt it all down and pay us good for it too. I'm thinking we should at least get ten grand."

"Ten grand! That one watch alone is worth more than that!" Cortez snapped thinking Chicago must have not known any better.

"I know; all of that shit together probably worth over a hundred grand, but you also got to remember that shit hot! On top of that, we didn't pay shit for it!"

Cortez's phone began to ring as DaMesha was calling him. "Hello." He answered.

"What you doing baby?" DaMesha asked.

"Shit! Chicago and me on our way back to your house; why? What's up?"

"I was just trying to see if you wanted to go to the movies or something because I'm bored; plus I wan'na do some other things too if you know what I mean?" DaMesha said with her head in the gutter."

"Okay, I'm feeling that! Be ready when we get there; we'll be there in about fifteen minutes."

Once they got back to DaMesha's house, Cortez got his money from Chicago; and then DaMesha and him went back to his crib to drop it off. After that, they went straight to the movies to spend some quality time together. When the movie was over and they were headed back to his house, Que called him. Cortez answered the phone, "What's up Que? How are you and my momma doing?"

"We good! Your momma out here holding it down; but I really called to check up on you! How you doing?"

"I'm good! Infact, Mesha and me are on the way to the house now; we just left the movies."

"Oh shit! Somebody fin'na get some cuddy huh?" Que said jokingly.

"Yes sir!" Cortez replied with a smile big as day on his face.

"Okay! Well another thing I call to tell you is that we set up that account for you today, so you can get that thousand dollars every month like we talked about. You should be getting a debt card with your name on it in the mail in a day or two."

"Thanks Que!" Cortez said as he quickly thought, *I'ma be spending that on Mesha; that way I don't have to really touch my own money.*

*E*verything was going perfect for Chicago, even though Barber was on his head about moving after he brought a new car. Everybody was starting to see a big change in the way that he dressed and carried his self; and thought that he was getting some real money now. He was consistent with being able to supply the dope that his clientele demanded; and it was consider the best dope on the streets. When folks seen him riding around in his new Lexus GS 450, they started to envy him for real. Then everything changed when he went to a dice game in the park one Sunday and revealed his hands.

Chicago started off losing big time. About thirty minutes went by and he had lost five grand easily. Drunk and feeling his self, he went home and got another ten thousand dollars to put in his pockets to play with; but his luck didn't change. Once he came back to the dice game, he quickly lost another four grand like it wasn't shit. Then all of a sudden, the tables began to turn and Chicago was on a roll. He was hitting people pockets hard, and talking big shit while he was at it.

"See ya'll lil' niggas' money ain't long enough to shoot against me! I'm playing with birds; while ya'll playing with crumbs! Come on, a thousand I shoot! I'm taking all bets. As a matter of fact, shoot the thousand, and if you lose I'll give you five hundred of it back so you can bet again!" Chicago replied as he hit another seven out the door and swiped up everything off the table. He then yelled out, "Chi-Town niggas'! Now that's how we do it in Chicago; send a motherfucker home sick! Now who wants to be next to lose their shit? You next?" he asked as the guy, Feeva, who he just hit stood up. "Say Feeva, I know your lil' broke ass sick; but don't go home and tell your baby momma you got robbed and shit!"

Everybody laughed at the statement Chicago made; but Feeva was pissed. He made up his mind right then and there; that as soon as this game was over, he was going to rob and kill Chicago. "A Chris; come holla' at me real quick!" Feeva said as he walked off.

"What's good bruh? You look mad as fuck!" Chris replied.

"I am! That motherfucker talking all shit; like he's playing with six figures or something!"

"I don't know about six figures, but he got some paper though. You seen how fast he left and came back with some more money didn't you?"

"Yeah, I peeped that! But fuck that; as soon as he gets up to leave, I'ma rob his dumb ass!"

"Shit, I want in too; but we shouldn't rob him right now! I know he went home and got that money; and then he talking about he playing with birds and shit! So fuck it, we should run up in his crib and see what he really got in there!"

"You know what, your right? Let's follow his drunk ass to his crib and get him for everything!"

"If he ain't got no birds for real, I'ma kill him!" Chris said.

"Shit, his smart mouth ass dead anyway it goes and I'm standing on that! I'ma show him how us St. Louis niggas' get down!" Feeva replied ready to take Chicago out.

"Alright then, it's a done deal; we on him!"

$\mathcal{M}$eanwhile, DaMesha was at home alone when Cortez called her asking her what she was doing. "I ain't doing anything; I'm just chilling looking at 106 & Park! Why; what you fin'na come get me or something?"

"*Naw*, I really wanted you to come over here and chill with me. I also wan'na taste your cooking you been bragging about too!"

"Oh, so you want me to cook for you huh? What you want me to cook?"

"I got a lil' bit of everything; so it really don't matter to me! I guess whatever you feel you can cook the best, that's what it's going to be!"

"Well just so you know, I know how to cook everything; but I got a taste for some fish. What you think about that?"

"That sounds good to me! I got some catfish nuggets in the freezer while I'm thinking about it too. I'ma even help you out a lil' bit. We can eat some French fries with it; and I'll peel and cut up the potatoes!" Cortez said laughing.

"Okay; I'm on my way. Take the fish out and let it soak in some water until I get there so it'll be ready. Do you need me to bring anything with me?"

"Nope; just you! I got everything else that we gone need."

DaMesha then said, "You so silly! I'm on my way." as she grabbed her all Black Prada bag and headed straight for the door.

As DaMesha was about to pull off, her momma and brother were pulling up. "Where you fin'na go lil' girl?" Barber asked her daughter through her window before she completely parked.

"Over Tez's house for awhile! Where ya'll coming from?"

"I just filed my taxes and picked your brother up from Jasmine's house."

"Oh yeah; how much money are you gone get back?"

"Nosey, I'm getting six thousand back this year! Is there anything else you wan'na know; or think you need to know that I ain't report to you ma'am?" Barber playfully responded as she made her way to the sidewalk.

"*Yep*! How much of that is me and my brother going to get?" DaMesha then asked with a smile on her face.

"That's the same thing I asked her!" Corey said as he made his way to the door.

"Look, I'ma tell you like I told him; I don't know yet! Whatever I give ya'll it's more than what ya'll got!"

"I ain't gone complain!" DaMesha said "I'm fin'na get out of here. I'll call you when I'm on my way home to see if you want me to bring you something!"

"Alright, tell Tez I said hi for me. Don't forget you got school in the morning; and be safe baby."

"I will; I love you momma!"

"I love you too, lil' ugly lil' girl!

"I look just like you!" DaMesha said as she pulled off.

Shortly after making it home, Barber called Chicago to see where he was. "Where you at? You at that damn park; ain't you?" Barber asked as she heard the crowd of people in the back ground.

"Yeah I'm up here killing these lil' niggas' in craps! Why; what's up?" Chicago said loudly slick side rubbing in that he was on a roll.

"I was expecting to see you when I got here; that's all. Anyway, I'ma let you get back to doing your thang; just don't be gone all night!"

"I'm not; I know these motherfuckers bout tired of me taking their money! I'll be home in about thirty minutes. Let me give these niggas' a chance to win some of their money back!"

"Alright baby; I got some stuff to talk to you about when you get home. Be careful because you know how those fools are out there."

"I am. I'll be there in a minute though." Chicago said before he hung up.

Feeva and Chris went to Feeva's car after hearing Chicago's conversation and waited on Chicago to come to his car. I mean they patiently waited on Chicago while smoking cigarettes back to back. When Chicago did come back to his car, he jumped straight in and pulled off; not even realizing that he was being followed. Feeva trailed Chicago home; but at the same time he kept his distance so that he wouldn't draw any attention to them. When they saw Chicago pulling over in front of his house, they slowed down and pulled over near the corner of his street and watched him make his way up the steps. Once Chicago made it halfway up the steps, Feeva pulled in front of the house and let Chris out of the car.

Chris ran up the steps and caught Chicago right before he put his key in the door and said, "Nigga' if you say anything or resist, I'ma blow the back of your brains out! Give me that motherfucking key!" he said with his gun pressed firmly up against Chicago's back.

Feeva finally parked the car and made his way up the steps where they were, and then took over things telling Chicago, "If you wan'na be hardheaded and get killed be my guest; but I ain't gone show you no sympathy!"

Chris opened the door and stepped in to see Corey sitting on the couch watching television; not paying any attention to the fact that Chicago was being held at gun point. Chris quickly turned his gun towards Corey and in a low but serious tone said, "Lil' nigga' if you say anything or try to run, your dead! Just be a good boy, and get your ass over here and lay down next to this bitch ass motherfucker!"

"Now who the fuck else is in here?" Feeva asked "And ya'll better tell me now or I'ma start shooting?"

Before the question got answered, Barber called out Corey's name and told him to, "Turn down that damn television some; it ain't got to be that loud!"

Feeva immediately looked at Chris and told him to go get her. Without a word Chris left headed towards the room Barber's voice came from. Seconds later he came back in the living room with Barber slightly resisting. She then screamed out, "What the fuck do ya'll want?" once see saw Feeva aiming his weapon at Corey and Chicago who were laying side by side on the floor.

"Your man here knows what the fuck we want! Don't you?" Feeva asked, but didn't wait on a response before he continue "Now we ain't got all day to play with ya'll; so lets keep this simple and just give it up! Where the bricks and shit at?"

Chicago quickly lied as he replied, "I was just fucking around and talking shit; ya'll know damn well I ain't got no motherfucking bricks! All I have is this money in my pockets!"

"I told you we should've been have moved!" Barber yelled at Chicago as she blamed him inside of her mind for what was going on.

"Yeah ya'll should've would've could've, but ya'll didn't! Chris turn that radio on; and turn it all the way up, so I can get my point across!" Feeva wickedly said.

Knowing what Feeva most likely had in mind Chicago bust out saying, "Okay, okay; I'll give it to ya'll! I got a hundred and forty thousand dollars and two and a half kilos. Ya'll can have it; just please don't hurt them!"

"Now that was a smart decision! Get the fuck up and take me to it! Chris, if either one of them attempt to get out of line, kill them!" Feeva replied.

"Baby don't worry; ya'll going to be alright." Chicago said, "I'ma give them what they want." On the way down to the basement Chicago kept thinking, *damn, karma a motherfucker!*

"Now you better be smart because if you try anything funny, I'ma kill you and them! Now where is everything at?"

"Everything is in the cooler under the steps!"

"Okay, well get it then; and don't attempt to open it either! Just slide it on out and over here!"

When Chicago pulled the cooler out, he slid it over to Feeva just like he was order to do. Feeva opened the cooler and saw the dope and money was piled up inside it just like Chicago said it was. "Okay, now you got what you want; just let us go!" Chicago angrily said.

"Motherfucker if you knew like I knew, you would shut the fuck up and pick this damn cooler up; and get it up stairs, without me having to tell you another damn thing! Now hopefully I made myself clear, and you realized that now is a really good time for you to shut the hell up and just do what I say do if you want you and your family to make it through this shit alive! Are we on the same page?" Feeva snapped. Chicago just nodded his head in a yes gesture motion. "Good; now that we got that understanding, let's go back upstairs in the living room." Feeva calmly said.

When they got back in the living room and Chris saw Chicago carrying the cooler he asked Feeva, "Is that everything in there?"

"Without a doubt; you know he knew better than to play with us!"

"Now that's what I'm talking about! So what are we going to do with them now?"

Feeva looked at Chicago, who was now staring directly at him to hear and see his response, and replied, "What was all of that Chicago shit you were talking earlier?"

"I was just fucking with ya'll man. You said you weren't going to hurt them; so what else is it that you want?"

"You right. I did say that I wasn't going to kill them; and I'm not. I'ma man of my word; but I got something that I want you to personally see. Chris, kill them!"

"No!" Chicago screamed as Chris began to shoot Barber and Corey in the back of their heads.

For a second, Chicago couldn't believe what he just witness. He just watched them lying on the floor lifeless. He felt like he was frozen in time because he couldn't move, nor talk, or do anything about what just took place. He was just simply ready to die; hoping that it would put an end to the pain he was feeling.

"Now that's how we do it in Saint Louis!" Feeva cold heartedly said to Chicago right before he shot him three times in the back. "Chris, take these keys and look in my trunk; and bring that gas can in here."

As Chris went to get the gas can, Feeva went inside the kitchen to the stove and blew out the pilot lights and turned on all of the stove's eyes; allowing gas to began filling the room. When Chris came back inside and gave him the gas can and his car keys back, he began pouring the gas all over Barber, Corey, and Chicago bodies. He then made a trail from the kitchen to the front door with the remaining gas.

"Say Chris, go make sure I cut the stove on so this motherfucker will blow the fuck up right!" Feeva replied plotting on the low.

"I-ight; I got you." Chris responded not knowing what was really going on.

As Chris went to make sure the stove was on, Feeva went to the front door with the cooler and waited on Chris to come back out of the kitchen. Once Chris made his way back into the living room, Feeva shot him too. He then stepped out the door, lit a cigarette, and then dropped it on the gas trail that he had made. "Swoosh!" was the sound made as the fire slowly but steady began to build. By the time Feeva made it back to his car and safely skirted off, the fire was just starting to pick up its speed in spreading. About five minutes later, the whole house blew.

Didn't nobody have a clue as to what had just took place, as people started coming outside to see what was going on from the sound of the explosion that they heard. A few of DaMesha's friends saw that it was their friend's house and immediately started calling and sending her text messages.

*M*eanwhile, DaMesha and Cortez was eating dinner when DaMesha's cellular phone started ringing like it wasn't a tomorrow. Taking a quick peep at her phone and seeing that it was only her friends calling her back to back, DaMesha decided to ignore all of her phone calls until her and Cortez was finish eating. By the time DaMesha did check her cellular phone and read the first text message that she received, she thought one of her friends were just playing just to get her to answer her telephone or to call them back; but the second text message that she received, was a text message that changed the rest of her life.

Chapter Twenty-Three
(Queen Penn)

*A*fter Keisha and Que got an understanding that if Keisha wanted Que to fall back, then she would have to step up to the plate; it was on and popping. Que had mapped out all of the spots that Keisha would have to make drop offs and pick ups from so they could get business back to flowing steady. Que also put it out there, that since he never made the connection with his plug, then Keisha would most definitely have to handle that on his behalf because eighteen kilos wasn't going to be enough to feed his whole organization. So he planned to set up a meeting.

After dialing the long distant phone number that Que had rememorized by heart, a familiar voice answered the phone speaking in broken English, "Hell-low."

"Hey Paco my friend; it's Win-Win! Did I catch you at a good time?" Que spoke into the receiver using his code name and phrase to let Paco know that everything was good on his end; but had to wait on a response back to determine whether they were going to continue their conversation.

"Any time is a good time my friend! Where you been? I haven't heard from you since our last conversation. Is my good friend Win-Win alright?" Paco replied using the code phrases to allow Que to know it was okay to talk.

After Que explain to Paco that he had been in a real bad car accident which caused him to leave him hanging up until now, Paco was ready to do business with him again. Que had to inform him that he wasn't able to travel yet, but had someone who he truly trusted that could meet up with him so they could get business back to flowing. Unfortunately, Paco wasn't feeling meeting someone new.

"My friend, we been doing real good business, but I don't know about meeting nobody new!" Paco said with serious concern in his voice.

"Come on Paco; this Win-Win! I wouldn't just send anybody to meet up with you; I'm sending the only person that I trust with my life my friend!"

Thinking about the words Que used along with how long they have been doing good business regularly up until the last few months, Paco agreed and said, "For you, I'll do my friend; but if anything shall go wrong or they not who you say they are, you know what's going to happen to you!"

"It's no need for all of that!" Que ensured Paco. "When and where do you want me to schedule the meeting?"

"What phone number do you have; the same as always?"

"Yeah." Que answered before hanging up, but knew exactly what Paco meant by the questions he asked. Que then told Keisha who was staring at him kind of confused, "Everything is a go. You just got to drop the money off, and he is going to make sure everything make it here."

"Okay that's cool with me; but how many nick names do you have Mr. Win-Win? And where do I suppose to be dropping this money off at?"

"Well, Win-Win is like saying you winning and I'm winning. You got what I want, and I got what you want; so it's a win/win situation for both of us every time we do business together. Now as far as where you dropping the money off at, I need you to catch the train out to Tucson, Arizona. When you get there you are going to go straight to the restaurant on the top floor of the station. Reservations will already be made for a Mr. and Mrs. Win-Win. Once they show you to the table just be calm, cool, and collective; and just go with the flow. When Paco shows up, follow his directions closely. Do not speak until you are spoken too; and everything will go smoothly. Alright!"

"I got you baby! What time do I need to be ready to head out?"

"I'm about to call and set up everything right now; so give me a minute and I'll have some answers for you." Que said as he started making all of the arrangements. Within twenty minutes Que had everything booked from Keisha's train ticket, to the reservation in Arizona. He even called Paco back and told him what time he could be expecting Keisha's arrival.

Before Keisha could even think about changing her mind, Que didn't waste any time with getting her booked to catch the next train available going to Tucson, Arizona. Within three hours, she was headed out. Not knowing that it was going to take her two days to get there, Keisha tried to sleep majority of her time on the train away as she became frustrated thinking to herself, *I can't believe Que got me on this damn train for two motherfucking days; but wait until I get back, I'ma be the new Queen Penn running shit!*

When the train finally arrived in Tucson, Arizona Keisha took a real good stretch before heading straight to the top floor of the train station looking for the restaurant that Que told her to go too. Once she spotted it, she checked her watch and saw that it was only a few minutes after four o'clock and quickly thought to herself while taking a deep breath, *It's show time now; I didn't come this far for nothing!* before heading into the restaurant.

As soon as she walked into the restaurant a hostess greeted her saying, "You need a table for one?"

"No ma'am. You should have a reservation reserved for a Mr. and Mrs. Win." Keisha replied almost giving the hostess her real name, but she quickly caught herself.

"Oh yes ma'am, we sure do. Please follow me right this way. Mr. Win hasn't arrived yet."

Keisha nodded her head and followed the hostess to a table in the far corner of the restaurant. Not knowing what Paco really looked like, Keisha eyed everyone that came towards her direction. Within a few minutes, the same host came walking back to the table where Keisha was seated smiling, and said, "Your guess Mr. Win is here." as a man slowly trailing the hostess came towards the table.

Keisha nodded her head and stood up, but didn't say a word until Paco said, "Win-Win!" studying her closely.

With a smile on her face barely revealing her teeth, Keisha said, "Win-Win!" as she walked over to Paco and gave him a friendly hug before returning to her seat as the hostess began walking off.

Once seated, Paco said, "Well I definitely wasn't expecting to meet a woman as beautiful as yourself! But listen closely, I know that you had a long train ride to get here, but that's over with now. You will be back home before the night is over with as long as things go smoothly. You have something for me?" Paco asked while still studying her closely.

Sitting on the opposite side of the table, Keisha had all kinds of thoughts running through her mind as nervously she became. She quickly thought, *How in the hell am I going to get home before the night is over with, when it took me two motherfucking days to get to this motherfucking hot ass place?* That thought sent a chill through her bones as she then thought, *What in the hell am I getting myself involved in? Please don't let this motherfucker kill me; and everything goes as smooth as Que said it would.* "Yes; what do you want me to do with it?" Keisha replied in return while signaling with her eyes that the bag was for him.

Sensing Keisha's uncomfortable ness and seeing the beads of sweat appearing on Keisha's forehead, Paco asked, "Are you alright? You look as if you are about to faint or cry! What's going on?" in concern.

Not wanting to tell Paco what she was really thinking, Keisha played it off as she gain control of herself and replied, "I'm sorry; everything is alright! I just have to use the bathroom really bad. What do you want me to do with this bag?"

"You can slide the bag under the table to me; but there is a ladies room over there if you must go." Paco said pointing in the direction of the restrooms.

Keisha slid the bag under the table to Paco without making it look noticeable; and then excused herself to the ladies room. Inside of the ladies room, Keisha had to talk to herself. "Girl, why in the fuck are you acting all nervous for? Pull yourself together! You know damn well Que wouldn't have sent you down here for some bullshit with no if, ands, or buts about it! They been doing business too long now, for some crazy shit to jump off all of a sudden. Besides, you here now; so whatever going to happen, going to happen. So get it together girl!" Keisha said to herself and then washed her hands and exit the restroom.

When she returned to the table Paco quickly asked, "Are you feeling better now?"

"Much better; I'm sorry if I caused any confusions! Now where were we?"

"I was going to tell you," Paco begin while reaching inside his inside jacket pocket and removing an envelope, "you have about two and a half hours before your plane leaves." he said while sliding Keisha the envelope containing an one-way plane ticket to Saint Louis, Missouri. "After we have dinner here, you are free to go. You can catch a taxi-cab right out front that will take you to the airport; and should have you there in ten to fifteen minutes top. Do you have any questions for me?"

"Not that I can think of; besides, what would you suggest that we order from here to eat?"

Saying nothing at all, Paco let out a laugh. When the waitress came to their table, Paco placed both of their orders; and then they continue making small talk until it was time for them to depart. Before leaving though, Paco told Keisha, "Tell my friend, sending you was a true win-win; and hurry up and recover. It was my pleasure meeting you!"

Once Keisha got on the plane, she felt relief knowing everything went smooth. She was only hoping that her plane ride would go just as smoothly; because honestly, she was ready to start calling shots. She knew Que was going to be proud of her; but she just had to gain the experience of knowing what it felt like to be a true boss running shit.

At eight twenty-two, Keisha plane landed at Lambert International Airport safely. Instead of catching a cab to quickly get back to her car that was parked at the Grey Hound Bus Station lot, Keisha jumped on the Metro Link since it would still take her directly where she needed to go anyway; and besides the fact that it was already there, she didn't have to wait but only a minute to leave.

Before nine o'clock came, Keisha had made it to her car; and was onto her next mission. Not wanting to call it a night just yet, Keisha drove straight to the trap house to pick up the kilos she had broken down already before Que had gotten into his car accident. Pulling out the list that Que had giving to her of who gets what, Keisha easily saw that they didn't have nearly enough supply to meet the whole organization demands. After quickly studying the list, Keisha decided that she wouldn't supply the two members that needed the most; but would at least give everybody else a kilo until the main shipment touch down.

Coming to a conclusion, Keisha headed to meet up with Tweezy first; since he was the closest out of all the drops that she was planning on making. As soon as she got to the spot that Que had mapped out for her to meet Tweezy at, she called him. After a couple of rings, he answered the telephone. "What's up Tweezy baby? Come holla' at your girl!" Keisha spoke into the receiver.

"Who in the fuck is this?" Antwon snapped.

"This the Queen Penn; step outside!" Keisha said feeling herself a lil' bit more.

"The Queen Penn!" Tweezy said, but quickly thought to his self, *who in the fuck is this bitch?* As he peeped out the window noticing Que's old all Black Range Rover. "Girl, you better quit playing so much! I'll be right out."

About ten minutes had past before Tweezy came emerging from his door. As soon as he jumped in the truck with Keisha, she flipped the script from what he was expecting. "Nigga', I don't give a fuck about what you was in there doing; but when I tell you to come holla' at me or step outside, you need to stop whatever you doing and get to it! You got me sitting out here with all this shit on me like it's legal! Here nigga'!" she said handing him a single kilo.

"Who in the hell do you think you are talking to like this; and what the fuck is this? Where Que at?" Tweezy replied pissed the fuck off and ready to smack the dog shit out of Keisha.

"Look, I'm not trying to let you fuck up my vibe; I been having a good day so far! Now I can have Que call you when he get some time; but for now, you can take this kilo and get to making some money until I plug you with what all you normal get! Other than that, you can get the fuck out my vehicle! Now, what are you going to do?"

Tweezy grudgingly took the kilo; but in his mind he planned on teaching Keisha a lesson the first chance he got. He didn't give a fuck about how much she thought she was the new Queen Penn; or even much the fact that she was suppose to be Que's woman. As far as he was concern, she was just another bitch that could be easily replaced. He felt like if anything, he should have been the new boss if Que was stepping down or was planning on passing it off since he been loyal since day one; but he didn't say anything as he walked off and Keisha pulled off heading to meet Pee Wee.

Pulling up on Pee Wee, Keisha was still kind of heated as she called Pee Wee and told him to step outside. Once Pee Wee saw the expression on Keisha's face he instantly said, "Damn sis, what brings you over here this time of night; and why you looking so mad?"

"I came over here to bring you a kilo and to let you know things are about to get back to normal; but before I got here, Tweezy monkey ass than struck my damn nervous with his bullshit! He had me waiting outside in that hot ass neighborhood, while he taking his sweet ass time and I got all this shit on me! Like where the fuck they do that at? And then he had the nervous to ask me who the fuck I thought I was talking too after I checked his ass!"

"Sis, don't even trip off that fool! I told Que that he was getting out of line and needed to be checked! I don't know why he just don't let me get rid of him; it won't cost him a thang!"

"Everything cool though. I'm just trying to make sure everybody get a lil' something to eat since we been missing in action for a minute. Let me get out of here, and finish making my moves. Oh yeah, where that money at? I needs that!"

"Hold up, and let me run inside to grab it." Pee Wee replied. When he came back out he handed Keisha seven thousand dollars and said, "I-ight sis. Be safe out here now." and then he went straight inside and began to set up shop.

The rest of the drops that Keisha made went by smoothly. Everybody pretty much had the same two concerns. Where Que been; and why they wasn't getting what they normally received? After explaining the same situation over and over, Keisha had her lines memorized. "Look, I know ya'll wondering where Que been at; but he's going to be getting in touch with ya'll soon. So until then, here's a kilo so ya'll can get back to eating until the next shipment comes in."

By the time Keisha made her last drop, she was damn near exhausted. Only being fueled with the excitement of knowing that she had completed her task, energize her enough to make the drive back to Que's house. Once she made it there, she kicked back as if everything she done was apart of her normal routine as she asked Que, "Baby, what you need me to do next?"

Happy to see Keisha return safely, Que said, "Well tomorrow, you can drop off them kilos we still have in the trap house; and spread the word that things are about to get back to normal. Other than that, you can go collect my money from Pee Wee; he still got seven grand for me. Besides that, I don't need for you to do anything until our shipment arrives."

Keisha let out a slight laugh as she replied, "Baby, I thought that you really had something for us to do tomorrow! I already took care of all that. Your money from Pee Wee, I put over there stacked on the dresser." She said as she pointed to it so he could see it.

After Que finally noticed the money stack neatly on his side of the bed on the dresser, Que smiled and then asked, "You didn't have any problems with getting it from him did you?"

As bad as Keisha wanted to tell Que who she had a slight confrontation with, she kept it to herself and replied, "*Naw*; everything went smoothly. I didn't have to ask him for it twice. Being the new Queen Penn and all, I even distributed the kilos we had sitting in the trap house; so everybody good until our shipment gets here. Speaking on our shipment, when will it be here?"

Que laughed and thought to his self, *now it's ours; and she the new Queen Penn!* But told her, "Mrs. Win-Win Queen Penn, it will be here within forty-eight hours." and they called it a night.

Chapter Twenty-Four
(Da Break Down)

$\mathcal{D}$aMesha finally looked at her phone to see thirteen missed calls and seven text messages from two of her friends; one which was LaKetia. The first message she saw read, Mesha, where are you? Are you alright? Then the next few messages were about her house being on fire. That's when DaMesha decided to called LaKetia back and give her a piece of her mind.

The phone bare made a complete ring before LaKetia answered it saying, "Hello Mesha! Thank God you are okay! I just wanted to make sure you and your momma, and everybody else wasn't in there."

"You and Destiny play too damn much! Ya'll need to stop calling and texting my phone like ya'll going crazy while I'm trying to chill with my boo!" DaMesha shot back at her.

"Mesha I wish I was playing; Destiny over here crying thinking you was in there! Don't you hear these damn fire trucks? As a matter of fact, hang up and I'ma send you a picture so you can see we ain't playing!"

"Whatever; girl bye!" A minute after DaMesha hung up, she got a picture message of her house on fire. Once she saw that it wasn't a joke, she jumped up screaming, "Baby, my house on fire! Tez, my house on fire for real; I got'ta get home to see what's going on!"

"Are you sure; or are you playing?" Cortez asked not knowing if she was just trying to trick him.

DaMesha then begin crying and said, "I got'ta check on my momma and brother!" as she tried calling her mother's cellular phone.

When Cortez saw the tears really rolling down DaMesha's cheeks, he knew then that she wasn't bullshitting. He quickly grabbed his car keys and told DaMesha, "Come on so we can find out what's going on!"

On the way there, DaMesha kept trying to call both Barber's and Corey's cellular phones, but they both kept going straight to the voice mail after the first ring. She even tried to call Chicago's phone several times; but got the exact same result. That sent her into a panic mode and she started flipping out. "What the fuck going on? Ain't nobody answering their motherfucking phones; and they all going straight to fucking voice mail! What the fuck?"

"Calm down baby! I'm pretty sure they all are okay! When was the last time you seen any of them?"

"I saw Corey and my momma right before I left; they were pulling up right as I was about to leave. We talked for a few seconds and then they went in the house."

"Okay; have you seen Chicago or got in touch with him yet?"

"Nope; his phone going straight to voice mail too!"

Cortez was flying down streets, running red lights and everything; trying to get to DaMesha's house as fast as he possible could. He tried to contact Chicago a few times as well his self; but he didn't get an answer either. That only made Cortez drive faster; as he bullet his way through intersections. Once they got close to Fairground Park, you could see smoke in the sky coming from about six blocks away. They both knew that whatever that was burning had to be burning bad. DaMesha's face turned astonish before she begin to say a prayer out loud, "God please let my family be okay!" As they turned onto her street and pulled up as close as they could get, DaMesha saw that her mother's car was still parked in the same spot that it was in before she left; and Chicago's new car was parked right in front of their house. All she could say was, "Oh God no; please say it ain't so!"

They jumped out of the car and began asking DaMesha's neighbors it they saw her momma or brother; but everybody kept saying no as they made their way closer to her house. They eventually bumped into LaKetia and Destiny who were still out there recording the house fire as firefighters tried to grain control of it. "I'm so happy you are alright!" Destiny said as soon as DaMesha got close to her and gave her a hug.

DaMesha only response was, "Have either of ya'll seen my momma or brother out here?"

"*Naw*; we ain't seen neither one of them!" replied Destiny.

"Oh no; don't tell me they were at home when all of this started!" LaKetia replied.

As they were talking, Cortez walked over to a group of firefighter and informed them that this was DaMesha's house; and that the rest of her family might still be inside of the burning house. Without wasting another moment, three firefighters stormed into the burning building to search and see if they could find anybody still trapped inside. About fifteen minutes later they all came back out empty handed. DaMesha was standing next to Cortez praying that her mother and brother would just pop up as the firemen walked up to them to break the news of what they discovered.

"Excuse me sir; is this the young woman who stays here?" one of the firemen asked Cortez.

"Yeah!" they both replied at the same time.

"Okay; ma'am, how many people stay here?" the fireman questioned.

"Just me, my momma, my brother, and my momma's boyfriend stay here!"

"Well I'm sorry to have to be the one that tells you this; but we found four bodies in there, and they all are dead!"

DaMesha heart felt like it hit the ground and exploded as she burst out screaming, "God; why you doing this to me? What I do? Why you take them from me? God why? I don't deserve this God!"

Cortez really didn't know how to comfort DaMesha at this point; all he was able to do was hold on to her and tell her, "You got'ta be strong Mesha! I'ma help you get through this; I promise!" other than that, he didn't know what to say or do to calm DaMesha down. He was just as lost as she was.

After awhile went by, a paramedic came to talk to DaMesha. It took her a minute to pull herself together, but she did as the paramedic began to ask her a few questions. "First and foremost, I'm sorry about your losses; but I will try to hurry this up as much as possible. I was told that you and three other people stayed here; is that correct?"

"Yes sir!" DaMesha replied but still not wanting to except the fact of what was going on.

"So it's a good chance that that's your family remains we found in there; but we still have to make sure that that's them. We're going to need you or one of your other family members to come down to the Saint Louis City Morgue located at 1300 Clark Avenue with dental records; because the only way we're going to be able to identify who they are is by their teeth."

"It's that bad?" DaMesha asked as she began to cry again.

"I'm afraid so ma'am; their burnt pretty bad! I wouldn't suggest for you to try to view them today; especially not without someone else who can give you some type of support in case you need it!" the paramedic bluntly said.

As the paramedic was finishing talking, a police officer walked up and asked DaMesha, "Ma'am, may I speak with you for a second?"

"Yes sir!"

"My name is Detective Morgan. I'll be the one handling this investigation. I have a few questions that I would like to ask you; but I know right now probably isn't a real good time to do so. So I'm just going to give you one of my cards, and you can call me whenever you're ready to talk."

"Alright, I will. I'ma let my grandma know what's going on; and then you can speak with the both of us."

Okay that sounds good; just remember the sooner the better." The detective said before turning to leave.

After the detective walked off Cortez said, "Come on baby, we need to go let your granny know what's going on." Even though DaMesha knew that her granny was going to take this news hard; especially after she just lost two grand kids and a daughter, she agreed.

$\mathcal{K}$eniesha was sitting on her porch looking at the Black clouds of smoke in the sky and wondering where the smoke was coming from as Cortez and DaMesha were pulling up to Ms. Rose's house. When they were getting out the car, Keniesha said, "Hey ya'll; what's up?" Then saw DaMesha's eyes were all swollen and watery, and she knew something was wrong. "What's wrong Mesha, baby?" Keniesha asked, "Is everything alright?"

"*Naw* auntie; it's real bad!" Cortez said as he walked up to Keniesha and DaMesha walked up to her grandma's door. "Auntie we just found out her house caught on fire!"

"Oh my God is everybody okay?"

"That's the bad part auntie; I'm afraid not! The firefighters found four bodies in their house."

"Four bodies!" Keniesha repeated. "Oh my God!"

$\mathcal{A}$s Cortez was telling Keniesha what happened, Ms. Ross opened her door to see DaMesha standing there crying. "What's wrong baby? Come in and talk to granny! Why your eyes so puffy? Mesha, girl what you crying about?"

"Granny, I need to talk to you; so come sit down with me!"

"Is it bad? What's going on?" Ms. Rose asked looking DaMesha in her teary eyes.

Reluctantly, DaMesha had to be the one to break the bad news to Ms. Rose. She burst out crying again as she began to tell her what happened.

$\mathcal{A}$s Cortez and Keniesha was outside talking, they heard a loud high pitch scream erupt from Ms. Rose's house causing them to run over there to see what was going on. DaMesha met them at the door screaming hysterically, "Call the ambulance! Something is wrong with my granny! She just fell to the floor holding her chest! Something wrong!"

Wasting no time, Keniesha pulled out her cellular phone and dialed 911 telling them to send an ambulance to Ms. Rose's address immediately. By the time the ambulance got there, it was too late though. Ms. Rose had died on her living room floor from a heart attack.

DaMesha really lost it. Everybody was trying to calm her down but nothing seemed to be working. Eventually the paramedics had to give her a shot of something to sedate her before she had a nervous break down.

*H*ours later, DaMesha woke up inside of Keniesha's house in Keisha's old room. At first she thought that she was still dreaming because she didn't have a clue as to where she was. When she saw Cortez was laying next to her in the bed, she glanced around the room and then realized where she was. At that point, things started coming back to her; and she began back crying. Cortez held and rocked DaMesha as he tried his best to comfort her; but he couldn't possibly understand how DaMesha felt. Here it was she just lost her whole family and everything that she had.

"What am I suppose to do now?" DaMesha asked Cortez. "I don't have any family or anywhere to go now!"

"Yes you do; you have me and my momma! Plus now, you can live with me; and I'm going to take care of you!"

"What about all of my stuff? I lost everything!"

"Anything that was materialistic can be replaced; I got money saved up. I'll buy you anything you want!" Cortez said.

DaMesha was grateful for all of Cortez's willingness to help her, and all the support he was giving her; but reality was strongly sinking in causing DaMesha to turn depressed.

Throughout the night, DaMesha kept thinking about how Chicago would always come through for her when her momma would tell her no on certain stuff. She also reminisced about going to all of Corey's fights; and how excited he was when he won the Golden Gloves Tournament. Most of all, she remember the good times her momma and her had together; but the main thing that stuck in her mind, was the fact that the last words her momma told her was I love you. When she thought about her granny, all of her good memories quickly faded away as she replayed her granny falling to the floor and dying right in front of her. That imaged along caused her to breakdown again and cry throughout the rest of the night.

Chapter Twenty-Five
(Spread Da Word)

*A*lthough Keisha really didn't know DaMesha and her family that well, to help DaMesha feel as if she was accepted as part of her family since she was dating Cortez, Keisha paid for all of her family funeral arrangements. She even went out and brought her a new wardrobe to try to ease her mind of the fact that she lost everything as she continue conducting business for Que in the streets.

Impressed by the way Keisha took the initiative to step up and claim Queen Penn as her title in the streets as she played her part in making sure everything was handled in an accordance manner, Que tried to match her eagle determination in his new position as a worker breaking down kilos. Que felt awkward at first; but he still wasn't ready to let anybody see him in a wheelchair that worked for him as he tired to regain his walking ability back, so he stayed low key.

*M*eanwhile, Keisha was becoming known as the Queen Penn title that she gave herself as she made drop after drop daily and collected the pick up money herself. Motherfuckers knew not to play with her when she came through taking care of business unless they wanted to see the bitch side of her come out on the spot. In which in that case, if you fell in that category, she was exposing and talking bad to you in front of whomever to get her point across that she wasn't taking shit off of nobody; but every now and then you would still have a stupid son-of-a-bitch that would press her button trying to be on some slick shit, and today it just so happen to be Tweezy.

Feed up with Keisha treating him like he was just another worker even when other people was around that didn't have anything to do with their business and not getting promoted to being the new boss since Que haven't been showing his face around, Tweezy clicked. "Why the fuck you always trying to put somebody on blast when you come around here?"
"I wouldn't be putting you on blast if you didn't act like rules didn't apply to you; but every time I come through this hot ass motherfucker, you be on some bullshit! Like you running shit and I work for you."

"See that's your motherfucking problem; bitch, I am running shit around here!"

"Bitch!" Keisha snapped in outrage. "Who the fuck are you calling a bitch? You got me fucked up!"

"*Naw*, you got me fucked up if you thought for one motherfucking second I was gone follow some bullshit ass rules you trying to make a nigga' like me follow!" Tweezy said while looking around making sure nobody was out witnessing their confrontation before he snatched his pistol from under his shirt and commenced to smacking Keisha with it until she blacked out.

When Keisha woke up, she didn't have the slightest clue as to where she was, nor what happen as she felt someone forcefully enter her rectum causing her to let out a scream of pain as she tried to wiggle herself free. "Bitch shut up; don't scream now!" Tweezy said as he shoved her swollen bloody face down into the pissy smelling mattress as he continue ramming his dick in her ass until she lost control of her bowels and began bleeding.

"Please stop!" Keisha pleaded in pain and tears trying to figure out how she ended up in this situation; and how she was going to get out.

"Please stop!" Tweezy mocked Keisha. "You nasty trifling bitch; you still think you running shit? And here it is you can't even control your own got damn bowels!" He said as he smacked her out of the bed sending her crashing face first into the floor. "Didn't I tell you, I'm running shit? Get your ass up and go in the bathroom." He ordered while kicking her across the floor while she scrambled trying to get out of the way and onto her feet.

As Keisha made it to the bathroom, she desperately hoped that she would find anything that she could use as a weapon as she quickly scanned the small confinements of the bathroom through her almost swollen shut eyes. Shit out of luck and nervous as hell, the only words Keisha could get to come out of her busted mouth was, "Please don't hurt me!" between sobs of tears followed by her stuttering, "I-I-I have to use the bathroom!" hoping Tweezy would give her a moment of privacy so she could try her last option and search the medicine cabinet in hope of finding anything that she could use against him.

Unfortunately, Keisha didn't get that break. Instead, Tweezy added more insults to her injuries; and embarrassed her even more. "Now bitch you want to st-st-stutter; and fucking use the bathroom! Bitch, ain't it too fucking late for that? You already shitted on me!" Not waiting on Keisha to respond back, Tweezy continued, "I tell you what, I'ma let you use the bathroom; but don't flush the toilet, so I can make sure you really had to use it. Let me find out you bullshitting, and we going to have a real long motherfucking night hoe! Do I make my motherfucking self clear?" Nodding her head in agreement, Keisha just stood there staring at Tweezy until he snapped again. "Bitch what the fuck are you waiting on; Christmas?"

"I-I-I was waiting on you-you to get out!"

"Get out! I ain't going no fucking where! You better get to using the bathroom while I'm letting you; before I change my motherfucking mind!"

Keisha knew she was in trouble as she nervously sat on the old dirty toilet trying to force herself to use the bathroom by any means; but the longer Tweezy stared at her, the more nervous she became making it harder for her to even release her bladder. Keisha didn't know what to do or think as she began to fear for her life. Just then, she began to release a few drops of piss as Tweezy stepped in front of her and got ready to say something. "I'm using it! I'm using it!" Keisha repeated herself petrified of what Tweezy was about to do to her.

Looking down at Keisha while hearing what sounded like only a couple of sprinkles of water hitting the water inside of the toilet already, Tweezy thought to his self, *Out of all of the shit this bitch talk, I wonder if she even can suck a dick right!* Pondering on that thought, Tweezy grabbed a handful of Keisha's hair and wrapped it around his hand; while with his other hand, he placed his pistol against her temple and said, "Now as big as your mouth is and as much shit that comes out of it, you better have a fire as head game! But bitch if you bit me or even let your teeth graze my shit just once or the slightest bit, you ain't gone have to worry about spreading the word of you being the new Queen Penn! You gone be known as the new Gum Queen; because I promise you, I'ma knock every last one of your motherfucking teeth out of your mouth! Now open up!" he said jamming his dick in Keisha's mouth and down her throat causing her to gag until she vomit.

As Keisha began to throw up, she knew she had fucked up the moment she felt her top teeth scrap against Tweezy's dick which caused his natural nerve reflexes to jump squeezing the trigger. *Boom!* Blood flew across the bathroom sink and mirror. As soon as Tweezy finished unwrapping Keisha's hair from around his hand, she slumped over hitting her head on the edge of the tub before coming to a rest on the floor.

Tweezy then said out loud but to his self, "Damn, I didn't mean to shot this bitch; at least not yet! I had more plans for her." as he walked out of the bathroom and back into the bedroom to get dress.

Once Tweezy was dressed, he left out of the old run down abandon motel room and jumped into Keisha's Range Rover as if nothing ever happen as he pulled off. Not wanting to drive the noticeable vehicle anywhere near his neighborhood or side of town, Tweezy decided to drive it over to the south side. When he reached Spring and Delor Avenue, he pulled onto the parking lot in front of their neighborhood liquor store and let down all of the windows halfway. Right before he exit the still running vehicular, he grabbed the Black Louis Vuitton duffel bag containing all of the kilos Keisha was suppose to have dropped off that day.

As Tweezy walked away from the running Range Rover, he knew it wouldn't be long before somebody would decide to jump into it and pull off. Laughing at the thought to his self, he then thought, *Yeah pretty soon somebody gone have to spread the word that since the new Queen Penn out of the picture, I'm the new Boss!*

Chapter Twenty-Six
(Moving On)

*A*while had went by and DaMesha was doing a good job at getting over the fact that her whole family had past. It took her awhile; but slowly she stopped crying about it everyday. Keisha would call and check on her everyday to make sure she was mentally holding it together. While Cortez did his best to keep her mind off of everything that had happened altogether.

One morning, DaMesha just woke up feeling different altogether. She had started growing accustom to the feeling of waking up missing her family; but this morning she didn't get that type of feeling at all. Instead, she awoke feeling as if her whole family had just sent her a blessing to ease her mind and heart. She felt like they all had spoken to her and told her what they each expected out of her so she could move on.

DaMesha kept it in her mind that she knew what her mother's expectation was for her; and she planned on making her mother proud of her even though she wasn't physically present anymore. Barber use to always tell her children to graduate from high school, and they could be whatever they wanted to be in life; and DaMesha was almost finished with high school now, and planned on going to a local college to become a register nurse.

On a few different occasions, DaMesha still tried to piece together what actually happen; but she had just about giving up on trying to figure it out. The one thing that she didn't give up on trying to figure out though was whom the fourth person was that died in her house; which still haven't been identified.

*C*ortez, on the other hand, was happy about seeing DaMesha trying to get back to her normal self; but he too had something racking his brain. Cortez wanted to know why everybody had gotten shot in the head execution style and burnt. He had his own speculations, but he couldn't prove what he thought. Cortez just wanted to know if this was about the dope that Chicago and him had came up on, then now who had the rest of the dope that Chicago had stashed away at home. It was a few unanswered questions out there that was just mind troubling and needed answered; but so far nobody had any answers, and Cortez wanted answers. He wanted to know who was behind this tragedy; and who actually did it.

With DaMesha doing so much better, Cortez figured he could go for a ride alone to get any information that he could get from the streets. He knew one thing for sure; and two things for certain. The streets talked; and it was only a matter of time before he would find out who actually did it. So when they made it home from school, Cortez told DaMesha he was about to make a few moves. "Baby, I'm about to go handle some business right quick; I won't be long at all! I'll grab us a movie to watch while I'm out. Do you want me to grab something to eat while I'm out as well?"

"*Naw*, I'ma cook today! What do you want; chicken or cheese burgers?"

"Cook the chicken!" Cortez answered.

"Okay, I'll call you when I'm almost done cooking. Just hurry up and take care of whatever it is that you need too, so you can hurry up and make it back home! Oh yeah baby, try to get the movie Avator; I wan'na see that tonight if you don't mind!"

"I know what you are talking about; the movie with the blue people in it. I wan'na see that too."

On the way out the door Cortez gave DaMesha a kiss and grabbed the keys to his Impala. Once he hit Fairgound Park, he noticed a few faces that he knew through Chicago. When he pulled up, he bumped into a hustler named Frank. Frank was one of the few hustlers that Chicago would sell ounces too. "Frank, what's good? Come holla' at me real quick!" Cortez requested.

"What's been up with you Tez? How you been living?"

"I been alright;" Cortez said as he lit up a blunt, "but I could be better! I know you heard about Chicago, and what the fuck happened!" Cortez said as he passed the blunt to Frank.

"I seen that shit on the news the day it happened, but at first I didn't know that was him. That was some fucked up shit that went down! They didn't deserve that shit at all!"

"I know; I been kind of fucked up about it for a minute!"

"It's crazy *cuzz* we were all just up here at the park earlier that day shooting dice, and Chicago stung all our asses and then slid out!"

"Who was all up here?"

"You know I smoke so much I don't remember everybody that was here; but I know Feeva was up here because Chicago hit him the hardest. Oh yeah, Chris was up here too now that I'm thinking about it. Chicago was talking so much shit to them as he was stinging their ass, that Feeva and Chris both quit and slid out together."

"I ain't seen neither one of them in a minute; when was the last time you seen them niggas'?"

"I ain't seen Chris since that day; I feel like he dodging me! I swung by his crib a few times to get some money he owes me, and his girl keep telling me some bullshit about she ain't seen him and he ain't welcome back there no more too keep me from coming over there if you ask me! But sooner or later, he gone bump heads with me! I saw Feeva yesterday. He got some fire ass dope; and the streets loving it! His shit so fire, that I had to buy a few ounces from him myself; but that motherfucker taxing!"

"What he charging for an ounce?"

"He wants twelve hundred; and he standing on it! He ain't trying to will or deal in no kind of way!"

"Straight up; well take my number down and fuck with me next time! I'll get you right for a thousand whenever you ready. You the only motherfucker out here that I trust fucking with this shit; so don't send anybody at me for nothing. Now on the other hand, if you know somebody trying to get right, you can tell them you got it and charge 'em twelve hundred; that way you can make two hundred off the top."

"I'm down with that shit too!" Frank said as he programmed Cortez's phone number in his phone. "Alright lil bruh, I got'ta get out of here so I can get my kids from daycare; but know that I should be calling you tomorrow for a few of those thangs!"

After Frank got out of the car, Cortez didn't even bother to go holla' at the rest of the folks that he knew in the park; besides he didn't know them or fuck with them like he did Frank. Feeva and the rest of the cats that hung out in the park only brought grams; so he didn't care to get to know them personally. He only knew who and what Feeva looked like because he was consistent; and damn near every time he rode with Chicago Feeva would call to re-up.

Cortez bent a few more corners and bumped into one of his classmates that he was cool with name Rasheed. Rasheed was a hustler at heart. He would sell you your own shit; if you gave him a chance to speak to you long enough. "Rasheed, what's cracking over here?" Cortez asked as he pulled up on him.

"Shit!" Rasheed replied as he bent over to look inside of Cortez's car from the passenger side window. "I'm just out here taking all these non hustlering ass motherfuckers sales. I got that A-1-YOLO!"

"Man whatever bruh! So you got that A-1-Yolo now? Where you get it from?"

"I got it from the big homie; Feeva!"

"Feeva!" Cotez replied as if he was shocked.

"Yeah; you know Feeva from the Dub! That nigga' over there off of East John Avenue booming!"

"Oh yeah; he can't be booming too hard over there!"

"I'll be shit if he ain't! That nigga' got whatever you need on that white girl tip; and he just coped the new F-150 truck, and put 28"s on that motherfucker already!"

"So you telling me that he came up over night huh?"

"I don't know; but I guess so! What I do know though, is that motherfuckering all candy brown F-150 killing shit! He straight shitting on the whip game right now!"

"That's cool," Cortez said, "but you seen what all I got; he ain't fucking with me when it comes to these whips! Anyway, I'm about to get out of here though. I'll see you at school tomorrow. Keep your head up!"

Cortez pulled off not giving a fuck about Feeva having a new truck; he felt like he had gotten enough information on him for one day so he decided to just go get the movie and head home. When he pulled up to Wal-Greens to rent a movie from the Red Box he saw Sam, the one who had sold him the Impala. "What's up Sam?" Cortez spoke as Sam headed in his direction looking at his old car.

"What's up bruh? How are you doing?" Sam replied, "I see you got the car still looking good!"

"I'm good; and the whip always going to look good!" Cortez said as they both smiled. "Did you hear about what happened to Chicago?"

"Yeah; I can't believe that shit!"

"Me neither; my momma end up paying for their funerals and everything."

"That's whats up! But check this out, I'm kind of in a rush right now; but you know where I'm at. Come fuck with me some time when you around my way; and tell DaMesha I said I got her in my prayers!" Sam said as he ran to his car; jumped in, and then pulled off. After Sam pulled off of the parking lot, Cortez proceeded to get the movie DaMesha requested; and then headed back home.

While driving from Wal-Greens Cortez all of a sudden thought to his self and said out loud, *hold the fuck up; Feeva was just selling grams a few weeks ago! Now you telling me he have whatever the fuck a motherfucker want! Let me find out he robbed and killed Chicago and 'em; and got our dope, and he one dead motherfucker on everythang!*

Cortez got back to the house before DaMesha could even call and tell him that she was ready for him to head back home. DaMesha finished making dinner, and they watched the movie that Cortez went and picked up and chill the rest of the day.

The following day, DaMesha got a phone call in the middle of class from an unfamiliar phone number. As her phone continued to viberate on her hip, DaMesha couldn't help wondering who it was as she raised her hand and asked to go to the restroom. When she made it to the restroom, she called the unfamiliar phone number back. After two rings she heard a white man's voice on the other end answer, "Hello, thank you for calling State Farm Insurance Company; how may I help you?"

"Yes, my name is DaMesha Smith and someone just called me from this number just a minute ago."

"Okay ma'am; can you hold on for one moment please?" the State Farm agent replied.

"I sure can!" DaMesha ansered as she thought to herself, *what the fuck does State Farm want with me? This has to be a fuck up.*

A moment later another State Farm agent came to the phone sounding happy to be speaking to DaMesha as he said, "Hello Ms. Smith; are you still there?"

"Yes sir, I'm still here."

"How are you doing Ms. Smith? My name is Justin Case; and I'm an insurance agent here at State Farm. I'm calling you because a Mrs. Rosemary Smith had a Home Owner's Insurance policy with us; and it seems that Mrs. Rosemary has recently passed away. From our records I can also see that it shows her husband, as well as her two daughters has also passed away too. Does this sound about right to you; or are our records inaccurate?"

"Yes, your records are correct." DaMesha said regretting thinking about her deceased relatives.

"Before I go any further, can you state your whole name for the record?"

"My name is DaMesha Machele Smith."

"Well you're definitely the person I was trying to contact according to our records, if everything you say is true; but let me jump straight to the reason why I'm calling you. With the passing of Mrs. Rosemary, her husband, and both of her daughters, you have become the sole owner of her property according to her policy; and we here at State Farm wanted to know if you would like to continue on with the Home Owner's Insurance plan Mrs. Rosemary had established?"

"Well right now I'm at school, and it's really not a good time for me to discuss this properly with you. Can I possible call you back when I have a lil' more free time?"

"Yes ma'am! Any time that's good for you, is good for me. I'm just about always here! We're open Monday through Saturday, from seven to seven; so feel free to call whenever you're ready Ms. Smith! I'll talk to you later."

"Okay Mr. Case, I'll be sure to call you back soon." DaMesha said before hanging up and going back to class.

*M*eanwhile, Cortez got a text message from Frank about buying three ounces of dope. Cortez immediately texted back in the middle of class telling Frank to give him about an hour and a half and he'll make it worth the while. After getting the text message back, Frank decided to wait and give Cortez a chance just so he could see if his dope was any better than Feeva's. Once Cortez got the text message back stating that Frank would wait, Cortez knew he couldn't waste any time after school.

After school, Cortez hurried DaMesha home. Cortez made the ride so quickly but calmly, that it made DaMesha get side tracked; tripping off of the rate of speed Cortez was driving. She straight forgot to mention Justin Case calling about the insurance policies.

When they made it home, Cortez ran up upstairs to his stash for the three ounces; and back down the steps. Without breaking his strive, he said in between breaths, "I'll be right back baby! I got'ta make a run real quick." and walked clean out the door.

Cortez met Frank in front of Ali's store in no time to make the transaction. "I put a few extra grams in here for the wait." Cortez said handling Frank the package as he got inside his car.

"Right on lil' bruh! I got a few moves I got'ta make right quick and got motherfuckers waiting on me; so I'll get at you later. I might be calling you right back if my cousin ain't bullshitting!"

"I-ight, just call me!" Cortez said as Frank got out his car; jumped into his own, and pulled off.

*B*ack at home, DaMesha got a phone call from Detective Morgan. "Hello; may I please speak to Ms. Smith?"

"This is she." DaMesha replied.

"Hello Ms. Smith; this is Detective Morgan. Do you have a minute so we can talk?"

"Yes I do. What's going on?"

"Well Ms. Smith, I was calling to let you know that we have finally identified whom the forth person was that was found in your home. Does the name Christopher Collins ring a bell to you at all?"

"No sir, I'm afraid not! Is it supposed too?"

"Well everybody calls him Chris on the streets! His last known address was 4154 Farlin Avenue. Does he ring a bell to you now?"

"Nope, I still don't know a Chris or Christapher that comes over to our house that I can think of!"

"Well I just wanted to get a lead; and keep you updated on our findings. If you get any information on whom this Christapher Collins a.k.a. Chris charater is or why he would be at your house, please feel free to call and inform me."

"I will do." DaMesha said and then hung up.

On the inside, DaMesha was puzzled as to who this Chris guy was. She just figured at this point what was done, was done. She had to move forward in order to get this behind her; but she still would run it by Cortez to see if he had an ideal of whom this Chris fellow might be before she would just leave it alone.

Cortez walked back through the door about thirty minutes after the detective had called. DaMesha was ready to sit Cortez down and tell him about all the news she had gotten. "Baby, sit down so I can tell you about these phone calls I've gotten today!" DaMesha smoothly but kind of anxiously said.

When Cortez finally sat down, DaMesha began telling him all about the phone call that she had gotten from the State Farm Insurance agent; and how they indicated to her that she is now the sole owner of her grandmother's old house, and wanted to know if she wanted to keep the same policy that her grandmother originally started. But with neither one of them knowing anything about insurance company policies, they both were clueless as to what to choose. With both of them being clueless DaMesha thought to call Keisha and ask her, her opinion on the situation before she blurted out, "Damn baby, when was the last time you talked to your momma; because she haven't called me in a few days?"

"I ain't talked to her in a few days myself."

"Well, I fin'na call her to see if she can help me out on what's going on with this house stuff."

"Don't call her; I have a better ideal! Lets just pop up on them! Besides, you haven't seen their new house yet anyway. You wan'na go? I know you going to love their house."

"Okay; let's go." DaMesha said, "I wan'na get out the house anyway."

They jumped on the highway and made it to Que's house with no problems; but on the way there though, DaMesha asked Cortez about the Christapher Collins guy the detective told her about. "Yeah, his name is Christapher Collins; but everybody supposed to call him Chris from what the detective say. He said that he was from off of Farlin Avenue."

When DaMesha said that he was from Farlin Avenue, Cortez knew exactly who she was talking about. He was sure he knew who killed DaMesha's family now. Feeva! Cortez put two and two together and instantly got pissed the fuck off; but he didn't let it show in none of his actions or expressions. He figured DaMesha was better off kept in the dark on about what he now knew; so he said, "I don't know no Chris that ya'll would now."

Pulling into Que's driveway, DaMesha said, "*DAMN*! Yeah, Que gots'ta be rich!"

"That's the same thing I first thought when I first seen this place and found out it was his." Cortez replied as he knocked on the door.

A servent quickly answered the knock. When Cortez said his name, the butler instantly knew who he was from a conversation that Que, Keisha, and him previously had; so he opened the door to allow him access as he said, "How do you do sir and Ms.?" stepping to the side.

"We good; but who are you? And where is my momma and Que at?" Cortez asked.

"Well my name is Jamar and I'm your butler. If there's anything you need done, please just let me know!"

"*DAMN*; they have a butler too!" DaMesha said.

"I guess so." Cortez replied before he asked Jamar, "So do you cook too?"

"No sir, I don't cook. There's a chef for that. Her name is Ms. Ann; and she's the best cook ever. She will be here to prepare shrimp pasta tonight. Will you all be staying for dinner?"

"Yes sir we will be Mr. Jamar; now if you will excuse me, I'm about to go up to my room. Come on Mesha."

As they stopped at the elevator door, DaMesha burst out and said, "What the fuck; they got a motherfucking elevator in here too!"

"*Yop*; but you ain't seen nothing yet. We fin'na let my momma and Que know that we're here; and then I'll show you the house."

Once they made it to the third floor where Que and Keisha was, Cortez got the shock of his life.

Chapter Twenty-Seven
(Honor Da Game)

*O*nce Cortez stepped in Keisha and Que's room and saw his mother's face, his heart dropped. He was ready to kill as he pulled his Glock-40 off his hip. Everybody went into shock when they saw Cortez pull out his gun. "Momma, what happened to you?" Cortez ferociously asked.

Keisha had two Black eyes, and one was swollen shut; which looked horrible on her due to the fact that she was light skinned. She also had bandges on both sides of her jaws; with her mouth wired shut from the gun shot wound Tweezy had inflicted on her. Keisha lost three teeth as well from the gun shot; and had a big gash on forehead from hitting her head on the edge of the tub after Tweezy had shot her. She was also suffering from two broken ribs.

Keisha was all fucked up; and Cortez wanted answers as he repeated, "Momma, what happen to you? Who did this to you?" but she couldn't replied through her own sobs. Cortez looked at Que with death in his eyes as he snapped, "Nigga', you put your motherfucking hands on my momma!" and turned his aim for Que's head.

Keisha jumped up mumbling, "Un-un! Un-un!" through the wires that held her mouth shut as she flaged her hands for Cortez to stop and put the gun down. But Cortez wasn't trying to hear nothing as tears began to well in his eyes. He was about to let Que feel his flesh be rearrange by the slugs in his Glock-40; before Keisha started running towards him to get the gun out of his hands.

Cortez brushed right pass Keisha though, and made his way to Que as he laid helpless in the bed. "What the fuck did you do to my momma?" Cortez asked with his gun barrel now touching Que's tempo.

"It's not what you think it is Cortez; I didn't touch her! I swear I didn't! I would never put my hands on her; I love your momma too much! Put the gun down and talk to me man to man; right now you gunning for the wrong person!"

"Tez! Baby, your momma trying to stop you; and get you to put the gun down too! She's trying to say something! Baby put the gun down; and see what they got'ta say at least!" DaMesha said trying to stop the situation from escalating out of control.

When Cortez turned his head and saw his mother shaking her head yes to what DaMesha was saying as DaMesha held her back, he lowered the gun from Que's tempo. Cortez was pissed to the maximum; but he was ready to hear what Que had to say. "Okay; I'm listening." Cortez said with the gun still in his hand. "Talk nigga'!"

"I-ight; it's all my fault!" Que said feeling responsible and the most guilties out of the entire room.

"What the fuck you mean it's your fault nigga'? I thought you just said you didn't do it!"

"Add I didn't! Just hear me out. I'ma real nigga'; and I'ma honor the game and tell you everything from the top so we don't get any future misunderstandings! I have been selling dope almost all my life; that's how I got where I am today. I own quite a few pieces of property; and I have ownership in quite a few establishments. I have ownership in the Royle Palace on Natural Bridge; which is there, where I meet your mother at. We clicked from day one; and I knew she was different, and someone I could trust. We went on a date once or twice; and then I put her on my pay roll, and in that Rover."

"What the fuck does that have to do with what happen to my motherfucking momma? All you telling me is that she have been working for you this whole fucking time we been up here; doing God knows what, to end up like this!" Cortez snapped trying his best to reason with Que.

"It's not like you thinking Tez! Now I'm being real with you; so try to understand where I'm coming from! I first started your momma off breaking kilos down at this trap spot I had fixed up just for her; but your mother showed me that she is so loyal, that I fell in love with her! I wanted to get to know her better; and get a chance to meet and know you too! I gave her the house you and Mesha staying in right now. Everything was going smooth until the accident. I took a nice hit as far as cash goes. Between the car and the cash I had inside it, I lost a million dollars easily! So yeah, being the hustler that I am, I felt like I needed to get my money back! Now selling dope is all I really know; I've been doing it since I was in the eighth grade. This is why I say it's all my fault! After the accident, when your momma got me here, she tried to talk me out of the game; but instead, I wouldn't listen! I talked her into switching positions with me; so I'm now breaking down the kilos, while she make all the drops and collect the money!"

"So you had my momma selling dope; what were you thinking Que? She could've been killed!"

"I know; but I thought that everything was cool because I only had her dealing with a handful of people that I trust. These are people that I've been dealing with for years. Two days ago though, she went to make a few drops and didn't come back home; and then I got a phone call saying she was almost killed. I've been trying to put everything together, but she won't tell me what happened and its confussing me! I don't know if it was one of my people, or if she tried to do some kind of side hustler or what!"

"Momma, why in the hell you ain't telling him what happened; or did he do this to you?" Cortez replied staring at Keisha waiting on some kind of expernation before he continued, "Whoever did this to you could have killed you; and you trying to keep it from us! Who are you trying to protect; and why?"

Keisha shook her head in a no gesture. She then went and grabbed her tablet to type and tell Cortez that she wasn't protecting anybody. When Cortez read what she wrote on the tablet, he angrily said, "How you not protecting anybody when you ain't telling us nothing? I know you know who did this to you! You know what though, if you don't tell us what happened to you, you ain't going to have to worry about telling me nothing else because I ain't gone deal with you no more. I don't care if you are my momma or not!"

Keisha began to cry as she started to type out what happened to her.

I went to drop Tweezy his package off and we got into it because he always have me waiting around ten to fifteen minutes; so I confronted him about it. That's when the argument started. He started telling me that he was supposed to be the next in charge; and that I wasn't shit! That's when I went off on him; and before I knew it, he started hitting me in the head with his gun. I don't even remember blacking out; but at some point I went unconscience. The next thing I know, I wake up to him raping me!

Keisha quickly had a flash back of being violated. It was bad enough knowing what happened, but having to tell her son and Que as well caused Keisha to start crying even more as she continued to type.

I couldn't get him off of me; but I tried! I tried so much that he got mad at me for resisting, and started beating me again! When he finished beating on me this ttime, he order me to go in the bathroom; where he forced me to perform oral sex on him until I threw up! And that's when he shot me! I don't remember anything else! I don't know what he did with the truck or the dope! I

*going to hurt you ten times more than what you already are! And, I can't lose
another baby!*

After they both finished reading what Keisha typed, she got her tablet
back; and quickly typed a message for Que to read before she slowly handed it
back to him. As Que began to read the tablet, Keisha grabbed ahold of
DaMesha's hand and led them to the elevator to go down stairs so Que and
Cortez could read her confessions in private. Feeling embarrassed enough
already, Keisha didn't want DaMesha to hear all of the details of what she just
experienced. She also didn't want to witness the looks on Cortez's and Que's
faces; when they discovered what all took place.

Que read Keisha's confession out loud. It had him and Cortez
devastated hearing what all Keisha went through. When he got to the part
about her losing another baby, he asked Cortez, "How many slibings have you
lost?"

"None; my momma ain't never had no other kids!" Cortez replied
looking at Que like where the fuck did that come from; but it was right at that
momemt that it clicked to Que and Cortez both.

When Keisha said that she couldn't lose another baby that was her
way of revealing to Cortez and Que at the same time that she was pregnant;
but she had lost her baby.

Chapter Twenty-Eight
(Deadly Revenge)

*F*ueled by a new hatred, Cortez felt like he just needed to get away and collect his thoughts. He just couldn't believe how someone violated his mother. Not only did this Tweezy character beat and rape his mother, but he left her for dead inside of an old rundown motel as well. This nigga' Tweezy even caused her to have a miscarriage; when all of Cortez's life he dreamed of having a sister or brother that he could grow up with. But now, this motherfucker they call Tweezy, than killed that dream of Cortez's; and Cortez wanted revenge. Deadly revenge!

Kissing Keisha on the forehead as he fought back the tears that wanted to freely fall from his eyes, Cortez told his momma, "I love you!" and then turned to look Que in the eyes and said, "I'll be in touch with you." before he grabbed DaMesha's hand to leave.

For the first time in a long time, it was an awkward silence between DaMesha and Cortez. They didn't even have the radio on as they drove down the highway in complete shock of learning what had done transpired. While both of their minds were wondering what was going to take place, DaMesha remembered she had a blunt in her purse already rolled up. Without saying a word, she pulled it out and sparked it up. While passing the blunt back and forth, DaMesha tried to break the silence by saying, "Tez, baby talk to me! Tell me what's going on in your mind because I can't imagine how you are feeling and I know you are hurt."

Hurt wasn't the right words to decrible how Cortez was feeling as he kept picturing the damage that was done to his mother. "I need a drink!"

Cortez finally replied, but that was it. His mind was too far gone to say anything else.

"Okay then; lets go to Ali's store because that's the only place I know that will sell us liquor." DaMesha said.

Cortez didn't respond what so ever; he just drove straight to Ali's store like DaMesha said. While riding through the neighborhood, Cortez quickly remembered that Feeva was on his shit list too; but he figured Feeva could wait for now, because he now wanted Tweezy's head before he did anything else.

"What kind of liquor do you want; Ciroc?" DaMesha asked exiting the car headed in the store.

"*Naw*; get a fifth of 1800!" Cortez responded. While DaMesha was in the store, Cortez set in the car full of rage. He was ready to kill the whole city if that's what it took to get to Tweezy. "Oh yeah, you're dead nigga'!" Cortez said out loud to his self before DaMesha came back out with a fifth of 1800 and a bottle of orange juice. As she attempted to open the passenger door, Cortez said, "Hold up baby; you drive! I'm so pissed right now I can't focus and think straight!"

DaMesha got them home safely. As soon as they got there, Cortez stormed up the steps and opened the door. He sat around for awhile drinking and thinking about his next move, but didn't say anything out loud. After awhile that's when DaMesha sat next to him and tried to get him to talk. "Baby, I know that you are upset; but I need for you to tell me where your head is at! Talk to me please!"

"Okay; you really want to know what I'm thinking! I'm thinking about how much I really want to kill this bitch ass motherfucker Tweezy! I got to kill 'em! He can't live to tell the story of what he did!"

"Are you really sure that's what you wan'na do? You sure you just don't wan'na let Que handle it?"

"Am I sure? I'm dead serious! I'm positive, that this is what I wan'na do! As for letting Que handle this, this is my momma they done fucked with; and they got me fucked up! I already got my mind made up, so it ain't no need to try to stop me; because and I ain't changing it!"

"I'm not going to try to stop you because I'd be ready to do the same thing if I was you. Infact, I stand behind you one hundred percent on this. I just don't want anything to go wrong. Tez if I was to lose you, I'll go crazy! So if you do decide to do it, just please be careful and make back home to me!" DaMesha said looking Cortez directly in the eyes.

"Nothing is going to go wrong! Tweezy motherfucker ass ain't even going to know what hit 'em when I'm finished; and I promise to make it home in one piece!" Cortez said as he stood up and kissed DaMesha on her forehead. He then pulled out his phone and called Que for the information that he needed on Tweezy.

"Hello; I've been waiting on your call." Que said, "I wan'na let you know that I got everything under control; so you don't have to worry about anything!"

"Well I'm calling to tell you that I ain't worried about anything; I just need that information on Tweezy, because I want to be the one that kill him!" Cortez replied.

"I got" Que began before Cortez cut him off saying.

"My daddy always told me that if you want something done right, then do it yourself! That's my damn momma; ant I wan'na kill 'em! I wan'na finish this shit; and I ain't taking no for an answer!" Cortez said pointing his finger as if Que was in front of him.

"I-ight, I guess I have to honor that; but let me let you know that I ain't sending you alone on this type of mission. You are going to have my partner, Pee Wee, with you."

"Que I said I want wan'na do this!" Cortez argued.

"And you can! You can pull the trigger if that's what you want to do; but Pee Wee going to be there to watch your back. I can't have shit happen to you; or your mother would kill me, and you know this!"

"I-ight, I'm cool with that! When can I get the nigga'?"

"When will you be ready?" Que asked.

"I'm ready now; the sooner the better!"

"*Naw*, not tonight; but ya'll can take care of him tomorrow night for sure. I want you to come over tomorrow, so I can hit you up with the plan. Also bring Mesha with you, so your mother can have somebody to chill with; because your auntie doesn't know what's going on, and your momma don't want her too. So don't tell her."

"I-ight, I won't. We'll be there tomorrow at seven o'clock."

"Good, because my therapist comes at four o'clock; and leaves at six."

"Okay, I'll see you then." Cortez said as he hung up the phone kind of relieved a little; at the thought of sweet deadly revenge.

Cortez and DaMesha continued to drink the night away until they both passed out.

*A*t seven o'clock the next day, Cortez was at Que's house ready for war. That's when he met Pee Wee; and Que told them the plan. "Now I had my people hunt the dumb ass nigga' down last night; and put a GPS under his car. I've been tracking his every move all day. His stupid ass is still in Saint Louis! I guess he think that he can't be found in South County. He's in Lemay, right off of Broadway; on a street called West Ripa Avenue. He's been ripping and running all day; but he's been coming back to this one particular location. So I made a few calls and got in touch with one of my Caucasian friends!"

MY HEART TURNED COLD

"One of your Caucasian friends!" Cortez interrupted

"Yeah, his name Josh; and he own a few houses out there on Clyde Avenue in which West Ripa Avenue runs into."

"I know about where that is." Pee Wee chipped in.

"Good, but anyway; I want you to walk right up on 'em Tez and tazer the shit out of 'em when you see 'em coming out the house or getting out his car! Pee Wee, once Cortez get his ass down you need to pull right in front of his car and park. Ya'll get the keys to his car and throw him in the trunk. When ya'll get his ass, call Josh so he can meet ya'll and take ya'll to the house on Clyde."

"Why we taking him to a house; and you sure we can trust this white boy?" Cortez asked.

"The house is for ya'll can have some privacy. That way ya'll can take ya'll time with him, and do whatever ya'll want to him; and don't have to rush. As for as trusting Josh, out of twenty plus years, Josh the only white person I've put it down with on several different occasions like this; and he ain't never said shit! I trust him more than I trust a lot of these motherfuckers that I deal with on the daily! Anyway, I've already paid him to get rid of the body when ya'll get finished with him. Ya'll going to have tarps and everything already there. I had Jamar run to Home Depot to grab ya'll a few tools. So far ya'll have: a hammer, a crow bar, a portable torch, a big ass knife, and a few more tarps just in case ya'll need them. I want ya'll to make him suffer for what he did! Tez, do you think you can stomach this kind of shit?"

"I don't think; I know that I can!" Cortez replied proudly.

"So do ya'll think this will work?" Que finally asked giving each Pee Wee and Cortez a chance to add in they own personal input.

"We gone make it work!" Cortez said.

"Yeah, like lil' bruh said, we'll make it work! You already know how I get down!" Pee Wee said rubbing his hands together.

"Okay then. I want ya'll to take this tablet and follow him until ya'll can get 'em!" Que replied as he handed Pee Wee the tablet with the GPS loaded on the screen already showing them exactly where Tweezy was parked. "Ya'll ain't got to rush this shit; so take ya'll time, and do it right!"

"I got you Que!" Pee Wee said, "Come on Tez, let's ride out!"

Once they loaded all the tools in the car, they jumped on the highway going south headed straight for West Ripa Avenue; since that's where the blinking dot on the tablet GPS locator screen was leading them too. As they got closer to the dot, it began to move again. "Hold on, he's on the move right now!" Cortez said to Pee Wee interrupting their conversation on getting to know each other.

Pee Wee quickly grabbed the tablet and studied where he was going before he replied anything. "It's okay; he still moving around on the south. Just let me know what street he stops on." He said while handling Cortez back the tablet.

After about eight minutes had past, Cortez finally replied, "It looks as if he just stopped on" but before he could get to the street name, the dot began to move again causing him to cut his self off.

"Where he stop at?" Pee Wee questioned.

"You got to hold up; the dot moving again." Cortez replied. After watching the movement of the dot for a few minutes, Cortez said, "If I didn't know any better, I'll say this motherfucker just made a drop off to somebody because it appears he's headed right back to the same place he started from."

"I bet that's exactly what he is doing." Pee Wee said, "Que said it looked like he been ripping and running; so I'm willing to bet that who's ever house it is on this West Ripa street, is where he's posted up at!" As they made there way to the street that the dot appeared to be on, Pee Wee peeped Tweezy's vehicle parked in a driveway as soon as they made the turn. After circling the block twice, Pee Wee decided to park down the street and said, "Check this out Cortez; that's that fool car right there." he motioned pointing at a two toned color Monte Carlo that didn't look as if it belong in the neighborhood. "I don't know how you are going to be able to get close up on him over here."

"Looking around and up and down the street that they were on, Cortez couldn't figure out how he could get up close to Tweezy either. That's when reality hit Cortez and he said, "You know what's so fucked up about this whole deal?"

"What's that?"

"I don't even know what this motherfucker even looks like!"

Pee Wee laughed before saying, "Trust me, you ain't going to miss this big bird looking ass motherfucker! He's a real tall and slinky ass motherfucker that you can't help but to noticed."

Right after Pee Wee finished describing Tweezy for Cortez; Tweezy came out of the house, and locked the door behind his self. "Damn, you mean to tell me that tall giraffe looking ass son-of-a-bitch is the motherfucker who fucked up my momma?" Cortez replied as Tweezy walked up to his car and opened the door as if he was about to get in; and then all of a sudden as if he forgotten something close the door back, and walked back to the house and went in without closing the door behind him. When Cortez peeped he had to open the door his self and left it open behind him, he told PeeWee, "Check game and peep play! I'm about to get up close to this motherfucker right now; just be ready to help put this fool in the trunk!" and then he grabbed the tazer, slide out of the car, and began jogging down the street towards Tweezy's car.

Pee Wee thought to his self, *what in the hell is this lil' nigga' about to do?* as he watched on clueless. Just as Cortez got halfway to Tweezy's car, he spotted Tweezy coming back out the house and locking it up.

"Fuck!" Cortez said to his self as he increased his speed to make sure he would make it to Tweezy's car before he got in.

Right as he made it two steps before reaching Tweezy's car, Cortez dove down as if he had tripped right in front of the car. Pee Wee looking on quickly thought, *what the fuck just happened? Get up nigga'; before he get away!*

Little did Pee Wee know that the whole fall scene was an act. Tweezy on the other hand, saw Cortez falling and bust out laughing to his self. After he heard Cortez fake some moan sounds that appeared to be real, he asked while walking closer to him, "Damn lil' clumsy, you alright? It looked like the sidewalk just grabbed ahold of you, and slammed you hard as a motherfucker!"

Playing the role as if he really injured his ankle, Cortez said, "Man, my ankle hurt; I think I might have broken it!" He then acted as if he was about to stand up, but couldn't and said, "Yeah, I think I definitely broken it! Can you help me get to the side; that way I won't be holding you up? I seen you were about to go somewhere."

"Yeah, I can do that!" Tweezy said as he reached him a hand to help him up.

Right when Cortez got to his feet, with the tazer in his left hand already, he lean up against Tweezy sending volts through his body causing him to collaspe like a ton of bricks. Pee Wee wasn't expecting for Cortez to get Tweezy like that, but then quickly realized that shit was real and quickly came hauling ass down the street.

As soon as Pee Wee hopped out of his car, he asked Cortez, "You got his keys already?"

Before Cortez even attempted to reach for Tweezy's keys, he said, "Look out Pee Wee." and tazered Tweezy again before he grabbed his keys. Cortez then said, "I got *'em* now!" as he ran an opened the trunk up.

Once they got Tweezy in the trunk, Pee Wee said, "Look, you drive my car; and I'll drive this fools. Just in case anything goes wrong, you won't have to worry about dealing with this motherfucker; and I can come up with a believable story. Just follow close behind me; and don't let anybody get in between us. I'm about to call Josh now; so we will know where to go with this clown." Pee Wee said as he jumped into Tweezy's Monte Carlo and pulled off.

Once Pee Wee got in touch with Josh, he gave him directions that led to an old run down building that you could tell was in desperate need of some reconstruction; but the good part about the place was it wasn't surrounded by a bunch of nosy neighbors. It was isolated just as they needed it to be for what Cortez had in mind.

Josh led them into the building and then opened it up for them. He then said, "I know it looks like shit; but the electric is on!" he replied while lifting a breaker switch up, and then continued, "But ya'll shouldn't have to worry about anybody coming out here, because I own everything on this strip; all the way to the dead end. Just give me a ring when ya'll finish and ready for me to come clean up the mess! Feel free to use any of my tools if ya'll run out or just want to use some more. Now I'ma let ya'll get to work. Here's the key." Josh said placing it inside of the lock on the door before leaving out.

Wasting no time, Cortez and Pee Wee went and grabbed Tweezy; bringing him inside the last place he would ever see.

Chapter Twenty-Nine
(Days Numbered)

After torturing Tweezy to death, Cortez felt as if he had gotten some type of justiced for his mother. Even though he couldn't turn back the hands of time, and prevent her from ever being hurt in the first place; he was satisfied knowing that Tweezy wouldn't be able to do shit else to anybody else.

For a moment, Cortez didn't think that he was going to be able to go through with all of the things that he had planned to do to Tweezy; but he did. If it wasn't for Pee Wee bringing him back to reality, telling him that Tweezy was dead; he couldn't imagined how much longer he would have been trying to do shit to him.

Once the phone call had been placed to Josh to come and clean up the remains of Tweezy; Cortez and Pee Wee were just about ready to get back to their normal lives, but they still had one more thing to do. Get rid of Tweezy's car. They pulled the door close behind them before they walked back to cars. On the walk there, Pee Wee asked Cortez, "You alright bruh?"

"Yeah, I'm straight!"

"That's whats up; but we still got to get rid of this bitch ass nigga' motherfuckering car! So check this out; just follow me the same way you did up here, and I know where to get rid of it at. Don't let nobody get in between us for anything!"

Pee Wee jumped back in Tweezy's car and led Cortez to the back of a Shop-N-Save grocery store parking lot; were nobody could see them pour gasoline all over and throughout Tweezy's car, before setting it on fire. Once the flames began to rise full fledge, they both jumped back into Pee Wee's car and skirted off.

Happy about the fact that they knew that they had gotten away with what they just done; they began to talk on an up to up level on the way back to Que's house. "Thanks for helping me get that low life sonofabitch; I owe you one now!" Cortez began the conversation off.

"You don't owe me shit: because I fuck with your moms! She's a good person, and we hella' cool! Plus I've been wanting to kill that bitch ass motherfucker anyway! He was a hard motherfucker to do business with! He would always do some ole bitch as shit; like trying to get Que to stop fucking with me on the low!"

"So ya'll sell crack for Que too?"

"*Naw*, we sell herion; but crack boom where I'm at! That's why Tweezy and me use to fall out about. He wanted me to have all of the money ready for a pick up from a drop, when he felt like that I should have had it ready; when this motherfucker really don't have shit to do with me and Que business! He had me all fucked up! Que and me already had an understanding; He knows crack sell faster in my hood!"

Hearing that was music to Cortez's ears. He figured he could supply Pee Wee; and then he thought of an even better plan in his book. "Check this out Pee wee; I be fucking with that hard." Cortez said "I know a motherfucker who has quite of bit of weight; and he has a hundred thousand in cash in his lil' trap spot. We can run up in his shit and take everything! Now when we done, I only want half of the money; and all the dope is yours as well. That's if you wan'na fuck with this lil' quick lick!"

"Who is this motherfucker you talking about; and where is he from?" Pee Wee asked suspiciously.

"His name Feeva; and he be on the Dub. That's where his trap is anyway."

"I don't know him; and my hood and Da Dub don't get along anyway, so fuck this motherfucker! Let's get *'em*! I'm down to hit him; if you got all the information we need!"

"I know everything we need to know about the motherfucker because I been plotting on *'em*! He did some fucked up shit! I ain't gone go into details; but this motherfucker got'ta be got and die! I'm just bring this to you because I figured since you just helped me, I can bless you with a lil' something that ain't gone cost you much of shit besides a few minutes of your time! I only need for you to watch my back; that's it. I'll do everything else on my own because this shit is going to be too easy! Easy as fuck infact! He money hungry; so he'll fuck with anybody and everybody!"

"Okay, enough said. When you wan'na get this motherfucker?" Pee Wee asked.

"We can meet up tomorrow night; and watch him until the weekend gets here. This way you can check shit out for your self; and see that I know what I'm talking about. Are we can hit his dumb ass up tomorrow? It's all up to you."

Pulling back up to Que's house where DaMesha and Que was awaiting their arrival, they parked and went in. Keisha didn't have a clue as to what took place; but with her and DaMesha up stairs, Cortez and Pee Wee let it be know to Que that the job was done and Tweezy didn't exist any more.

Que got happy and told Pee Wee, "I got something for you before you leave!"

"I'm about to go now because I got a few things I need to do. As far as what you got for me, keep it. This was on the house! Besides, Tez did everything his damn self. I didn't have to do shit, but help put the clown in the trunk and get him out." Pee Wee said as he oponed the door and left empty handed.

"I like him!" Cortez said "He's a cool dude to have on your squard Que!"

Que didn't respond to what Cortez said. He just looked deeply at Cortez before asking, "Are you alright?"

"I couldn't feel any better!"

"Seriously?"

"I'm serious! I told you I had it in me; and everything went perfectly as planned!"

Que continued to stare at Cortez for a moment before he finally said, "I want you to know, that I'm proud of you for riding for your mother! You stand in a whole new light light in my eyes; and I'ma start treating you like a grown ass man from now on! But any, fill me in; and tell me what all you did to the motherfucker! Did you use all the tools I gave you?"

"Hell yeah I used everything you gave us; and a lil' more!" Cortez said as he began to give Que a full run down of everything he did to Tweezy in full detail.

By the time Cortez was finished telling Que everything that he had done, Que was in disbelief; as he tried to picture Cortez doing all the stuff that he said he had done. Que silently thought to his self, *I'ma really have to watch Tez a lil' more closer now; especially since I know now, he really got the heart to get down with this murder shit!* But, he didn't say anything that he was thinking.

After their conversation, Cortez went and talked to his mother for awhile; before DaMesha and him decided to head home theirselves. When they got there, DaMesha noticed that Cortez was back to his normal self; and she was happy to see her man in such a good mood. She was just hoping that being involved with killing would be a one time thing; and not become a habbit. But, little did she know that Cortez had already killed five people before he killed Tweezy; and he was planning on killing Feeva any day now.

DaMesha was the type of female who let her man do his thing, and stayed out of his business; so she wasn't the type to question any of the moves he might have made, but for some strange reason she felt like Cortez was keeping something from her.

Cortez was eating dinner with DaMesha when he got the phone call from Pee Wee letting him know that he was going to meet him on Grand and Natural Bridge Boulevard at the gas station. Cortez agreed to be there at eight o'clock, and then hung up without saying a word because he didn't want to do too much talking in front of DaMesha about what he was up too.

"Baby, will you be home before twelve o'clock?" DaMesha asked knowing Cortez was about to leave by him glancing at his watch.

"I don't know; Pee Wee and me got to wrap up a few things, but it shouldn't take long." Cortez replied.

Shortly after DaMesha and Cortez finished eating dinner, Cortez shot out to go meet Pee Wee. Upon meeting Pee Wee at the gas station, Pee Wee pulled up on the side of Cortez and told him to park his car in the back of the lot, and jump into his car. When Cortez got in Pee Wee's car, the first thing he asked was, "Why you just didn't follow me?"

"I ain't following you because we don't need to be in two cars. I got this geek rental just for this mission!"

"So you wan'na hit this lick now?"

"Yeah; it ain't no point in playing around! You do know what you talking about; right?"

"Yeah, I'm absolutely sure I know what I'm talking about; it's my dope! He robbed and killed my partner a few weeks ago for two kilos and almost two hundred thousand dollars in cash! I know he ain't spent all of that money yet; and I'm quite sure he ain't got rid of all the dope either!"

"I-ight; well are you ready to push up on this motherfucker? Did you come prepared?"

"What's up with everybody asking me am I ready?" Cortez asked as he pulled out his gun and then replied, "I stay prepared and ready; everyday and all day!"

"Well let's go get this money!" Pee Wee said, "Where at on the Dub are we going?"

"We're going on the Dub and East John Avenue. Once we get on East John Avenue, I'll show you what house it is."

When they hit East John Avenue, Feeva was sitting on his porch smoking a blunt while talking on his cellular phone. Cortez quickly spotted him and told Pee Wee to pull to the corner as he pointed out Feeva and the house to him. Feeva was about to go pick up one of his female friends; and bring her back to his trap house. He was just waiting on a sale to come through; and then he was out. The whole time while he was talking on the phone though, he didn't notice the strange car that Pee Wee and Cortez were sitting in sitting on the corner.

"How many people you think are in there?" Pee Wee asked while plotting to his self.

"Every time I been up there, he was by his self. Plus he's hella' scary; so I doubt if he have anybody else in there!"

"I-ight! So check this out; and tell me what you think about it!" Pee Wee began "We can hit the alley right here, and break in the back; and then just wait on him to come in. If he ain't got anybody else in there, by time he figures out what's going on it'll be too late!" As Pee Wee was talking, a car pulled up and Feeva ran down to it to make a sell. After he made the exchange, he ran back up on the porch and locked the door to his house.

Feeva then ran and jumped into his truck and pulled off. "Oh yeah, now is the perfect time for us to run up in there!" Pee Wee said, "We can tear his shit up before he makes it back; so peep play, I'ma about to ride around to the back of his crib now so we can get this over with!"

Once they kicked the back door in and got in the house, they were out done. Feeva's trap house was super nasty. Shit was everyehere. Old beer cans, molded half eaten sandwiches, and Chinamen boxes were scattered just about everywhere throughout the house.

While rambling through the house, under the kitchen sink in a cabnet, Cortez spotted a cooler. It was the same cooler Chicago had. Cortez was about to move it to the side, but then quickly became curious to know what was left in it because it looked like the cleanest thing in the whole house by far. "Jackpot!" Cortez screamed to get Pee Wee's attention, "I found the dope!"

Pee Wee came running in the kitchen where Cortez was and asked, "Is the money in there too?"

"Nope; but it's in here somewhere, we just got'ta keep looking!"

"Fuck that! We just gone wait until this nasty ass motherfucker make it back here; and make him give it to us!" Pee Wee said as Cortez agreed with him.

They posted up for almost an hour; while every so often continue searching before they heard Feeva coming through the door. They knew Feeva wasn't alone this time because they heard a female voice too. They could hear Feeva telling the chick that he was with, "You know I'm about to fuck the shit out of you!" but he didn't have the slightest clue that they weren't alone. That's when Pee Wee and Cortez made their move; and let it be known that they were in the house. Feeva was dumb founded. "How the fuck did ya'll get in here? Tez, what's this all about? I thought we were cool!"

"I though you were cool too; but you're a snake! And not only are you a snake, but you wan'na play dumb with me!"

"Tez bruh, I don't know what you're talking about!"

"So you just came up over night huh? That's what you're telling me? Cause word on the streets is Feeva the man! You were just walking; buying grams and shit; and now I just found a whole kilo in your shit! Plus you're riding in a new whip! What's really going on?"

"My people put me on Tez! I ain't did shit! I ain't whoever it is that you're looking for!"

"Oh yes you are; you ole bitch ass motherfucker! I just got two questions for you though. First, where's the money; and second, why you kill Chicago?"

"Look, I don't know shit about who killed Chicago!" Feeva began before Cortez cut him off.

"Hold up one second!" Cortez said focusing his attention on the female Feeva had brought into the house with him. "Who are you; and why are you with this clown?"

The scared chick replied, "My name is Kayla; and I-I was just about to chill with him. I don't know what all he's invovled in; but it doesn't have anything to do with me! Can I please leave? I swear I ain't seen shit, or don't know shit! Please! I promise I won't say anything!"

"How about this; you sit down, and let me think about what I wan'na do with you! Now back to you! I'ma ask you one last time, and then I'ma smoke you if you're still bullshitting me! Where is my motherfucking money?"

"Okay! Okay! I got a hundred and seventy eight thousand left! It's all in the air condition vent in the kitchen!"

"Where is the vent at in the kitchen nigga'?"

"It's right over the refrigerator. It's all there; just take it and go!" Feeva said thinking if he gave them what they asked for, then they would spare his life.

"Go get it bruh!" Cortez said to Pee Wee, "If this motherfucker lying, it's going to be the last motherfucking lie he ever tells!"

Pee Wee went straight to the vent and snatched it out the wall. Once he removed an old dirty Black bag from inside of the vent and looked inside it, he said, "Yeah, it's in here. I got it."

"I know you killed my nigga'; so it ain't no need to lie about it bruh! Just tell the truth; because you know you than already fucked up!"

"Bruh, I didn't!" Feeva pleaded.

"Bruh my ass! You fucked up!" Cortez said as he pointed his gun to Feeva's neck.

"Tez, please bruh!" Feeva began.

Boom! Boom! Cortez shot Feeva in the neck twice trying to dislocate his head from the rest of his body. Feeva fell over and died instantly. Cortez then looked at Kayla and said, "Girl, hurry up and get your ass out of here; before I change my mind!"

"Thank you!" Kayla replied, "I-."

"Stop talking; and get the fuck out of here before I change my mind!" Cortez snapped. When Kayla got up and turned to run, Cortez shot her in the back four times. By the time her body hit the floor, she was stiff as a door knob. Cortez then turned and made his way to the back door where Pee Wee was waiting for him.

On the way back to Cortez's car, Pee Wee said, "You out here for real!

I thought for a second, that you were going to let that girl go for real; and I was going to have to knock her off!"

Smiling and shaking his head at the same time, Cortez replied, "*Naw*, I couldn't let her live; she was guilty by association! Plus my father always taught me to make sure I finish whatever I start!"

Chapter Thirty
(Da Ultimatum)

$\mathcal{B}$y the time Cortez finally made it back home, DaMesha was still up waiting on his return. Sensing that something had to be wrong, the first thing Cortez did was check to see what time it was. Once he saw that it was just turning midnight, he couldn't figure out what was suppose to be wrong as he made his way up stairs to put his share of the money and his guns away.

Although the television was on in the bedroom, DaMesha had it on mute as she just sat on the edge of the bed facing it in silence. "What's wrong Mesha? Why you got t.v. on mute? You heard or hear something that don't sound right?" Cortez asked while getting undressed so he could take a shower.

"I don't know where to begin!" DaMesha said in a tone that alerted Cortez letting him know something was definitely wrong.

"What are you talking about baby? What do you mean by, you don't know where to begin? Did I miss something?" Cortez asked in concern; while at the same time, trying to figure out what had done transpire since he left home and came back. "Baby, talk to me! What's going on with you? What's on your mind?" DaMesha's eyes began to tear up; but she didn't say what was bothering her before Cortez asked, "Is something hurting on you; or do you need to go to the hospital?"

Shaking her head in a no gesture, DaMesha finally said in a real low voice, "No; it's nothing like that! I just really need to seriously talk to you about a few things that I've been noticing, but haven't said anything about; that are really starting to bother me big time."

Taking a seat on the bed next to DaMesha, while grabbing a hold of her hands after whipping away a few of her tears, Cortez replied, "Mesha, talk to me! Tell me what's bothering you so bad! You know you can tell me anything; and I'll listen to you any time of the day or night!"

After taking a couple of deep breaths, DaMesha said, "I'ma tell you everything, just please don't interrupt me; and let me get everything I've been holding in off of my chest. You can say whatever afterwords; but I just need to get everything out first!"

"Go ahead Mesha baby; and run whatever you want down to me! I ain't going to interrupt you! Get whatever you need to get off of your chest! Do and say whatever that's going to make you feel better! I'm listening!"

DaMesha looked Cortez directly in the eyes and began, "Tez, when I first laid eyes on you, I knew I wanted to be with you. You were just so laid back and calm! Our conversations were great, and still are; but I know its a few things that you are keeping from me, and that's what's starting to bother me! Every since the Ej situation happened, you been acting kind of different. And sometimes, I trip off the fact that you knew what Ej had planned to do; yet when you asked me where Lil' T lived, the very next day he and his family popped up dead!"

"I didn't have any-." Cortez began before DaMesha cut him off.

"Stop; just let me talk! I kind of feel in my heart, that you did have something to do with it; but I'm not sure and couldn't prove it, so I left it alone! Then I seen how you and Chicago got super tight with each other; and that was a good thing to me, because it's very important to me that your family likes me and my family likes you because I'm a very family orientated person. So on that note, everything was going good; because everybody in my house hold liked you too! Chicago had been around in our lives for about ten years or more; so I viewed him like a father to us! Shit, my real father got killed when I was just turning four; so I never really had the chance to get to know him like talked about! Chicago was all Corey and me knew; and he treated me and Corey like we were made out of gold and were his own kids from day one! I mean I watched him for years; and knew his routines as if they were the back of my hands! All of a sudden, I started bringing you around, and all of his normal routines changed! He started doing everything differently once he got around you! And then you just popped up with some cars, jewel, and money out of the blue and started buying me anything I wanted; which I'm thankful for and you know that I'm am, but I ain't a fool! Chicago started doing the same stuff with my momma; and all of this started around the same time Doe got killed! Ring any bells yet? But don't even bother answering that, because ya'll just came up! I thought for a second that ya'll probably done it! But then I said to myself, ain't neither one of ya'll the type of people that would do some shit like that; and left it alone. But now I don't know! I'll say a few weeks later, everything was different as far as money goes. Chicago would bring home large amounts of cash at a time. One day I saw him with my on eyes with over a hundred thousand dollars in cash in our house; and called you talking about your cut!"

"We were-!"

"I'm not done Tez; just listen to me! I'm not dumb by a long shot! I didn't hear everything; but I know he said your cut! And I know if you got your cut like Chicago said and from what I seen, then it had to be a lot! You started driving that 750, and then Chicago ran out and got that expensive ass car he brought! It was like ya'll were in competition with each other on the low; but in a friendly manner! Like ya'll were bringing out the best in each other; making each other step up to a new level of shining! Then all of a sudden my house gets set on fire; and everybody inside of there was shot dead! I'm no fool! I know Chicago had something in that house; and whoever it was that set our house on fire, that's what they came for. I probably would've been dead too, but thank God I was with you! You had me feeling like you were my angel; but I don't know now. It's like I lost my whole family since you came into my life! Shit, the first day I met you Ej got shot!"

"I didn't have anything to do-." Cortez began before DaMesha cut him short again.

"I know you didn't have anything to do with that; I was there, I saw what happened! It's just starting to seem like you are bad luck to a degree! Everybody around you are getting hurt badly; if not killed! Then lately you been ripping and running; and staying out all late and stuff! You doing exactly what Chicago was doing before he ended up dead! I know you are not cheating on me; that's not a thought of mines at all! I think you were selling dope with Chicago; well I'm sure you were even though I can't prove it. The truth be told, I think you still are right now today! The only thing that gets me is I don't know why you would choose to when your momma and Que take damn good care of you! I just hope it's not to impress me or to buy me shit because I don't too much care for money; and it ain't shit in this world more important to me than you right now! I lost my momma, brother, and Chicago due to dope and this street shit! I can't lose you; at least not like that! Then on top of everything, I'm scared for myself! I don't wan'na die over no bullshit drugs or money! I'll be eighteen years old in two weeks. I'll get a job and support us; just so you don't have to do this shit! Then to make matters even worse, I know you killed a man the other day! Now I know he had it coming, and I ain't mad at you for defending your momma; but I don't want you turning into a killer!"

"Fuck that bitch ass motherfucker; he got what he deserved, and I'll do it again for how he violated my mother! I'd do the same for you!"

"I know you would! It's just everybody that I know who has killed somebody, says it fucks with their head; and they have nightmares and shit! But to me, it's like you did it and got a kick out of it. I just got a feeling that you think that you can get away with anything now; and it's going to become a habbit! It's like your heart just turned so cold; like you don't care if you live or die, or if you even get locked up. If you get in trouble and have to do some real hard time, it's going to kill me. Most of all, it's going to kill your mother because you are the only baby she have; and she don't want to lose you! I need you to wake up and realize that there are people that truly love you out here! And you know damn well if you had to go to prison ten, twenty, or thirty years it would kill you; but it would kill me and your momma even more! I'm begging you to slow down because shit fucked up out here; and you don't even know where you are for real! You need GPS to get where you're going most of the time!" DaMesha said wiping away her tears from her face as she smiled. "I'm not trying to be your mother; its just I love you! Fuck that, I'm in love with you; and I don't want you to fall victom to these streets. These fake ass people out here will smile in your face; and then stab you in your back as soon as you turn around! Trust me, I know; I've been living here all of my life!" DaMesha said.

Cortez knew that everything DaMesha was saying was true, and came from her heart. Especially after seeing what Feeva did to Chicago, Chris, and the rest of DaMesha's family; and how motherfuckers were running their mouths good enough to give him all the information that he needed to get up on Feeva without them even knowing that they were setting him up to meet his death.

While DaMesha had Cortez sitting next to her thinking hard and seriously about everything she said she went on, "Now I know that you have done some shit since you've been here; but you need to stop it! You too damn smart to get caught up in some bullshit! I want my old Tez back! I don't ask you where you're going, or what you are doing when you leave; because you're my man, and I trust you a hundred percent! You got my life in your hands Tez. Hell, I be thinking about marrying you all the time; you just don't know it because I've never shared what I be thinking about with you on that level! You've been here for me through the worst of the worst of my times! You support everything I do to the fullest; and I'd be a fool to let you just fuck up your life and I just sit back and watch! I know that you have a nice lil' bit of money; and I might have a house. If everything works out, we can rent that house out; and fall back until we find us some good jobs. Until then we can try to come up with a better plan for our future. But there are a few things that I'm not going to do. I'm not going to be with a drug dealer! I'm not going to be with a person who deliberately murder people for materialistic things either! And most of all, I'm not going to sit back and watch you fuck up your life; or lose it! I love you enough to let you go before I do that! I'm not trying to hit you with an ultimatum; but I'm dead serious about what I'm telling you right now! All I'm asking you to do is to take some time out to think about everything; and figure out what you really wan'na do. That's all I'm asking! Please do that for me Tez!" DaMesha pleaded. By the time DaMesha was finished talking, Cortez was at a lost for words.

Chapter Thirty-One
(Da Confessions)

About three days went by since DaMesha told Cortez what was on her mind and troubling her heart; but the whole conversation was still fresh in Cortez's head. Cortez totally agreed with everything DaMesha said; and couldn't blame her one bit for what she wanted. Then after seeing so much bullshit go down over the last few days, he quickly made up his mind on what he was about to do.

Cortez felt as if it was time to put DaMesha on game. He felt he held things in long enough; and today was going to be the best day for his confessions. After school, Cortez took DaMesha home; where he decided he would tell her just about everything that she wanted to know, and just hope for the best out come. Once they walked in the house, DaMesha asked Cortez, "What do you want to eat today baby?"

Cortez replied, "Don't worry about that right now; we can go out to eat. But check this out; I really need to talk to you on the up and up!"

"Is it good or bad?" DaMesha asked.

"It's a little bit of both! It's about the conversation we had the other day. I really want you to know what's been going on lately!"

"Hold up and let me have a seat before you get started!" DaMesha said while feeling a little uncomfortable about where this conversation was going to end up at.

After DaMesha took a seat Cortez began, "Now I don't want you to judge me! I'm just hoping that you can understand where I'm coming from; forgive me, and we can move on!" Cortez paused and took a deep breath before he continued, "I feel as if I'm in love with you; and I want you to know the honest to God truth about me! I feel it's only fair for you to know; besides I don't want to have any secrets between us!"

"I don't want to have any secrets between us either baby. So go ahead and talk to me; I'm listening!" DaMesha said, but wasn't fully prepared to hear what Cortez was about to tell her.

"Well Mesha baby, it's a lot of fucked up shit that's been going on; and I've been in the middle of it all, so I'm going to tell you everything starting from the top! Remember when I told you that Lil' T said he was going to shoot me if he seen me at the store again?"

"Yeah I remember that!" DaMesha replied.

"Well baby, what I didn't tell you was that he said that he was going to shoot you too if he saw you with me! I couldn't take his threat lightly, especially after seeing Ej getting shot! So I called Ej up, and got a gun from him so I could handle my business; and then I had you show me where Lil' T lived."

"So you mean to tell me that you-!" DaMesha began before Cortez cut her off.

"Mesha baby, just listen! I listened to you; but now I need for you to just hear me out! I got that gun from Ej, but then I started having second thoughts about the whole situation; so I figured that I'd give the gun back in a day or two after I really thought the whole situation through. But the more I thought about the situation, and the possibility of you and me getting hurt or even worse; I said fuck it, he had to go! I looked at it as if I would be doing Ej, you, and me a favor! So the next morning I killed him! I didn't really care about his momma and brother being innocent; because to me you and me were innocent, yet he chose to put us in his beef with Ej. Besides, they both had seen my face, so they both had to go!" Cortez coldly said. DaMesha couldn't believe her ears as her jaw dropped. She was totally speechless. Cortez then continued, "I didn't originally plan on killing his momma and brother; but fuck *'em*, it was what it was! I then got a phone call from Ej panicking; saying that everybody thought that he was the one who killed Lil' T bitch ass, and his family because of their beef. I told him not to trip off of what everybody else thought; because it was obvious that they didn't know what they were talking about, and they were just assuming and fishing for information! I never thought that somebody would send the police to his house behind that shit and they couldn't prove if he did it or didn't! The day you and me went over to his house and the cops kicked his door in, was the same day that I went over to his house to talk to him about it in person instead of over the telephone. I gave him fifty dollars for the bullets I used since he had said something about the gun being empty. I didn't know anything about the police was going to come there like they did!"

"So my cousin dead because of something you did!" DaMesha said as she shook her head in disgust.

"I didn't mean for shit to happen the way it did! Like I said, I thought that I was doing us all a favor! Everything that happened, still would've happen because Juan and him were going to do it anyway; it was just a matter of time, and he still would've got the blame when it was all said and done!" Cortez said trying his best to justify his actions.

"I can't believe you been keeping this from me all of this time!" DaMesha snapped.

"Hold up Mesha baby, let me put everything out there while I'm clearing the air and getting everything off of my chest! After everything happened with Lil' T and *em*, I felt like I couldn't be stopped! I felt invincible! So I robbed Doe. He kept bullshitting with me, and pissed me off; so I shot him!" Cortez replied temporary reliving the moment. DaMesha's eyes got big as she listened to Cortez tell his story about what he did to Doe. "Doe was my up! I simply robbed him to get me some money to buy a car; but I ended up getting way more than what I planned on! I got pounds of weeds out of him: regular and Kush, hundreds of different kinds of Ecstasy pills, dope, and some cash. After I got rid of everything I made about twenty-eight thousand dollars; maybe a lil' bit more. We were smoking his Kush on your porch the day Chicago and me really started fucking with each other! Remember, he wanted to get an ounce from me?"

"I remember that day!" DaMesha replied recalling that day.

"Well when we went to go get the weed, he called a few people and helped me get it all off. That day we came up with an agreement."

"What was the agreement Tez?" DaMesha asked determined to know.

"The agreement was if he helped me get rid of the weed and shit, then I was to help take care of you. And I was cool with that because I planned on doing that anyway; you my baby! Anyway, after the weed was gone, Chicago took me to get the Chevy Impala; and that was the same day that he asked me to go half on a dope package with him. The dope that I got from Doe was an ounce shorter than what Chicago was trying to get; so I just gave him what I had to work with." Cortez honestly replied. Cortez quickly realized that was the same day that he exposed Carla and Raykel relationship to Ej to Que; but just as quickly thought to his self that maybe he shouldn't tell DaMesha about that, and he didn't. He just moved on straight to telling her about Hector. "Everything was going good for a few weeks. Chicago and me were eating good! You were happy! Shit was straight! Then Chicago came to me with the ideal to rob his connect, Hector. When he came to me with the ideal, I was down from jump; and we hit him for thirteen kilos, and about a quarter million dollars!"

Cortez was trying to stay away from telling DaMesha the fact that he killed Hector; but she brought the truth out of him by asking a question. "So this Hector drug lord person is the person responsible for killing my family?" DaMesha asked with an angry hatred expression type of look on her face.

"No; Hector is dead!"

"So you killed him too?"

Cortez didn't want to make Chicago look too bad; so he took the blame for killing Hector as well.

"So you telling me that you had at least a hundred thousand dollars since we been together? Come on now; keep it real with me! Don't start telling me no any ole thing Tez! I want the truth!"

"I'm for real! I got, well we got, three hundred thousand dollars right now down stairs! I'll show it to you as soon as we get done talking! Anyway, once we got that dope and money from Hector, everything went to a whole different level! Chicago was serving everybody; and motherfuckers started hating! Then before you knew it, you got that phone call about your house being on fire. After the funeral, I started leaving you here; and hitting the streets more to find out what the word on the streets was as to what happened. I know you noticed that! But anyway, that's when I bumped into Frank at Fairground Park, and got a good clue as to what actually happened; and who the forth person might have been in your house. Then I got some more information that Feeva, which is the same motherfucker that Frank was telling me about, was suppose to be the new king of the streets when it came down to having that dope. That's when I put two and two together; because just a week before the funeral Feeva was just buying grams from Chicago. Now all of a sudden he's the new king penn! After Pee Wee and me got rid of the son-of-a-bitch that almost killed my momma, we paid Feeva a lil' visit; and it wasn't pretty! I had to do him in! I had to kill him!"

"So the motherfucker that killed my family is dead?" DaMesha asked.

"Yeah; he's dead as a doorknob, and ain't coming back Mesha! Come with me and check this out baby!" Cortez said as he grabbed DaMesha's hand and led her to the basement where he had his money stashed at.

Once he opened the door to the furnace room, he pulled out a nice size sum of money that he still had sitting out before allowing DaMesha to enter. DaMesha instantly looked inside of the small room and seen all of the guns Cortez was storing inside. Shocked and surprised, DaMesha asked, "Where did you get all of these guns from Tez? What are you really up too?"

"Chicago and me got 'em out of Hector's house." Cortez replied as he began opening his safe he had inside of the furnace room. Once he got the safe opened, he showed DaMesha that he wasn't bullshitting about having three hundred thousand dollars in cash. He also had six kilos left inside of the safe; which he knew DaMesha wasn't fond of. Before she could say a word about the dope that he had left, Cortez replied, "Now I know that you don't want me out here selling dope any more; and I'm going to honor that. I'm just going to give all of what I have left to Pee Wee for helping me get even with that bitch ass nigga' that I needed to get even with!"

"I-ight; so you are telling me that you are just going to give away the rest of that shit, and then you're done with the dope game?" DaMesha asked Cortez searching for the truth.

"That's exactly what I'm going to do! I'm not about to lose you over this shit! I just want to do what you said, and chill out! We got everything we need right now; and then some! I'm comfortable with the way things are; but right now it's not just about me. The question is, are you comfortable; and can you see yourself continuing to be with me?"

DaMesha didn't hesitate to answer Cortez's questions in the order that he asked 'em. "I'm absolutely comfortable with the way we living; and I'm comfortable with you too! And yes, I can see myself continuing being with you! I understand why you did what you did; even though I don't totally agree with most of the things you done. I understand Tez! And baby, I love you for telling me the truth about everything; and I'm not mad at you at all! I just want you to really put an end to all of this unnecessary shit that you been getting involved in; so we can move on!"

"I promise that I'm done with it all! I got what I was trying to get; so now it's over with."

"I'm holding you to that Tez!"

"Trust me; you got my word on that! Anyway, where do we go from here? Is there anything in particular that you wan'na do; or somewhere that you wan'na go?"

"I just wan'na do something nice today. We can celebrate the truth; and our new beginning!"

"I-ight; we can do that! It's the weekend; so we got plenty of time to do us! Is there anything specific that you want to do?" Cortez asked again.

"Nope; I just want you to surprise me! And you don't need to go all out the way to do so; we can just do something simple for a change."

"I-ight Mesha; that sounds good to me!" Cortez replied feeling relief at the fact that everything worked out in his favor; and DaMesha was going to remain with him after all.

<u>*Epilogue*</u>

*F*our months had past and everything was going great. Cortez kept his word to DaMesha; and decided to help Pee Wee and Frank out by giving each of them three kilos a piece free of charge. When they questioned why he was giving them that much dope for free for, his only reply was, "I'm getting out of the game before I get trapped in it. The only thing that I ask is for you to take good care of your family; and try to stay out of trouble. That's it; no more, or no less." After agreeing to Cortez's terms, they departed on a good note.

*K*eisha and Que were doing good as well. Keisha had healed up real good. She know had a scar on each side of her cheeks; but besides that, she was good as new. Que had healed pretty well his self too. He even began walking around again. He wasn't walking as fast as he use too; but he was convinced that he would get back there in a matter of time if God said the same. He was mainly just thankful that God gave him a second chance in life; and allowed him to get out of that wheelchair that he been confined too. Que also left the dope game alone. His new full time hustle was buying and flipping houses; and investing his profits from that into anything that made more dollars and cents. I guess you can't stop a true hustler from hustling. Surprisingly though, as soon as Que felt comfortable enough walking, he proposed to Keisha and asked her to marry him as soon as possible; and of course you know she said yes.

DaMesha had a beautiful eighteenth birthday. Cortez had did it big for her. With the help of Que, she found out that she was the sole full owner of the house her grandmother, Mrs. Rose, had left her. DaMesha and Cortez decided to keep the house; and just rent it out for the time being, just to keep some type of money coming in every month. The biggest surprising news DaMesha had, was when DaMesha found out that she was three weeks pregnant by nobody else other than Cortez. She was extremely happy to share the news with him; and to know that they had plenty of funds to take of the baby once it would be born, only made her happier.

Cortez.his self was on cloud nine. He was learning things from Que that nobody every show him; and before long, he was making small investments in properties as well. Cortez began buying two and four family flats; fixing them up, and then renting them out. The one thing that he did smart by him still being young was, he put all of his properties in his mother's name to keep the insurance cost low. Even though Chicago wasn't alive any more to witness how Cortez and DaMesha was living, Cortez kept his word to him; and was taking damn good care of DaMesha, and he wasn't in the streets robbing or selling drugs any more. He was loving the fact that DaMesha was having his baby; and that he had a few things establish to were they would always be able to take care of their baby once DaMesha had him or her.

Cortez, DaMesha, Keisha, and Que would have a family meeting once a month to discuss what their next power move would be; and to see how each of them was personally doing. So far, everything was working out; and life was great for them all. They had beaten the odds against them; and had became very successful. In the end, Saint Louis was the best move Keisha and Cortez could've ever made; and they both were happy that they came. They owed all of their happiness to Keniesha; for letting them both come and stay with her when they felt like they were stuck at the bottom of the barrow.

~ *The End* ~

If you like this urban novel, then you should also check out my previous release. Here's a sneak peep inside of it.

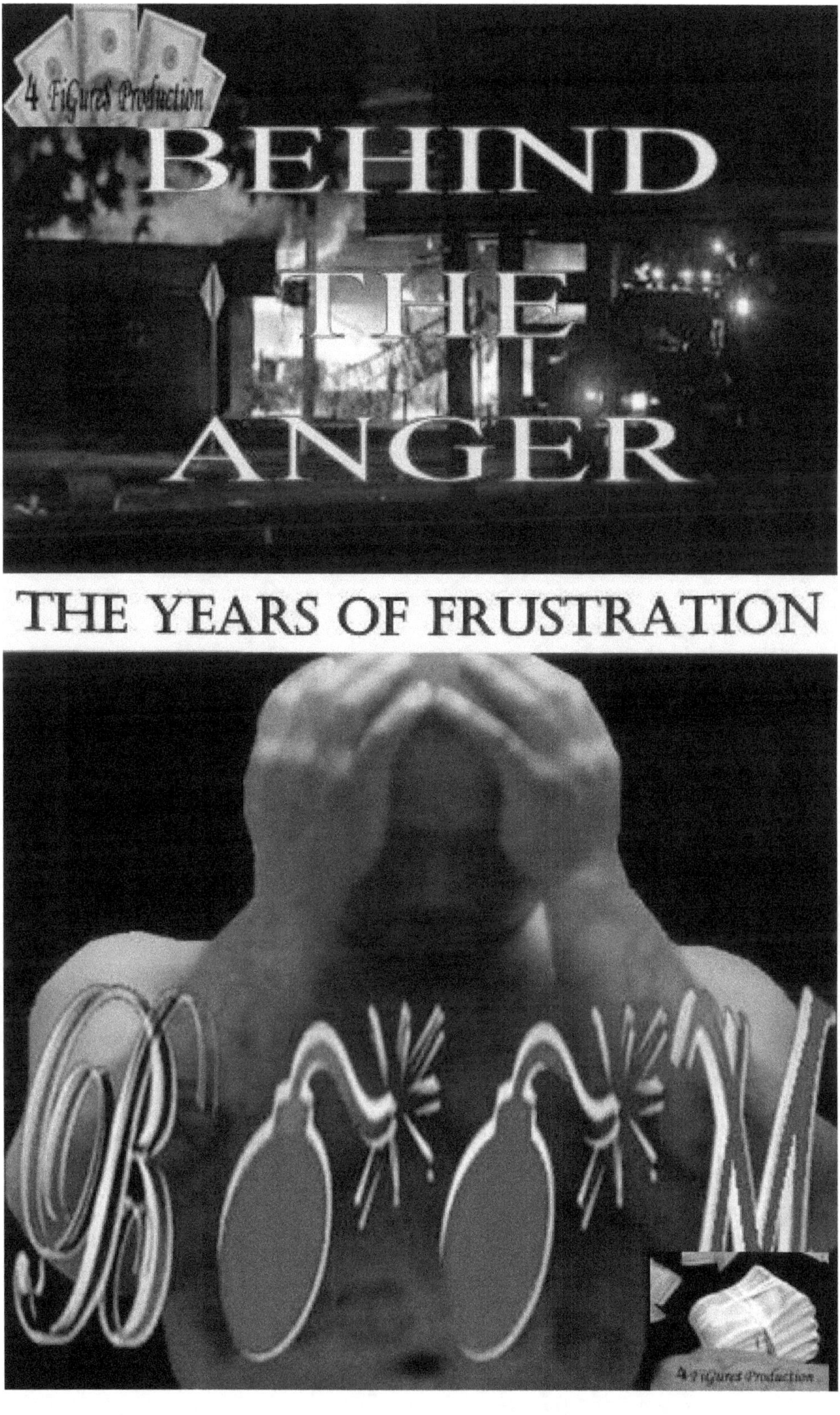

BEHIND THE ANGER

THE YEARS OF FRUSTRATION

<u>*Prologue*</u>

$\mathcal{M}$y name is Tj Green; but I'm also known as Boom. The story I'm about to tell is not only for you common folks, but for every individual whoever had dreams to get rich legal or illegal. Due to unwise decisions that I made as a youth, I ended up losing my freedom time after time after time. In the process of all the years I spent incarcerated, it overall affected my way of thinking and changed the way that I lived.

I grew up in poverty on the streets of Saint Louis, Missouri. I have an older sister who is physically attractive to whomever eyes set upon her, male or female. Although she is physically beautiful, mentally she is immature. Eventually, my bigger sister decided to run away from home; and never again have I seen her.

My mother was only twenty-two years old when she gave birth to me. Due to the stress that we caused her, as a single parent, she gave up on life. My mother later on fell in love with a pimp; who not only turned her on to tricks, but drugs as well.

As conditions became worse in our unsteady house hold, my own mother ended up abandoning me on a couples' porch; who decided to raise me as their own, instead of giving me to the state. Shortly afterwards, a fatal accident occurred; leaving me stuck without a place to go.

As far as my birth father, I never had a chance to meet him. By me never meeting him, I decided that he was the one person that I didn't want to be like in life. So with no father figure or mother in my life, I ended up looking up to those selling drugs and packing guns in the communities I grew up in.

When I was small growing up, I never imagined some of life's struggles that I would go through. I can recall when we were doing bad, going from place to place just to sleep. I even remember sleeping in car-shop garages during the winter just to keep warm; not knowing that the hard parts of life were just about to start.

Chapter One

*I*f you never experienced having to do without, you couldn't possibly imagine how life was for me growing up. I was raised by my momma, Sparkle, in a one bedroom apartment in the projects with my bigger sister, Precious. To say we had different daddies, we looked alike; just like both of our fathers had nothing to do with either of us growing up.

My mother worked days at a fast food restaurant getting paid three dollars and twenty-five cents an hour. While at night, she would leave us alone in the apartment and tell us not to open the door for anyone or she would beat us to death. My bigger sister and me would never know what time our mother would come home; but every morning she faithfully would wake us up, even if we didn't have to go to school.

Precious would always ask momma where she was going, but her only reply was, "I'm grown! I don't have to tell you nothing; but for your information, I'm going to work. So watch your brother and ya'll bet not mess up my damn house!"

My sister would always be mad, so most of the time we would fight after mom left. Normally I lost, and then my sister would make up with me and talk about how she felt. "Momma always saying she's going to work and don't never take us nowhere. Ever since you came along, she makes me sleep on the floor with you; and the lights stay getting cut off. If you wasn't here I'll probably have my bed by now."

"It's not my fault we got to sleep on the floor. That's why you got a bug crawling on you."

She would kill the bug and then say, "I hate you! I wish you would die just like these roaches." Then we would begin fighting again.

I think we use to fight with each other just to take our minds off the roaches and rats that might as well been family since they always crawled on us and ate just about anything we had. It wasn't always bad for us at first. Momma use to take us places and cooked for us all the time. But as time went along, I didn't know what seemed to be worse; momma sending us next door all the time to get food to eat, or having to wear the same clothes three and four times a week.

I hated to go to school because all the children would make fun of me for wearing the same clothes every other day. So I stayed getting into fights and sent home with a note for my mother to come back to school with me. Momma would punish me at home, and then hit me in front of the class for having to bring me back. The whole class would laugh at me and as soon as she would leave they would start back picking on me and I'd be right back in trouble. So I started skipping school.

If I wouldn't have started skipping school, I would have never known my sister was skipping school too. "Boy, why you not at school? You going to get in trouble." she replied.

"I hate school. Everybody always messing with me. Anyway, why you not at school?"

"I'm going by my friend's house."

"I can go with you?"

"No and you bet not tell momma!"

"Forget you. I don't want to go with you anyway." I would be mad because I didn't have anywhere to go. I knew I couldn't go home; and if momma would have found out that I was skipping school, she would have beaten me until I seen Jesus. So I would just hang out at the park until school was over.

After missing so many days at school, my teacher started asking for a note from my mother explaining why I was missing so many days. When that happened I started making up excuses on how I kept forgetting to get the note from her until that story got worn out. After that, I had to talk my sister into writing letters for me and signing momma's name on them. At first, I didn't think the letters would work; but it did for awhile. At least until report cards came out.

"Tj, bring your ass here! Why you have all these damn D's and F's? Better yet, why you have so many fucking absents? You better tell me something got damn it!" my momma snapped.

I would be scared to say anything because I knew I was going to get punished and if she found out I was lying to her it would be even worse. So I would say, "I don't understand everything in class. Then everybody be picking on me all the time."

"Why do you have so many absents then?"

"I don't know. They must have made a mistake on that."

"I'm going to see. I'm taking ya'll to school tomorrow."

I knew I was going to get a beating. I was just hoping it wouldn't happen in front of the whole class; but I knew it was coming. When momma left Precious started going off on me, "Now look at what you done did. Because of you I'm going to get punished too! At least I was going to school. You missed damn near three months straight. Momma going to beat the shit out of you!"

I knew she was right even though I didn't want to admit it. All I could say was, "I don't care. I'm still not going back."

"Oh you going to go when momma finish whipping your ass tomorrow!"

"You going to get a whipping too; or I'm going to tell her you wrote them notes and be with that boy."

"Oh you little motherfucker!" Precious would say before we would start fighting. By the time we would finish fighting she would then say, "I wish all of ya'll would just die!"

That use to hurt my feelings because I still loved my sister and mother even though they both treated me like they didn't want me around and called me stupid all the time.

When momma brought us to school the next day, I was hoping my heart would just stop because I knew we were in for it. "Hello Tj; and you must be Mrs. Sparkle Green. I've been waiting to meet you!" my teacher said in a tone of seriousness.

"Oh really! Any reason in particular you wanted to meet me?" My mother responded.

"To be frankly honest, yes Mrs. Green!"

"Please call me Sparkle."

"I'm majorly concerned with all the days Tj seem to be constantly missing. Is there some kind of personal problem you are having at home causing him to miss so many days?"

"Excuse me! I don't understand what you are talking about. I was coming to find out how could you possibly say my child done missed a hundred and seven days when I send him to school everyday."

"Well Mrs. Green, excuse me Sparkle. I'm afraid you might be sending him; but he's not making it here. I haven't seen him in bout three months until today!"

"Tj, you mean to tell me you haven't been coming to school?" my mother angrily snapped, but I didn't even get a chance to say anything before she hit me three times.

"Sparkle! You can't hit him like that in here."

"What you mean I can't hit him? This is my child!"

"I understand you are upset; but you can't hit a child on school property ma'am. The only thing I can do is to allow him to make up his work so that he won't fail."

"Thank you so much ma'am. He will do all of it too. When I'm finished with him, he will not miss anymore days either. Isn't that right Tj?"

"Yes ma'am!" I said on the verge of crying. Then we went to meet my sister's teacher. Along the way there, I caught a few more hits across the head while she cursed me out.

When we met my sister's teacher, I knew momma was really mad and we were going to get beat like it wasn't a tomorrow. "Hello Precious, and you must be her mother." my sister's teacher said.

"Yes I'm Precious mother. Just call me Sparkle."

"Since you insist Sparkle. I don't know where to begin. I've been having problems with Precious all year!"

"What type of problems are you having with her?"

"She refuses to stop talking in class when she comes! And I'm ashamed to say it, but we had no other choice but to send her home a few times because of the way she dresses."

"What is wrong with the way my child dress?"

"Today she is dress fine; but some days, she comes to school with short mini-skirts on revealing just too much."

When the teacher said that, momma eyes turned red as a demon. I could already feel the beating we had coming. Somehow momma controlled her temper and said, "I'm sorry for any disturbance Precious has caused; but after today she won't give you anymore problems. Isn't that right Precious?"

"Uh-huh."

"It's yes, not uh-huh! You understand me?"

"Yes."

Normally it would have taken us almost thirty minutes to walk home, but not today. Momma was cursing us out and smacking us all the way home, so we made it there in a little bit over fifteen minutes. As soon as we made it home, one of my cousins that just moved from California seen us and asked, "Can ya'll come out and play?"

I was wishing we could, but I had to tell him, "Not today, we about to be on a punishment!"

He just stood there with a blank expression on his face, then ask, "Well can I come over?"

"I doubt it! But you can ask my momma and see what she says." Precious said.

When he asked momma could he come over, she blew on him. "Didn't they just tell you they on a punishment? No you can't come over! They can't have company or come outside for a month!"

He got the picture when she finished talking, and then ran off without anymore questions. As soon as we stepped in the door momma said, "You motherfuckers get out them damn clothes! Ya'll think ya'll can do whatever the fuck ya'll want to do! I'm going to show ya'll, ya'll can't outsmart me!"

Once she started whipping me with her favorite leather belt, I was screaming hoping Jesus would stop her from hitting me again. I mean she hit me so hard so many times, that the belt broke. I thought my prayers were answered until she grabbed an extension cord and begun whipping me all over. By the time she was finished, I was bleeding with red extension cord marks all over my body. That was the first time I really felt like I hated my momma and wished she would've died; but it wasn't the last time.

Chapter Two

*T*hat evening when my momma went out like usually, my sister asked me, "Are you alright?"

I really didn't want too answer her because I felt like momma took it easy on her compared to the whipping I received. Then I said, "Momma make me sick! She be beating on me like she don't love me. She beat on you too, but she don't beat on you like she do me. Why?"

"I guess because you a boy she figure she don't be hurting you."

"She don't be hurting me! Look at all these marks she put on me! You think they don't hurt?"

"I know they hurt. I got some too. Well you better go to sleep before momma get back."

That's exactly what I did. When I did wake up, all I heard was momma cursing. I thought I was dreaming at first; until I seen that boy my sister be with running out the door. When I realize who I just seen, I knew we were going to get another whipping so I kept my eyes closed until I fell back asleep. All of a sudden, momma woke me back up, "Where is your fucking sister at? You knew that boy was in my house? Precious, where the fuck are you?"

I didn't know what to do or say. I knew momma was real pissed off even more than she was earlier. So I didn't say anything and acted like I wasn't all the way awoke.

"Got damn it, I know you hear me talking to you! Where is your sister at?"

"I don't know. She ain't in the bathroom?"

"You mean to tell me you didn't know that man was in my damn house?"

"What man was in the house? What are you talking about momma?"

Before I knew it, I was getting another whipping for something I didn't even know about and I wasn't even lying this time. By the time my mother realized I didn't know what she was talking about, she broke down crying. I never saw my mother cry like she did that day. The way she broke down crying, made me start crying and it wasn't because I just gotten a whipping.

I was telling her everything was going to be okay, even though I didn't really understand what she was crying for. Precious and me always talked about leaving home, but I never figured she would leave for real. "Tj, you don't have an ideal where your sister might have gone?"

"No ma'am. She's going to come home though."

"You don't know who that boy was? He looked like he could have been grown."

"I don't know who you talking about, but Precious going to come home."

I was trying to put things together in my mind why Precious had left without telling me. At first I couldn't come up with a clue. Then when I thought about seeing that boy running out of the house, I knew why Precious had left. Momma would have damn near killed her if she wouldn't have left.

For the first time in about a year, momma sat down on a crate that we used as furniture in the living room and began talking to me. Half of the time I didn't know if she was speaking to me, or just out loud while she was rocking back and forth. All I really knew was that momma was hurt; and if my sister would have walked through the door somebody would have died that night. After sitting there for hours rocking back and forth, momma realized I was still up watching her and said, "Tj. You know I love you, don't you?"

"I know you love me momma and I love you too."

"It's just I don't know what to do with ya'll anymore. I bust my ass to make sure ya'll have; but somehow I seem to fail. I'm sorry for taking my anger out on you. I hope you don't hate me. You my baby and I love you. I just don't know what I would do if I was to lose either one of you."

"You not going to lose us momma. Everything is going to be alright."

"I hope so son. You can go sleep in my bed."

I knew something had to be seriously wrong when momma told me I could go sleep in her bed. As far back as I could remember, momma never allowed me to sleep in her bed. So I said, "That's alright momma; I'll sleep on the floor like I normally do."

She started crying again when I told her that. I didn't know if I did something wrong or not; so I just grabbed my blanket and went in the corner where I normally slept and went to sleep.

The next morning when I woke up momma was already up. When I looked at the clock, it was ten-thirty-three. Since I was old enough to go to school and tell time, momma never allowed us to sleep past eight o'clock in the morning; so I knew she had to have a lot on her mind. Once I gotten all the way up I asked momma how she was doing, but I could tell she hadn't slept a wink when I seen how red and swollen her eyes were. She just looked at me and said, "When you finish brushing your teeth, get dressed so we can go."

I didn't know where we were going, but I didn't ask any questions. I just did what momma said because I couldn't take another whipping. I was already hurting from yesterday and I had enough extension cord marks to last me for a month. As soon as I gotten dressed, I told momma I was ready to go. Then we left.

We stopped at a pay-phone where I thought momma was calling the police until I started paying attention to what she was saying. "She still haven't came home. I don't know. He right next to me. Uh-huh. No. Okay, I'll see you then." then she turned to me and said, "I'm sorry I got you out here without eating. Let's go get something to eat."

I was expecting us to begin walking back home thinking about how much butter and sugar I was going to put on my rice, but we wasn't walking towards the house so I asked, "Where we going? I thought we were going home to eat."

"I'm going to take you to White Castle's. I know you haven't had that in a long time."

I couldn't believe she was actually taking me to White Castle's. The hamburgers were only thirty-six cents, but we only ate there about three times a year unless our neighbors had leftovers or extras. When we arrived there momma ordered me three castle burgers and asked me, "What kind of soda do you want?"

I didn't want to push my luck, so I said, "None! I'll drink some water!"

Once we sat down, I couldn't believe I was really about to eat some White Castle's at White Castle's. I ate them as if I hadn't ate in a week. When momma seen how quickly I at them, she said, "You must have been hungry. You want some more?"

"Yes ma'am if I can!" I replied.

She went back to the counter and ordered me three more castle burgers. When she came back she said, "Now you sit right here and eat them slow while I go make a phone call."

"You don't want none momma?" I asked because I realized that she didn't order herself anything to eat. She just shook her head and walked out of the place. I didn't know what else to expect out of the day. To say we didn't know where my sister was, momma was actually treating me like I was her child instead of someone she couldn't stand.

When she came back I was finish eating the castle burgers. She said, "You didn't save me any. Not even one!"

I just knew I was going to get a whipping. I said, "I thought you were shaking your head no when I asked you if you wanted any."

"It's alright. I'm not hungry." Then momma finally asked me the big question, "Be honest with me Tj. You know where your sister would have went or who that man was that was in my bed?"

When she asked me that, it took me a second to catch on that she said in her bed. That right there explained to me why my sister really left and haven't came back home. I said, "Momma I really don't know where Precious might be or who was in the house. You woke me up last night. I had went to sleep a little while after you left, and Precious was still in the house with me then."

"Where do you be going when you skip school then?"

"To the park."

"Well lets go, our ride is here." I didn't even know we had a ride coming or waiting. When we went outside, momma walked up to a clean Lincoln Continental and told me to get in the back.

Inside was an older Black man. He introduced his self as Mr. Wayne. To me he looked like an old high roller and spoke as if it wasn't a thing in the world that could get him upset. Right off the back I could tell he was the type of man that wanted his presence to be known; but it was something about him that I just didn't like.

He rode us around for a long time looking for my sister as if he was really concerned. After a few hours of just riding around, he offered to buy us something to eat. Momma said, "I'm not hungry, just get him something to eat."

"Well lil' man, what do you want to eat?" Mr. Wayne asked me.

I didn't know what to say because momma always told us not to take food from folks we didn't know. Then again here was my chance to get anything I wanted to eat and momma was right here so I couldn't see it being a problem. I replied, "White Castle's."

"You sure that's what you want?"

I looked at momma and she seemed to be in her own world so I answered him, "Yes sir, Mr. Wayne."

"You don't have to call me Mr. Wayne. Just call me Money."

"Okay Mr. Money." He didn't say anything about me calling him Mr. Money. He just smiled as if he was turned on by hearing the word money.

He drove us to the same White Castle's that we went to earlier then said, "Sparkle, you sure you don't want anything to eat?"

"I'm alright!" she answered in a low tone.

"Look Sparkle, you have to eat something! I'm just going to get enough so if you get hungry later you will have some."

She didn't say anything. She just remained looking spaced out.

After we gotten our food, he brought us home. I said, "Thank you Mr. Wayne. I mean Mr. Money," then got out of his car. Momma stayed sitting in there for a minute before getting out. I guess they had something to talk about that they didn't want me to hear.

Once we opened the door to the apartment, I knew things were back to normal. Bugs were crawling all over the place as if they lived there and we were visiting them. I use to hate coming inside because I knew they were going to crawl all over me eventually and that use to drive me. I shook a sheet free from roaches that we used to cover a box in which we used as a table,

then placed the food on it. After I did that, I asked momma, "Are you going to come eat with me?"

This time she came and ate two burgers; and then said, "You just eat what you want and save me some." Then she went into her bedroom and closed the door behind her.

When I finished eating, I realized I didn't have nothing to do since Precious was gone. I asked momma did she want me to put the rest of the food in the oven or in the refrigerator. It took her a few moments to tell me in the refrigerator, but I didn't pay it no mind. I thought she might have been laying down until she came out of her room and went into the bathroom.

When she opened her bedroom door, it smelt like she was smoking crack in there. I couldn't help but noticed that smell being that I smelt it all the time in the building we stayed in. I thought it was just coming through the window being that the window was cracked; but I just didn't know, my momma was really getting high.

Chapter Three

*L*ater on that night, momma came out of her room and said, "You can warm up them burgers; and then take a bath. When you finish you can go to sleep in my bed. I have to go to work tonight. While I'm gone you can answer the door, but you bet not open it for anyone but your sister; if she comes back. Do you understand me?"

"Yes ma'am."

When momma left I was really lonely. It felt strange being in the house by myself. I didn't have anything to do. I couldn't watch television because we didn't have one; and I didn't want to mess with the radio on the clock because I might have messed up the time and momma would have known it was me. So I just laid in the bed and listened to the neighbors until I fell asleep.

The next morning momma woke me up like usual for school. Once I got ready, momma said, "Don't tell anyone your sister ran away. You understand me?"

"Yes."

"And, you better go to school and come straight home afterwards. Is that clear?"

"Yes."

It felt real funny going to school without my sister. On the way there, I bumped into my cousin and we began to walk to school together. "Say *cuzz*, what did ya'll do to get on punishment? Your momma was mad!"

"We just been getting into a lot of trouble at school; and momma just got sick of it."

"She really going to keep ya'll on punishment for a month?"

"I don't know. She might!"

"Where Precious at?"

Now when he asked me that, I thought about what momma said; but she didn't tell me what to say. So I asked him, "What you said?" trying to buy some time to come up with an excuse.

"Where your sister?"

"Oh, she sick so she got to stay home today." and that was that.

Once we arrived at school we went our own way and the day went on normal. By lunch time I was ready to go; but I knew I couldn't skip a few classes without it really being noticed; so I just went to all of them. By the time I went to gym, my normal day made a sudden turn. The gym teacher told us, "Change into ya'll gym clothes." When I took off the long sleeve shirt I was wearing, the tee-shirt under it came up revealing some of the extension cord marks that I had and he pulled me to the side, "Tj, are you having problems at home you want to talk about?"

I thought he knew my sister had ran away, but he couldn't have known. I didn't tell anybody! I said, "Why would you ask something like that?"

He said, "You don't have to be afraid to tell me if you are having problems. I saw the marks on your side. Are you getting beatings at home?"

"No sir. I just got a whipping because of my report card."

"I can understand you might get a whipping or some type of punishment; but looking at how many marks you have on you, that's considered child abuse! Now I don't want to put Family Service on your parents causing more problems for you, but I will have to suspend you until those marks heal on you."

"Suspend me! If I get suspended I'm really going to get punished. Please don't do that, I'll participate in class!"

"I'm sorry, but it's not about participating in class. If any other teacher here would happen to see all of those marks on you, they would call Family Service; and nobody could stop them once they step in."

I just dropped my head. How was I going to explain I just been suspended to my momma? I knew momma wasn't going to give me a chance to say anything or explain. I just made my last plea of hope to the teacher, "Since you going to suspend me, can you at least write me a note explaining it's not my fault this time?"

"I'll tell you what, I'll call your parents and talk to them."

"That sound good, but we don't have a telephone."

"Oh, is that so? Well I'll write you a letter, and then you can go ahead and leave before anybody else sees you."

Once he gave me the note he wrote, I left. I already knew I was going to get in trouble; so I figured I'll go straight home and deal with it. But on my way home, I saw Mr. Wayne. From where I was standing at, it looked like he was arguing with four women. Then all of a sudden, I saw them all taking money out of their bras and pocket books and hand it over to him. I guess that's why he called his self Money.

When I got close enough that they could see me, I recognized that the four women were neighborhood prostitutes. I was wondering why they would have been giving Mr. Wayne money; but when I really looked at the picture it didn't take a genius to see that Mr. Wayne was a pimp.

"Hello Mr. Money." I said walking by.

"Oh, how you doing Tj?"

"I'm alright. How about you?"

"Just fine! Where are you going this time of day?"

"Home."

"Well come on, let me give you a ride." Once I got in the car he asked, "Are you hungry?"

"No sir, I'm alright."

"Have you heard from your sister yet?"

"No. She didn't even come to school today."

"She'll come home sooner or later."

"I hope so; I actually miss her!"

"It's going to be okay! I'll see you later on." then he dropped me off.

I wasn't expecting my momma to be at home when I got there, so I figured I'll have enough time to get my story together on how I was going to tell her I gotten suspended. When I opened the door I thought somebody must have broken in because the whole house smelt as if someone was smoking crack cocaine; and I knew for sure it was crack I was smelling.

"What the fuck are you doing home early?" momma snapped.

"I got suspended and they sent me home."

"What your dumb ass get suspended for this time?"

I didn't bother to say anything; I just handed her the note my teacher wrote for me. When she finished reading it she said, "Motherfucker you going around telling people I'm beating on you! You my motherfucking child! If I feel I want to whip you until I get tired, it ain't a motherfucker that could stop me!"

I knew she was going to find some kind of way to make it seem like I had gotten suspended on purpose; and the way she was looking, I knew she was smoking that stuff. When she cooled down, I told her, "I saw Mr. Wayne. I guess he's going to come over because he said he'll see me later."

"Where you seen him at?"

"On the way home; he the one who brought me home."

For the rest of the day I was drove. I was hoping Money would come over, but I guess I wasn't that lucky. Around seven o'clock momma cooked some rice and warmed up the left over White Castle's we had. When she finished she said, "Eat all you want, and then go to bed. I'm about to go!"

In a sense I was happy she was leaving. I couldn't stand the thought of knowing that my mother was turning into a dope fiend. I wished I knew where Precious was; I would have left and went by her.

It was three eleven in the morning when momma returned home. I noticed she was wearing: a short skirt, a shirt revealing her stomach, and some red lip stick. At first I thought I was dreaming because I knew that wasn't how my momma left. I soon realized that I wasn't dreaming, when I heard her running some bath water and smelt crack burning again. I just covered my head up and made myself go to sleep.

ALSO

COMING

SOON

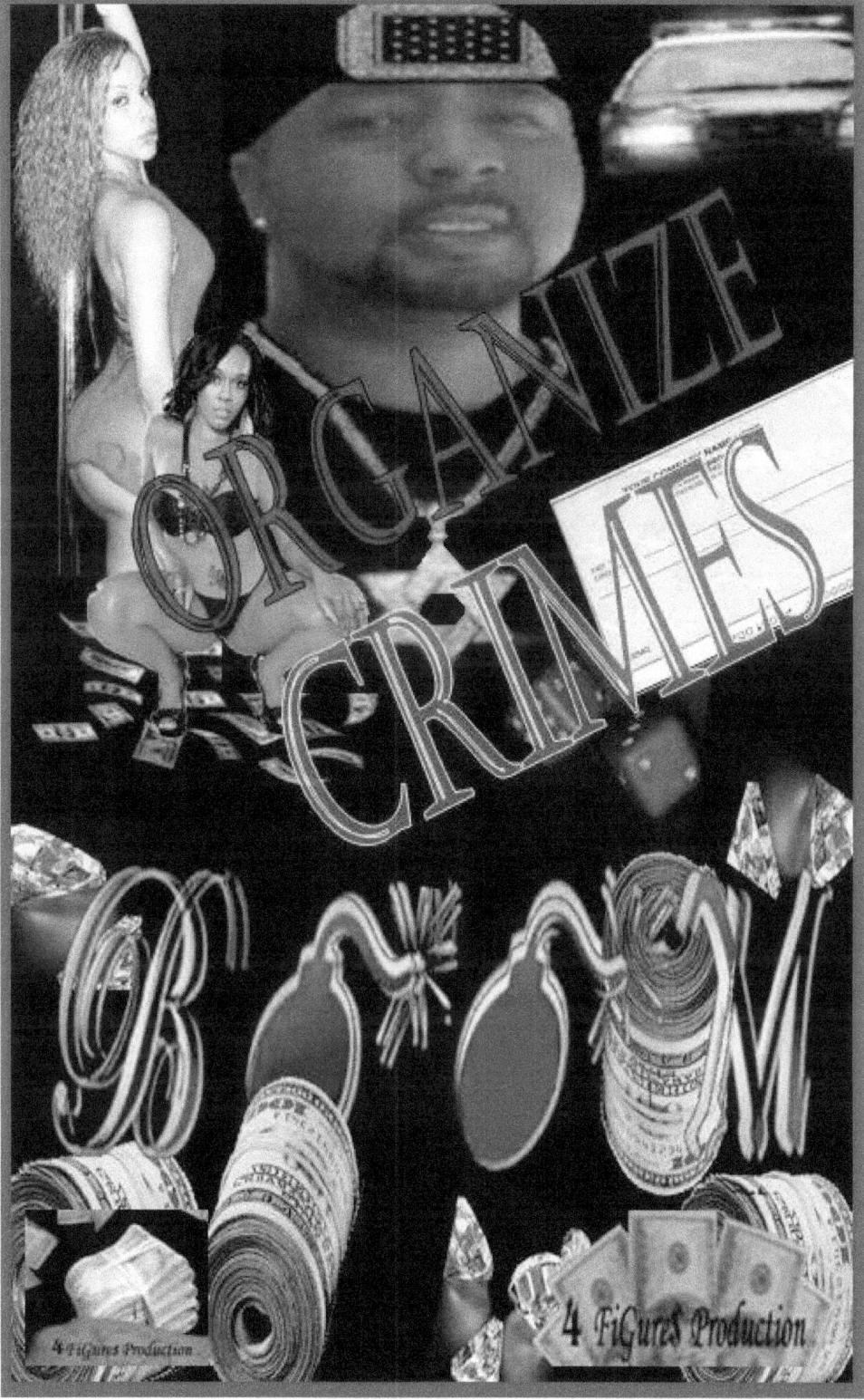

4 FiGureS Production

SPECIAL THANKS

TO ALL WHO HAS
SUPPORTED
THIS BOOK

AND MAY YOU KEEP ON SUPPORTING
MY FUTURE PROJECTS